PRAISE FOR JOHN SANDFORD AND *WINTER PREY*

Turn the page for more rave reviews . . .

P9-CEC-485

RULES OF PREY

**John Sandford's smash bestselling debut
—introducing detective Lucas Davenport . . .**

"Sleek and nasty . . . it's a big, scary, suspenseful read, and I loved every minute of it."

—Stephen King

"Tough, gritty, genuinely scary."   —Robert B. Parker

"A haunting, unforgettable, ice-blooded thriller."

—Carl Hiaasen

SHADOW PREY

**Lieutenant Davenport returns
—on a city-to-city search for
a bizarre ritualistic killer . . .**

"Ice-pick chills . . . excruciatingly tense . . . a double-pumped roundhouse of a thriller."

—*Kirkus Reviews*

"The pace is relentless . . . a classic."   —*Boston Globe*

"Harrowing."   —*West Coast Review of Books*

"MR. SANDFORD KNOWS ALL THERE IS TO KNOW ABOUT DETONATING THE GUT-LEVEL SHOCKS OF A GOOD THRILLER."
—*New York Times Book Review*

EYES OF PREY

Davenport risks his sanity to stalk the most brilliant and dangerous man he's ever known, a doctor named Michael Bekker . . .

"Savage . . . suspenseful . . . gripping from start to finish."

—*Kirkus Reviews*

"Engrossing . . . one of the most horrible villains this side of Hannibal the Cannibal."

—*Richmond Times-Dispatch*

"Relentlessly swift. Genuine suspense . . . excellent."

—*Los Angeles Times*

SILENT PREY

Michael Bekker, the psychopath Davenport captured in *Eyes of Prey*, escapes. And the nightmare begins again . . .

"*Silent Prey* terrifies . . . just right for fans of *The Silence of the Lambs*."

—*Booklist*

"Readers will speed through the surprise twists . . . Sandford delivers!"

—*Publishers Weekly*

"Superb!"

—*St. Paul Pioneer Press*

Berkley Books by John Sandford

WINTER PREY

JOHN SANDFORD

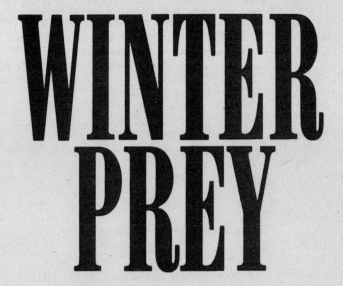

B
BERKLEY BOOKS, NEW YORK

WINTER PREY

A Berkley Book / published by arrangement with
the author

PRINTING HISTORY
G. P. Putnam's Sons edition/March 1993
Published simultaneously in Canada
Berkley edition/March 1994

ISBN: 0-425-14123-3

BERKLEY®
Berkley Books are published by
The Berkley Publishing Group, 200 Madison Avenue,
New York, New York 10016.
BERKLEY and the "B" design are trademarks of
Berkley Publishing Corporation.

PRINTED IN THE UNITED STATES OF AMERICA

10 9 8 7 6 5 4 3 2 1

CHAPTER

✳ ✳ ✳

1

The wind whistled down the frozen run of Shasta Creek, between the blacker-than-black walls of pine. The thin naked swamp alders and slight new birches bent before it. Needle-point ice crystals rode it, like sandpaper grit, carving arabesque whorls in the drifting snow.

The Iceman followed the creek down to the lake, navigating as much by feel, and by time, as by sight. At six minutes on the luminous dial of his dive watch, he began to look for the dead pine. Twenty seconds later, its weather-bleached trunk appeared in the snowmobile headlights, hung there for a moment, then slipped away like a hitchhiking ghost.

Now. Six hundred yards, compass bearing 37 . . .

Time time time . . .

He almost hit the lake's west bank as it came down from the house, white-on-white, rising in front of him. He swerved, slowed, followed it. The artificial blue of a yard-light burrowed through the falling snow, and he eased the sled up onto the bank and cut the engine.

The Iceman pushed his faceplate up, sat and listened. He heard nothing but the pat of the snow off his suit and helmet, the ticking of the cooling engine, his own breathing, and the wind. He was wearing a full-face woolen ski mask with holes for his eyes and mouth. The snow caught on the soft wool, and after a moment, melt-water began trickling from the eye holes down his face beside his nose. He was dressed for the weather and the ride: the snowmobile suit was windproof and insulated, the legs fitting into his heavyweight pac boots, the wrists overlapped by expedition ski mitts. A heavyweight polypropylene turtleneck overlapped the face mask, and the collar of the suit snapped directly to the black helmet. He was virtually encapsulated in nylon and wool, and still the cold pried at the cracks and thinner spots, took away his breath . . .

A set of bear-paw snowshoes was strapped behind the seat, on the sled's carry-rack, along with a corn-knife wrapped in newspaper. He swiveled to a sidesaddle position, keeping his weight on the machine, fumbled a miniature milled-aluminum flashlight out of his parka pocket, and pointed it at the carry-rack. His mittens were too thick to work with, and he pulled them off, letting them dangle from his cuff-clips.

The wind was an ice pick, hacking at his exposed fingers as he pulled the snowshoes free. He dropped them onto the snow, stepped into the quick-release bindings, snapped the bindings and thrust his hands back into the mittens. They'd been exposed for less than a minute, and already felt stiff.

With his mittens on, he stood up, testing the snow. The latest fall was soft, but the bitter cold had solidified the layers beneath it. He sank no more than two or three inches. Good.

The chimes sounded in his mind again: Time.

He paused, calmed himself. The whole intricate clock-work of his existence was in danger. He'd killed once already, but that had been almost accidental. He'd had to improvise a suicide scene around the corpse.

And it had almost worked.

Had worked well enough to eliminate any chance that they might catch him. That experience changed him, gave him a taste of blood, a taste of *real* power.

The Iceman tipped his head back like a dog testing for scent. The house was a hundred feet farther along the lake shore. He couldn't see it; except for the distant glow of the yard-light, he was in a bowl of darkness. He pulled the corn-knife free of the carry-rack and started up the slope. The corn-knife was a simple instrument, but perfect for an ambush on a snowy night, if the chance should present itself.

✳

In a storm, and especially at night, Claudia LaCourt's house seemed to slide out to the edge of the world. As the snow grew heavier, the lights across the frozen lake slowly faded and then, one by one, blinked out.

At the same time, the forest pressed in: the pine and spruce tiptoed closer, to bend over the house with an unbearable weight. The arbor vitae would paw at the windows, the bare birch branches would scratch at the eaves. All together they sounded like the maundering approach of something wicked, a beast with claws and fangs that rattled on the clapboard siding, searching for a grip. A beast that might pry the house apart.

When she was home alone, or alone with Lisa, Claudia played her old Tammy Wynette albums or listened to the television game shows. But the storm would always come through, with a thump or a screech. Or a line would go down somewhere: the lights would stutter and go out, the music would stop, everybody would hold their breath . . . and the storm would be there, clawing. Candlelight made it worse; hurricane lanterns didn't help much. For the kinds of wickedness created by the imagination during a nighttime blizzard, only modern science could fight: satellite-dish television, radio, compact disks, telephones, computer games. Power drills. Things that made machine noise. Things that banished the dark-age claws that pried at the house.

Claudia stood at the sink, rinsing coffee cups and stacking them to dry. Her image was reflected in the window over the sink, as in a mirror, but darker in the eyes, darker in the lines that framed her face, like an old daguerreotype.

From outside, she'd be a madonna in a painting, the only sign of light and life in the blizzard; but she never thought of herself as a madonna. She was a Mom with a still-shapely butt and hair done with a red rinse, an easy sense of humor, and a taste for beer. She could run a fishing boat and swing a softball bat and once or twice a winter, with Lisa staying over at a friend's, she and Frank would drive into Grant and check into the Holiday Inn. The rooms had floor-to-ceiling mirrors on the closet doors next to the bed. She *did* like to sit on his hips and watch herself fuck, her head thrown back and her breasts a burning pink.

Claudia scraped the last of the burnt crust from the cupcake tin, rinsed it and dumped it in the dish rack to air-dry.

A branch scraped against the window. She looked out, but without the chill: she was humming to herself, something old, something high school. Tonight, at least, she and Lisa weren't alone. Frank was here. In fact, he was on the stairs, coming up, and *he* was humming to *himself*. They did that frequently, the same things at the same time.

"Um," he said, and she turned. His thinning black hair fell over his dark eyes. He looked like a cowboy, she thought, with his high cheekbones and the battered Tony Lamas poking out of his boot-cut jeans. He was wearing a tattered denim shop apron over a t-shirt and held a paintbrush slashed with blood-red lacquer.

"Um, what?" Claudia asked. This was the second marriage for each of them. They were both a little beat-up and they liked each other a lot.

"I just got started on the bookcase and I remembered that I let the woodstove go," he said ruefully. He waggled the paintbrush at her. "It's gonna take me another hour to finish the bookcase. I really can't stop with this lacquer."

"Goddammit, Frank . . ." She rolled her eyes.

"I'm sorry." Moderately penitent, in a charming cowboy way.

"How about the sheriff?" she asked. New topic. "Are you still gonna do it?"

"I'll see him tomorrow," he said. He turned his head, refusing to meet her eyes.

"It's nothing but trouble," she said. The argument had been simmering between them. She stepped away from the sink and bent backwards, to look down the hall toward Lisa's room. The girl's door was closed and the faint sounds of Guns 'N Roses leaked out around the edges. Claudia's voice grew sharper, worried. "If you'd just shut up . . . It's *not* your responsibility, Frank. You *told* Harper about it. Jim was *his* boy. *If* it's Jim."

"It's Jim, all right. And I told you how Harper acted." Frank's mouth closed in a narrow, tight line. Claudia recognized the expression, knew he wouldn't change his mind. Like what's-his-name, in *High Noon*. Gary Cooper.

"I wish I'd never seen the picture," she said, dropping her head. Her right hand went to her temple, rubbing it. Lisa had taken her back to her bedroom to give it to her. Didn't want Frank to see it.

"We can't just let it lay," Frank insisted. "I told Harper that."

"There'll be trouble, Frank," Claudia said.

"And the law can handle it. It don't have nothing to do with us," he said. After a moment he asked, "Will you get the stove?"

"Yeah, yeah. I'll get the stove."

Claudia looked out the window toward the mercury-vapor yard-light down by the garage. The snow seemed to come from a point just below the light, as though it were being poured through a funnel, straight into the window, straight into her eyes. Small pellets, like birdshot. "It looks like it might be slowing down."

"Wasn't supposed to snow at all," Frank said. "Assholes."

He meant television weathermen. The weathermen said it would be clear and cold in Ojibway County, and here they were, snowing to beat the band.

"Think about letting it go." She was pleading now. "Just think about it."

"I'll think about it," he said, and he turned and went back down to the basement.

He might think about it, but he wouldn't change his mind. Claudia, turning the picture in her mind, put on a sweatshirt and walked out to the mudroom. Frank had gotten his driving gloves wet and had draped them over the furnace vent; the room smelled of heat-dried wool. She pulled on her parka and a stocking cap, picked up her gloves, turned on the porch lights from the switch inside the mudroom and stepped out into the storm.

The picture. The people might have been anybody, from Los Angeles or Miami, where they did these things. They weren't.

They were from Lincoln County. The printing was bad and the paper was so cheap it almost crumbled in your fingers. But it was the Harper boy, all right. If you looked close, you could see the stub of the finger on the left hand, the one he'd caught in a log splitter; and you could see the loop earring. He was naked on a couch, his hips toward the camera, a dulled, wondering look on his face. He had the thickening face of an adolescent, but she could still see the shadow of a little boy she'd known, working at his father's gas station.

In the foreground of the picture was the torso of an adult man, hairy-chested, gross. The image came too quickly to Claudia's mind; she was familiar enough with men and their physical mechanisms, but there was something about this, something so bad . . . the boy's eyes, caught in a flash, were black points. When she'd looked closely, it seemed that somebody at the magazine had put the pupils in with a felt-tipped pen.

✳

She shivered, not from the cold, and hurried down the snow-blown trench that led out to the garage and woodshed. There were four inches of new snow in the trench: she'd have to blow it out again in the morning.

The trench ended at the garage door. She shoved the door open, stepped inside, snapped on the lights and stomped her feet without thinking. The garage was insulated and heated with a woodstove. Four good chunks of oak would burn slowly enough, and throw off enough heat, to keep the inside temperature above the freezing point on even the coldest nights. Warm enough to start the cars, anyway. Out here, in the Chequamegon, getting the cars to start could be a matter of life and death.

The stove was still hot. Down to coals, but Frank had cleaned it out the night before—she wouldn't have to do that, anyway. She looked back toward the door, at the woodpile. Enough for the night, but no more. She tossed a few wrist-thin splits of sap-heavy pine onto the fire, to get some flame going, then four solid chunks of oak. That would do it.

She looked at the space where the woodpile should have been, sighed, and decided she might as well bring in a few chunks now—give it a chance to thaw before morning. She went back outside, pulling the door shut, but not latched, walked along the side of the garage to the lean-to that covered the woodpile. She picked up four more chunks of oak, staggered back to the garage door, pushed the door open with her foot and dropped the oak next to the stove. One more trip, she thought; Frank could do his share tomorrow.

She went back out to the side of the garage, into the dark of the woodshed, picked up two more pieces of oak.

And felt the short hairs rise on the back of her neck.

Somebody was here with her . . .

Claudia dropped the oak splits, one gloved hand going to her throat. The woodlot was dark beyond the back of the garage. She could feel it, but not see it, could hear her heart pounding in her ears, and the snow hitting her hood with a delicate pit-put-pit. Nothing else: but still . . .

She backed away. Nothing but the snow and the blue circle of the yard-light. At the snow-blown trench, she paused, straining into the dark . . . and ran.

Up to the house, still with the sense of someone behind her, his hand almost there, reaching for her. She pawed at the door handle, smashed it down, hit the door with the heel of her hand, followed it into the heat and light of the mudroom.

"Claudia?"

She screamed.

❋

Frank stood there, with a paint rag, eyes wide, startled. "What?"

"My God," she said. She pulled down the zip on the snowmobile suit, struggled with the hood snaps, her mouth working, nothing coming out until: "My God, Frank, there's somebody out there by the garage."

"What?" He frowned and went to the kitchen window, looked out. "Did you see him?"

"No, but I swear to God, Frank, there's somebody out there. I could *feel* him," she said, catching his arm, looking past him through the window. "Call nine-one-one."

"I don't see anything," Frank said. He went through the kitchen, bent over the sink, looked out toward the yard-light.

"You *can't* see anything," Claudia said. She flipped the lock on the door, then stepped into the kitchen. "Frank, I swear to God there's somebody . . ."

"All right," he said. He took her seriously: "I'll go look."

"Why don't we call . . . ?"

"I'll take a look," he said again. Then: "They wouldn't send a cop out here, in this storm. Not if you didn't even see anybody."

He was right. Claudia followed him into the mudroom, heard herself babbling: "I loaded up the stove, then I went around to the side to bring some wood in for tomorrow morning . . ." and she thought, *I'm not like this.*

Frank sat on the mudroom bench and pulled off the Tony Lamas, stepped into his snowmobile suit, sat down, pulled on his pacs, laced them, then zipped the suit and picked up his gloves. "Back in a minute," he said. He sounded exasperated; but he knew her. She wasn't one to panic.

"I'll come," she blurted.

"Nah, you wait," he said.

"Frank: take the gun." She hurried over to the service island, jerked open the drawer. Way at the back, a fully loaded Smith and Wesson .357 Magnum snuggled behind a divider. "Maybe it's Harper. Maybe . . ."

"Jesus," he said, shaking his head. He grinned at her ruefully, and he was out the door, pulling on his ski gloves.

On the stoop, the snow pecked his face, mean little hard pellets. He half-turned against it. As long as he wasn't looking directly into the wind, the snowmobile suit kept him comfortable. But he couldn't see much, or hear anything but the sound of the wind whistling over the nylon hood. With his head averted, he walked down the steps onto the snow-blown path to the garage.

❈

The Iceman was there, next to the woodpile, his shoulder just at the corner of the shed, his back to the wind. He'd been in the woodlot when Claudia came out. He'd tried to get to her, but he hadn't dared use the flashlight and in the dark, had gotten tangled in brush and had to stop. When she ran back inside, he'd almost turned away, headed back to the snowmobile. The opportunity was lost, he thought. Somehow, she'd been warned. And time was pressing. He looked at his watch. He had a half hour, no more.

But after a moment of thought, he'd methodically untangled his snowshoes and continued toward the dark hulk of the garage. He had to catch the LaCourts together, in the kitchen, where he could take care of both of them at once. They'd have guns, so he'd have to be quick.

The Iceman carried a Colt Anaconda under his arm. He'd stolen it from a man who never knew it was stolen. He'd done that a lot, in the old days. Got a lot of good stuff. The Anaconda was a treasure, every curve and notch with a function.

The corn-knife, on the other hand, was almost elegant in its crudeness. Homemade, with a rough wooden handle, it looked something like a machete, but with a thinner blade and a squared end. In the old days it had been used to chop cornstalks. The blade had been covered with a patina of surface rust, but he'd put the edge on a shop grinder and the new edge was silvery and fine and sharp enough to shave with.

The corn-knife might kill, but that wasn't why he'd brought it. The corn-knife was simply horrifying. If he needed a threat to get the picture, if he needed to hurt the girl bad but not kill her, then the corn-knife was exactly right.

Standing atop the snow, the Iceman felt like a giant, his head reaching nearly to the eaves of the garage as he worked his way down its length. He saw Frank come to the window and peer out, and he stopped. Had Claudia seen him after all? Impossible. She'd turned away, and she'd run, but he could hardly see her, even with the garage and yard-lights on her. He'd been back in the dark, wearing black. Impossible.

The Iceman was sweating from the short climb up the bank, and the struggle with the brush. He snapped the releases and pulled the bindings loose, but stayed balanced on the shoes. He'd have to be careful climbing down into the trench. He glanced at his watch. *Time time time . . .*

He unzipped his parka, pulled his glove and reached inside to touch the wooden stock of the Anaconda. Ready. He was turning to step into the trench when the back door opened and a shaft of light played out across the porch. The Iceman rocked back, dragging the snowshoes with his boots, into the darkness beside the woodshed, his back to the corrugated metal garage wall.

Frank was a dark silhouette in the light of the open door, then a three-dimensional figure shuffling down the snow trench out toward the garage. He had a flashlight in one hand, and played it off the side of the garage. The Iceman eased back as the light crossed the side wall of the garage, gave Frank a few seconds to get farther down the path, then peeked around the corner. Frank had gotten to the garage door, opened it. The Iceman shuffled up to the corner of the garage, the gun in his left hand, the corn-knife in his right, the cold burning his bare hands.

Frank snapped on the garage lights, stepped inside. A moment later, the lights went out again. Frank stepped out, pulled it tight behind him, rattled the knob. Stepped up the path. Shone the flashlight across the yard at the propane tank.

Took another step.

The Iceman was there. The corn-knife whipped down, *chunked*. Frank saw it coming, just soon enough to flinch, not soon enough to avoid it. The knife chocked through Frank's parka and into his skull, the shock jolted through the Iceman's arm. A familiar shock, as though he'd chopped the blade into a fence post.

The blade popped free as Frank pitched over. He was dead as he fell, but his body made a sound like a stepped-on snake, a tight exhalation, a ccccuuuhhhhh, and blood ran into the snow.

For just a second then, the wind stopped, as though nature were holding her breath. The snow seemed to pause with the wind, and something flicked across the edge of the woods, at the corner of the Iceman's vision. Something out there . . . he was touched by an uneasiness. He watched, but there was no further movement, and the wind and snow were back as quickly as they'd gone.

The Iceman stepped down into the trench, started toward the house. Claudia's face appeared in the window, floating out there in the storm. He stopped, sure he'd been seen: but she pressed her face closer to the window, peering out, and he realized that he was still invisible. After a moment, her face moved back away from the window. The Iceman started for the house again, climbed the porch as quietly as he could, turned the knob, pushed the door open.

"Frank?" Claudia was there, in the doorway to the kitchen. Her hand popped out of her sleeve and the Iceman saw the flash of chrome, knew the flash, reacted, brought up the big .44 Mag.

"Frank?" Claudia screamed. The .357 hung in her hand, by her side, unready, unthought-of, a worthless icon of self-defense. Then the V of the back sight and the i of the front sight crossed the plane of her head and the .44 bucked in the Iceman's hand. He'd spent hours in the quarry doing this, swinging on targets, and he knew he had her, felt the accuracy in his bones, one with the target.

The slug hit Claudia in the forehead and the world stopped. No more Lisa, no more Frank, no more nights in the Holiday Inn with the mirrors, no memories, no regrets. Nothing. She didn't fly back, like in the movies. She wasn't hammered down. She simply dropped, her mouth open. The Iceman, bringing the Colt back to bear, felt a thin sense of disappointment. The big gun should batter them down, blow them up; the big gun was a Universal Force.

From the back room, then, in the silence after the shot, a young girl's voice, not yet afraid: "Mom? Mom? What was that?"

The Iceman grabbed Claudia's parka hood, dragged her into the kitchen and dropped her. She lay on the floor like a puppet with the strings cut. Her eyes were open, sightless. He ignored her. He was focused now on the back room. He needed the picture. He hefted the corn-knife and started back.

The girl's voice again. A little fear this time: "Mom?"

CHAPTER
❊ ❊ ❊

Lucas Davenport climbed down from his truck. The light
on the LaCourt house was brilliant. In the absolutely clear
air, every crack, every hole, every splinter of glass was as
sharp as a hair under a microscope. The smell of death—the
smell of pork roast—slipped up to him, and he turned his
face toward it, looking for it, like a stone-age hunter.

The house looked oddly like a skull, with its glassless
windows gaping out at the snowscape. The front door was
splintered by fire axes, while the side door, hanging from
the house by a single hinge, was twisted and blackened
by the fire. Vinyl siding had melted, charred, burned. Half
of the roof was gone, leaving the center of the ruin open to
the sky. Pink fiberglass insulation was everywhere, sticking
out of the house, blowing across the snow, hung up in the
bare birch branches like obscene fleshy hair. Firehose ice,
mixed with soot and ash, flowed around and out of the
house like a miniature glacier.

On the land side of the house, three banks of portable
stadium-style lights, run off an ancient gas-powered Army
generator, poured a hundred million candlepower of blue-
white light onto the scene. The generator underlined the
shouting of the firemen and the thrumming of the fire truck

pumps with a ferocious jackhammer pounding.

All of it stank.

Of gasoline and burning insulation, of water-soaked plaster and barbecued bodies, diesel fumes. The fire had moved fast, burned fiercely, and had been smothered in a hurry. The dead had been charred rather than cremated.

Twenty men swarmed over the house. Some were firemen, others were cops; three or four were civilians. The snow had eased, at least temporarily, but the wind was like a razor, slashing at exposed skin.

❅

Lucas was tall, dark-complected, with startling blue eyes set deep under a strong brow. His hair was dark, but touched with gray, and a bit long; a sheath of it fell over his forehead, and he pushed it out of his eyes as he stood looking at the house.

Quivering, almost—like an expensive pointer.

His face should have been square, and normally was, when he was ten pounds heavier. A square face fit with the rest of him, with his heavy shoulders and hands. But now he was gaunt, the skin stretched around his cheekbones: the face of a boxer in hard training. Every day for a month he'd put on either skis or snowshoes, and had run up through the hills around his North Woods cabin. In the afternoon he worked in the woodlot, splitting oak with a mall and wedge.

Lucas stepped toward the burnt house as though hypnotized. He remembered another house, in Minneapolis, just south of the loop, a frozen night in February. A gang leader lived in the downstairs apartment; a rival group of 'bangers decided to take him out. The top floor was occupied by a woman—Shirleen something—who ran an illegal overnight child-care center for neighborhood mothers. There were six children sleeping upstairs when the Molotov cocktails came through the windows downstairs. Shirleen dropped all six screaming kids out the window, breaking legs on two of them, ribs on two more, and an arm on a neighbor who was trying to stop their fall. The woman was too big to jump herself and burned to death trying to get down the single stairway. Same deal: the house like a skull, the firehose ice, the smell of roast pork. . . .

Lucas unconsciously shook his head and smiled: he'd had good lines into the crack community and gave homicide the 'bangers' names. They were locked in Stillwater, and would be for another eight years. In two days he'd done a number on them they still didn't believe.

Now this. He stepped back to the open door of his truck, leaned inside, took a black cashmere watch cap off the passenger seat and pulled it over his head. He wore a blue parka over jeans and a cable-knit sweater, pac boots, and expedition-weight polypropylene long underwear. A deputy walked around the Chevy Suburban that had pulled into the yard just ahead of Davenport's Ford. Henry Lacey wore the standard tan sheriff's department parka and insulated pants.

"Shelly's over here," Lacey said, jerking a thumb toward the house. "C'mon—I'll introduce you . . . what're you looking at, the house? What's funny?"

"Nothing."

"Thought you were smiling," Lacey said, looking vaguely disturbed.

"Nah . . . just cold," Lucas said, groping for an excuse. Goddamn, he loved this.

"Well . . . Shelly . . ."

"Yeah." Lucas followed, pulling on his thick ski gloves, still focused on the house. The place might have been snatched from a frozen suburb of hell. He felt at home.

❊

Sheldon Carr stood on a slab of ice in the driveway, behind the volunteer tanker and pumper trucks. He wore the same sheriff's cold-weather gear as Lacey, but black instead of khaki, with the sheriff's gold star instead of the silver deputy's badge. A frozen black hose snaked past his feet down to the lake, where the firefighters had augered through three feet of ice to get at the lake water. Now they were using a torch to free the hose, and the blue flame flickered at the edge of Carr's vision.

Carr was stunned. He'd done what he could, and then he stopped functioning: he simply stood in the driveway and watched the firemen work. And he froze. His cold-weather gear wasn't enough for this weather. His legs were stiff and his feet numb, but he couldn't go into the garage, couldn't tear himself away. He stood like a dark snowman, slightly fat, unmoving, hands away from his side, staring up at the house.

"Piece a . . ." A fireman slipped and fell, cursing. Carr had to turn his whole body to look at him. The fireman was smeared with ash and half-covered with ice. When they'd tried to spray the house, the wind had whipped the water back on them as sleet. Some of the firemen looked like small mobile icebergs, the powerful lights glistening off them as they worked across the yard. This one was on his back, looking up at Carr, his mustache white with frost from his own breath, face red from the wind and exertion. Carr moved to help him, hand out, but the fireman waved him away. "I'd just pull you down," he said. He clambered awkwardly to his feet, struggling with a frozen firehose. He was trying to load it into a pickup truck and it fought back like an anaconda on speed. "Piece a shit . . ."

Carr turned back to the house. A rubber-encased fireman was helping the doctor climb through the shattered front door. Carr watched as they began to pick their way toward the back bedroom. The little girl was there, so burnt that God only knew what had happened to her. What had happened to her parents was clear enough. Claudia's face had been partly protected by a fireproof curtain that had fallen over her. A fat bullet hole stared out of her forehead like a blank third eye. And Frank . . .

"Heard anything from Madison?" Carr called to a deputy in a Jeep. The deputy had the engine turning over, heater on high, window down just far enough to communicate.

"Nope. It's still snowin' down there. I guess they're waitin' it out."

"Waitin' it out? Waitin' it out?" Sheldon Carr was suddenly shouting, eyes wild. "Call the fuckers back and tell them to get their asses up here. They've heard of four-by-fours, haven't they? Call them back."

"Right now," the deputy said, shocked. He'd never heard Sheldon Carr say anything stronger than *gol-darn.*

Carr turned away, his jaw working, the cold forgotten. *Waiting it out?* Henry Lacey was walking toward him, carefully flatfooted on the treacherous slab of ice that had run down into the yard. He was trailed by a man in a parka. Lacey came up, nodded, said, "This is Davenport."

Carr nodded: "Th–th–thanks f–f–for coming." He suddenly couldn't get the words out.

Lacey took his elbow. "Have you been out here all the time?"

Carr nodded numbly and Lacey tugged him toward the garage, said, "My God, Shelly, you'll kill yourself."

"I'm okay," Carr ground out. He pulled his arm free, turned to Lucas. "When I heard you were up here from the Cities, I figured you'd know more about this kind of thing than I do. Thought it was worth a try. Hope you can help us."

"Henry tells me it's a mess," Lucas said.

He grinned as he said it, a slightly nasty smile, Carr thought. Davenport had a chipped tooth, never capped, the kind of thing you might have gotten in a fight, and a scar bisected one eyebrow. "It's a . . ." Carr shook his head, groping for a word. "It's a gol-darn *tragedy,*" he said finally.

Lucas glanced at him: he'd never heard a cop call a crime a tragedy. He'd never heard a cop say gol-darn. He couldn't see much of Carr's face, but the sheriff was a large man with an ample belly. In the black snowmobile suit, he looked like the Michelin tire man in mourning.

"Where's LES?" Lucas asked. The Division of Law Enforcement Services did mobile crime-scene work on major crimes.

"They're having trouble getting out of Madison," Carr said grimly. He waved at the sky. "The storm . . ."

"Don't they have four-by-fours? It's all highway."

"We're finding that out right now," Carr snapped. He apologized: "Sorry, that's a tender subject. They shoulda been halfway here by now." He looked back at the house, as if helpless to resist it: "Lord help us."

"Three dead?" Lucas asked.

"Three dead," Carr said. "Shot, chopped with some kind of ax or something, and the other one . . . shoot, there's no way to tell. Just a kid."

"Still in the house?"

"Come on," Carr said grimly. He suddenly began to shake uncontrollably, then, with an effort, relaxed. "We got tarps on 'em. And there's something else . . . heck, let's look at the bodies, then we'll get to that."

"Shelly, are you okay?" Lacey asked again.

"Yeah, yeah . . . I'll show Davenport—Lucas?—I'll show Lucas around, then I'll get inside. Gosh, I can't believe this cold."

❋

Frank LaCourt lay faceup on a sidewalk that led from the house to the garage. Carr had one of the deputies lift the plastic tarp that covered the body and Lucas squatted beside it.

"Jesus," he said. He looked up at Carr, who'd turned away. "What happened to his face?"

"Dog, maybe," Carr said, looking sideways down at the mutilated face. "Coyotes . . . I don't know."

"Could have been a wolf," Lacey said from behind him. "We've had some reports, I think there are a few moving down."

"Messed him up," Lucas said.

Carr looked out at the forest that pressed around the house: "It's the winter," he said. "Everything's starving out there. We're feedin' some deer, but most of them are gonna die. Shoot, most of them are already dead. There're coyotes hanging around the dumpsters in town, at the pizza place."

Lucas pulled off a glove, fumbled a hand-flash from his

parka pocket and shone it on what was left of the man's face. LaCourt was an Indian, maybe forty-five. His hair was stiff with frozen blood. An animal had torn the flesh off much of the left side of his face. The left eye was gone and the nose was chewed away.

"He got it from the side, half-split his head in two, right through the hood," Carr said. Lucas nodded, touched the hood with his gloved finger, looking at the cut fabric. "The doc said it was some kind of knife or cleaver," Carr said.

Lucas stood up. "Henry said snowshoes . . ."

"Right there," Lacey said, pointing.

Lucas turned the flashlight into the shadows along the shed. Broad indentations were still visible in the snow. The indentations were half drifted-in.

"Where do they go?" Lucas asked, staring into the dark trees.

"They come up from the lake, through the woods, and they go back down," Carr said, pointing at an angle through the jumble of forest. "There's a snowmobile trail down there, machines coming and going all the time. Frank had a couple sleds himself, so it could have been him that made the tracks. We don't know."

"The tracks come right up to where he was chopped," Lucas said.

"Yeah—but we don't know if he walked down to the lake on snowshoes to look at something, and then came back up and was killed, or if the killer came in and went out."

"If they were his snowshoes, where are they now?"

"There's a set of shoes in the mudroom, but they were so messed up by the firehoses that we don't know if they'd just been used or what . . . no way to tell," Lacey said. "They're the right kind, though. Bearpaws. No tails."

"Okay."

"But we still got a problem," Carr said, looking reluctantly down at the body. "Look at the snow on him. The firemen threw the tarps over them as soon as they got here, but it looks to me like there's maybe a half-inch of snow on him."

"So what?"

Carr stared down at the body for a moment, then dropped his voice. "Listen, I'm freezing and there's some strange stuff to talk about. A problem. So do you want to see the other bodies now? Woman was shot in the forehead, the girl's burned. Or we could just go talk."

"A quick look," Lucas said.

"Come on, then," Carr said.

Lacey broke away. "I gotta check that commo gear, Shelly."

Lucas and Carr trudged across a layer of discolored ice to the house, squeezed past the front door. Inside, sheetrock walls and ceiling panels had buckled and folded, falling across burned furniture and carpet. Dishes, pots and pans, glassware littered the floor, along with a set of ceramic collector's dolls. Picture frames were everywhere. Some were burned, but every step or two, a clear, happy face would look up at him, wide-eyed, well-lit. Better days.

Two deputies were working through the house with cameras: one with a video camera, the power wire running down his collar under his parka, the other with a 35mm Nikon.

"My hands are freezing," the video man stuttered.

"Go on down to the garage," Carr said. "Don't get yourself hurt."

"There're a couple gallon jugs of hot coffee and some paper cups in my truck. The white Explorer in the parking lot," Lucas said. "Doors are open."

"Th–thanks."

"Save some for me," Carr said. And to Lucas: "Where'd you get the coffee?"

"Stopped at Dow's Corners on the way over and emptied out their coffeemaker. I did six years on patrol and I must've froze my ass off at a hundred of these things."

"Huh. Dow's." Carr squinted, digging in a mental file. "That's still Phil and Vickie?"

"Yeah. You know them?"

"I know everybody on Highway 77, from Hayward in Sawyer County to Highway 13 in Ashland County," Carr said matter-of-factly. "This way."

He led the way down a charred hall past a bathroom door to a small bedroom. The lakeside wall was gone and blowing snow sifted through the debris. The body was under a burnt-out bedframe, the coil springs resting on the girl's chest. One of the portable lights was just outside the window, and cast flat, prying light on the scorched wreckage, but left the girl's face in almost total darkness: but not quite total. Lucas could see her improbably white teeth smiling from the char.

Lucas squatted, snapped on the flash, grunted, turned it off and stood up again.

"Made me sick," said Carr. "I was with the highway patrol before I got elected sheriff. I saw some car wrecks you wouldn't believe. They didn't make me sick. This did."

"Accidents are different," Lucas agreed. He looked around the room. "Where's the other one?"

"Kitchen," Carr said. They started down the hall again. "Why'd he burn the place?" Carr asked, his voice pitching up. "It couldn't have been to hide the killings. He left Frank's body right out in the yard. If he'd just taken off, it might have been a day or two before anybody came out. Was he bragging about it?"

"Maybe he was thinking about fingerprints. What'd LaCourt do?"

"He worked down at the res, at the Eagle Casino. He was a security guy."

"Lots of money in casinos," Lucas said. "Was he in trouble down there?"

"I don't know," Carr said simply.

"How about his wife?"

"She was a teacher's aide."

"Any marital problems or ex-husbands wandering around?" Lucas asked.

"Well, they were both married before. I'll check Frank's ex-wife, but I know her, Jean Hansen, and she wouldn't hurt a fly. And Claudia's ex is Jimmy Wilson and Jimmy moved out to Phoenix three or four winters back, but he wouldn't do this, either. I'll check on him, but neither one of the divorces was really nasty. The people just didn't like each other anymore. You know?"

"Yeah, I know. How about the girl? Did she have any boyfriends?"

"I'll check that too," Carr said. "But, uh, I don't know. I'll check. She's pretty young."

"There's been a rash of teenagers killing their families and friends."

"Yeah. A generation of weasels."

"And teenage boys sometimes mix up fire and sex. You get a lot of teenage firebugs. If there was somebody hot for the girl, it'd be something to look into."

"You could talk to Bob Jones at the junior high. He's the principal and he does the counseling, so he might know."

"Um," Lucas said. His sleeve touched a burnt wall, and he brushed it off.

"I'm hoping you'll stay around a while," Carr blurted. Before Lucas could answer, he said, "Come on down this way."

They picked their way toward the other end of the house, through the living room, into the kitchen by the back door. Two heavily wrapped figures were crouched over a third body.

The larger of the two people stood up, nodded at Carr. He wore a Russian-style hat with the flaps pulled down and a deputy sheriff's patch on the front. The other, with the bag, was using a metal tool to turn the victim's head.

"Can't believe this weather," the deputy said. "I'm so fuck—uh, cold I can't believe it."

"Fucking cold is what you meant to say," said the figure still crouched over the body. Her voice was low and uninflected, almost scholarly. "I really don't mind the word, especially when it's so fucking cold."

"It wasn't you he was worried about, it was me," Carr said bluntly. "You see anything down there, Weather, or are you just fooling around?"

The woman looked up and said, "We've got to get them down to Milwaukee and let the pros take a look. No amateur nights at the funeral home."

"Can you see anything at all?" Lucas asked.

The doctor looked down at the woman under her hands. "Claudia was shot, obviously, and with a pretty powerful weapon. Could be a rifle. The whole back of her head was shattered and a good part of her brain is gone. The slug went straight through. We'll have to hope the crime lab people can recover it. It's not inside her."

"How about the girl?" Lucas asked.

"Yeah. It'll take an autopsy to tell you anything definitive. There are signs of charred cloth around her waist and between her legs, so I'd say she was wearing underpants and maybe even, um, what do you call those fleece pants, like uh . . ."

"Sweat pants," Carr said.

"Yes, like that. And Claudia was definitely dressed, jeans and long underwear."

"You're saying they weren't raped," Lucas said.

The woman stood and nodded. Her parka hood was tight around her face, and nothing showed but an oval patch of skin around her eyes and nose. "I can't say it for sure, but just up front, it doesn't look like it. But what happened to her might have been worse."

"Worse?" Carr recoiled.

"Yes." She stooped, opened her bag, and the deputy said, "I don't want to look at this." She stood up again and handed Carr a Ziploc bag. Inside was something that looked like a dried apricot that had been left on a charcoal grill. Carr peered at it and then gave it to Lucas.

"What is it?" Carr asked the woman.

"Ear," she and Lucas said simultaneously. Lucas handed it back to her.

"Ear? You can't be serious," Carr said.

"Taken off before or after she was killed?" Lucas asked, his voice mild, interested. Carr looked at him in horror.

"You'd need a lab to tell you that," Weather said in her professional voice, matching Lucas. "There are some crusts that look like blood. I'm not sure, but I'd say she was alive when it was taken off."

The sheriff looked at the bag in the doctor's hand and

turned and walked two steps away, bent over and retched, a stream of saliva pouring from his mouth. After a moment, he straightened, wiped his mouth on the back of a glove, and said, "I gotta get out of here."

"And Frank was done with an ax," Lucas said.

"No, I don't think so. Not an ax," the woman said, shaking her head. Lucas peered at her, but could see almost nothing of her face. "A machete, a very sharp machete. Or maybe something even thinner. Maybe something like, um, a scimitar."

"A what?" The sheriff goggled at her.

"I don't know," she said defensively. "Whatever it was, the blade was very thin and sharp. Like a five-pound razor. It *cut* through the bone, rather than smashing through like a wedge-shaped weapon would. But it had weight, too."

"Don't go telling that to anybody at the *Register,*" Carr said. "They'd go crazy."

"They're gonna go crazy anyway," she said.

"Well, don't make them any crazier."

"What about the guy's face?" Lucas asked. "The bites?"

"Dog," she said. "Coyote. God knows I see enough dog bites around here and it looks like a dog did it."

"You can hear them howling at night, bunches of them," the deputy said. "Coyotes."

"Yeah, I've got them up around my place," Lucas said.

"Are you with the state?" the woman asked.

"No. I used to be a Minneapolis cop. I've got a cabin over in Sawyer County and the sheriff asked me to run over and take a look."

"Lucas Davenport," the sheriff said, nodding at him. "I'm sorry, Lucas, this is Weather Karkinnen."

"I've heard about you," the woman said, nodding.

"Weather was a surgeon down in the Cities before she came back home," the sheriff said to Lucas.

"Is that Weather, like 'Stormy Weather'?" Lucas asked.

"Exactly," the doctor said.

"I hope what you heard about Davenport was good," Carr said to her.

The doctor looked up at Lucas and tilted her head. The

light on her changed and he could see that her eyes were
blue. Her nose seemed to be slightly crooked. "I remember
that he killed an awful lot of people," she said.

❋

The doctor was freezing, she said, and she led the way
toward the front door, the deputy following, Carr stum-
bling behind. Lucas lingered, looking down at the dead
woman. As he turned to leave, he saw a slice of nickeled
metal under a piece of crumbled and blackened wallboard.
From the curve of it, he knew what it was: the forepart of
a trigger guard.

"Hey," he called after the others. "Is that camera guy still
in the house?"

Carr called back, "The video guy's in the garage, but the
other guy's here."

"Send him back here, we got a weapon."

Carr, Weather, and the photographer came back. Lucas
pointed out the trigger guard, and the photographer took
two shots of the area. Moving carefully, Lucas lifted the
wallboard. A revolver. A nickel-finish Smith and Wesson
on a heavy frame, walnut grips. He pushed the board back
out of the way, then stood back as the photographer shot
the gun in relation to the body.

"You got a chalk or a grease pencil?" Lucas asked.

"Yeah, and a tape measure." The photographer groped in
his pocket, came up with a grease pencil.

"Shouldn't you leave it for the lab guys?" Carr asked
nervously.

"Big frame, could be the murder weapon," Lucas said.
He drew a quick outline around the weapon, then measured
the distance of the gun from the wall and the dead woman's
head and one hand, while the photographer noted them.
With the measurements done, Lucas handed the grease
pencil back to the photographer, looked around, picked
up a splinter of wood, pushed it through the fingerguard,
behind the trigger, and lifted the pistol from the floor. He
looked at the doctor. "Do you have another one of those
Ziplocs?"

"Yes." She opened her bag, supported it against her leg, dug around, and opened a freezer bag for him. He dropped the gun into it, pointed the barrel at the floor, and through the plastic he pushed the ejection level and swung the cylinder.

"Six shells, unfired," he said. "Shit."

"Unfired?" Carr asked.

"Yeah. I don't think it's the murder weapon. The killer wouldn't reload and then drop it on the floor . . . at least I can't think why he would."

"So?" Weather looked up at him.

"So maybe the woman had it out. I found it about a foot from her hand. She might have seen the guy coming. That means there might have been a feud going on; she knew she was in trouble," Lucas said. He read the serial number to the photographer, who noted it: "You could try to run it tonight. Check the local gun stores, anyway."

"I'll get it going," Carr said. Then: "I n–n–need some coffee."

"I think you're fairly hypothermic, Shelly," Weather said. "What you need is to sit in a tub of hot water."

"Yeah, yeah."

As they climbed down from the front door, Lucas carrying the pistol, another deputy was walking up the driveway. "I got those tarps, Sheriff. They're right behind me in a Guard truck."

"Good. Get some help and cover up the whole works," Carr said, waving at the house. "There'll be guys in the garage." To Lucas he said, "I got some canvas sheets from the National Guard guys and we're gonna cover the whole house until the guys from Madison get here."

"Good." Lucas nodded. "You really need the lab guys for this. Don't let anybody touch anything. Not even the bodies."

✳

The garage was warm, with deputies and firemen standing around an old-fashioned iron stove stoked with oak splits. The deputy who'd been doing the filming spotted them and came over with one of Lucas' Thermos jugs.

"I saved some," he said.

"Thanks, Tommy." The sheriff nodded, took a cup, hand shaking, passed it to Lucas, then took a cup for himself. "Let's get over in the corner where we can talk," he said. Carr walked around the nose of LaCourt's old Chevy station wagon, away from the gathering of deputies and firemen, turned, took a sip of coffee. He said, "We've got a problem." He stopped, then asked, "You're not a Catholic, are you?"

"Dominus vobiscum," Lucas said. "So what?"

"You are? I haven't been in the Church long enough to remember the Latin business," Carr said. He seemed to think about that for a moment, sipped coffee, then said, "I converted a few years back. I was a Lutheran until I met Father Phil. He's the parish priest in Grant."

"Yeah? I don't have much interest in the Church anymore."

"Hmph. You should consider . . ."

"Tell me about the problem," Lucas said impatiently.

"I'm trying to, but it's complicated," Carr said. "Okay. We figure whoever killed these folks must've started the fire. It was snowing all afternoon—we had about four inches of new snow. When the firemen got here, though, the snow'd just about quit. But Frank's body had maybe a half-inch of snow on it. That's why I had them put the tarp over it, I thought we could fix an exact time. It wasn't long between the time he was killed and the fire. But it was *some* time. That's important. *Some* time. And now you tell me the girl might have been tortured . . . *more* time."

"Okay." Lucas nodded, nodding at the emphasis.

"Whoever started the fire did it with gasoline," Carr said. "You can still smell it, and the house went up like a torch. Maybe the killer brought the gas with him or maybe he used Frank's. There're a couple boats and a snowmobile out in the back shed but there aren't any gas cans with them, and no cans in here. The cans'd most likely have some gas in them."

"Anyway, the house went up fast," Lucas said.

"Yeah. The folks across the lake were watching television. They say that one minute there was nothing out the window but the snow. The next minute there was a fireball. They called the firehouse."

"The one I came by? Down at the corner?"

"Yeah. There were two guys down there. They were making a snack and one of them saw a black Jeep go by. Just a few seconds later, the alarm came in. They thought the Jeep belonged to Phil . . . the priest. Father Philip Bergen, the pastor at All Souls."

"Did it?" Lucas asked.

"Yes. They said it looked like Phil was coming out of the lake road. So I called him and asked him if he'd seen anything unusual. A fire or somebody in the road. And he said no. Then, before I could say anything else, he said he was here, at the LaCourts'."

"Here?" Lucas eyebrows went up.

"Yeah. Here. He said everything was all right when he left."

"Huh." Lucas thought about it. "Are we sure the time is right?"

"It's right. One of the firemen was standing at the microwave with one of those prefab ham sandwiches. They take two minutes to cook and it was about ready. The other one said, 'There goes Father Phil, hell of a night to be out.' Then the microwave alarm went off, the guy got his sandwich out, and before he could unwrap it, the alarm came in."

"That's tight."

"Yeah. There wasn't enough time for Frank to have that snow pile up on him. Not if Phil's telling the truth."

"Time is weird," Lucas said. "Especially in an emergency. If it *wasn't* just a minute, if it was five minutes, then this Father Phil *could* have . . ."

"That's what I figured . . . but doesn't look that way." Carr shook his head, swirled coffee around the coffee cup, then set it on the hood of the Chevy and flexed his fingers, trying to work some warmth back in them. "I got the firemen and went over it a couple of times. There just isn't time."

"So the priest . . ."

"He said he left the house and drove straight out to the highway and then into town. I asked him how long it took him to get from the house, here, to the highway, and he said three or four minutes. It's about a mile, so that's about right, with the snow and everything."

"Hmp."

"But if he had something to do with it, why'd he admit being here? That doesn't make any gol-darned sense," the sheriff said.

"Have you hit him with this? Sat him down, gone over it?"

"No. I'm not real experienced with interrogation. I can take some kid who's stolen a car or ripped off a beer sign and sit him down by one of the holding cells and scare the devil out of him, but this would be . . . different. I don't know about this kind of stuff. Killers."

"Did you tell him about the time bind?" Lucas asked.

"Not yet."

"Good."

"I was stumped," Carr said, turning to stare blankly at the garage wall, remembering. "When he said he was here, I couldn't think what to say. So I said, 'Okay, we'll get back to you.' He wanted to come out when we told him the family was dead, do the last rites, but we told him to stay put, in town. We didn't want him to . . ."

". . . Contaminate his memory."

"Yeah." Carr nodded, picked up the coffee he'd set on the car hood, and finished it.

"How about the firemen? Would they have any reason to lie about it?"

Carr shook his head. "I know them both, and they're not particular friends. So it wouldn't be like a conspiracy."

"Okay."

Two firemen came through the door. The first was encased in rubber and canvas, and on top of that, an inch-thick layer of ice.

"You look like you fell in the lake," Carr said. "You must be freezing to death."

"It was the spray. I'm not cold, but I can't move," the fireman said. The second fireman said, "Stand still." The fireman stood like a fat rubber scarecrow and began chipping the ice away with a wooden mallet and a cold chisel.

They watched the ice chips fly for a moment, then Carr said, "Something else. When he went by the fire station, he was towing a snowmobile trailer. He's big in one of the snowmobile clubs—he's the president, in fact, or was last year. They'd had a run today, out of a bar across the lake. So he was out on the lake with his sled."

"And those tracks came up from the lake."

"Where nobody'd be without a sled."

"Huh. So you think the priest had something to do with it?"

Carr looked worried. "No. Absolutely not. I know him: he's a friend of mine. But I can't figure it out. He doesn't lie, about anything. He's a moral man."

"If a guy's under pressure . . ."

Carr shook his head. Once they'd been playing golf, he said, both of them fierce competitors. And they were dead even after seventeen. Bergen put his tee shot into a group of pines on the right side of the fairway, made a great recovery and was on the green in two. He two-putted for par, while Carr bogied the hole, and lost.

"I was bragging about his recovery to the other guys in the locker room, and he just looked sadder and sadder. When we were walking down to the bar he grabbed me, and he looked like he was about to cry. His second shot had gone under one of the evergreens, he said, and he'd kicked it out. He wanted to win so bad. But cheating, it wrecked him. He couldn't handle it. That's the kind of guy he is. He wouldn't steal a dime, he wouldn't steal a golf stroke. He's absolutely straight, and incapable of being anything else."

The fireman with the chisel and mallet laid the tools on the floor, grabbed the front of the other fireman's rubber coat, and ripped it open.

"That's got it," said the second man. "I can take it from here." He looked at Carr: "Fun in the great outdoors, huh?"

✳

The doctor was edging between the wall and the nose of the station wagon, followed by a tall man wrapped in a heavy arctic parka. The doctor had light hair spiked with strands of white, cut efficiently short. She was small, but athletic with wide shoulders, a nose that was a bit too big and a little crooked, bent to the left. She had high cheekbones and dark-blue eyes, a mouth that was wide and mobile. She had just a bit of the brawler about her, Lucas thought, with the vaguely Oriental cast that Slavs often carry. She was not pretty, but she was strikingly attractive. "Is this a secret conversation?" she asked. She was carrying a cup of coffee.

"No, not really," Carr said, glancing at Lucas. He gave a tiny backwards wag of his head that meant, *Don't say anything about the priest.*

The tall man said, "Shelly, I hit every place on the road. Nobody saw anything connected, but we've got three people missing yet. I'm trying to track them down now."

"Thanks, Gene," Carr said, and the tall man headed toward the door. To Lucas, he said, "My lead investigator."

Lucas nodded, and looked at Weather. "I don't suppose there was any reason to do body temps."

The doctor shook her head, took another sip of coffee. Lucas noticed that she wore no rings. "Not on the two women. The fire and the water and the ice and snow would mess everything up. Frank was pretty bundled up, though, and I did take a temp on him. Sixty-four degrees. He hadn't been dead that long."

"Huh," said Carr, glancing at Lucas.

The doctor caught it and looked from Lucas to Carr and asked, "Is that critical?"

"You might want to write it down somewhere," Carr said.

"There's a question about how long they were dead before the fire started," Lucas said.

Weather was looking at him oddly. "Maddog, right?"

"What?"

"You were the guy who killed the Maddog after he sliced up all those women. And you were in that fight with those Indian guys."

Lucas nodded. "Yeah." *The Crows coming out of that house in the dark, .45s in their hands. . . . Why'd she have to bring that up?*

"I had a friend who did that New York cop, the woman who was shot in the chest? I can't remember her name, but at the time she was pretty famous."

"Lily Rothenburg." *Damn. Sloan on the steps of Hennepin General, white-faced, saying, "Got your shit together? . . . Lily's been shot." Sweet Lily.*

"Oh, yes," Weather said, nodding. "I knew it was a flower name. She's back in New York?"

"Yeah. She's a captain now. Your friend was a redheaded surgeon? I remember."

"Yup. That's her. And she was there when the big shootout happened. She says it was the most exciting night of her career. She was doing two ops at the same time, going back and forth between rooms."

"My God, and now it's here," Carr said, appalled. He looked at Lucas. "Listen, I spent five years on the patrol before I got elected up here, and that was twenty years ago. Most of my boys are off the patrol or local police forces. We really don't know nothin' about multiple murder. What I'm askin' is, are you gonna help us out?"

"What do you want me to do?" Lucas asked, shaking away the memories.

"Run the investigation. I'll give you everything I can. Eight or ten guys, help with the county attorney, whatever."

"What authority would I have?"

Carr dipped one hand in his coat pocket and at the same time said, "Do you swear to uphold the laws of the state of Wisconsin and so forth and so on, so help you God?"

"Sure." Lucas nodded.

Carr tossed him a star. "You're a deputy," he said. "We can work out the small stuff later."

Lucas looked at the badge in the palm of his hand.

"Try not to shoot anybody," Weather said.

CHAPTER

✳ ✳ ✳

The Iceman's hands were freezing. He fumbled the can opener twice, then put the soup can aside and turned on the hot water in the kitchen sink. As he let the water run over his fingers, his mind drifted. . . .

He hadn't found the photograph. The girl didn't know where it was, and she'd told the truth: he'd nearly cut her head off before she'd died, cut away her nose and her ears. She said her mother had taken it, and finally, he believed her. But by that time Claudia was dead. Too late to ask where she'd put it.

So he'd killed the girl, chopping her with the corn-knife, and burned the house. The police didn't know there was a photo, and the photo itself was on flimsy newsprint. With the fire, with all the water, it'd be a miracle if it had survived.

Still. He hadn't *seen* it destroyed. The photo, if it were found, would kill him.

Now he stood with his fingers under the hot water. They slowly shaded from white to pink, losing the putty-like consistency they'd had from the brutal cold. For just a moment he closed his eyes, overwhelmed by the sense of things undone. And time was trickling away. A voice at the back of his head said, *Run now. Time is trickling away.*

But he had never run away. Not when his parents had beaten him. Not when kids had singled him out at school. Instead, he had learned to strike first, but slyly, disguising his aggression: even then, cold as ice. Extortion was his style: *I didn't take it, he gave it to me. We were just playing, he fell down, he's just a crybaby, I didn't mean anything.*

In tenth grade he'd learned an important lesson. There were other students as willing to use violence as he was, and violence in tenth grade involved larger bodies, stronger muscles: people got hurt. Noses were broken, shoulders were dislocated in the weekly afternoon fights. Most importantly, you couldn't hide the violence. No way to deny you were in a fight if somebody got hurt.

And somebody got hurt. Darrell Wynan was his name. Tough kid. Picked out the Iceman for one of those reasons known only to people who pick fights: in fact, he had seen it coming. Carried a rock in his pocket, a smooth sandstone pebble the size of a golf ball, for the day the fight came.

Wynan caught him next to the football field, three or four of his remora fish running along behind, carrying their books, delight on their faces. A fight, a fight . . .

The fight lasted five seconds. Wynan came at him in the stance of an experienced barehanded fighter, elbows in. The Iceman threw the rock at Wynan's forehead. Since his hand was only a foot away when he let go, there was almost no way to miss.

Wynan went down with a depressive fracture of the skull. He almost died.

And the Iceman to the cops: I was scared, he was coming with his whole gang, that's all he does is beat up kids, I just picked up the rock and threw it.

His mother had picked him up at the police station (his father was gone by then, never to be seen again). In the car, his mother started in on him: *Wait till I get you home,* she said. *Just wait.*

And the Iceman, in the car, lifted a finger to her face and said, *You ever fuckin' touch me again I'll wait until you're asleep and I'll get a hammer and I'll beat your head in.*

You ever touch me again, you better never go to sleep.

She believed him. A good thing, too. She was still alive.

❄

He turned off the hot water, dried his hands on a dish towel. *Need to think. So much to do.* He forgot about the soup, went and sat in his television chair, stared at the blank screen.

He had never seen the photograph as it had been reproduced, although he'd seen the original Polaroid. He had been stupid to let the boy keep it. And when the boy had sent it away . . .

❄

"We're gonna be famous," the kid said.

"What?" They were smoking cigarettes in the trailer's back bedroom, the boy relaxing against a stack of pillows; the Iceman had both feet on the floor, his elbows on his knees.

The boy rolled over, looked under the bed, came up with what looked like a newspaper. He flipped it at the Iceman. There were dozens of pictures, boys and men.

"What'd you do?" the Iceman asked; but in his heart he knew, and the anger swelled in his chest.

"Sent in the picture. You know, the one with you and me on the couch."

"You fuck."

The Iceman lurched at him; the boy giggled, barely struggling, not understanding. The Iceman was on his chest, straddling him, got his thumbs on the boy's throat . . . and then Jim Harper knew. His eyes rolled up and his mouth opened and the Iceman . . .

Did what? Remembered backing away, looking at the body. Christ. He'd killed him.

❄

The Iceman jumped to his feet, reliving it and the search for a place to dump the body. He thought about throwing it in a swamp. He thought about shooting him with a shotgun, leaving the gun, so it might look like a hunting accident. But Jim didn't hunt. And his father would know, and his father was nuts. Then he remembered the kid talking about something he'd read about in some magazine, about people using towel racks, the rush you got, better than cocaine . . .

The Iceman, safe at home, growled: thinking. Everything so difficult. He'd tried to track the photo, but the magazine gave no clue to where it might be. Nothing but a Milwaukee post office box. He didn't know how to trace it without showing his face. After a while he'd calmed down. The chances of the photo being printed were small, and even if it was printed, the chances of anyone local seeing it were even smaller.

And then, when he'd almost forgotten about it, he'd gotten the call from Jim Harper's insane father. The LaCourts had a photo.

Remember the doctor.

Yes. Weather . . .

If the photo turned up, no one would immediately recognize him except the doctor. Without the doctor, they might eventually identify him, but he'd know they were looking, and that would give him time.

He got to his feet, went to wall pegs where he'd hung his snowmobile suit over a radiator vent. The suit was just barely enough on a night like this. Even with the suit, he wouldn't want to be out too long. He pulled it on, slipped his feet into his pac boots, laced them tight, then dug into his footlocker for the .44. It was there, wrapped in an oily rag, nestled in the bottom with his other guns. He lifted it out, the second time he'd use it today. The gun was heavy in his hand, solid, intricate, efficient.

He worked it out, slowly, piece by piece:

Weather Karkinnen drove a red Jeep, the only red Jeep at the LaCourt home. She'd have to take the lake road out to Highway 77, and then negotiate the narrow, windblown road back to town. She'd be moving slow . . . if she was still at the LaCourt house.

❄

Weather's work was finished. The bodies were covered and would be left in place until the crime lab people arrived from Madison. She'd performed all her legal duties: this was her year to be county coroner, an unpleasant job rotated between the doctors in town. She'd made all the necessary notes for a finding of homicide by persons unknown. She'd write the notes into a formal report to the county attorney and let the Milwaukee medical examiner do the rest.

There was nothing holding her. But standing in the shed, drinking coffee, listening to the cops—even the cops coming over to hit on her, in their mild-mannered Scandinavian way—was something she didn't want to give up right away.

And she wouldn't mind talking to Davenport again, either, she thought. Where'd he go to? She craned her neck, looking around. He must be outside.

She flipped up her hood, pulled it tight, put on her gloves. Outside, things were more orderly. Most of the fire equipment was gone, and the few neighbors who'd walked to the house had been shooed away. It still stank. She wrinkled her nose, looked around. A deputy was hauling a coil of inch-thick rope up toward the house, and she asked, "Have you seen, uh, Shelly, or that guy from Minneapolis?"

"I think Shelly's up to the house, and the other guy went with a bunch of people down to the lake to look at the snowmobile trail, and they're talking to snowmobile guys."

"Thanks."

She looked down toward the lake, thought about walking down. The snow was deep, and she was already cold again. Besides, what'd she have to contribute?

She went back to the garage for another cup of coffee, and found that it was gone, Davenport's Thermoses empty.

Davenport. God, she was acting like a teenager all of a sudden. Not that she couldn't use a little . . . friendship. She thought back to her last involvement: how long, a year? She counted back. Wait, jeez. More than two years. God, it was nearly three. He'd been married, although, as he said charmingly, *not very,* and the whole thing was doomed from the start. He'd had a nice touch in bed, but was a little too fond of network television: it became very easy to see him as a slowly composting lump on a couch somewhere.

Weather sighed. No coffee. She put on her gloves, went back out and trudged toward her Jeep, still reluctant to go. In the whole county, this was the place to be this night. This was the center of things.

But she was increasingly feeling the cold. Even with her pacs, her toes were feeling brittle. Out on the lake, the lights from a pod of snowmobiles shone toward the house. They'd been attracted by the fire and the cops and by now, undoubtedly, the whole story of the LaCourt murders. Grant was a small town, where nothing much happened.

❉

The Iceman sliced across the lake. A half-dozen sleds were gathered on the ice near the LaCourt house, watching the cops work. Two more were cruising down the lakeshore, heading for the house. If the temperature had been warmer, a few degrees either side of zero, there'd have been a hundred snowmobiles on the lake, and more coming in.

Halfway across, he left the trail, carved a new cut in the soft snow and stopped. The LaCourt house was a half mile away, but everything around it was bathed in brilliant light. Through a pair of pocket binoculars he could see Weather's Jeep, still parked in the drive.

He grunted, put the glasses in a side pocket where they'd stay cold, gingerly climbed off the sled and tested the snow. He sank in a foot before the harder crust supported his weight. Good. He trampled out a hole and settled into it, in the lee of the sled. Even a five-mile-an-hour wind was a killer on a night like this.

From his hole he could hear the beating of a generator and the occasional shouts of men working, spreading what appeared to be a canvas tent over the house. Their distant voices were like pieces of audible confetti, sharp isolated calls and shouts in the night. Then his focus shifted, and for the first time, he heard the other voices. They'd been there, all along, like a Greek chorus. He turned, slowly, until he was facing the darkness back along the creek. The sound was unearthly, the sound of starvation. Not a scream, like a cat, but almost like the girl, when he'd cut her, a high, quavering, wailing note.

Coyotes.

Singing together, blood songs after the storm. He shivered, not from the cold.

❉

But the cold had nearly gotten to him twenty minutes later when he saw the small figure walking alone toward the red Jeep. Yes. Weather.

When she climbed inside her truck, he brushed the snow off his suit, threw a leg over the sled and cranked it up. He watched as she turned on the headlights, backed out of her parking space. She had further to go than he did, so he sat and watched until he was sure she was turning left, heading out. She might still stop at the fire station, but there wasn't much going on there except equipment maintenance.

He turned back toward the trail, followed it for a quarter mile, then moved to his right again, into new snow. Stackpole's Resort was over there, closed for the season, but marked with a yard-light. He could get off the lake on the resort's beach, follow the driveway up to the highway, and wait for her there.

He'd had an image of the ambush in his mind. She'd be driving slowly on the snowpacked highway, and he'd come alongside the Jeep with the sled. From six or ten feet away, he could hardly miss: the .44 Magnum would punch through the window like it was toilet paper. She'd go straight off the road, and he'd pull up beside her, empty the pistol into her. Even if somebody saw him, the sled was the perfect escape vehicle, out here in the deep snow. Nothing could follow him, not unless it had skis on the front end. Out here, the sled was virtually anonymous.

❉

The snow-covered beach came up fast, and he braked, felt the machine buck up, took it slowly across the resort's lakeside lawn and through the drifts between two log cabins. The driveway had been plowed after the last storm, but not yet after this one, and he eased over the throw-piles down into it. He stopped just off the highway, where a blue fir windbreak would hide the sled. He felt like a motorcycle cop waiting behind a billboard.

Waiting. Where was she?

There was a movement to his left, at the corner of his eye, sudden but furtive, and his head snapped around. Nothing. *But there had been something . . .* There. A dog, a small German shepherd, caught in the thin illumination of the yard-light. No. Not a shepherd, but a coyote. Looking at him from the brush. Then another. There was a snap, and a growl. They never did this, never. Coyotes were invisible.

He pulled down the zip on his suit, took the .44 out of the inside pocket, looked nervously into the brush. They were gone, he thought. Somewhere.

Headlights turned the corner down at the lake road. Had to be Weather. He shifted the pistol to his other hand, his brake hand. And, for the first time, tried to figure out the details of the attack. With one hand on the accelerator and the other on the brake. . . . He was one hand short. Nothing to shoot with. He'd have to improvise. He'd have to use his brake hand. But . . .

He put the gun in his outside leg pocket as the headlights closed on him. The Jeep flashed by and he registered a quick flickering image of Weather in the window, parka hood down, hat off.

He gunned the sled, started after her, rolling down the shallow ditch on the left side of the road. The Jeep gained on him, gained some more. Its tires threw up a cloud of ice and salt pellets, which popped off his suit and helmet like BBs.

She was traveling faster than he'd expected. Other snowmobiles had been down the ditch, so there was the semblance of a trail, obscured by the day's snow; still, it wasn't an official trail. He hit a heavy hummock of swamp grass and suddenly found himself up in the air, holding on.

The flight might have been exhilarating on another day,

when he could see, but this time he almost lost it. He landed with a jarring impact and the sled bucked under him, swaying. He fought it, got it straight. He was fifty yards behind her. He rolled the accelerator grip forward, picking up speed, rattling over broken snow, the tops of small bushes, invisible bumps . . . his teeth chattered with the rough ride.

A snowplow had been down the highway earlier in the evening, and the irregular waves of plowed snow flashed by on his right. He moved further left, away from the plowed stuff: it'd be hard and irregular, it'd throw him for sure. Weather's taillights were right *there*. He inched closer. He was moving so fast that he would not be able to brake inside his headlight's reach: if there was a tree down across the ditch, he'd hit it.

He'd just thought of that when he saw the hump coming; he knew what it was as soon as he picked it up, a bale of hay pegged to the bottom of the ditch to slow spring erosion. The deep snow made it into a perfect snowmobile jump, but he didn't want to jump. But he had no time to go around it. He had no time to do anything but brace himself, and he was in the air again.

He came down like a bomb, hard, bounced, the sled skidding through the softer snow up the left bank. He wrestled it to the right, lost it, climbed the right bank toward the plowed snow, wrestled it left, carved a long curve back to the bottom.

Got it.

The Iceman was shaken, thought for an instant about giving it up; but she was right *there,* so close. He gritted his teeth and pushed harder, closing. Thirty yards. Twenty . . .

❄

Weather glanced in her side mirror, saw the sled's headlight. He was coming fast. Too fast. Idiot. She smiled, remembering last year's countywide outrage. Intersections of snowmobile trails and ordinary roads were marked with diamond-shaped signs painted with the silhouette of a snowmobile. Like deer-crossing signs, but wordless. The year

before, someone had used black spray paint to stencil IDIOT
CROSSING on half the snowmobile signs in Ojibway County.
Had done the job neatly, with a stencil, a few signs every
night for a week. The paper had been full of it.

Davenport.

An image of his face, shoulders, and hands popped into
her mind. He was beat-up, wary, like he'd been hurt and
needed help; at the same time, he looked tough as a railroad
spike. She'd felt almost tongue-tied with him, found herself
trying to interest him. Instead, half the things she'd said
sounded like borderline insults. *Try not to shoot anyone.*

God, had she said that? She bit her tongue. Why? Trying
to impress him. When he'd focused on her, he seemed to
be looking right into her. And she liked it.

The bobbing light in her side mirror caught her eye again.
The fool on the snowmobile was still in the ditch, but had
drawn almost up beside her. She glanced back over her
shoulder. If she remembered right, Forest Drive was coming up. There'd be a culvert, and the guy would catapult into
Price County if he tried to ride over the embankment at this
speed. Was he racing her? Maybe she should slow down.

❋

The Iceman was befuddled by the mechanics of the assassi-
nation; if he'd had a sense of humor, he might have laughed.
He couldn't let go of the accelerator and keep up with her.
If he let go of the brake . . . he just didn't feel safe without
some connection with the brake. But he had no choice: he
took his hand off the brake lever, pulled open the Velcro-
sealed pocket flap, got a good grip on the pistol, slid it out
of his pocket. He was fifteen feet back, ten feet. Saw her
glance back at him . . .

Five feet back, fifteen feet to the left of her, slightly
lower . . . the snow thrown up by the Jeep was still pelting
him, rattling off his helmet. Her brake lights flashed, once,
twice, three times. Pumping the brakes. Why? Something
coming? He could see nothing up ahead. He lifted the gun,
found he couldn't keep it on the window, or even the truck's
cab, much less her head. He saw the edge of her face as she

looked back, her brake lights still flashing . . . What? What was she doing?

He pushed closer, his left hand jumped wildly as he held it awkwardly across his body; the ride was getting rougher. He tried to hold it, the two vehicles ripping along at fifty miles an hour, forty-five, forty, her brakes flashing . . .

Finally, hissing to himself like a flattening tire, he dropped the gun to his leg and rolled back the accelerator. The whole thing was a bad idea. As he slowed, he slipped the pistol back into his pocket, got his hand back on the brake. If he'd had a shotgun, and he'd been in daylight, then it might have worked.

He looked up at the truck and saw her profile, the blonde hair. So close.

He slowed, slowed some more. She'd stopped pumping her brakes. He turned to look back, to check traffic. And suddenly the wall was there, in front of him. He jerked the sled to the right, squeezed the brake, leaned hard right, wrenched the machine up the side of the ditch. A block of frozen snow caught him, and the machine spun out into the road and stalled.

He sat in the sudden silence, out of breath, heart pounding. The Forest Road intersection: he'd forgotten all about it. If he'd kept moving on her, he'd have hit the ends of the steel culvert pipes. He'd be dead. He looked at the embankment, the cold moving into his stomach. Too close. He shook his head, cranked the sled and turned toward home. He looked back before he started out, saw her taillights disappear around a curve. He'd have to go back for her. And soon. Plan it this time. Think it out.

❄

Weather saw the snowmobile slow and fall back. Forest Road flashed past and she came up on the highway. He must have read her taillights. She'd seen the road-crossing sign in her headlights, realized she wouldn't have time to stop, to warn him, and had frantically pumped her brakes, hoping he'd catch on.

And he had.

Okay. She saw his taillight come up, just a pinprick of red in the darkness, and touched the preset channel selector on her radio. Duluth public radio was playing Mozart's *Eine kleine Nachtmusik.*

Now about Davenport.

They really needed to talk again. And that might take some planning.

She smiled to herself. She hadn't felt like *this* for a while.

CHAPTER

4

Lucas followed Carr down the dark, snow-packed highway. A logging truck, six huge logs chained to the trailer, pelted past them and enveloped them in a hurricane of loose snow. Carr got his right wheels in the deep snow on the shoulder, nearly didn't make it out. A minute later, a snowplow pushed glumly past them, then a pod of snowmobiles.

He leaned over the steering wheel, tense, peering into the dark. The night seemed to eat up their headlights. They got past the snowplow and the highway opened up for a moment. He groped in the storage bin under the arm rest, found a tape, shoved it in the tape player. Joe Cocker came up, singing "Black-Eyed Blues."

❋

Lucas felt like he was waking from an opium dream, spiderwebs and dust blowing off his brain. He'd come back from New York and a brutal manhunt. In Minneapolis, he'd found . . . nothing. Nothing to do but work for money and amuse himself.

In September he'd left the Cities for two weeks of muskie fishing at his Wisconsin cabin east of Hayward. He'd never gone back. He'd called, kept in touch with his programmers, but could never quite get back to the new office. The latest in desktop computers waited for him, a six-hundred-dollar swivel chair, an art print on the wall beside the mounted muskie.

He'd stayed in the north and fought the winter. October had been cold. On Halloween, a winter storm had blown in from the southern Rockies. Before it was done, there were twenty inches of snow on the ground, with drifts five and six feet high.

The cold continued through November, with little flurries and the occasional nasty squall. Two or three inches of new snow accumulated almost every week. Then, on the Friday after Thanksgiving, another major storm swept through, dumping a foot of additional snow. The local papers called it Halloween II and reported that half the winter snowplow budget had been used. Winter was still four weeks away.

December was cold, with off-and-on snow. Then, on January second and third, a blizzard swept the North Woods. Halloween III. When it ended, thirty-four more inches of snow had been piled on the rest. The drifts lapped around the eaves of lakeside cabins.

People said, "Well you shoulda been here back in . . ." But nobody had seen anything like it, ever.

And after the blizzard departed, the cold rang down.

On the night of the third, the thermometer on his cabin deck fell to minus twenty-nine. The following day, the temperature struggled up to minus twenty: schools were closed everywhere, the radio warned against anything but critical travel. On this night, the temperature in Ojibway County would plunge to minus thirty-two.

Almost nothing moved. A rogue logging truck, a despondent snowplow, a few snowmobile freaks. Cop cars. The outdoors was dangerous; so cold as to be weird.

He'd been napping on the couch in front of the fireplace when he first heard the pounding. He'd sat up, instantly alert, afraid that it might be the furnace. But the pounding stopped. He frowned, wondered if he might have imagined it. Rolled to his feet, walked to the basement stairs, listened. Nothing. Stepped to the kitchen window. He saw the truck in the driveway and a second later the front doorbell rang. Ah. Whoever it was had been pounding on the garage door.

He went to the door, curious. The temperature was well into the minus twenties. He looked through the window inset in the door. A cop, wearing a Russian hat with the ear flaps down.

"Yeah?" Lucas didn't recognize the uniform parka.

"Man, we gotta big problem over in Ojibway County. The sheriff sent me over to see if you could come back and take a look at it. At least three people murdered."

"C'mon in. How'd you know about me?"

Lacey stepped inside, looked around. Books, a few wild-life watercolors on the walls, a television and stereo, pile of embers in the fireplace, the smell of clean-burning pine. "Sheriff read that story in the Milwaukee *Journal* 'bout you in New York, and about living up here. He called around down to Minneapolis and they said you were up here, so he called the Sawyer County sheriff and found out where you live. And here I am."

"Bad night," Lucas said.

"You don't know the half of it," said Lacey. "So cold."

❋

Carr's taillights blinked, then came up, and he slowed and then stopped, turned on his blinkers. Lucas closed up behind, stopped. Carr was on the highway, walking around to the front of his truck.

Lucas opened his door and stepped out: "You okay?"

"Got a tree down," Carr yelled back.

Lucas let the engine run, shut the door, hustled around Carr's truck. The cold had split a limb off a maple tree and it had fallen across the roadside ditch and halfway across the right traffic lane. Carr grabbed the thickest part of it, gave it a tug, moved it a foot. Lucas joined him, and together they dragged it off the road.

"Cold," Carr said, and they hurried back to their trucks.

Weather, Lucas thought. Her image popped up in his mind as he started after Carr again. Now *that* might be an efficient way to warm up, he thought. He'd been off women for a while, and was beginning to feel the loss.

✳

Grant appeared as a collection of orange sodium-vapor streetlights, followed by a Pines Motel sign, then a Hardee's and a Unocal station, an LP gas company and a video-rental store with a yellow-light marquee. The sheriff turned right at the only traffic light, led him through the three-block-long business district, took a left at a half-buried stop sign and headed up a low hill. On the left was a patch of pines that might have been a park.

A white clapboard church stood at the top of the hill, surrounded by a grove of red pine, with a small cemetery in back. The sheriff drove past the church and stopped in the street in front of a small brick house with lighted windows.

Lucas caught a sign in his headlights: RECTORY. Below that, in cursive letters, REV. PHILIP BERGEN. He pulled in behind Carr, killed the engine, and stepped down from the truck. The air was so cold and dry that he felt as though his skin were being sandpapered. When he breathed, he could feel ice crystals forming on his chin and under his nose.

"That logging truck almost did us," Lucas said as Carr walked back from his Suburban. Gouts of steam poured from their mouths and noses.

"Gol-darned fool. I called back and told somebody to pull him over," Carr said. "Give him a breath test, slow him down." And as they started across the street, he added, "I'm not looking forward to this."

They scuffed through the snow on the rectory walk, up to the covered porch. Carr pushed the doorbell, then dropped his head and bounced on his toes. A man came to the door, peered out the window, then opened it.

"Shelly, what happened out there?" Bergen held the door open, glanced curiously at Lucas, and said, "They're dead?"

"Yeah, um . . . let's get our boots off, we gotta talk," Carr said. "This is our new deputy, Lucas Davenport."

Bergen nodded, peered at Lucas, a wrinkle forming on his forehead, between his eyes. "Pleased to meet you."

The priest was close to fifty, a square, fleshy Scandinavian with blond hair and a permanently doubtful look on his pale face. He wore a wool Icelandic sweater and black slacks, and was in his stocking feet. His words, when he spoke, had a softness to them, a roundness, and Lucas thought that Bergen would not be a fire-and-brimstone preacher, but a mother's-milk sort.

Lucas and Carr dumped their pac boots in the front hallway and walked in stocking feet down a short hall, past a severe Italianate crucifix with a bronze Jesus, to the living room. Carr peeled off his snowmobile suit and Lucas dumped his parka next to a plain wood chair, and sat down.

"So what happened?" Bergen said. He leaned on the mantel over a stone fireplace, where the remnants of three birch logs smoldered behind a glass door. A Sacred Heart print of the Virgin Mary peered over his shoulder.

"There was an odd thing out there." Carr dropped the suit on the floor, then settled on the edge of an overstuffed chair. He put his elbows on his knees, laced his fingers, leaning toward the priest.

"Yes?" Bergen frowned.

"When I called, you said the LaCourts were okay when you left."

"Yes, they were fine," Bergen said, his head bobbing. He was assured, innocent. "They didn't seem nervous. How were they killed, anyway? Is it possible that one of them . . ." He answered his own question, shaking his head. "No, not them."

"A fireman saw your Jeep passing the station," Carr continued. "A few seconds later the fire call came in. When the firemen got there, maybe five or six minutes later, it appeared that the LaCourts had been dead for some time. A half hour, maybe more."

"That's not possible," Bergen said promptly. He straightened, looked from Lucas to Carr, a shadow in his eyes. Suspicion. "Shelly . . . you don't think *I* was involved?"

"No, no, we're just trying to straighten this out."

"So what were they doing when you left?" Lucas asked.

Bergen stared at him, then said, "You're the homicide fellow who lives over in Sawyer County. The man who was fired from Minneapolis."

"What were you doing?" Lucas repeated.

"Shelly?" The priest looked at the sheriff, who looked away.

"We've got to figure this out, Phil."

"Mr. Davenport is a mercenary, isn't he?" Bergen asked, looking again at Lucas.

"We need him, Phil," Carr said, almost pleading now. "We've got nobody else who can do it. And he's a good Catholic boy."

"What were you doing?" Lucas asked a third time. He put glass in his voice, a cutting edge.

The priest pursed his lips, moving them in and out, considering both Lucas and the question, then sighed and said, "When I left, they were fine. There was not a hint of a problem. I came right back here, and I was still here when Shelly called."

"The firemen say there's no mistaking the time," Lucas said. "They're certain."

"I'm certain, too," Bergen snapped.

Lucas: "How long were you there at the house?"

"Fifteen minutes, something like that," Bergen said. He'd turned himself to face Lucas more directly.

"Did you eat anything?"

"Cupcakes. A glass of milk," Bergen said.

"Were the cupcakes hot?"

"No, but as a matter of fact, she was frosting them while we talked."

"When you left, did you stop anywhere on the way out? Even pause?"

"No."

"So you went right out to your Jeep, got in, drove as fast as seemed reasonable to get out of the road."

"Well . . . I probably fiddled around in the Jeep for a minute before I left, a minute or two," Bergen said. He knew where they were going, and began to stretch the time. "But I didn't see any sign of trouble before I left."

"Was the television on?" Lucas asked.

"Mmm, no, I don't think so."

"How about the radio?"

"No. We were talking," Bergen said.

"Was there a newspaper on the table?"

"I just can't remember," Bergen said, his voice rising. "What are these questions?"

"Can you remember anything that would be peculiar to this day, that you saw inside the LaCourt house, that might still be there, that might have survived the fire? A book sitting on a table? Anything?"

"Well . . ." The priest scratched the side of his nose. "No, not particularly. I'll think about it. There must be something."

"Did you look at the clock when you got home?"

"No. But I hadn't been here long when Shelly called."

Lucas looked at Carr. "Shelly, could you call in and have somebody patch you through to the LaCourt house, and tell somebody to go into the kitchen and check to see if there was a bowl of frosting."

He turned his head back to Bergen: "Was the frosting in a bowl or out of one of those cans?"

"Bowl."

To Carr: ". . . check and see if there was a frosting bowl or a cupcake tin in the sink or around the table."

"Sure."

"She might have washed the dishes," Bergen suggested.

"There couldn't have been too much time," Lucas said.

"Use the office phone, Shelly," the priest said to Carr.

He and Lucas watched the sheriff pad down the hall, then Lucas asked, "Did Frank LaCourt come outside when you left?"

"No. He said good-bye at the door. At the kitchen table, actually. Claudia came to the door. Did you go to Catholic schools?"

"Through high school," Lucas said.

"Is this what they taught you? To interrogate priests?"

"Your being a priest doesn't cut any ice with me," Lucas said. "You've seen all the scandals these last few years. That stuff was out there for years and you guys hid it. There were a half a dozen gay brothers at my school and everybody knew it. And they affected more than a few kids."

Bergen stared at him for a moment, then half-turned and shook his head.

"Was Frank LaCourt wearing outdoor clothing or look like he was getting ready to go outside?" Lucas asked, returning to the questions.

"No." Bergen was subdued now, his voice gone dark.

"Did you see anyone else there?"

"No."

"Did Frank have a pair of snowshoes around?" Lucas asked.

"Not that I saw."

"Did you see any snowshoe tracks outside the door?"

"No." Bergen shook his head. "I didn't. But it was snowing."

"Did you pass any cars on the way out?"

"No. How far is it from the corner by the firehouse back to LaCourts'?"

"One-point-one miles," Lucas said.

Bergen shook his head. "I'm a careful driver. I said it took a minute or two to get out to the corner, but two minutes would be thirty miles an hour. I wasn't doing thirty. I was probably going a lot slower than that. And I was pulling my trailer."

"Snowmobile?"

"Yes, I'd been out with the club, the Grant Scramblers, you can check with them."

Carr came back: "They're looking," he said. "They'll call back."

Lucas looked at Carr. "If we have somebody waiting for Father Bergen to leave, and if he lures Frank LaCourt outside somehow, right away, kills him, then kills the other two, burns the place immediately and gets out, in a frenzy, and if you build a little extra time in between the firemen's arrival at the place and finding the bodies—we could almost make it."

Carr looked at Bergen, who seemed to ponder what Lucas had said. He'd chosen Lucas as the enemy, but now Lucas had changed direction.

"Okay," Carr said, nodding. To Bergen: "I hated to hit you with it, Phil, but there did seem to be a problem. We can probably figure it out. When you were there, what were you talking about? I mean, it's not confessional stuff, is it? I . . ."

"Actually, we were talking about the Tuesday services and the concept of an exchange with Home Baptist. I wanted to get some ground rules straight."

"Oh." Now Carr looked uncomfortable. "Well, we can figure that out later."

"What's all this about?" Lucas asked.

"Church stuff, an argument that's going around," Carr said.

"Could somebody get killed over it?"

Bergen was startled. "Good grief, no! You might not get invited to a party, but you wouldn't get killed."

Carr glanced at him, frowned. The phone rang down the hallway, and the priest said, "Let me get that." A moment later he returned with a portable handset and passed it to Carr. "For you."

Carr took it, said, "This is the sheriff," then, "Yeah." He listened for a moment, said, "Okay, okay, and I'll see you out there in a bit . . . okay." He pushed the clear button and turned to Lucas: "There was a bowl in the sink that could have been used to make frosting. No frosting in it, but it was the right kind of bowl."

"Like I told you," said Bergen.

"Okay," Lucas said.

"If we're done here, I'm going back out to the LaCourt place," Carr said. He picked up his snowmobile suit and began pulling it over his feet. "I'm sorry we bothered you, Phil, but we had to ask."

"These killings are . . . grotesque," the priest said, shaking his head. "Obscene. I'll start thinking about a funeral service, something to say to the town."

"That'll be a while yet. We'll have to send them down to Milwaukee for autopsies," Carr said. "I'll stay in touch."

✳

When they were outside again, Carr asked, "Are you coming back out to LaCourts'?"

Lucas shook his head. "Nah. There's nothing there for me. I'd suggest you button the place up. Post some deputies to keep out the curiosity-seekers and coyotes, and wait for the Madison guys."

"I'll do that. Actually, I could do it from here, but . . . politics." He was apologetic. "I gotta be out there a lot the next couple of days."

Lucas nodded. "Same way in the Cities."

"How about Phil? What do you think?"

"I don't know," Lucas said. Far away, somebody started a chain saw. They both turned to look up the street toward the sound, but there was nothing visible but garage and yard lights. The sound was an abrasive underline to the conversation. "We still don't have enough time. Not really. The bowl thing hardly clears him. But who knows? Maybe a big gust of wind scoured off the roof and put that snow on LaCourt in two minutes."

"Could be," Carr said.

"This Baptist thing—that's no big deal?" Lucas asked.

"It's a bigger deal than he was making it," Carr said. "What do you know about Pentecostals?"

"Nothing."

"Pentecostals believe in direct contact with God. The Catholic Church has taught that only the Church is a reliable interpreter of God's word. The Church doesn't trust the idea of direct access. Too many bad things have come of it in the past. But some Catholics—more and more all the time—believe you can have a valid experience."

"Yeah?" Lucas had been out of touch.

"Baptists rely on direct access. Some of the local Pentecostal Catholics, like Claudia, were talking about getting together with some of the Baptists to share the Spirit."

"That sounds pretty serious," Lucas said. The cold was beginning to filter through the edges of the parka, and he flexed his shoulders.

"But nobody would kill because of it. Not unless there's a nut that I don't know about," Carr said. "Phil was upset about Claudia talking to Home Baptist, but they were friends."

"How about Frank? Was he a friend of Bergen's?"

"Frank was Chippewa," said Carr. He stamped his feet, and looked back in the direction of the irritating chain saw. "He thought Christianity was amusing. But he and Phil were friendly enough."

"Okay."

"So what are you gonna do now?" Carr asked.

"Bag out in a motel. I brought clothes for a couple of days. We can get organized tomorrow morning. You can pick some people, and I'll get them started. We'll need four or five. We'll want to talk to the LaCourts' friends, kids at school, some people out at the Res. And I'll want to talk to these fire guys."

"Okay. See you in the morning, then," Carr said. The sheriff headed for his Suburban and muttered, mostly to himself, "Lord, what a mess."

"Hey, Sheriff?"

"Yeah?" Carr turned back.

"Pentecostal. I don't mean to sound impolite, but really—isn't that something like Holy Rollers?"

After a moment Carr, looking over his shoulder, nodded and said, "Something like that."

"How come you know so much about them?"

"I am one," Carr said.

CHAPTER

✳ ✳ ✳

5

The morning broke bitterly cold. The clouds had cleared and a low-angle, razor-sharp sunshine cut through the red pines that sheltered the motel. Lucas, stiff from a too-short bed and a too-fat pillow, zipped his parka, pulled on his gloves and stepped outside. His face was soft and warm from shaving; the air was an icy slap.

The oldest part of Grant was built on a hill across the highway from the motel, small gray houses with backyard clotheslines awash in the snow. Wavering spires of gray woodsmoke curled up from two hundred tin chimneys, and the corrosive smell of burning oak bark shifted through town like a dirty tramp.

Lucas had grown up in Minneapolis, had learned to fish along the urban Mississippi, in the shadow of smokestacks and powerlines and six-lane bridges, with oil cans, worn-out tires and dead carp sharing space on the mud flats. When he began making serious money as an adult, he'd bought a cabin on a quiet lake in Wisconsin's North Woods. And started learning about small towns.

About the odd comforts and discomforts of knowing everyone; of talking to people who had roads, lakes, and entire townships named after their families. People who made their living in the woods, guiding tourists, growing Christmas trees, netting suckers and trapping crawdads for bait.

Not Minneapolis, but he liked it.

He yawned and walked down to his truck, squinting against the sun, the new snow crunching underfoot. A friendly, familiar weight pulled at his left side. The parka made a waist holster impractical, so he'd hung his .45 in a shoulder rig. The pistol simply felt *right*. It had been a while since he'd carried one. He touched the coat's zipper tag with his left hand, pulled it down an inch, then grinned to himself. Rehearsing. Not that he'd need it.

Ojibway County *wasn't* Minneapolis. If someone came after him in Ojibway County, he'd bring a deer rifle or a shotgun, not some bullshit .22 hideout piece. And if somebody came with a scoped .30-06, the .45 would be about as useful as a rock. Still, it felt good. He touched the zipper tag again with his left hand and mentally slipped the right hand into the coat.

The truck had been sitting in the brutal cold overnight, but the motel provided post outlets for oil-pan heaters. Lucas unplugged the extension cord from both the post and the truck, tossed the cord in the back seat, cranked up the engine and let it run while he went down to the motel office for a cup of free coffee.

"Cold," he said to the hotel owner.

"Any colder, I'd have to bring my brass monkey inside," the man said. He'd been honing the line all morning. "Have a sweet roll, too, we got a deal on them."

"Thanks."

Cold air was still pouring from the truck's heater vents when Lucas returned to it, balancing the coffee and sweet roll. He shut the fan off and headed into town.

There were only two real possibilities with the LaCourt killings, he thought. They were done by a stranger, a traveling killer, as part of a robbery, picked out because the house was isolated. Or they were done for a reason. The fire suggested a reason. A traveler would have hauled Frank LaCourt's body inside, locked the doors, turned off the

lights, and left. He might be days away before the murders
were uncovered. With the fire, he couldn't have been more
than fifteen or twenty minutes away.

A local guy who set a fire meant either a psychotic
arsonist—unlikely—or that something was being covered.
Something that pointed at the killer. Fingerprints. Semen.
Personal records. Or might the fire have been set to distract
the investigation?

The gun he'd found with Claudia LaCourt, unfired, suggested that the LaCourts knew something was happening,
but they hadn't called 9-1-1. The situation may have been
somewhat ambiguous . . . Huh.

And the girl with the missing ear might have been inter-
rogated. Another suggestion that something was going on.

The image of the ear in the Ziploc bag popped into his
mind. Carr had bent and retched because he was human,
as the LaCourt girl had once been. She'd been alive at this
time yesterday, chatting with her friends on the telephone,
watching television, trying on clothes. Making plans. Now
she was a charred husk.

And to Lucas, she was an abstraction: a victim. Did that
make him less than human? He half-smiled at the introspec-
tive thought; he tried to stay away from introspection. Bad
for the health.

But in truth he didn't feel much for Lisa LaCourt. He'd
seen too many dead children. Babies in garbage cans, killed
by their parents; toddlers beaten and maimed; thirteen-year-
olds who shot each other with a zealous enthusiasm scraped
right off the TV screen. Not that their elders were much
better. Wives killed with fists, husbands killed with ham-
mers, homosexuals slashed to pieces in frenzies of sexual
jealousy. After a while it all ran together.

On the other hand, he thought, if it were *Sarah* . . . His
mouth straightened into a thin line. He couldn't put his
daughter together with the images of violent death that
he'd collected over the years. They simply would not fit.
But Sarah was almost ready for school now, she'd be moving out into the bigger world.

His knuckles were white on the steering wheel. He shook

off the thought and looked out the window.

Grant's Main Street was a three-block row of slightly shabby storefronts, elbow to elbow, like a town in the old west. The combinations that would have been strange in other places were typical for the North Woods: a Laundromat-bookstore-bar, an Indian souvenir store-computer outlet, a satellite dish-plumber. There were two bakeries, a furniture store, a scattering of insurance agents and real estate dealers, a couple of lawyers. The county courthouse was a low rambling building of fieldstone and steel at the end of Main. A cluster of sheriff's trucks sat in a parking lot in back and Lucas wheeled in beside them. A Bronco with an unfamiliar EYE3 logo was parked in a visitor's slot by the door.

A deputy coming out nodded at him, said, "Mornin'," and politely held the door. The sheriff's outer office was behind a second door, decorated with curling DARE antidrug posters and the odors of aging nicotine and bad nerves. A reporter and a cameraman were slumped in green leatherette chairs scarred with cigarette burns and what looked like razor cuts. The reporter was working on her lipstick with a gold compact and a small red brush. She looked up when Lucas stepped in. He nodded and she nodded back. A steel door and a bulletproof glass window were set in the wall opposite the reporter. Lucas went to the window, looked at the empty desk behind it, and pushed the call button next to the window.

"It'll just piss them off," the reporter said. She had a tapered fox-face with a tiny chin, big eyes and wide cheekbones, as though she'd been especially bred for television. She rubbed her lips together, then snapped the compact shut, dropped it in her purse, and gave him a reflexive smile. The cameraman was asleep.

"Yeah? Where're you guys from?" Lucas asked. The reporter was very pretty, with her mobile eyes and trained expressions, like a latter-day All-American geisha girl. Weather could never work for television, he thought. Her features were too distinctive. Could be a movie star, though.

"Milwaukee," she said. "Are you with the *Star-Tribune?*"

"Nope." He shook his head, giving her nothing.

"A cop?" The reporter perked up.

"An interested onlooker," Lucas said, grinning at her. "Lots of reporters around?"

"I guess so," she said, a frown flitting across her face. "I heard Eight talking on their radios, so they're up here somewhere, and I heard the *Strib* came in last night. Probably out at the lake. Are you one of the lab people from Madison?"

"No," Lucas said.

A harried middle-aged woman bustled up behind the glass, peered through, and said, "Davenport?"

"Yes." The reporter was wearing perfume. Something slightly fruity.

"I'll buzz you in," the woman said.

"FBI?" the reporter pressed.

"No," he said.

The woman inside pressed her entry button and as Lucas slipped through the door, the reporter called, "Tell Sheriff Carr we're gonna put something on the air whether he talks to us or not."

❋

Carr had a corner office overlooking the parking lot, the county garage and a corroded bronze statue of a World War I doughboy. The beige walls were hung with a dozen photographs of Carr with other politicians, three plaques, a bachelor's degree certificate from the University of Wisconsin/River Falls, and two fish-stamp prints with the actual stamps mounted in the mats below the prints. A computer and laser printer sat on a side table, and an intricate thirty-button decorator-blue telephone occupied one corner of an expansive walnut desk. Carr was sitting behind the desk, looking gloomily across a tape recorder at Henry Lacey.

"You got reporters," Lucas said, propping himself in the office door.

"Like deer ticks," Carr said, looking up. "Morning. Come in."

"All you can get from deer ticks is Lyme's disease," said Lacey. "Reporters can get your ass *fired.*"

"Should I let them shoot pictures of the house?" Carr asked Lucas. "They're all over me to let them in."

"Why wouldn't you?" Lucas asked. He stepped into the office and dropped into a visitor's chair, slumped, got comfortable.

Carr scratched his head. "I dunno . . . it doesn't seem right."

"Look, it's all bullshit," Lucas said. "The outside of a burnt house doesn't mean anything to anybody, especially if they live in Milwaukee. Think about it."

"Yeah." Carr was still reluctant.

"If I were you, I'd draw up a little site map and pass it out—where the bodies were and so on," Lucas said. "That doesn't mean shit either, but they'll think you're a hell of a guy. They'll give you a break."

"I could use a break," Carr said. He scratched his head again, working at it.

"Did the guys from Madison get here?" Lucas asked.

"Two hours ago," said Lacey. "They're out at the house."

"Good." Lucas nodded. "How's it look out there?"

"Like last night. Uglier. There was a lump of frozen blood under Frank's head about the size of a milk jug. They're moving the bodies out in an hour or so, but they say it could take a couple of weeks to process the house."

"We gotta push them: there's something in there we need, or the guy wouldn't have burned the place," Lucas said irritably. Two weeks? Impossible. They needed information *now.* "Anything more new?"

"Yeah. We got a call," Carr said. He reached across his desk and pushed a button on the tape recorder. There was a burst of music, a woman country-western singer, then a man's voice: *You tell them goddamned flatheads down at FNR to stay away from white women or they'll get what LaCourt got.*

Lucas stuck out his bottom lip, shook his head: this was bullshit.

The music swelled, as if somebody had taken his mouth away from the phone, then a new voice said, *Give'm all a six-pack of Schlitz and send them down to Chicago with the niggers.*

The music came up, then there were a couple of indistinguishable words, a barking laugh, a click and a dead line.

"Called in on the 9-1-1 number, where we got an automatic trace. Went out to a pay phone at the Legion Hall. There were maybe fifty people out there," Lacey said. "Mostly drunk."

"That's what it sounded like, drunks," Lucas agreed. A waste of time. "What's the FNR? The Res?"

"Yeah. Forêt Noire," Carr said. He pronounced it For-A Nwa. "The thing is, most everybody in town'll know about the call before this afternoon. The girl on the message center talked it all over the courthouse. The guys from the tribe'll be up here. We're gonna have to tell the FBI. Possible civil rights whatchamajigger."

"Aw, no," Lucas groaned, closing his eyes. "Not the feebs."

"Gonna have to," Carr said, shaking his head. "I'll try to keep them off, but I bet they're here by the weekend."

"Tell him about the windigo," Lacey said.

"There's rumors around the reservation that a windigo's been raised by the winter," Carr said, looking even gloomier.

"I've heard of them," Lucas said. "But I don't know . . ."

"Cannibal spirits, roaming the snowdrifts, eating people," Lacey said. "If you see one, bring him in for questioning."

He and Carr started to laugh, then Carr said, "We're getting hysterical." To Lucas he said, "Didn't get any sleep. I picked out some guys to work with you, six of them, smartest ones we got. They're down in the canteen. You ready?"

"Yup. Let's do it," Lucas said.

❄

The deputies arranged themselves around a half-dozen rickety square tables, drinking coffee and chewing on candy bars, looking Lucas over. Carr poked his finger at them and called out their names. Five of the six wore uniforms. The sixth, an older man, wore jeans and a heavy sweater and carried an automatic pistol just to the left of his navel in a cross-draw position.

". . . Gene Climpt, investigator," Carr said, pointing at him. Climpt nodded. His face was deeply weathered, like a chunk of lake driftwood, his eyes careful, watchful. "You met him out at the house last night."

Lucas nodded at Climpt, then looked around the room. The best people in the department, Carr said. With two exceptions, they were all white and chunky. One was an Indian, and Climpt, the investigator, was lean as a lightning rod. "The sheriff and I worked out a few approaches last night," Lucas began. "What we're doing today is talking to people. I'll talk to the firefighters who were the first out at the house. We've also got to find the LaCourts' personal friends, their daughter's friends at school, and the people who took part in a religious group that Claudia LaCourt was a member of."

They talked for twenty minutes, dividing up the preliminaries. Climpt took two deputies to begin tracking the LaCourts' friends, and he'd talk to the tribal people about any job-related problems LaCourt might have had at the casino. Two more deputies—Russell Hinks and Dustin Bane, Rusty and Dusty—would take the school. The last man would canvass all the houses down the lake road, asking if anyone had seen anything unusual before the fire. The night before, Climpt had been looking for immediate possibilities.

"I'll be checking back during the day," Lucas said. "If anybody finds anything, call me. And I mean anything."

As the deputies shuffled out, pulling on coats, Carr turned to Lucas and said, "I've got some paperwork before you leave. I want to get you legal."

"Sure." He followed Carr into the hallway, and when they were away from the other deputies asked, "Is this

Climpt guy . . . is he going to work with me? Or is he gonna be a problem?"

"Why should he be?" Carr asked.

"I'm doing a job that he might have expected to get."

Carr shook his head. "Gene's not that way. Not at all."

❄

Bergen stumbled into the hallway, looked around, spotted Carr. "Shelly . . ." he called.

Carr stopped, looked back. Bergen was wearing wind pants and a three-part parka, a Day-Glo orange hunter's hat, ski mitts and heavy-duty pac boots. He looked more like an out-of-shape lumberjack than a priest. "Phil, how'r you feeling?"

"You ought to know," Bergen said harshly, stripping his mitts off and slapping them against his leg as he came down the hall. "The talk all over town is, Bergen did it. Bergen killed the LaCourts. I had about half the usual congregation at Mass this morning. I'll be lucky to have that tomorrow."

"Phil, I don't know . . ." Carr started.

"Don't BS me, Shelly," Bergen said. "The word's coming out of this office. I'm the prime suspect."

"If the word's coming out of this office, I'll stop it—because you're not the prime suspect," Carr said. "We don't have any suspects."

Bergen looked at Lucas. His lower lip trembled and he shook his head, turned back to Carr: "You're a little late, Shelly; and I'll tell you, I won't put up with it. I have a reputation and you and your hired gun"—he looked at Lucas again, then back to Carr—"are ruining it. That's called slander or libel."

Carr took him by the arm, said, "C'mon down to my office, Phil." To Lucas he said, "Go down there to the end of the hall, ask for Helen Arris."

Helen Arris was a big-haired office manager, a woman who might have been in her forties or fifties or early sixties, who chewed gum and called him dear, and who did the paperwork in five minutes. When they finished with the paper, she took his photograph with a Polaroid camera, slipped the photo into a plastic form, stuck the form into a hot press, slammed the press, waited ten seconds, then handed him a mint-new identification card.

"Be careful out there," she said, sounding like somebody on a TV cop show.

❉

Lucas got a notebook from the Explorer and decided to walk down to Grant Hardware, a block back toward the highway. This would be a long day. If they were going to break the killings, they'd do it in a week. And the more they could get early, the better their chances were.

A closet-sized book-and-newspaper store sat on the corner and he stopped for a *Wall Street Journal;* he passed a t-shirt store, a shoe repair shop, and one of the bakeries before he crossed in midblock to the hardware store. The store had a snowblower display in the front window, along with a stack of VCRs and pumpkin-colored plastic sleds. A bell rang over the door when Lucas walked in, and the odor of hot coffee hung in the air. A man sat on a wooden stool, behind the cashier's counter, reading a *People* magazine and drinking coffee from a deep china cup. Lucas walked down toward the counter, aging wooden floor creaking beneath him.

"Dick Westrom?"

"That's me," the counterman said.

"Lucas Davenport. I'm . . ."

"The detective, yeah." Westrom stood up and leaned across the counter to shake hands. He was big, fifty pounds too heavy for his height, with blond hair fading to white and large watery cow eyes that looked away from Lucas. He tipped his head at another chair at the other end of the counter. "My girl's out getting a bite, but there's nobody around . . . we could talk here, if that's all right."

"That's fine," Lucas said. He took off his jacket, walked around the counter and sat down. "I need to know exactly what happened last night, the whole sequence."

Westrom had found Frank LaCourt's body, nearly tripping over it as he hauled hose off the truck.

"You didn't see him right away, laying there?" Lucas asked.

"No. Most of the light was from the fire, it was flickering, you know, and Frank had a layer of snow on him," Westrom said. He had a confidential manner of talking, out of the side of his mouth, as though he were telling secrets in a prison yard. "He was easy to see when you got right on top of him, but from a few feet away . . . hell, you couldn't hardly see him at all."

"That was the first you knew there were dead people?"

"Well, I thought there might be somebody inside, there was a smell, you know. That hit us as soon as we got there, and I think Duane said something like, 'We got a dead one.' "

Westrom insisted that the priest had passed the fire station within seconds of the alarm.

"Look. I got nothing against Phil Bergen," Westrom said, shooting sideways glances at Lucas. "Shelly Carr was trying to get some extra time out of me last night, so I know where *he's* at. But I'll tell you this: I was nukin' a couple of ham sandwiches . . ."

"Yeah?" Lucas said, a neutral noise to keep Westrom rolling.

"And Duane said, 'There goes Father Phil. Hell of a night to be out.' Duane was standing by the front window and I saw Phil going by. Just then the buzzer went off on the microwave. I mean *right then,* when I was looking at the taillights. I says, 'Well, he's a big-shot priest with a big-shot Grand Cherokee, so he can go *where* he wants, *when* he wants.' "

"Sounds like you don't care for him," Lucas said. And Lucas didn't care for Westrom, the eyes always slipping and sliding.

"Well, personally, I don't. But that's neither here nor there, and he can go about his business," Westrom said. He pursed his lips in disapproval. His eyes touched Lucas' face and then skipped away. "Anyway, I was taking the sandwiches out, they're in these cellophane packets, you know, and I was just trying to grab them by the edges and not get burned. I said 'Come and get it,' and the phone rang. Duane picked it up and he said, 'Oh, shit,' and punched in the beeper code and said, 'It's LaCourts', let's go.' I was still standing there with the sandwiches. Never got to open them. Phil hadn't gone by more'n ten seconds before. Shelly was trying to get me to say it was a minute or two or three, but it wasn't. It wasn't more'n ten seconds and it might have been five."

"Huh." Lucas nodded.

"Check with Duane," Westrom said. "He'll tell you."

"Is Duanc a friend of yours?"

"Duane? Well, no. I like him okay. We just don't, you know . . . relate."

"Do you know of anything that Father Bergen might have against the LaCourts?"

"Nope. But he was close to Claudia," Westrom said, with a distinct spin on the word *close*.

"How close?" Lucas asked, tilting his head.

Westrom's eyes wandered around Lucas without settling. "Claudia had a reputation before she married Frank. She got around. She was a pretty thing, too, she had big . . ." Westrom cupped his hands at his chest and bounced them a couple of times. "And Phil . . . He *is* a man. Being a priest and all, it must be tough."

"You think he and Claudia could have been fooling around?" Lucas asked.

Westrom edged forward in his chair and said confidentially, "I don't know about that. We probably would have heard if she was. But it might go way back, something with Father Phil. Maybe Phil wanted to get it started again or something." Westrom's nose twitched.

"How many black Jeeps in Ojibway County?" Lucas asked. "There must be quite a few."

"Bet there aren't, not in the winter. Not Grand Cherokees—those are mostly summer-people cars. I can't think of any besides Phil's." He looked at Lucas curiously: "Are you a Catholic?"

"Why?"

" 'Cause you sound like you're trying to find an excuse for Phil Bergen."

❄

Lucas' notebook cover said, "Westrom, Helper." He drew a line through Westrom, started the Explorer, headed out Highway 77 to the fire station.

In the daytime, with sunlight and the roads freshly plowed, the half-hour trip of the night before was cut to ten minutes. From the high points of the road, he could see forever across the low-lying land, with the contrasting black pine forests cut by the silvery glint of the frozen lakes.

The firehouse was a tan pole barn built on a concrete slab, nestled in a stand of pine just off the highway. One end of the building was dominated by three oversized garage doors for the fire trucks. The office was at the other end, with a row of small windows. Lucas parked in one of four plowed-out spaces and walked into the office, found it empty. Another door led out of the office into the back and Lucas stuck his head through.

"Hello?"

"Yeah?" A heavyset blond man sat at a worktable, a fishing reel disassembled in the light of a high-intensity lamp. A thin, almost transparent beard covered his acne-pitted face. His eyes were blue, careful. A small kitchen area was laid out along one wall behind him. At the other end of the room, a broken-down couch, two aging easy chairs and two wooden kitchen chairs faced a color television. Lockers lined a third wall, each locker stenciled with a man's last name. Another door led back into the truck shed. A flight of stairs went up to a half-loft.

"I'm looking for Duane Helper," Lucas said.

"That's me. You must be Davenport," Helper said. He had a heavy, almost Germanic voice, and stood up to shake hands. He was wearing jeans with wide red suspenders over a blue work shirt. His hand was heavy, like his body, but crusted with calluses. "A whole caravan of TV people just came out of the lake road. The sheriff let them in to take pictures of the house."

"Yeah, he was going to do that," Lucas said.

"I heard Phil Bergen is the main suspect." Helper said it bluntly, as a challenge.

Lucas shook his head. "We don't have any suspects yet."

"That's not the way I heard it," Helper said. The television was playing a game show and Helper picked up a remote control and punched it off.

"Then what you heard is wrong," Lucas said sharply. Helper seemed to be looking for an edge. He was closed-faced, with small eyes; when he played his fingers through his beard, the fingers seemed too short for their thickness, like sausages. Lucas sat down across the round table from him and they started through the time sequence.

"I remember seeing the car, but I didn't remember it was right when the alarm came in," Helper said. "I thought maybe I'd walked up and looked out the window, saw the car, and then we'd talked about something else and I'd gone back to the window again and that's when the alarm came in. That's not the way Dick remembers it."

"How sure are you? Either way?"

Helper rubbed his forehead. "Dick's probably right. We talked about it and he was sure."

"If you went to the window twice, how much time would there have been between the two trips?" Lucas asked.

"Well, I don't know, it would have only been a minute or two, I suppose."

"So even if you went twice, it wasn't long."

"No, I guess not," Helper said.

"Did you actually see Bergen's Jeep come out of the lake road?"

"No, but that's the impression I got. He was moving slow when he went past, even with the snow, and he was accelerating. Like he'd just turned the corner onto 77."

"Okay." Lucas stood up, walked once around the room. Looked at the stairs.

"What's up there?"

"There's a bunk room right at the top. I live in the back. I'm the only professional firefighter here."

"You're on duty twenty-four hours a day?"

"I have time off during the day and early evenings, when we can get volunteers to pick it up," Helper said. "But yeah, I'm here most of the time."

"Huh." Lucas took a turn around the room, thumbnail pressed against his upper teeth, thinking. The time problem was becoming difficult. He looked at Helper. "What about Father Bergen? Do you know him?"

"Not really. I don't believe I've spoken six words to him. He drinks, though. He's been busted for drunk driving, but . . ." He trailed off and looked away.

"But what?" Helper was holding something back, but he wanted Lucas to know it.

"Sheriff Carr's on the county fire board," Helper said.

"Yeah? So what?" Lucas made his response a little short, a little tough.

"He's thick with Bergen. I know you're from the outside, but if I talk, and if it gets back to Shelly, he could hurt me." Helper let the statement lie there, waiting.

Lucas thought it over. Helper might be trying to build an alliance or drive a wedge between himself and Carr. But for what? Most likely he was worried for exactly the reason he claimed: his job. Lucas shook his head. "It won't get back to him if it doesn't need to. Even if it needs to, I can keep the source to myself. If it seems reasonable."

Helper looked at him for a moment, judging him, then looked out the window toward the road. "Well. First off, about that drunk driving. Shelly fixed it. Fixed it a couple of times and maybe more."

He glanced at Lucas. There was more to come, Lucas thought. Helper mentioned the ticket-fixing as a test. "What else?" he pressed.

Helper let it go. "There're rumors that Father Bergen's . . . that if you're a careful dad, you wouldn't want your boy singing in his choir, so to speak."

"He's gay?" Gay would be interesting. Small-town gays felt all kinds of pressure, especially if they were in the closet. And a priest . . .

"That's what I've heard," Helper said. He added, carefully, "It's just gossip. I never gave it much thought. In fact, I don't think it's true. But I don't know. With this kind of thing, these killings, I figured you'd probably want to hear everything."

"Sure." Lucas made a note.

They talked for another five minutes, then three patrol deputies stomped in from duty at the LaCourt house. They were cold and went straight to the coffee. Helper got up to start another pot.

"Anything happening down at the house?" Lucas asked.

"Not much. Guys from Madison are crawling around the place," said one of the deputies. His face was red as a raw steak.

"Is the sheriff down there?"

"He went back to the office, he was gonna talk to some of the TV people."

"All right."

Lucas looked back at Helper, fussing with the coffee. Small-town fireman. He heard things, sitting around with twenty or thirty different firemen every week, nothing much to do.

"Thanks," he said. He nodded at Helper and headed for the door, the phone ringing as he went out. The wind bit at him again, and he hunched against it, hurried around the truck. He was fumbling for his keys when Helper stuck his head out the door and called after him: "It's a deputy looking for you."

Lucas went back inside and picked up the phone. "Yeah?"

"This is Rusty, at the school. You better get your ass up here."

✳

Grant Junior High was a red-brick rectangle with blue-spruce accents spotted around the lawn. A man in a snowmobile suit worked on the flat roof, pushing snow off. The harsh scraping sounds carried forever on the cold air. Lucas parked in front, zipped his parka, pulled on his ski gloves. Down the street, the bank time-and-temperature sign said

– 21. The sun was rolling across the southern sky, as pale as an old silver dime.

Bob Jones was waiting outside the principal's office when Lucas walked in. Jones was a round-faced man, balding, with rosy cheeks, a short black villain's mustache and professional-principal's placating smile. He wore a blue suit with a stiff-collared white shirt, and his necktie was patriotically striped with red, white, and blue diagonals.

"Glad to see you," he said as they shook hands. "I've heard about you. Heck of a record. Come on, I'll take you down to the conference room. The boy's name is John Mueller." The school had wide halls painted an institutional beige, with tan lockers spotted between cork bulletin boards. The air smelled of sweat socks, paper, and pencil-sharpener shavings.

Halfway down the hall, Jones said, "I'd like you to talk to John's father about this. When you're done with him. I don't think there's a legal problem, but if you could talk to him . . ."

"Sure," Lucas said.

Rusty and Dusty were sitting at the conference table drinking coffee, Rusty with his feet on the table. They were both large, beefy, square-faced, white-toothed, with elaborately casual hairdos, Rusty a Chippewa, Dusty with the transparent pallor of a pure Swede. Rusty hastily pulled his feet off the table when Lucas and Jones walked in, leaving a ring of dirty water on the tabletop.

"Where's the kid?" Lucas asked.

"Back in his math class," said Dusty.

"I'll get him," Jones volunteered. He promptly disappeared down the hall, his heels echoing off the terrazzo.

Dusty wiped the water off the tabletop with his elbow and pushed a file at Lucas. "Kid's name is John Mueller. We pulled his records. He's pretty much of an A-B student. Quiet. His father runs a taxidermy shop out on County N, his mother works at Grotek's Bakery."

Lucas sat down, opened the file, started paging through it. "What about this other kid? You said on the phone that another kid was murdered."

Rusty nodded, taking it from Dusty. "Jim Harper. He went to school here, seventh grade. He was killed around three months back," Rusty said.

"October 20th," said Dusty.

"What's the story?" Lucas asked.

"Strangled. First they thought it was an accident, but the doc had the body sent down to Milwaukee, and they figured he was strangled. Never caught anybody."

"First murder of a local resident in fourteen years," Rusty said.

"Jesus Christ, nobody told me," Lucas said. He looked up at them.

Dusty shrugged. "Well . . . I guess nobody thought about it. It's kind of embarrassing, really. We got nothing on the killing. Zero. Zilch. It's been three months now; I think people'd like to forget it."

"And he went to this school, and he was in classes with the LaCourt girl . . . I mean, Jesus. . . ."

Jones returned, ushering a young boy into the room. The kid was skinny and jug-eared, with hair the color of ripe wheat, big eyes, a thin nose and wide mouth. He wore a flannel shirt and faded jeans over off-brand gym shoes. He looked like an elf, Lucas thought.

"How are you? John? Is that right?" Lucas asked as Jones backed out of the room. "I understand you have some information about Lisa."

The kid nodded, slipped into the chair across the table from Lucas, turned a thumb to the other two deputies. "I already talked to these guys," he said.

"I know, but I'd like to hear it fresh, if that's okay," Lucas said. He said it serious, as though he were talking to an adult. John nodded just as seriously. "So: how'd you know Lisa?"

"We ride the bus together. I get off at County N and she goes on."

"And did she say something?" Lucas asked.

"She was really scared," John said intently. His ears reddened, sticking out from his head like small Frisbees. "She had this picture, from school."

"What was it?"

"It was from a newspaper," John said. "It was a picture of Jim Harper, the kid who got killed. You know about him?"

"I've heard."

"Yeah, it was really like . . ." John looked away and swallowed, then back. "He was naked on the bed and there was this naked man standing next to him with, you know, this, uh, I mean it was stickin' up."

Lucas looked at him, and the kid peered solemnly back. "He had an erection? The man?" Lucas asked.

"Yup," John said earnestly.

"Where's the picture?" Lucas felt a tingle: this was something.

"Lisa took it home," John said. "She was going to show it to her mom."

"When? What day?" Lucas asked. Rusty and Dusty watched the questioning, eyes shifting from Lucas to the kid and back.

"Last week. Thursday, 'cause that's store night and Mom works late, and when I got home Dad was cooking."

"Do you know where she got the picture?" Lucas asked.

"She said she got it from some other kid," John said, shrugging. "I don't know who. It was all crinkled up, like it had been passed around."

"What'd the man look like? Did you recognize him?"

"Nope. His head wasn't in the picture," the boy said. "I mean, it looked like the whole picture was there, but it cut off his head like somebody didn't aim the camera right."

Dammit. "So you could only see his body."

"Yeah. And some stuff around him. The bed and stuff," John said.

"Was the man big or small? His body?" Lucas asked.

"He was pretty big. Kind of fat."

"What color was his hair?" asked Lucas.

John cocked his head, his eyes narrowing. "I don't remember."

"You didn't notice a lot of chest hair or stomach hair or hair around his crotch?" Lucas fished for a word the kid could relate to: "I mean, like really kind of gross?"

"No. Nothing like that . . . but it was a black-and-white picture and it wasn't very good," John said. "You know those newspapers they have at the Super Valu . . . ?"

"National Enquirer," Rusty said.

"Yeah. The picture was like from that. Not very good."

If the hair didn't strike him as gross, then the guy was probably a blond, Lucas thought. Black hair on cheap paper would blot. "If it wasn't very good, could you be sure it was Jim?" Lucas asked.

The boy nodded. "It was Jim, all right. You could see his face, smiling like Jim. And Jim lost a finger and you could see if you looked real close that the kid in the picture didn't have a finger. And he had an earring and Jim wore an earring. He was the first guy in the school to get one."

"Mph. You say Lisa was scared? How do you know she was scared?"

"Because she showed it to me," John said.

"What?" Lucas frowned, missing something.

"She's a girl. And the picture—you know . . ." John twisted in his chair. "She wouldn't show something like *that* to a boy if she wasn't scared about it."

"Okay." Lucas ran over the questions one more time, probed the contents of the picture the boy had seen, but got nothing more. "Is your dad out at his shop?"

"Sure—I guess," the kid said, nodding.

"Did you tell him about the picture?"

"No." John looked uncomfortable. "I mean . . . how could I tell him about that?"

"Okay," Lucas said. "Let's ride out there and I'll tell him about you talking to us. Just so everything's okay. And I think we ought to keep it between us."

"Sure. I'm not going to tell anybody else," John said. "Not about that," he said earnestly, eyes big.

"Good," Lucas said. He relaxed and smiled. "Go get your stuff, and let's go out to your place."

"Did we do good?" Rusty asked lazily when John had gone.

"Yeah, you did good," Lucas said.

The two deputies slapped hands and Lucas said, "You're all done with Lisa's friends?"

"Yeah, all done," Rusty said.

"Great. Now do this other kid's friends. The Harper kid. Look for connections between Lisa and Harper," Lucas said. "And if this picture was passed around, find out who passed it."

❄

Lucas used a pay phone in the teachers' lounge to call the sheriff's office. "You sound funny," he said when Carr came on.

"You're being relayed. What'd you need?"

"Are we scrambled?"

"Not really."

"I'll talk to you later. Something's come up."

"I'm on my way to the LaCourts'."

"I'm heading that way, so I'll see you there," Lucas said. He hung up momentarily, then redialed the sheriff's office, got Helen, the office manager, and asked her to start digging up the files on the Harper murder.

John Mueller had gone to put his books away and get his coat and boots. As Lucas waited for him at the front door, a bell rang and kids flooded into the hallways. Another, non-student head bobbed above the others in the stream, caught his eye. The doctor. He took a step toward her. He'd been a while without a woman friend; thought he could get away from the need by making a hermit of himself, by working out. He was wrong, judging from the tension in his chest . . . unless he was having a heart attack. Weather was pulling on her cap as she came toward him, and oversized mittens with leather palms. She nodded, stopped and said, "Anything good?"

"Not a thing," he said, shaking his head. *Not pretty,* he thought, *but very attractive. A little rough, like she might enjoy the occasional fistfight. Who is she dating? There must be someone. The guy is probably an asshole; probably has little tassels on his shoes and combs them straight in the morning, before he puts the mousse on his hair.*

"I was doing TB patches down there." She nodded back down the hall, toward a set of open double doors. A gymnasium. "And one kid was scared to death that somebody was going to come kill him in the night."

Lucas shrugged. "That's the way it goes." As soon as he said it, he knew it was wrong.

"Mr. Liberal," she said, her voice flat.

"Hey, nothing I can do about it except catch the asshole," Lucas said, irritated. "Look, I didn't really . . ." He was about to go on but she turned away.

"Do that," she said, and pushed through the door to the outside.

Annoyed, Lucas leaned against the entryway bulletin board, watching her walk to her car. Had a nice walk, he decided. When he turned back to the school, looking for John, he saw a yellow-haired girl watching *him*.

She stood in a classroom doorway, staring at him with a peculiar intensity, as though memorizing his face. She was tall, but slight, angular with just the first signs of an adolescent roundness. And she was pale as paper. The most curious thing was her hair, which was an opaque yellow, the color of a sunflower petal, and close-cropped. With her pointed chin, large tilted eyes and short hair, she had a waifish look, like she should be selling matches. She wore a homemade dress of thin print material, cotton, with short sleeves: summer wear. She held three books close to her chest. When he looked at her, she held his eyes for a moment, a gaze with a solid sexuality to it, speculative, but at the same time, hurt, then turned and walked away.

John arrived in a heavy parka with a fur-lined hood and mittens. "Do you have a cop car?" he asked.

"No. A four-by-four," Lucas said.

"How come?"

"I'm new here."

❄

John's father was a mild, round-faced man in a yellow wool sweater and corduroys. "How come you didn't tell me?" he asked his son. He sat on a high stool. On his bench, a fox skin was half-stretched over a wooden form. John shrugged, looked away.

"Embarrassed," Lucas said. "He did the right thing, today. We didn't want you to think we were grilling him. We'd have called you, to get you in, but I was right there and he was . . ."

"That's okay, as long as John's not in trouble," his father said. He patted John on the head.

"No, no. He did the right thing. He's a smart kid," Lucas said.

✳

The picture was critical. He felt it, knew it. Whistled to himself as he drove out to the LaCourt house. Progress.

Helper was working in the fire station parking lot, rolling hose onto a reel, when Lucas passed on his way to the LaCourts'. A sheriff's car was parked in a cleared space to one side of the LaCourts' driveway, and a deputy waved him through. A half-dozen men were working around or simply standing around the house, which was tented with sheets of Army canvas, and looked like an olive-drab haystack. Power lines, mounted on makeshift poles, ran through gaps in the canvas. Lucas parked at the garage and hurried inside. Two sheriff's deputies were warming themselves at the stove, along with a crime tech from Madison.

"Seen the sheriff?" Lucas asked.

"He's in the house," one of the deputies said. To the tech he said, "That's Davenport."

"Been looking for you," the tech said, walking over. "I'm the lab chief here . . . Tod Crane." Crane looked like he might be starving. His fingers and wrists were thin, bony, and the skin on his balding head seemed to be stretched over his skull like a banjo covering. When they shook hands, an unexpected muscle showed up: he had a grip like a pair of channel-lock pliers.

"How's it going?" Lucas asked.

"It's a fuckin' mess," Crane said. He held up his hands, flexed them. They were bone-white and trembling with cold. "Whoever did it spread gas-oil premix all over the house. When he touched it off, Boom. We're finding stuff blown right through some of the internal walls."

"Premix from the boats?"

"Yeah, that's what we think. Maybe some straight gas from the snowmobiles. We've found three six-gallon cans. The LaCourts had two boats, a pontoon and a fishing rig, and there aren't any gas cans with them. And premix, you put it in a bottle with a wick, it's called a Molotov cocktail."

"Any chance our man was hurt? Or burned?" Lucas asked.

"No way to tell, but he'd have to be careful," Crane said. "He spread around quite a bit of gas. We've got an arson guy coming up this afternoon to see if we can isolate where the fire started."

Lucas nodded. "I'm looking for a piece of paper," he said. "It was a picture, apparently torn from a magazine or a newspaper. It shows a naked man and a naked boy on the bed behind him. It might be in the house."

"Yeah? That's new?" Crane's eyebrows went up.

"Yup."

"Think he was trying to burn it up?" Crane asked.

"The thought crossed my mind."

"I'll tell you right now, there were a couple of filing cabinets that were dumped and doused with gas, and he shot some gas into a closet full of paper stuff, photographs, like that. He did the same thing on the chests of drawers in the parents' bedroom, after he dumped them."

"So maybe . . ."

"There ought to be some reason he torched the place. I mean, besides being nuts," Crane said. "If he'd just killed them and walked, it might of been a day or two before anybody found them. He'd have time to set up an alibi. This way he tipped his hand right away."

"So find the paper," Lucas said.

"We'll look," Crane said. "Hell, it's nice to have something specific to look for."

❊

Carr came in while they were talking. He'd mellowed since morning, a small satisfied smile on his face. "They're gone, the reporters. Most of them, anyway," he said. "Poof."

"Probably found a better murder," Lucas said.

"I talked to Helen, back at the office," Carr said. "What's this about Jim Harper?"

"Rusty and Dusty found a kid at the junior high who says Jim Harper posed for sex photos with an adult male," Lucas said. "That'd be a long-term felony and might be worth killing somebody for. The picture came out of a pulp-paper magazine or newspaper. Some kids got hold of it and it may have been passed around the school. Lisa LaCourt had it last. She took it home on Thursday and showed it to this kid who talked to me."

"Who is it? The kid at the school?"

"John Mueller. His father's a taxidermist," Lucas said.

Carr nodded. "Sure, I know him. That's an okay family. Damn, these things could be tied."

Lucas shrugged. "It's a possibility. The Harper kid's parents, are they around?"

"One of them is, the old man, Russ. The wife left years ago, went out to California. She was back for the funeral, though."

"What does Harper do?" Lucas asked.

"Runs an Amoco station out at Knuckle Lake."

"Okay, I'll head out there."

"Whoa, whoa." Carr shook his head. "Better not go alone. Are you gonna be up late?"

"Sure."

"Harper's open till midnight. He'd never talk to us if he didn't have to: never to a cop. Why don't I pick up a search warrant for Jim Harper's stuff out at his house, and we'll get a couple deputies and go out there late? I got church."

"All right," Lucas said. "Harper's an asshole?"

"He is," Carr said, nodding. And he said, "Lord, if these two cases are tied together and we could nail them down in a day or two . . . that'd make me a very happy man."

"Will Father Bergen be at your service tonight?" Lucas asked.

"Probably not. He's pretty shook up. You heard him this morning."

"Yeah." Lucas crossed his arms, watching Carr. "The Mueller kid said the adult in the photo was a big guy. And probably blond or fair. The kid didn't remember the guy as being hairy, which means he probably didn't have much."

"Like Father Phil," Carr said, flushing. "Well, it wasn't Phil. There are a thousand chunky blonds in this county. I'm one."

"I talked to the firemen. Westrom thinks Bergen did it. He says so. And he looks like someone who'd talk about it."

"Dick's the gossip-central for the whole town," Carr said. Then, his voice dropping almost to a whisper, "God damn him."

"Have you ever heard anything about Bergen being involved in sexual escapades?"

Carr stepped back. "No. Absolutely not. Why?"

"Just bullshit, probably. There are rumors around that he's messed with both women and men."

"A homosexual?" Carr was flabbergasted. "That's ridiculous. Where'n the heck are you getting this stuff?"

"Just asking around. Anyway, we've gotta talk to him again," Lucas said. "After your service? Then we can hit Harper."

Carr looked worried. "All right. I'll see you at the church at nine o'clock. Are we still meeting with the other guys at five?"

"Yeah. But I don't think there's much, except for Rusty and Dusty coming up with the photo thing."

"You're not going to tear Phil up, are you?" Carr asked.

"There's something out of sync, here," Lucas said, avoiding a direct answer. "He's not telling us something, maybe. I gotta think about it."

CHAPTER

✳ ✳ ✳

6

The yellow-haired girl sat on a broken-legged couch, smoking an unfiltered Camel, working on her math problems; old man Schuler would be on her ass if she didn't finish all ten of them. She hated Schuler. He had a way of embarrassing her.

The couch cushions were stained with Coke and coffee spills, the cushions pulled out of shape by shrunken upholstery. The yellow-haired girl's brother had seen the couch sitting on the street late one rainy night, waiting for the annual spring trash pickup, and had hauled it away himself. Almost good as new, except for the cushions.

She exhaled, playing with the smoke with her mouth and nose. Snorted it. Trying to think. Across the room, the letter-woman, what's-her-name, the blonde, was turning letters on "Wheel of Fortune." She turned two *t*'s and the audience applauded.

A train is traveling west at twenty-five miles an hour. Another train is traveling east at forty-five . . .

Bullshit.

The yellow-haired girl looked back at the television. The letter-woman wore a silky white dress with a deep neckline, some kind of an overlap on the material, with padding at the shoulders. She looked good in the dress; but she had the complexion and the body for it.

The yellow-haired girl checked herself every morning in the mirror on the back of her door, lifting her small breasts with her hands, squeezing them to make a cleavage, looking at herself sideways and straight-on, at her back over her shoulders. She tried all of Rosie's clothes and some of her brother Mark's. Mark's t-shirts were best. She'd wear them downtown next summer, to Juke's, without a bra. If she lightly brushed the tips of her nipples, they'd firm up and faintly indent the t-shirt material, if she arched her back. Very sexy.

If the trains start two hundred miles apart, how long will . . .

Doritos sacks littered the floor at her feet. A round cardboard tray, marked with scrapings of chocolate-cake frosting, sat on a spindly-legged TV-dinner table. An aluminum ashtray was piled with cigarette butts, and she'd just dropped another burning butt into the hole of a mostly empty Coke can. The butt guttered in the dampness at the bottom, and the stench of burning wet tobacco curdled the air; and beneath that, the smell of old coffee grounds, spoiled bananas, rotting hamburger.

On the "Wheel of Fortune," the contestants had found the letters *T-- --n-t- ---n-n-*. She stared at them, moving her lips. *Turn? No, it couldn't be "turn," you just thought that because you could see the* t*'s and the* n*'s.*

Huh. Could be two . . . ?

The truck rattled into the driveway and her heart skipped. The girl hopped to her feet, peered out the window, saw him climbing down, felt her breath thicken in her chest. His headlights were still on and he walked around to the front of the truck, peered at a tire. Sometimes, in her young-old eyes, he looked like a dork. He weighed too much, and had that turned-in look, like he wasn't really in touch with the world. He had temper tantrums, and did things he was sorry for. Hit her. Hit Mark. Always apologized . . .

At other times, when he was with her, or with Mark or Rosie or the others, when they were having a fuck-in . . . then he was different. The yellow-haired girl had seen a penned wolf once. The wolf sat behind a chain-link fence and looked her over with its yellow eyes. The eyes said, *If only I was out there . . .*

His eyes were like that, sometimes. She shivered: he was no dork when he looked like that. He was something else.

And he was good to her. Brought her gifts. Nobody had ever brought her gifts—not good ones, anyway—before him. Her mom might get her a dress that she bought at the secondhand, or some jeans at K Mart. But he'd given her a Walkman and a bunch of tapes, probably twenty now. He bought her Chic jeans and a bustier and twice had brought her flowers. Carnations.

And he took her to dinner. First he got a book from the library that told about the different kinds of silverware—the narrow forks for meat, the wide forks for salad, the little knives for butter. After she knew them all, they talked about the different kinds of salads, and the entrées, and the soups and desserts. About scooping the soup spoon away from you, rather than toward you; about keeping your left hand in your lap.

When she was ready, they did it for real. She got a dress from Rosie, off-the-shoulder, and some black flats. He took her to Duluth, to the Holiday Inn. She'd been awed by the dining room, with the view of Superior. Two kinds of wine, red and white. She'd remember it forever.

She loved him.

Her old man had moved away two years before, driven out by Rosie and her mom, six months before the cancer had killed her mom. All her old man had ever given her were black eyes—and once he'd hit her in the side, just below her armpit, so hard that she almost couldn't breathe for a month and thought she was going to die.

He was worse with Rosie: he tried to fuck Rosie and everybody knew that wasn't right; and when Rosie wouldn't fuck him, he'd given her to Russ Harper for some tires.

When he'd started looking at the yellow-haired girl—
started showing himself, started peeing with the bathroom
door open when he knew she'd walk by, when he came
busting in when she was in the shower—that's when Rosie
and her mom had run him off.

Not that they'd had to.

Her old man had worn shapeless overalls, usually covered with dirt, and old-fashioned sleeveless undershirts that
showed off his fat gut, hanging from his chest like a pig
in a hammock. She couldn't talk to him, much less look at
him. If he'd ever come into her bedroom after her, she'd
kill him.

Had told him that.

And she would have.

❊

This man was different. His voice was soft, and when he
touched her face he did it with his fingertips or the backs of
his fingers. He never hit her. Never. He was educated. Told
her about things; told her about sophisticated women and
the things they had to know. About sophisticated love.

He loved her and she loved him.

The yellow-haired girl tiptoed into the back of the double-
wide and looked into the bedroom. Rosie was facedown on
the bed, asleep, a triangle of light from the hallway crossing her back. One leg thrust straight down the bed and was
wrapped from knee to ankle with a heavy white bandage.
The yellow-haired girl eased the door shut, pulling the handle until she heard the bolt click.

He was climbing the stoop when she got to the door, a
sack of groceries in his arms. There was a puddle of cold
water on the floor and she stepped in it, said, "Shit," wiped
her foot on a rag rug and opened the door. His heavy face
was reddened with the cold.

"Hi," she said. She lifted herself on her tiptoes to kiss
him on the cheek: she'd seen it done on television, in the
old movies, and it seemed so . . . right. "Rosie's asleep."

"Cold," he said, as though answering a question. He
pushed the door shut and she walked away from him into

the front room, hips moving under her padded housecoat. "Is Rosie still hurting?"

"Yeah, she bitches all day. The doctor was back and took the drain out, but it'll be another week before she takes out the stitches . . . stunk up the whole house when she took the drain out. Bunch of gunk ran out of her leg."

"Nasty," he said. "How was the birthday party?"

"Okay, 'cept Rosie was so bitchy because of her leg." The yellow-haired girl had turned fourteen the day before. She looked at the cake ring on the floor. "Mark ate most of the cake. His friend had some weed and we got wrecked."

"Sounds like a good time." His cheeks were red like jolly old St. Nick's. "Get anything good? For your birthday?"

"The fifty bucks from you was the best," she said, taking his hand, smiling into his eyes. "Rosie gave me a Chili Peppers t-shirt and Mark gave me a tape for the Walkman."

"Well, that sounds pretty good," he said. He dumped the groceries on the kitchen table.

"There was a cop at school today, one I never seen before," the yellow-haired girl said.

"Oh, yeah?" He took a six-pack of wine coolers out of the sack, but stopped and looked at her. "Guy looks like an asshole, a big guy?"

"He was kinda good-looking but he looked like he could be mean, yeah," she said.

"Did you talk to him?"

"No. But he had some kids in the office," she said. "Lisa's friends."

"What'd they tell 'em?" He was sharp, the questions rapping out.

"Well, everybody was talking about it in the cafeteria. Nobody knew anything. But the new cop took John Mueller home with him."

"The taxidermist's kid?" His thin eyebrows went up.

"Yeah. John rode on the bus with Lisa."

"Huh." He dug into the grocery sack, a thoughtful look on his face.

"The cop was talking to the doctor," she said. "The one who takes care of Rosie."

"What?" His head came around sharply.

"Yeah. They were talking in the hall. I saw them."

"Were they talking about Rosie?" He glanced down the hall at the closed door.

"I don't know; I wasn't that close. I just saw them talking."

"Hmm." He unscrewed the top of one of the wine bottles, handed it to the yellow-haired girl. "Where's your brother?"

Jealousy scratched at her. He was fond of Mark and was helping him explore his development. "He's over at Ricky's, working on the car."

"The Pinto?"

"Yeah."

The man laughed quietly, but there was an unpleasant undertone in the sound. Was *he* jealous? Of Ricky, for being with Mark? She pushed the thought away.

"I wish them the best," he said. He was focusing on her, and she walked back to the couch and sat down, sipping the wine cooler. "How have you been?"

"Okay," she said, and wiggled. She tried to sound cool. *Okay.*

He knelt in front of her and began unbuttoning her blouse, and she felt the thickness in her chest again, as though she were breathing water. She put down the wine cooler, helped him pull the blouse off, let him reach around her and unsnap the brassiere; he'd shown her how he could do it with one hand.

She had solid breasts like cupcakes, and small stubby nipples.

"Wonderful," he whispered. He stroked one of her nipples, then stood up and his hand went to his fly. "Let's try this one."

She was aware of him watching, of his intent blue eyes following her; he pushed her hair out of her face.

Behind him the blonde woman on "Wheel of Fortune" was turning around the last of the letters.

Two Minute Warning, the sign said.

❆

When the Iceman left, he drove out to the county road, to the first stop sign, and sat there, smoking, thinking about John Mueller and Weather Karkinnen. So many troubling paths were opening. He tried to follow them in his mind, and failed: they tangled like a rats' nest.

If the photograph turned up, and if they identified him, they'd have him on the sex charge. That's all he'd wanted to stop. When Harper called and said Frank LaCourt had the photo but didn't know who was in it, all he'd wanted was to get it back. Get it before the sheriff got it.

Then he'd killed Claudia too quickly and hadn't gotten the photo. Now the photo would mean they'd look at him for the killings. More than that: when they saw the photo, they'd figure the whole thing out.

He was in a perfect position to monitor the investigation, anyway. He'd know when they found the photo. He'd probably have a little time: until Weather saw it, anyway.

He'd been crazy to let the kid take the picture. But there was something about seeing yourself, contemplating yourself at a distance. Now: had John Mueller seen? Did he have a copy or know where it came from?

If they found the photo, they'd have a place to start. And if they showed it to enough people, they'd get him. He had to have it. Maybe it had burned in the fire. Maybe not. Maybe the Mueller kid knew.

And Weather Karkinnen. If *she* saw the photo, she'd know him for sure.

Dammit.

He rolled down the window a few inches, flipped the cigarette into the snow.

He'd once seen himself in a movie. A comedy, no less. *Ghostbusters.* Silly scene—a jerk, a nebbish, is possessed by an evil spirit, and talks to a horse. When the cabriolet driver yells at him, the nebbish growls and his eyes burn red, and the power flares out at the driver.

Good for a laugh—but the Iceman had seen himself there,

just for an instant. He also had a force inside, but there was nothing funny about it. The force was powerful, unafraid, influential. Manipulating events from behind the screen of a bland, unprepossessing face.

Flaring out when it was needed.

He had a recurring dream in which a woman, a blonde, looked at him, her eyes flicking over him, unimpressed. And he let the force flare out of his eyes, just a flicker, catching her, and he could feel the erotic response from her.

He'd wondered about Weather. He'd stood there, naked under his hospital gown, she examined him. He'd let the fire out with her, trying to look her into a corner, but she'd seemed not to notice. He'd let it go.

He often thought about her after that encounter. Wondering how she saw him, standing there; she must've thought *something,* she *was* a woman.

The Iceman looked out at the frozen snowscape in his headlights.

The Mueller kid.

Weather Karkinnen.

CHAPTER

✳ ✳ ✳

7

An hour after dark, the investigation group gathered in Carr's office. Climpt, the investigator, and two other men had worked the LaCourts' friends and found nothing of significance. No known feud, nothing criminal. The Storm Lake road had been run from one end to the other, and all but two or three people could account for themselves at the time of the killings; those two or three didn't seem to be likely prospects. Several people had seen Father Bergen loading his sled on his trailer.

"What about the casino?" Lucas asked Climpt.

"Nothing there," Climpt said, shaking his head. "Frank didn't have nothing to do with money; never touched it. There was no way he could rig anything, either. He was in charge of physical security for the place, mostly handling drunks. He just didn't have the access that could bring trouble."

"Do the tribe people think he's straight?"

"Yup. No money problems that they know of. Didn't gamble himself. Didn't use drugs. Used to drink years back, but he quit. Tell you the truth, it felt like a dead end."

"All right . . . Rusty, Dusty, how about that picture."

"Can't find anybody who admitted seeing it," Rusty said. "We're talking to Lisa LaCourt's friends, but there's been some flu around, and we didn't get to everybody yet."

"Keep pushing."

The next day would be more of the same, they decided. Another guy to help Rusty and Dusty check Lisa's friends. "And I'll want you to start interviewing Jim Harper's pals, if you can find any."

❄

The sheriff's department's investigators shared a corner office. One did nothing but welfare investigations, worked seven-to-three, and was out of the murder case. A second had gotten mumps from his daughters and was on sick leave. The third was Gene Climpt. Climpt had said almost nothing during the meeting. He'd rolled an unlit cigarette in his fingers, watching Lucas, weighing him.

Lucas moved into the mumps-victim's desk and Helen Arris brought in a lockable two-drawer file cabinet for papers and personal belongings.

"I brought you the Harper boy's file," she said. She was a formidable woman with very tall hair and several layers of makeup.

"Thanks. Is there any coffee in the place? A vending machine?"

"Coffee in the squad room, I can show you."

"Great." He tagged along behind her, making small talk. He'd recognized her type as soon as Carr sent him to her for his ID. She knew everybody and tracked everything that went on in the department. She knew the forms and the legalities, the state regs and who was screwing who. She was not to be trifled with if you wanted your life to run smoothly and end with a pension.

She wouldn't be fooled by false charm either. Lucas didn't even try it: he got his coffee, thanked her, and carried it back to the office, left the door open. Deputies and a few civilian clerks wandered past, one or two at a time, looking him over. He ignored the desultory parade as he combed through the stack of paper on the county's first real homicide in six years.

Jim Harper had been found hanging from a pull-down towel rack in the men's room of a Unocal station in Bon Plaine, seventeen miles east of Grant. The boy was seated on the floor under the rack, a loop of the towel around his neck. His Levi's and Jockey shorts had been pulled down below his knees. The door had been locked, but it was a simple push-button that could be locked from the inside with the door open and remain locked when the door was pulled shut, so that meant nothing. The boy had been found by the station owner when he opened for business in the morning.

Harper's father had been questioned twice. The first time, the morning after the murder, was perfunctory. The sheriff's investigators were assuming accidental death during a masturbation ritual, which was not unheard of. The only interesting point on the preliminary investigation was a scrawled note to Carr: *Shelly, I don't like this one. We better get an autopsy. —Gene.*

Climpt. His desk was in the corner, and Lucas glanced at it. The desk was neatly kept, impersonal except for an aging photograph in a silver frame. He pushed the chair back and looked closer. A pretty woman, dressed in the styles of the late fifties or early sixties, with a baby in her arms. Lucas called Arris, asked her to find Climpt, and went back to the Harper file.

After an autopsy, a forensic pathologist from Milwaukee had declared the death a strangulation homicide. Russ Harper, the boy's father, was interviewed again, this time by a pair of Wisconsin state major-crime investigators. Harper didn't know anything about anything, he said. Jim had gone wild, had been drinking seriously and maybe smoking marijuana.

They were unhappy about it, but had to let it go. Russ Harper was not a suspect—he had been working at his gas station when the boy was murdered, and disinterested witnesses would swear to it. His presence was also backed by computer-time-stamped charge slips with his initials on them.

The state investigators interviewed a dozen other people, including some Jim's age. They'd all denied being his friend. One had said Jim didn't have any friends. Nobody had seen the boy at the crossroads gas station. On the day he was killed, nobody had seen him since school.

❋

"Hear you want to talk to me?"

Climpt was a big man in his middle fifties, deep blue eyes and a hint of rosiness about his cheeks. He was wearing a blue parka, open, brown pac boots with wool pants tucked inside, and carried a pair of deerhide gloves. A chrome pistol sat diagonally across his left hip bone, where it could be crossdrawn with his right hand, even when he was sitting behind a steering wheel. His voice was like a load of gravel.

Lucas looked up and said, "Yeah, just a second." He pawed through the file papers, looking for the note Climpt had sent to Carr. Climpt peeled off his parka, hung it on a hook next to Lucas', ambled over to his own desk and sat down, leaning back in his chair.

"How'd it go?" Lucas asked as he looked through the file.

"Mostly bullshit." The words came out slow and country. "What's up?"

Lucas found the note, handed it to him: "You sent this to Shelly after you handled that death report on the Harper kid. What was wrong out there? Why'd you want the autopsy?"

Climpt looked at the note, then handed it back to Lucas. "The boy was sittin' on the floor with his dick in his hand, for one thing. I never actually tried hanging myself, but I suspect that right near the end, you'd know something was going wrong and you'd start flapping. You wouldn't sit there pumpin' away until you died."

"Okay." Lucas nodded, grinned.

"Then there was the floor," Climpt continued. "There aren't many men's room floors *I'd* sit on, and this wasn't one of them. The gas station gets cleaned in the morning—maybe. There's a bar across the highway and guys'd come out of the bar at night, stop at the station for gas, the cold air'd hit 'em and they'd realize they had to take a whiz. Being half drunk, their aim wasn't always so good. They'd pee all over the place. I just couldn't see somebody sitting there voluntarily."

Lucas nodded.

"Another thing," Climpt said. "Those damn tiles were cold. You could frostbite your ass on those tiles. I mean, it'd hurt."

"So you couldn't add it up."

"That's about it," Climpt said.

"Got any ideas about it?"

"I'd talk to Russ Harper if I was gonna go back into it," Climpt said.

"They talked to him," Lucas said, flipping through the stack of paper. "The state guys did."

"Well . . ." His eyes were on Lucas, judging: "What I mean was, I'd take him out back to my workshop, put his hand in the vise, close it about six turns and *then* ask him. And if that didn't work, I'd turn on the grinder." He wasn't smiling when he said it.

"You think he knows who killed his boy?" Lucas asked.

"If you asked me the most likely guy to commit a sneaky-type murder in this county, I'd say Russ Harper. Hands down. If his *son* gets killed, sneaky-like . . . that's no coincidence, to my way of thinkin'. Russ might not know who killed him, but I bet he'd have some ideas."

"I'm thinking of going out there tonight, talking to Harper," Lucas said. "Maybe take him out back to the shop."

"I'm not doin' nothing. Invite me along," Climpt said, stretching his legs out.

"You don't care for him?"

"If that son-of-a-bitch's heart caught on fire," Climpt said, "I wouldn't piss down his throat to put it out."

❄

Climpt said he'd get dinner and hang around his house until Lucas was ready to go after Harper. Helen Arris had already gone, and much of the department was dark. Lucas tossed the Jim Harper file in his new file cabinet and banged the drawer shut. The drawer got off-track and jammed. When he tried to pull it back open, it wouldn't come. He knelt down, inspecting it, found that a thin metal rail had bent, and tried to pry it out with his fingernails. He got it out, but his hand slipped and he ripped the fingernail on his left ring finger.

"Mother—" He was dripping blood. He went down to the men's room, rinsed it, looked at it. The nail rip went deep and it'd have to be clipped. He wrapped a paper towel around it, got his coat, and walked out through the darkened hallways of the courthouse. He turned a corner and saw an elderly man pushing a broom, and then a woman's voice echoed down a side hallway: "Heck of a day, Odie," it said.

The doctor. Weather. Again. The old man nodded, looking down a hall at right angles to the one he and Lucas were in. "Cold day, miz."

She walked out of the intersecting corridor, still carrying her bag, a globe light shining down on her hair as she passed under it. Her hair looked like clover honey. She heard him in the hallway, glanced his way, recognized him, stopped. "Davenport," she said. "Killed anybody yet?"

Lucas had automatically smiled when he saw her, but he cut it off: "That's getting pretty fuckin' tiresome," he snapped.

"Sorry," she said. She straightened and smiled, tentatively. "I didn't mean . . . I don't know what I didn't mean. Whatever it was, I didn't mean it when I saw you at the school, either."

What? He didn't understand what she'd just said, but it sounded like an apology. He let it go. "You work for the county, too?"

She glanced around the building. "No, not really. The board cut out the public health nurse and I do some of her old route. Volunteer thing. I go around and see people out in the country."

"Pretty noble," Lucas said. The line came out sounding

skeptical instead of wry. Before she could say anything, he put up a hand. "Sorry. That came out wrong."

She shrugged. "I owed you one." She looked at his hand. He was holding it at his side, waist height, clenching the towel in his fist. "What happened to your hand?"

"Broke a nail."

"You oughta use a good acrylic hardener," she said. And then quickly, "Sorry again. Let me see it."

"Aw . . ."

"Come on."

He unwrapped the towel and she held his finger in her hand, turned it in the weak light. "Nasty. Let me, uh . . . come more under the light." She opened her bag.

"Listen, why don't I . . . Is this gonna hurt?"

"Don't be a baby," she said. She used a pair of surgical scissors on the nail, trimming it away. No pain. She dabbed on a drop of an ointment and wrapped it with a Band-Aid. "I'll send you a bill."

"Send it to the sheriff, I got it on the job," he said. Then: "Thanks."

They stopped at the door, looked out at the snow. "Where're you going?" Lucas asked.

She glanced at her wristwatch. No rings. "Get something to eat."

"Could I buy you dinner?" he asked.

"All right," she said simply. She didn't look at him. She just pushed through the door and said *all right*.

"Where?" following her onto the porch.

"Well, we have six choices," she said.

"Is that a guess?"

"No." A grin flickered across her face and she counted the restaurants off on her fingertips. Lucas noticed that her fingers were long and slender, like a pianist's were supposed to be. Or a surgeon's. "There's Al's Pizza, there's a Hardee's, the Fisherman Inn, the Uncle Steve's American Style, Granddaddy's Cafe, and the Mill."

"What's the classiest joint?"

"Mmm." She tilted her head, thought about it, and said,

"Do you prefer stuffed ducks or stuffed fish? On the wall, I mean, not the menu."

"That's a hard one. Fish, I guess."

"Then we'll go to the Inn," she said.

"Do you play piano?"

"What?" She stopped and looked up at him. "Have you been asking about me?"

"Huh?" He was puzzled.

"How did you know I play?"

"I didn't," he said. "I was just thinking your hands . . . they look like a pianist's."

"Oh." She looked at her hands. "Most of the pianists I've known have heavy hands."

"Like a surgeon's hands, then," he said.

"Most surgeons' hands are ordinary."

"Okay, okay." He started to laugh.

"Ordinary. They are."

"Why are you grumping at me?" Lucas asked.

She shrugged. "We're just getting over being awkward. It's always hard on a first date."

"What?" he asked, following down the sidewalk. He had the sense that something had just flown past him.

❉

The restaurant had been built from two double-wide trailers set at right angles to each other, both covered with vinyl siding disguised as weathered wood. A neon Coors sign hung in the window. Lucas pulled into the parking lot and killed his light, trailed a few seconds later by Weather in her Jeep.

"Elegant," he said.

She pivoted her feet out of the Jeep, pulled off her pac boots. "I want to change shoes . . . elegant, what? The restaurant?"

"I think the vinyl siding combined with the sparkle of the Coors sign gives it a certain European ambiance. Swiss, I'd say, or possibly Old Amsterdam."

"Wait'll you find out that each table has its own red votive candle, personally lit by the maitre d', and a basket

of cellophane-wrapped crackers and breadsticks," Weather said.

"Hey, it's a gourmet joint," Lucas said. "I expected nothing less. And a choice of wines, I bet."

"Yup."

And they both said, simultaneously, "Red or white," and
laughed. Weather added, "If you ask for rosé, they say fine,
and you see the bartender running into the back with a bottle
of white and bottle of red."

"Where'd you get your name?" Lucas asked.

"My father was a sailboat freak. Homemade fourteen-
foot dinghys and scows. He used to build them in the
garage in the summer," she said. She pulled on the second
loafer, tossed the pac boot onto the floor on the passenger
side, stood up and slammed the car door with authority.
And left it unlocked. "Anyway, Mom says he was always
talking about the weather—'If the weather holds, if the
weather turns.' Like that. So when I was born, they called
me Weather."

"Does your mother live in town?"

"No, no. Dad died ten years ago, and then she went, three
or four years later," Weather said, with just a color of sad-
ness. "There was nothing particularly wrong with her. She
just sorta died. I think she wanted to."

❄

The maitre d' was a chubby man with a neatly clipped black
mustache and a Las Vegas manner. "Hello, Weather," he
said. His eyes shifted to Lucas' throat and refused to lift
any higher. "Two? No smoking?"

"Yeah, two," Lucas said.

"A booth," said Weather.

When he left them with the menus, Weather leaned forward and muttered, "I forgot about Arlen. The maitre d'.
He'd like to get me in bed. Not actually leave Mother and
the Kids, you understand, just do a little Mm-hmm with the
lady doctor, preferably in some place like Hurley, where we
might not get caught."

"What are his chances?" Lucas asked.

"Zero," she said. "There's something about the Alfred Hitchcock profile that turns me off."

The salad came with a French dressing redolent of catsup, sprinkled with a handful of croutons.

"I remember the news stories when you left Minneapolis. Very strange, all those stories about a cop. A lot of people at the ER knew you, I guess. They were all pissed. It made an impression on me."

"I used to come in there quite a bit," Lucas said. "I'd have these street guys working for me, and they'd get messed up and not have anybody to call. I'd go over and try to fix them up."

"Why'd you leave? Tired of the bullshit?"

"No . . ." He found himself opening up, told her about the internal games played in the department.

And the lure of money: "When you're a cop, you're always running into rich assholes who treat you like some kind of servant. Guys who oughta be in jail, but they're driving around in Lexuses and Cadillacs and Mercedes," he said, toying with his wine. "People tell you, yeah, but you're doing a public service, blah blah blah, but after twenty years, you realize you wouldn't mind having a little money yourself. Nice house, nice car."

"You had a Porsche. You were famous for it."

"That was different. A rich guy has a Porsche, he does it because he's an asshole. A cop has a Porsche, it's like a comment on the assholes," he said. "Every cop in the department liked me driving a Porsche. It was like a fuck-you to the assholes."

"God, you have a rich ability to rationalize," she said, laughing at him. "Anyway, what're you doing now? Just consulting?"

"No, no. Actually, I write games. That's where I made my money. And I've started another little sideline that . . ."

"Games?"

"Yeah. I've done it for years, now I'm doing it full time."

"You mean like Monopoly?" she asked. She was interested.

"Like Dungeons and Dragons, and sometimes war games. They used to be mostly on paper, now it's mostly computers. I'm in a semipartnership with this college kid—he's a graduate student in computer science. I write the games and he programs them."

"And you can make a living at this?"

"Yeah. And now I've started writing simulation software for police crisis management, for training dispatch people. Most of that's computers, dispatch is. And you get in a crisis situation, the dispatchers are virtually running things for a while. This software lets them simulate it, and scores them. It's kind of taking off."

"If you're not careful, you could get rich," Weather said.

"I kind of am," Lucas said gloomily. "But goddamn, I'm bored. I don't miss the bullshit part of the PD, but I miss the *movement.*"

✳

And later, over walleye in beer batter:

"You can't hold together a heavy-duty relationship when you're in medical school and working to pay for it," Weather said. He enjoyed watching her work with her knife, taking the walleye apart. *Like a surgeon.* "Then a surgical residency kills you. You've got no time for anything. You sit there and think about men, but it's impossible. You can fool around, but if you get serious about somebody, you can get torn apart between the work and the relationship. So you find it's easiest, if you meet somebody you might love, to turn away. Turning away isn't that hard if you do it right away, when you first meet."

"Sounds lonely," Lucas said.

"Yeah, but you can tolerate it if you're working all the time and you're convinced that you're right. You keep thinking, if I can just clear away this last thing, if I can just make it through next Wednesday or next month or through the winter, then I can get my life going. But time passes. Sneaks past. And all of a sudden your life is rushing up on you."

"Ah . . . the old biological clock," Lucas said.

"Yeah. And it's not just ticking for women. Men get it just as bad."

"I know."

She rolled on: "How many men do you know who decided that life was passing them by, and they jumped out of their jobs or their marriages and tried to . . . escape, or something?"

"A few. More felt trapped but hung on," said Lucas. "And got sadder and sadder."

"You're talking about me, I think," she said.

"I'm talking about everybody," Lucas said. "I'm talking about me."

❋

After a carafe of wine: "Do you worry about the people you've killed?" She wasn't joking. No smile this time.

"They were hairballs, every one of them."

"I asked that wrong," she said. "What I meant to ask was, has killing people screwed up your head?"

He considered the question for a moment. "I don't know. I don't brood about them, if that's what you mean. I had a problem with depression a couple of years ago. The chief at the time . . ."

"Quentin Daniel," she said.

"Yeah. You know him?"

"I met him a couple of times. You were saying . . ."

"He thought I needed a shrink. But I decided I didn't need a shrink, I needed a philosopher. Someone who knows how the world works."

"An interesting idea," she said. "The problem isn't you, the problem is Being."

"My God, that *does* make me sound like an asshole."

❋

"Carr seems like a decent sort," Lucas said.

"He is. Very decent," Weather agreed.

"Religious."

"Very. You want pie? They have key lime."

"I'll take coffee; I'm bloated," Lucas said.

Weather waved at the waitress, said, *two coffees,* and turned back to Lucas. "Are you a Catholic?"

"Everybody asks me that. I am, but I'm seriously lapsed," he said.

"So you won't be going to the Tuesday meetings, huh?"

"No."

"But you're going over tonight, to talk to Phil." She made it a statement.

"I really don't . . ."

"It's all over town," Weather said. "He's the main suspect."

"He's not," Lucas said with a touch of asperity.

"That's not what I heard," she said. "Or everybody else hears, for that matter."

"Jesus, that's just wrong," Lucas said, shaking his head.

"If you say so," she said.

"You don't believe me."

"Why should I? You're going to question him again tonight after Shelly gets out of the Tuesday service."

The coffee came and Lucas waited until the waitress was gone before he picked up the conversation. "Is there anything that everybody in town doesn't know?"

"Not much," Weather admitted. "There are sixty people working for the sheriff and only about four thousand people in town, in winter. You figure it out. And have you wondered why Shelly's going to Tuesday service when he should be questioning Phil?"

"I'm afraid to ask," Lucas said.

"Because he wants to see Jeanine Perkins. He and Jeanine have been screwing at motels in Hayward and Park Falls."

"And everybody in town knows?" Lucas asked.

"Not yet. But they will."

"Carr's married."

"Yup. His wife is mad," Weather said.

"Uh . . ."

"She has a severe psychological affliction. She can't stop doing housework."

"What?" He started to laugh.

"It's true," Weather said solemnly. "It's not funny, buster. She washes the floors and the walls and the blinds and the toilets and sinks and pipes and the washer and drier and the furnace. And then she washes all the clothes over and over. Once she washed her own hands so many times that she rubbed a part of the skin off and we had to treat her for burns."

"My God." He still thought it was mildly funny.

"Nothing anybody can do about it. She's in therapy, but it doesn't help," Weather said. "A friend told me that she won't have sex with Shelly because it's dirty. I mean, not psychologically dirty, but you know—dirty. Physically dirty."

"So Carr solves his problem by having it off with a woman in his Pentecostal group."

"*Having it off* is such a romantic way to put it; British, isn't it?" she teased.

❄

"You don't act like a doctor," Lucas said.

"You mean because I gossip and flirt?"

"Mmmm."

"You have to live here a while," she said with a hint of tension in her voice. She looked around the room, at the people talking over the red votive candles. "There's nothing to do but work. Nothing."

"Then why stay?"

"I have to," she said. "My dad came here from Finland, and spent his life working in the woods, in the timber. And sailing on the lakes. Never had any money. But I maxed out in everything at school."

"You went to the high school here in Grant?"

"Yup. Anyway, I was trying to save money to go to college, but it looked tough. Then some of the teachers got together and chipped in, and this old fart county commissioner who I didn't know from Adam called down to Madison and pulled some strings and got me a full-load scholarship. And they kept the money coming all the way through medical school. I paid it all back. I even set up a little scholarship fund at the high school while I was working in Minneapolis, but that's not what everybody wanted."

"They wanted you back here," Lucas said.

"Yes." She nodded. She picked up her empty wineglass and turned it in her hands. "Everything around here is timber and tourism, with a little farming. The roads are not much good and there's a lot of drinking. The timber accidents are terrible—you ought to see somebody caught by a log when it's rolling down to a sawmill. And with tractor accidents and people run over with boat propellers . . . They had an old guy here who could do enough general surgery to get you on a helicopter to Duluth or down to the Cities, and as long as he was here I didn't feel like I had to come back."

"Then he retired."

"Kicked off," Weather said. "Heart attack. He was sixty-three. He ate six pancakes with butter and bacon every morning, cream in his coffee, cheeseburger for lunch, steak for dinner, drank a pint of Johnnie Walker every night and smoked like a chimney. It was amazing he made it as long as he did."

"They couldn't get anybody else?"

She laughed, not a pleasant laugh, looked out the window at the snow: "Are you kidding? Look outside. It's twenty-five below zero and still going down and the movie theater is closed in the winter."

"So what do you do for entertainment?"

"That's a little personal," she said, grinning, reaching across the table to touch the back of his hand, "for this stage of our relationship."

"What?"

CHAPTER

✳ ✳ ✳

8

The dinner left Lucas vaguely mystified but not unhappy. They said good-bye in the restaurant parking lot, awkwardly. He didn't want to leave. The talk ran on in the snow, the air so cold that it felt like after-shave. Finally they stepped apart and Weather got in her Jeep.

"See you," she said.

"Yeah." Definitely.

Lucas watched her go, pulled his hat on, and drove the six blocks to the church. Carr was waiting in the vestibule with two women, the three of them chatting brightly, nodding. One of the women was as large as Lucas and blond, and wore a red knitted hat with snowflakes and reindeer on it. Her coat carried a button that said *Free the Animals*. The other woman was small and dark, with gray streaks in her hair, lines at the corners of her eyes. Carr called the dark one *Jeanine* as Lucas came up.

"This is Lucas Davenport . . ." Carr was saying.

"Lieutenant Davenport," Jeanine said. She had soft, warm hands and a strong grip. "And our friend Mary . . ."

Mary fawned and Lucas retreated a couple of steps, said to Carr, "We better go."

"Yeah, sure," Carr said reluctantly. "Ladies, we gotta work."

They walked out together and Lucas asked Carr, "Did you talk to Bergen?"

"Not myself—Helen Arris got him. I had to go back out to the house. They're taking the place apart."

"How about the Harper warrant?"

"Got it." Carr patted his chest and then yawned. "It's getting to be a long day."

"How about the Harper place? What can we do?"

"We're allowed to go into the kid's room and the other principal rooms of the house, not including any office or Harper's own bedroom if that's separate from the kid's. We can look at anything we believe is the kid's, or that Harper says is the kid's."

"I'd like to poke around."

"So would I, but the judge didn't want to hear about it," Carr said. "He was gonna confine us to the boy's room, but I got him to include his other personal effects—we can look inside closets and cupboards and so on, in the main rooms. Of course, if we *see* anything that's clearly illegal . . ."

"Yeah. By the way, Gene Climpt . . ."

". . . invited himself along, which is fine with me. Gene's a tough old bird. And Lacey's coming; said he didn't want to miss it."

They'd walked around the church and started down the carefully shoveled sidewalk to the rectory.

"How many accidents has Bergen had? Car accidents?" Lucas asked.

Carr looked at him, frowning, and said, "Why?"

"I heard you fixed a couple of drunk-driving tickets for him," Lucas said. "I just wondered if he ever hit anything."

"Where'd you hear . . ."

"Rumors, Shelly. Has he ever hit anything?"

They'd stopped on the sidewalk and Carr stared at him for a moment and said, finally, "I got no leverage with you. You don't need the job."

"So . . ."

Carr started down the walk again. "He was in a one-car accident three years ago, hit a pylon at the end of a bridge, totaled out the car. He was drunk. He got caught two other times, drunk. One was pretty marginal. The other time he was on his butt."

"Gotta be careful about your relationship with him," Lucas said. "People are talking about this. The driving problems."

"Who?"

"Just people," Lucas said.

Carr sighed. "Darn it, Lucas."

"Bergen lied to me yesterday," Lucas said. "He told me he was a good driver . . . a small lie but it kind of throws some doubt on the rest of what he said."

"I don't understand it," Carr said. "I know in my soul that he's innocent. I just can't understand what he's hiding. If he's hiding anything. Maybe we just don't understand the sequence."

They were at the rectory door. Carr pushed the doorbell and they fell silent, hands in their pockets, breathing long gouts of steam out into the night air. After a moment Carr frowned, pushed the doorbell again. They could hear the chimes inside.

"I know he's here," Carr said. He stepped back from the porch, looked at the lighted windows, then pushed the doorbell a third time. There was a noise from inside, a thump, and Carr stood on his tiptoes to peer through the small window set in the door.

"Oh, no," he groaned. He pulled open the storm door and pushed through the inner door, Lucas trailing behind. The priest stood in the hallway, leaning on one wall, looking at them. He was wearing a white t-shirt, pulled out of his black pants, and gray wool socks. His hair stood almost straight up, as though he'd been electrocuted. He was holding a glass and the room smelled of bourbon.

"You idiot," Carr said quietly. He walked across the room and took the glass from the priest, who let it go, his hand slack. Carr turned back toward Lucas as though looking for a place to throw it.

"You know what they're saying," Bergen said at Carr's back. "They're saying I did it."

"Jesus, we've been trying . . ." Lucas started.

"Don't you blaspheme in this house!" the priest shouted.

"I'll kick your ass if you give me trouble," Lucas shouted back. He crossed the carpet, walking around Carr, who caught at his coat sleeve, and confronted the priest: "What happened out at the LaCourts'?"

"They were alive when I saw them!" Bergen shouted. "They were alive—every one of them!"

"Did you have a relationship with Claudia LaCourt? Now or ever?"

The priest seemed startled: "A relationship? You mean sexual?"

"That's what I mean," Lucas snapped. "Were you screwing her?"

"No. That's ridiculous." The wind went out of him, and he staggered to a La-Z-Boy and dropped into it, looking up at Lucas in wonder. "I mean, I've never . . . What are you asking?"

Carr had stepped into the kitchen, came back with an empty Jim Beam bottle, held it up to Lucas.

"I've heard rumors that the two of you might be involved."

"No, no," Bergen said, shaking his head. He seemed genuinely astonished. "When I was in the seminary, I slept with a woman from a neighboring college. I also got drunk and was talked into . . . having sex with a prostitute. One time. Just once. After I was ordained, never. I never broke my vows."

His face had gone opaque, either from whiskey or calculation.

"Have you ever had a homosexual involvement?"

"Davenport . . ." Carr said, a warning in his voice.

"What?" Bergen was back on his feet now, face flushed, furious.

"Yes or no," Lucas pressed.

"No. Never."

Lucas couldn't tell if Bergen was lying or telling the

truth. He sounded right, but his eyes had cleared, and Lucas could see him calculating, weighing his responses. "How about the booze? Were you drinking that night, at the LaCourts'?"

The priest turned and let himself fall back into the chair. "No. Absolutely not. This is my first bottle in a year. More than a year."

"There's something wrong with the time," Lucas said. "Tell us what's wrong."

"I don't know," Bergen said. He dropped his head to his hands, then ran his hands halfway up to the top of his head and pulled out at the hair until it was again standing up in spikes. "I keep trying to find ways . . . I wasn't drinking."

"The firemen. Do you have any trouble with them?"

Bergen looked up, eyes narrowing. "Dick Westrom doesn't particularly care for me. I take my business to the other hardware store, it belongs to one of the parishioners. The other man, Duane . . . I hardly know him. I can't think what he'd have against me. Maybe something I don't know about."

"How about the people who reported the fire?" Lucas asked, looking across the room at Carr. Carr was still holding the bottle of Jim Beam as though he were presenting evidence to a jury.

"They're okay," Carr said. "They're out of it. They saw the fire, made the call. They're too old and have too many physical problems to be involved."

The three of them looked at each other, waiting for another question, but there were none. The time simply didn't work. Lucas searched Bergen's face. He found nothing but the waxy opacity.

"All right," he said finally. "Maybe there was another Jeep. Maybe Duane saw Father Bergen's Jeep earlier, going down the lake road, and it stuck in his mind and when he saw a car go by, he thought it was yours."

"He didn't see a Jeep earlier," Carr said, shaking his head. "I asked him that—if he'd seen Phil's Jeep go down the lake road."

"I don't know," Lucas said, still studying the priest. "Maybe . . . I don't know."

Carr looked at Bergen. "I'm dumping the bottle, Phil. And I'm calling Joe."

Bergen's head went down. "Okay."

"Who's Joe?" Lucas asked.

"His AA sponsor," Carr said. "We've had this problem before."

Bergen looked up at Carr, his voice rasping: "Shelly, I don't know if this guy believes me," he said, tipping his head at Lucas. "But I'll tell you: I'd swear on the Holy Eucharist that I had nothing to do with the LaCourts."

"Yeah," Carr said. He reached out and Bergen took his hand, and Carr pulled him to his feet. "Come on, let's call Joe, get him over here."

✳

Joe was a dark man, with a drooping black mustache and heavy eyebrows. He wore an old green Korean War–style olive-drab billed hat with earflaps. He glanced at Lucas, nodded at Carr and said, "How bad?"

"Drank at least a fifth," Carr said. "He's gone."

"Goddammit." Joe looked up at the house, then back to Carr. "He'd gone more'n a year. It's the rumors coming out of your office, Shelly."

"Yeah, I know. I'll try to stop it, but I don't know . . ."

"Better more'n try. Phil's got the thirst as bad as anyone I've ever seen." Joe stepped toward the door, turned, about to say something else, when Bergen pulled the door open behind him.

"Shelly!" he called. He was too loud. "Telephone—it's your office. They say it's an emergency."

Carr looked at Lucas and said, "Maybe something broke."

He hurried inside and Joe took Bergen by the shoulder and said, "Phil, we can handle this."

"Joe, I . . ." Bergen seemed overcome, looked glassily at Lucas, still on the sidewalk, and pulled Joe inside, closing the door.

Lucas waited, hands in his pockets, the warmth he'd accumulated in the house slowly dissipating. Bergen was a smart guy, and no stranger to manipulation. But he didn't have the sociopath edge, the just-below-the-surface glassiness of the real thing.

Thirty seconds after he'd gone inside, Carr burst out.

"Come on," he said shortly, striding past Lucas toward the trucks.

"What happened?"

"That kid you talked to, the one that told you about the picture?" Carr was talking over his shoulder.

"John Mueller." Jug-ears, off-brand shoes, embarrassed.

"He's missing. Can't be found."

"What?" Lucas grabbed Carr's arm. "Fuckin' tell me."

"His father was working late at his shop, out on the highway," Carr said. They were standing in the street. "He'd left the kid at home watching television. When his mother got home, and the kid wasn't there, she thought he was out at the shop. It wasn't until his parents got together that they realized he was gone. A neighbor kid's got a Nintendo and John's been going down there after school a couple nights a week, and sometimes stays for dinner. They called the neighbors but there wasn't anybody home, and they thought maybe they'd all gone down to the Arby's. So they drove around until they found the neighbors, but they hadn't seen him either."

"Sonofabitch," Lucas said, looking past Carr at nothing. "I might of put a finger on him."

"Don't even think that," Carr said, his voice grim.

❋

They headed for the Mueller house, riding together in the sheriff's truck, crimson flashers working on top.

"You were hard on him," Carr said abruptly. "On Phil."

"You've got four murder victims and now this," Lucas said. "What do you expect, violin music?"

"I don't know what I expected," Carr said.

The sheriff was pushing the truck, moving fast. Lucas caught the bank sign: minus twenty-eight.

He said it aloud: "Twenty-eight below."

"Yeah." The wind had picked up again, and was blowing thin streamers of snow off rooftops and drifts. The sheriff hunched over the steering wheel. "If the kid's been outside, he's dead. He doesn't need anybody to kill him."

A moment passed in silence. Lucas couldn't think about John Mueller: when he thought about him, he could feel a darkness creeping over his mind. Maybe the kid was at another friend's house, maybe . . .

"How long has Bergen had the drinking problem?" he asked.

"Since college. He told me he went to his first AA meeting before he was legal to drink," Carr said. His heavy face was a faint unhealthy green in the dashboard lights.

"How bad? DTs? Memory loss? Blackouts?"

"Like that," Carr said.

"But he's been dry? Lately?"

"I think so. Sometimes it's hard to tell, if a guy keeps his head down. He can drink at night, hold it together during the day. I used to do a little drinking myself."

"Lot of cops do."

Carr looked across the seat at him: "You too?"

"No, no. I've abused a few things, but not booze. I've always had a taste for uppers."

"Cocaine?"

Lucas laughed, a dry rattle: the kid's face kept popping up. Small kid, sweet-faced. "I can hear the beads of sweat popping out of your forehead, Shelly. No. I'm afraid of that shit. Might be too good, if you know what I mean."

"Any alcoholic'd know what you mean," Carr said.

"I've done a little speed from time to time," Lucas continued, looking out at the dark featureless forest that lined the road. "Not lately. Speed and alcohol, they're for different personalities."

"Either one of them'll kill you," Carr said.

They passed a video rental shop with three people standing outside; they all turned to watch the sheriff's truck go by. Lucas said, "People do weird things when they're drunk. And they forget things. If he was drunk, the time . . ."

"He says he wasn't," Carr said.

"Would he lie about it?"

"I don't think so," Carr said. "Under other circumstances, he might—drinkers lie to themselves when they're starting again. But with this, all these dead people, I don't think he'd lie. Like I told you, Phil Bergen's a moral man. That's why he drinks in the first place."

❋

There were twenty people at the Muellers', mostly neighbors, with three deputies. A half-dozen men on snowmobiles were organizing a patrol of ditches and trails within two miles of the house.

Carr plunged into it while Lucas drifted around the edges, helpless. He didn't know anything about missing persons searches, not out here in the woods, and Carr seemed to know a lot about it.

A few moments after Carr and Lucas arrived, the boy's father hurried out into the yard, pulling on a snowmobile suit. A woman stood in the door in a white baker's dress, hands clasped to her face. The image stuck with Lucas: it was an effect of pure terror.

Mueller said something to Carr and they talked for a moment, then Carr shook his head. Lucas heard him say "Three of them up north. . . ."

The father had been looking around the yard, as though his son might walk out of the woods. Instead of the boy, he saw Lucas and stepped toward him. "You sonofabitch," he screamed, eyes rolling. A deputy caught him, jostled him, stayed between them. Faces in the yard turned toward Lucas. "Where's my boy, where's my boy?" Mueller screamed.

Carr came over and said, "You better leave. Take my truck. Call Lacey, tell him to get Gene, and the three of you go on out to Harper's place. There's nothing you can do here."

"Must be something," Lucas said. A deputy was talking to Mueller, Mueller's eyes still fixed on Lucas.

"There's nothing," Carr said. "Just get out. Go on down to Harper's like we planned."

❋

Lucas met Lacey and Climpt at the 77 Tap, a bar ten miles east of Grant. The bar was an old one, a simple cube with shingle siding and a few dark windows up above, living rooms upstairs for the owner. An antique gas pump sat to one side of the place, with a set of rusting, unused bait tanks, all of it awash in snow. A Leinenkugel's sign provided most of the exterior lighting.

Inside, the bar smelled of fried fish and old beer; an Elton John song was playing on the jukebox. Lacey and Climpt were sitting in one of the three booths.

"No sign of the kid?" Lacey asked as he slid out of the booth. Climpt threw two dollars on the table and stood up behind him, chewing on a wooden matchstick.

"Not when I left," Lucas said.

Lacey and Climpt looked at each other and Climpt shook his head. "If he ain't at somebody's house . . ."

"Yeah."

"Ain't your fault," Climpt said, looking levelly at Lucas. "What're you supposed to do?"

"Yeah." Lucas shook his head and they started for the door. "So tell me about Harper."

Lacey was pulling on his gloves. "He's our local hood. He spent two years in prison over in Minnesota for ag assault—this was way back, must've been a couple of years after he got out of high school. He's been in jail since then, maybe three or four times."

"For?"

"Brawling, mostly. Fighting in bars. He'd pick out somebody, get on them, goad them into a fight and then hurt them. You know the type. He's beat up some women we know of, but they never wanted to do anything about it. Either because they were still hoping to get together with him or because they were scared. You know."

"Yeah."

"He's carried a gun off and on, smokes a little marijuana, maybe does a little coke, we've heard both," Lacey continued. "He says he needs the gun to protect himself when he's taking cash home from the station."

"He's a felon," Lucas said.

"Got his rights back," Lacey said. "Shouldn't of. There's been rumors that when he's been hard up for money, he'd go down to the Cities and knock over a liquor store or a 7-Eleven. Maybe that's just bar talk."

"Maybe," Climpt grunted. He looked at Lucas: "He's not like a TV bully. He's a bully, but he's not a coward. He's a mean sonofabitch."

✳

Climpt and Lacey rode together, and Lucas followed them out, occasional muted cop chatter burbling out of the radio. The roads had cleared except for icy corners and intersections, and traffic was light because of the cold. They made good time.

Knuckle Lake popped up as a fuzzy ball of light far away down the highway, brightening and separating into business signs and streetlights as they got closer. There were a half dozen buildings scattered around the four corners: a motel, two bars, a general store, a cafe, and the Amoco station. The station was brightly lit, with snow piled twenty feet high along the back property lines. One car sat at a gas pump, engine off, the driver elsewhere. An old Chevy was visible through the windows of the single repair bay. They stopped in front of the big window, the other two trucks swinging in behind. A teenager in a ragged trench coat and tennis shoes peered through the glass at them: he was all by himself, like a guppie in a well-lit aquarium.

Lucas followed Climpt inside. Climpt nodded at the kid and said, "Hello, Tommy. How you doing?"

"Okay, just fine, Mr. Climpt," the kid said. He was nervous, and a shock of straw-colored hair fell out from under his watch cap, his Adam's apple bobbing spasmodically.

"How long you been out?" Climpt asked.

"Oh, two months now," the kid said.

"Tommy used to borrow cars, go for rides," Climpt said.

"Bad habit," Lucas said, crossing his arms, leaning against

the candy machine. "Everybody gets pissed off at you."

"I quit," the kid said.

"He's a good mechanic," Climpt said. Then: "Where's Russ?"

"Down to the house, I guess."

"Okay."

"It'd be better if you didn't call him," Lucas said.

"Whatever," the kid said. "I'm, you know, whatever."

"Whatever," Climpt said. He pointed a finger at the kid's face, and the kid swallowed. "We won't be tellin' Russ we talked to you."

Back outside, Climpt said, "He won't call."

"How far is Harper's place?"

"Two minutes from here," Carr said.

"Think he'll be a problem?"

"Not if we get right on top of him," Climpt said. "He won't win no college scholarship, but he's not stupid enough to take on a whole . . . whatever we are."

"A posse," Lucas said.

Climpt laughed, a short bark. "Right. A posse."

✳

John Mueller came back to Lucas' mind, like a nagging toothache, a pain that wouldn't go away but couldn't be fixed. Maybe he was at a friend's; maybe they'd already found him. . . .

Harper's house huddled in a copse of birch and red pine, alone on an unlit stretch of side road, a free-standing garage in back, a mercury-vapor yard-light overhead. Windows were lit in the back of the house. Climpt killed his lights and pulled into the end of the drive, and Lucas pulled in behind him.

Climpt and Lacey got out, pushed the truck doors shut instead of slamming them. "Are you carrying?" Climpt asked.

"Yeah."

"Might loosen it up. Russ's always got something around."

"All right." Lucas turned to Lacey, who had his hands in

his pockets and was staring up at the house. "Henry, why don't you sit out here by the truck. Get the shotgun and just hang back."

Lacey nodded and walked back toward the Suburban.

"I'll try to get a little edge on him right away," Lucas told Climpt as they started up the driveway. "I won't pull any real shit, but you can act like you think I might."

Woodsmoke drifted down on them, an acrid odor that cut at the nose and throat. Two feet of pristine snow covered the front porch. "Looks like he doesn't use the front door at all," Climpt said.

As they walked around the side of the house, they heard the gun rack rattle as Lacey unlocked the shotgun and took it out, then the ratcheting sound of a twelve-gauge shell being pumped home. At the back door, Lucas could hear the sounds of a television—not the words but the rhythms.

"Stand down at the bottom where he can see you," Lucas told Climpt. He went to the top of the stoop and knocked on the door, then stepped to the side. A moment later the yellow porch light came on, and then a curtain pulled back. A man's head appeared behind the window glass. He looked at Climpt, hesitated, made a head gesture, and fumbled with the doorknob.

"We're okay," Lucas muttered.

Harper pulled open the inner door, saw Lucas, frowned. He was an oval-faced man, with a narrow chin, thick, short lips, and scar tissue on his forehead and under his eyes. His eyes were the size of dimes, and black, like a lizard's. He was unshaven. He pushed open the storm door, looked down at Climpt and said, "What do you want, Gene?"

"We need to talk to you about the death of your son, and we need to look through Jim's stuff again," Climpt said.

Harper's thick lips twisted. "You got a warrant?"

"Yeah, we got a warrant."

After another long moment Harper said, "Now what the fuck are you fuckin' with me for, Climpt?" The question came in a low voice, rough and guttural, angry but unafraid.

"We're not fuckin' with you," Lucas snapped back. He

hooked the storm door handle with his left hand and jerked it open. Harper pulled back an inch, then settled in a fighting stance, ready to swing. He was round-shouldered but hard, with hands that looked granite-gray in the bad light. Lucas took his right hand out of his pocket, a bare hand with a .45. "Swing on me and I'll beat the shit out of you," he said. "And if I start to lose I'll blow your fuckin' nuts off."

"What?" Harper stepped back, dropping his right hand.

"You heard me, asshole."

"Oh, yeah," Harper said. He straightened, let the left hand drop. "You're the big city guy, uh? Big city guy, big city asshole gonna blow my nuts off." He took another step back, the anger spreading from his eyes over his face, ready to go again.

"Come on, motherfucker," Lucas said. He lifted the .45 out to the side. "You put your own boy out on the corner givin' blowjobs to fat guys, there's nobody in this county'd blame me if I spread your brains all over the house. So you wanna do it? Come on, come on . . ."

"You're fuckin' nuts," Harper said. But his voice had changed again, uncertainty near the surface, and his eyes shifted past Lucas to Climpt. "Why are you fuckin' with me, Gene?"

"The LaCourt girl, the one who was killed, had a picture of your boy, naked, with a grown-up male," Climpt said.

Lucas dropped the gun to his side, moved forward, one foot inside, shoulder against the door, forcing Harper back. "She showed it around and then the family was wiped out," he said. "We want to look at Jim's things, see if there's anything that might indicate who it was."

"Sure as shit wasn't me."

"We're looking for a guy who's blond and a little fat," Lucas said. He stepped through the storm door into a mudroom, crowding Harper, who backed through an inner door into the kitchen. Climpt was a step behind. "You don't have any friends that look like that, do you?"

Climpt called out to the truck, "Henry, c'mon."

"I want to see that warrant," Harper said, backing far-

ther into the kitchen. The kitchen smelled of onions and
bad meat and old soured milk.

"Henry's got it," Climpt said. Harper looked past Lucas
as Lacey walked up. Lacey pulled a paper out of his pocket
and handed it to Lucas, who handed it to Harper. While
Harper looked at it, Lucas decocked the .45. At the latching
sound, Harper looked up and said, "Smith and Wesson. Is
that the .40 or the .45?"

"The .45," Lucas said.

"I'd have gone with the .40," Harper said as the
two deputies came in behind Carr. He'd gone into
the asshole-cooperative mode, an almost imperceptible
groveling learned in prisons.

"Right," said Lucas, ignoring the comment. He put the
pistol back in his coat pocket. "Where's the kid's room?"

"You don't think I know about guns? I . . ."

"I don't give a fuck what you know," Lucas snapped.
"Where's the kid's room?"

Harper muttered *shit,* crumbled the warrant in his hand
and threw it on the floor, turned and led them through a
narrow archway into the living room. The TV was tuned
to professional wrestling, and a cardboard tray, stained
orange from the sauce of an instant spaghetti dinner, sat
on a round oak table with an empty crockery coffee cup.
Harper brushed past it, into a hallway. The first door on the
right was open, into a bathroom; the next door, to the left,
was half-open, and Harper pulled it closed. "That's mine.
Nothin' of Jim's in there."

At the last door, on the right, he stopped and gestured
with his thumb: "That was Jim's."

Lucas pushed the door open. Jim Harper had been dead
for more than two months, but his room was like he'd left
it: a pair of dirty jeans, a t-shirt and pair of underpants
tossed in a corner, now covered with dust. The bed was
unmade, a discolored flat-sheet and an olive-drab Army
blanket tangled on a yellowed fitted sheet. The pillow was
small, gray, dotted with what might have been blood. Lucas
looked closer: blood, all right, but only in small spots, as
though the kid had acne and picked at the sores. Clothes

were pinched in the drawers of the single bureau, and two of the drawers hung open.

"The cops already been through it, messed it up," Harper said over Lucas' shoulder. "Didn't find anything."

Lucas looked back down the hall at Lacey. "Henry, why don't you and Mr. Harper here go sit and watch some TV? Gene and I'll look around."

"Hey . . ." Harper said.

"Shut up," said Lucas.

✳

"They turned the room over and didn't find anything," Lucas said to Climpt. "If you were a kid, hiding something, where'd you put it?"

"What I've been thinking is, Russ's such an asshole, why would a kid hide anything from him? Nothing the kid could do would bother him much."

Lucas shrugged. "Maybe he'd hide something just so he could keep it."

"That's a point," Climpt said. After a moment: "I always hid stuff in the basement. Maybe in a closet if it was just overnight and small—dirty magazines, that sort of thing. I suppose the attic, if they got one."

"Let's do a quick run through this, then maybe look around a little."

The house was an old one, with hardwood planked floors covered with patches of linoleum, and lath-and-plaster walls. Lucas dug through the kid's closet, shaking out a stack of magazines and comic books, checking shoes and the few shirts hanging inside. There were no loose floorboards and the plaster wall was cracked but intact. Climpt tossed the bureau again, pulling out each drawer to turn it over, checked the heat register, found it solid. In ten minutes they'd decided the room was clean.

"Attic or basement?" asked Climpt.

"Let's see how much trouble the attic is."

The attic access was through a hatch in the bathroom. Standing on a chair, Lucas pushed up the hatch and was showered with dust and asbestos insulation. He pulled it shut again and climbed down, brushing the dirt out of his hair.

"Hasn't been open in a while," he said.

"Basement," said Climpt. They headed for the basement stairs, found Lacey digging through a freestanding wardrobe in the living room while Harper slumped in a chair.

"Anything?" Lucas asked.

"Nope."

"We'll be down the basement," Lucas said.

Harper watched them go, but said nothing. "I wish that fucker'd give me a reason to slam him up alongside the head," Climpt said.

The basement smelled of cobwebs, dust, engine oil, and coal. The walls' granite fieldstone was mortared with crumbling, sandy concrete. Two bare bulbs, dangling from ancient fraying wire, provided all the light. There were two small rooms, filled with the clutter of a rural half-century: racks of dusty Ball jars, broken crocks, an antique lawnmower, a lever-action .22 covered with rust. A dozen leg-hold jump traps hung from a nail, and hanging next to them, two dozen tiny feet tied together with twine.

"Gophers," Climpt said, touching them. They swayed like a grisly wind chime. "County used to pay a bounty on them, way back, nickel a pair on front feet."

A railroad-tie workbench was wedged into a corner with a rusting vise fitted at one end. A huge old coal furnace hunkered in the middle of the main room like a dead oak, stone cold. A diminutive propane burner stood in what had once been a coal room, galvanized ducts leading to the rooms above. The coal room was the cleanest place in the basement, apparently cleaned when the furnace was installed. At a glance, there was no place to hide anything.

Lucas wandered over to the coal furnace, pulled open the furnace door, looked at a pile of old ashes, closed it. "This could take a while," he said.

They took fifteen minutes, Climpt repeating, "Someplace where he could get it quick. . . ." They found nothing, and started up the steps, unsatisfied. The basement had too many nooks and crannies. "If one of those fieldstones pulled out . . ." Lucas started.

"We'd never find it: there must be two thousand of them," Climpt said.

And Lucas said, "Wait a minute," went back down the stairs and looked toward the propane burner.

"If that's the coal room, shouldn't there be a coal chute?" he asked.

"Yeah, there should," Climpt said.

They found the chute door set in the wall behind the propane burner, four feet above the floor and virtually invisible in the bad light. Lucas reached back, unlatched the door and felt inside. His hand fell on a stack of paper.

"Something," he said. "Paper." He pulled it out. Three glossy sex magazines and two sex comics. He handed them to Climpt, reached back inside for another quick check, came up with a small corner of notebook paper, blank, that might have been used as a bookmark. Lucas stuck the paper in his pocket.

"Porn," said Climpt, standing under one of the hanging light bulbs. They shook out the magazines, found nothing inside.

"Check 'em," Lucas said. "We're looking for a picture of a kid on a bed."

They flipped through the magazines, but all of the pictures were obviously commercial and involved women. The Mueller kid had described the photo he'd seen as rough, printed on newsprint.

"Nothing much," Climpt said. "I mean, a lot of pussy . . . Goddamn Shelly'd have a heart attack."

Lucas went back to the coal chute for a final check, reached far inside, felt just a corner of a piece of plastic. He had to stretch to fish it out.

A Polaroid.

Climpt came to look over his shoulder.

A young boy, slender, nude, standing in front of a crouched woman, pushing into her mouth. His hands were wrapped around her skull. All that was visible of the woman was her dark hair, the lower part of her face from her nose down, and part of her neck. She was obviously older, probably in her forties.

The boy's left hand was visible and a finger was gone.

"Don't know the woman, just from that," Climpt said. "But that's Jim doin' her."

"Hey, Lucas," Lacey called from upstairs.

"Yeah?"

"It's like . . . ah, Christ!" Lacey blurted.

Lucas looked at Climpt, who shrugged, and they headed up the stairs. Lacey was standing in the door to the living room, his face dead white. Harper sat in a chair, a half-amused look on his face. They were looking at the television. The video was cheap, clear enough: two men were lying on a bed, fondling each other.

"You sell this shit?" Climpt growled at Harper.

"I told Henry—it all belonged to Jim. I don't look at homo shit."

"Found it in the wardrobe," Lacey said. "There weren't any labels."

Lucas handed Lacey the Polaroid.

"Sonofagun," Lacey whispered.

"Yeah," Lucas said. "You want to look at this, Harper?" No more *Russ* or *Mr. Harper*. He held it out in front of Harper, who reached for it, but Lucas pulled it back. "Just look—don't touch."

Harper peered at the picture and drawled, "Looks like Jim, gettin' him some head. Damn, I wish I knew her—she looks like she knows what she's doing."

He still had the slightly amused look on his face. He was about to say something else when Climpt stepped past Lucas, grabbed Harper by the shirt, and hauled him out of the chair. "You motherfucker."

Harper covered his gut with his elbows, kept his hands up in front of his face. He didn't want to get hurt, but he wasn't scared, Lucas thought.

"Hey, hey," said Lacey, trying to intervene. "Let him . . ."

Climpt shoved Harper at Lucas, who caught him, still off-balance, said, "Fuck, I don't want him," and spun him into the wall. Climpt caught him on the rebound, dragged him backwards by the collar and as Lacey shouted, "Hey," banged the back of Harper's head against the opposite wall, then pulled him forward, letting go as Lucas put his hand in Harper's face and snapped him backwards into the chair.

"Knock it off," Lacey said.

"Set your own kid up for this shit, didn't you?" Climpt said, his face an inch from Harper's. Harper spit at him, a spray of spittle. Climpt caught him by the shirt collar and the skin under his neck and hoisted him a foot out of the chair. "Sold his ass to faggots and anybody else who wanted some young stuff. You know what they're gonna do to you in the joint? You know what they do to child fuckers? You're gonna wear out your kneecaps kneeling on the floors, blowing those guys."

Lacey, face red, had Climpt by the shoulder, pulling at him. Lucas put his arm between Harper and Climpt, said, "Gene, let him go. Gene . . ."

Climpt looked blindly at Lucas, then dropped Harper back in the chair, turned away, wiped his face with his forearm.

"Motherfucker," Harper said, pulling down his shirt.

Lucas turned to Lacey. "Could you get Shelly on the radio? Don't mention the Polaroid directly, but tell him we got something. And we need to see him."

Lacey stepped back, reluctantly. "You guys won't . . ."

"No, no," Lucas said. "And listen, ask him about the Mueller kid, if there's been any progress."

"What about the Mueller kid?" Harper asked.

"He's missing," Lucas said, turning back to him.

Lacey was walking out through the kitchen. When the back door banged shut, Lucas stepped up to Harper. "I believe you spit on deputy Climpt, and I feel kinda short-changed, you know. You didn't spit on me."

"Fuck you," Harper said. He looked from Lucas to Climpt and back. "I got my rights."

Lucas took him by the shirt as Climpt had, jerked him out of the chair, ran him straight back at the wall, slammed him against it. Harper covered, still not ready to resist. Climpt caught his right arm, twisted it. Both Lucas and Climpt were bigger than Harper, and pinned him on the wall.

"Remember what you said about your vise?" Lucas asked, face half-turned to Climpt. Climpt grunted. "Watch this—this is nasty."

He caught the flesh between Harper's nostrils by his thumb and middle fingers and squeezed, his fingernails digging into the soft flesh. Harper's mouth dropped as though he were going to scream, but Climpt's hand came up and squeezed his throat.

Lucas squeezed, squeezed, then said, "Who's the woman in the picture? *Who is it?*"

Harper, his body bucking, shook his head. "Better let go of his throat for a minute, Gene," Lucas said, and he let go of Harper's nose. Harper groaned, thrashed, sucked air, and Lucas asked, "Who is that, asshole? Who's the woman?"

"Don't know . . ."

"Let me try," Climpt said, and he caught Harper's nose as Lucas had, his thick yellow fingernails squeezing. . . .

The sound that came from Harper's throat might have been a scream if it had been pitched lower. As it was, it was a kind of blackboard scratching squeak, and he shuddered.

"Who is it?" Lucas asked.

"Don't . . ."

Climpt looked at Lucas, who shook his head, and they both released him at the same moment. Tears were running down Harper's face and he caught his head in his hands and dropped to his knees. Lucas squatted beside him.

"You know some stuff," Lucas said. "You know the woman or you know somebody who knows the woman."

Harper got one foot beneath him, then heaved himself up. His eyes were red, and tears still poured down his face. "Motherfuckers."

Climpt cuffed him on the side of the head. "You ain't listening. You know who this is, this woman. If you don't spit out the name . . ."

"You're gonna what? Beat me around?" Harper asked, defiant. "I been beat around before, so go ahead. I'll get my fuckin' lawyer."

"Yeah, you put a fuckin' lawyer out there and I'll pin this fuckin' picture on the bulletin board at the goddamn Super Valu with the note that you sold Jim's ass," Climpt said. "They'll find your fuckin' skin hanging from a tree out here, and you won't be in it."

"Go fuck yourself," Harper snarled. There was blood on his upper lip, trickling down from his nose.

Climpt pulled back his hand but Lucas blocked it. "Let it go," he said.

❋

Outside, as they were loading into the trucks, Lacey said, "Where's Harper?"

"Probably fixin' some dinner," Climpt said. Then, "He's okay, Henry, don't get your ass in an uproar."

Lacey shook his head doubtfully, then said, "Can I see that Polaroid again, just for a minute?"

Lucas handed it to him and Lacey turned on his truck's dome light and peered at the photo.

"Check this, right here," Lacey said. He touched the edge of the photograph with a fingernail. Lucas took it.

"It looks like a sleeve."

"Sure does," said Lacey, holding the photo four inches from his face. "Now, this here is a Spectra Polaroid. Spectras come with a remote control, a radio thing, so it might of been that there were only the two of them. But if that's a sleeve, and if there's somebody else behind the camera . . ."

"The camera angle's downward," Lucas said. "That'd be high for a tripod."

"So there must be a bunch of them," Lacey said.

"Yeah, probably," Lucas said, nodding. "We already know he was with a heavy white guy and here's a woman."

"Damn—if it's a bunch of people, it's gonna tear this county up," Climpt said.

"I'd say the county's already torn up," Lucas said.

Climpt shook his head: "This'd be worse'n the murders, a bunch of people screwing children. Believe me, around here, this'd be worse."

CHAPTER

✳ ✳ ✳

9

They headed back to town, Climpt riding with Lucas.

"Kind of liked your style back there," Climpt said.

"Thanks. I've worked on it," Lucas said.

The radio burped: Carr. *Need to see you guys at the courthouse.*

"Did you find the kid?" Lucas asked.

Nothing yet, Carr said.

Off the air, Lucas told Climpt, "I fucked up. The school principal was worried about cops talking to kids without the parents' permission. I took the kid out to his house so I could explain to his father. Goddammit."

"You didn't fuck up," Climpt said. He fumbled a cigarette out of a crumpled pack and lit it with a paper match. "That's not the kind of thing you can know. You're dealing with a crazy man. And you've got a reputation. People around here think you're Sherlock Holmes."

"I'm not. But I have dealt with psychos before. I should have known better than to show an interest in one witness," Lucas said. "I . . . Oh, shit."

"What?"

"Do you know where the doctor's house is? Weather

Karkinnen?" Lucas asked, his voice urgent.

"Sure. Down on Lincoln Lake."

❋

Weather lived in a rambling, white-clapboard house with a steep, snow-covered roof. A fieldstone chimney, webbed with naked vines, climbed one end, a double garage anchored the other. A stand of red pines protected it from the north wind. Two huge white pines, one with a rope dangling from a lower branch, stood in back, along the edge of the frozen lake. The neighboring homes were as large or larger than Weather's, most of them with aging boathouses at the edge of the lake.

As Lucas and Climpt pulled into the driveway, a pod of snowmobiles whipped by on the lake, heading for a bar sign at the far end.

Weather's house was dark.

"Just be a minute or two," Lucas said, but a chilly anxiety plucked at his chest, growing heavier as he climbed out of the truck and hurried up to the house. He rang the doorbell, and when he didn't get a response, pounded on the front door and rattled the knob. The door was locked. He stepped back off the porch and started down the sidewalk, intending to try the garage doors, when a light came on inside.

He felt like a boulder had been lifted off his back. He turned and hurried back to the door, rang the doorbell again. And suddenly he was nervous again, afraid that she might think he was here to hustle her.

A moment later Weather opened the inner door, peered through the glass of the storm door, then pushed the storm door open. She was wearing a heavy throat-to-ankle terrycloth robe. She pulled the robe together at the neck as she leaned out and looked past him at the truck, still running in the driveway, and said, "Okay, what happened?"

Another boulder came off his back. She *didn't* think . . .

"There's a kid missing—after I talked to him at school today," Lucas blurted. "He might have wandered away from his house, but nobody really thinks so. He may have been taken by whoever did the LaCourts. Since we've spent some time together, you and I . . . You see . . ."

"Who's out in the truck?" Weather asked.

"Gene Climpt."

She waved at the truck, then said to Lucas, "Come on in for a moment and tell me about it."

Lucas kicked snow off his boots and stepped inside. The house smelled subtly of baking and herbs. A modern watercolor of a vase of flowers hung on an eggshell-white wall that faced the entry. Lucas knew almost nothing about modern art, but he liked it.

"Who's the kid?" Weather asked.

"John Mueller," Lucas said. "Do you know him?"

"Oh, God. His mom works at the bakery?"

"I guess . . ."

"Aw, jeez, I've seen him up there doing his homework. Aw, God . . ." She had her arms crossed over her chest, and was gripping the material on the sleeves of her robe, her knuckles white.

"If the killer took the kid, then he's out of control. Nuts," Lucas said. He felt large and awkward in the parka and boots and hat and gloves, looking down at her in her bathrobe. "It'd be best if you got out of here. At least until we can set up some security."

Weather shook her head: "Not tonight. I've got surgery in"—she looked at her watch—"seven hours. I've got to be up in five."

"Can you cancel?" Lucas asked.

"No." She shook her head. "My patient's already in the hospital, fasting and medicated. It wouldn't be right."

"I've got to go downtown," Lucas said. "I could come back and bag out on your couch."

"In other words, wake me up again," she said, but she smiled.

"Look, this is getting nasty." He was so serious that she tapped his chest, to hold him where he was standing, and said, "Wait a minute." She walked into the dark part of the house and a light came on. There was a moment of rattling, then she came back with a garage-door opener.

"C'mere . . . don't worry about the snow on your boots, it's only water." She led him through the living room to the hallway, opened the first door in the hall. "Guest room. The right bay in the garage is empty. You come through the garage door to the kitchen, then through here. I'll leave a couple of lights on."

Lucas took the garage-door opener, nodded, said, "I'll walk around your house, look in back. Keep your doors locked and stay inside. You've got dead bolts?"

"Yes."

"Then lock the doors," he said. "You've got a lock on your bedroom door?"

"Yes, but just a knob lock. It's not much."

"It'd slow somebody down," Lucas said. "Lock it. How about a gun. Do you have a gun?"

"A .22 rifle. My dad shot squirrels off the roof with it."

"Know how to use it? Got any shells?"

"Yes, and there's a box of shells with the gun."

"Load it and put it under your bed," Lucas said. "We'll talk tomorrow morning. Wake me up when you get up."

"Lucas, be careful."

"*You* be careful. Lock the doors."

He went to the entry, pulled open the inner door. As he was about to go out, she caught his sleeve, tugged him back, stood on her tiptoes and kissed him, and in almost the same movement, gave him a little shove that propelled him out through the storm door.

"See you in the morning," she said and closed the door. He waited until he heard the lock snap, then went back down the walk to the truck, still feeling the fleeting pressure of her lips on his.

"She okay?" Climpt asked.

"Yeah. Gimme the flashlight. In the glove compartment." Climpt grunted, dug around in the glove compartment, handed him the flash, and Lucas said, "I'll be right back."

The snow around the house was unbroken as far back as he could see. A low railed deck stuck out of the back, in front of a long sliding-glass door. A bird feeder showed hundreds of bird tracks and the comings and goings of a squirrel, but nothing larger. As he waded ponderously through the snow, returning to the truck, another pod of snowmobiles roared by on the lake, and Lucas thought about the sled used in the LaCourt attack.

Climpt was standing next to the truck, smoking an unfiltered Camel. When he saw Lucas coming, he dropped the cigarette on the driveway, stepped on it, and climbed back into the passenger seat.

"Find anything?" he asked as Lucas got in.

"No."

"We could get somebody down here, keep an eye on her."

"I'm gonna come back and bag out in her guest room," Lucas said. "Maybe we can figure something better tomorrow."

Lucas backed out of the drive and they rode in silence for a few minutes. Then Climpt, slouching against the passenger-side door, drawled, "That Weather's a fine-looking woman, uh-huh. Got a good ass on her." He was half-grinning. "She's single, I'm single. I'm quite a bit older, of course, but I get to feeling pretty frisky in the spring," Climpt continued. "I been thinking about calling her up. Do you think she'd go out with an old guy like me? I might still be able to show her a thing or two."

"I don't believe she would, Gene," Lucas said, looking straight out through the windshield.

Climpt, still smiling in the dark, said, "You don't think so, huh? That's a damn shame. I think she could probably show a fellow a pretty good time. And it's not like puttin' a little on me would leave her with any less of it, if you know what I mean."

"Stick a sock in it, Gene," Lucas said.

Climpt broke into a laugh that was half a cough, and after a minute, Lucas laughed with him. Climpt said, "Looking at you when you went up to her door, I'd say you're about half-caught, my friend. If you don't want to get all-caught, you better be careful. If you want to be careful."

❅

Carr was gray-faced, exhausted. Old.

"I've got to get back out there, on the search line," he said when Climpt and Lucas walked into his office. Lacey was with him and four other deputies. "It's a mess. We got people who want to help who just aren't equipped for it. Not in this cold. They'll be dying out there, looking for the kid."

"The kid's dead if he's not inside," Climpt said bluntly. "And if he's inside somewhere, looking for him outside won't help."

"We thought of that, but you can't really quit, not when there's a chance," Carr said. "Where's this photograph Henry's been telling me about?"

Lucas took it out of his pocket and flipped it on Carr's desk. Carr looked at it for a moment and said, "Mother of God." To one of the deputies, he said, "Is Tony still down the hall?"

"Yeah, I think so."

Carr picked up the phone, poked in four numbers. They all heard a ringing far down the hall, then Carr said, "Tony? Come on down to my office, will you?"

When he'd hung up, Lucas said, "I had dinner with Weather Karkinnen and people have seen us talking. Gene and I stopped at her place. She's all right for now."

"I'll send somebody over," Carr suggested.

Lucas shook his head. "I'll cover it tonight. Tomorrow I'll try to push her into a safer place, maybe out of town, until this thing is settled. I just hope it doesn't start any talk in the town."

The sheriff shrugged. "It probably will, but so what? The truth'll get out and it'll be okay."

"There's another problem," Lucas said. "Everything we do seems to be all over town in a few minutes. You need to put the lid on, tight. If John Mueller's missing, and if he's missing because he talked to me, it's possible that our killer heard about it from a teacher or another kid. But it's also possible that it came out of the department here. Christ, everything that we've done . . ."

Carr nodded, pointed a finger at Lacey. "Henry, write up a memo. Anyone who talks out of place, to anyone, about this case, is gonna get terminated. The minute I hear about it. And I don't want anybody talking about substantive stuff on the radios, either. Okay? There must be a hundred police-band monitors in this town, and every word we say is out there."

Lacey nodded and opened his mouth to say something when a short dark-haired man stuck his head in the office and said, "Sheriff?"

Carr glanced up at him, nodded and said, "I need to talk to Tony for a minute. Could we get everybody out of here except Lucas and Henry? And Gene, you stay . . . Thanks."

When the others had gone, Carr said, "Shut the door." To Lucas: "Tony's my political guy." When the dark-haired man had closed the door, Carr handed him the Polaroid and said, "Take a look at this picture."

Tony took it, studied it, turned it, said "Huh," and nibbled on a thumbnail. Finally he looked up and said, "Sheriff?"

"You know that woman?"

"There're half-dozen people it could be," he said. "But something about her jaw . . ."

"Say the name."

"Judy Schoenecker."

"Damn," the sheriff said. "That's what I thought soon as I saw it. Gene?"

Gene took the photo, looked at it, shook his head. "Could be, but I don't know her that well."

"Let's check it out," Carr said. "Lucas, what're you going to do? It'd be best if you stayed away from the Mueller search, at least for a while."

Lucas looked at his watch. "I'm going back to Weather's. I'm about to drop dead anyway." He reached across the desk and tapped the photograph. "Why don't you call this a tentative identification and see if you can get a search warrant?"

"Boy, I'd hate to . . ." the sheriff started. Then: "Screw it. I'll get one as soon as the judge wakes up tomorrow."

"Have somebody call me," Lucas said.

"All right. And Lucas: You couldn't help it about the kid, John Mueller," Carr said. "I mean, if he's gone."

"You really couldn't," Lacey agreed.

"I appreciate your saying it," Lucas said bleakly. "But you're both full of shit."

CHAPTER

***

10

Sleep had always been difficult. The slights and insults of the day would keep him awake for hours, plotting revenge; and there were few days without slights and insults.

And night was the time that he worried. There was power in the Iceman—movement, focus, clarity—but at night, when he thought things over, the things he'd done during the day didn't always seem wise.

Lying awake in his restless bed, the Iceman heard the three vehicles arrive, one after another, bouncing off the roadway into the snow-packed parking lot. He listened for a moment, heard a car door slam. A clock radio sat on the bedstand: the luminous red numbers said it was two o'clock in the morning.

Who was out in the pit of night?

The Iceman got out of bed, turned on a bedside lamp, pulled on his jeans, and started downstairs. The floor was cold, and he stooped, picked up the docks he'd dropped on the floor, slipped them on, and went down the stairs.

A set of headlights still played across his side window, and he could hear—or feel—an engine turning over, as if people were talking in the lot. As he reached the bottom of the stairs, the headlights and engine sounds died and a moment later someone began pounding on the door.

The Iceman went to the window, pulled back the gingham curtain, and peered out. Frost covered the center of the window in a shattered-paisley pattern, but through a clear spot he could see the roof-mounted auxiliary lights on Russ Harper's Toyota truck, sitting under the blue yard-light.

"Harper," he muttered. Bad news.

The pounding started again and the Iceman yelled "Just a minute" and went to the door and unlocked it. Harper was on the concrete stoop, stamping the snow off his boots. He looked up when the Iceman opened the door, and without a word, pushed inside, shoving the door back, his face like a chunk of wood. He wore a red-and-plaid wool hunting coat and leather gloves. Two other men were behind him, and a woman, all dressed in parkas with hoods and heavy ski gloves, corduroy or wool pants, and pac boots, faces pale with winter, harsh with stress.

"Russ," said the Iceman, as Harper brushed past. "Andy. Doug. How're you doin', Judy?"

"We gotta talk," Harper said, pulling off his gloves. The other three wouldn't directly meet the Iceman's inquiring eyes, but looked instead to Harper. Harper was the one the Iceman would have to deal with.

"What's going on?" he said. On the surface, his face was slack, sleepy. Inside, the beast began to stir, to unwind.

"Did you kill the LaCourts?" Harper asked, stepping close to him. The Iceman's heart jumped, and for just a moment he found it hard to breathe. But he was a good liar. He'd always been good.

"What? No—of course not. I was here." He put shock on his face and Harper said "Motherfucker," and turned away, shaking his head. He touched his lip and winced, and the Iceman saw what looked like a tiny rime of blood.

"What are you talking about, Russ?" he asked. "I didn't have a goddamned thing to do with it. I was here, there were witnesses," he complained. Public consumption: *I didn't mean to; they just fell down* . . .

As his voice rose, Harper was pulling off his coat. He tossed it on a card table, hitched his pants. "Motherfucker," he said again, and he turned and grabbed the Iceman by his pajama shirt, pulled him forward on his toes, off-balance.

"You motherfucker—you better not have," Harper breathed in his face. His breath smelled of sausage and bad teeth, and the Iceman nearly retched. "We don't want nothing to do with no goddamned half-assed killer."

The Iceman brought his hands up, shoulder height, shrugged, tried not to struggle against Harper's hold, tried not to breathe. *Kill him now . . .*

Of the people in their group, Harper was the only one who worried him. Harper might do anything. Harper had a craziness, a killer feel about him: scars on his shiny forehead, lumps. And when he was angry, there was nothing calculated about it. He was a nightmare you met in a biker bar, a man who liked to hurt, a man who never stopped to think that he might be the one to get damaged. He worried the Iceman, but didn't frighten him. He could deal with him, in his own time.

"Honest to God, Russ," he said, throwing his hands out to his sides. "I mean, calm down."

"I'm having a hard time calmin' down. The cops was out to my house tonight and they flat jacked me up," Harper said. "That fuckin' guy from Minneapolis and old Gene Climpt, they jacked my ass off the floor, you know what I'm telling you?" Spit was spraying out of his mouth, and the Iceman averted his face. "You know?"

"C'mon, Russ . . ."

Harper was inflexible, boosted him an inch higher, his work-hardened knuckles cutting into soft flesh under the Iceman's chin. "You know what we been doing? We been diddlin' kids. Fuckin' juveniles, that's what we been doin', all of us. All that fancy bullshit talk about teachin' 'em this or that—it don't mean squat to the cops. They'd put us all in the fuckin' penitentiary, sure as bears shit in the woods."

"There's no reason to think I did it," the Iceman said, forcing sincerity into his voice. And the beast whispered, *Let's kill him. Now now now . . .*

"Horseshit," Harper snarled. He snapped the Iceman away as though he were a bug. "You sure you didn't have nothing to do with it?" Harper looked straight into his eyes.

"I promise you," the Iceman said, his eyes turning away, down, then back up. He pushed the beast down, caught his breath. "Listen, this is a time to be calm."

The man called Doug was bearded, with the rims of old pock-scars showing above the beard and dimpling his purple nose. "The Indians think a windigo did it," he said.

"That's the most damn-fool thing I ever did hear," Harper said, turning his hostility toward Doug. "Fuckin' windigo."

Doug shrugged. "I'm just telling you what I hear. Everybody's talking about it, out at the Res."

"Jesus Christ."

"Judy and I are outa here," the man called Andy said abruptly, and they all turned to him. Judy nodded. "We're going to Florida."

"Wait—if you take off . . ." the Iceman began.

"No law against taking a vacation," Andy said. He glanced sideways at Harper. "And we're out of this. Out of the whole deal. I don't want to have nothing to do with you. Or any of the others, neither. We're taking the girls."

Harper stepped toward them, but Andy set his feet, unafraid, and Harper stopped.

"And I won't talk to the cops. You know I can't do that, so you're all safe. There's no percentage in any of you coming looking for us," Andy finished.

"That's a bullshit idea, running," Harper said. "Runnin'll only make people suspicious. If something does break, bein' in Florida won't help none. They'll just come and get you."

"Yeah, but if somebody just wants to come and talk, offhand, and we're not around . . . Well, then, maybe they'll just forget about it," Andy said. "Anyway, Judy and I decided: we're outa here. We already told the neighbors. Told them this weather was too much, that we're going away for a while. Nobody'll suspect nothing."

"I got a bad feeling about this," said Doug.

A car rolled by outside, the lights flashing through the

window, then away. They all looked at the window.

"We gotta get going," Andy said finally, pulling on his gloves. To the Iceman he said, "I don't know whether to believe you or not. If I thought you did it . . ."

"What?"

"I don't know . . ." Andy said.

"Why did you people think . . ."

"Because of that goddamn picture Frank LaCourt had. As far as I know, the only person he talked to was me. And the only person I talked to was you."

"Russ . . . I . . ." The Iceman shook his head, put a sad look on his face. He turned to Andy. "When're you leaving?"

"Probably tomorrow night or the next day," Judy said. Her husband's eyes flicked toward her, and he nodded.

"Got a few things to wind up," he muttered.

❋

Andy and Judy left first, flipping up their hoods, stooping to look through the window for car lights before they went out into the parking lot. As Harper zipped his parka he said, "You better not be bullshitting us."

"I'm not." The Iceman stood with his heels together, fingertips in his pants pockets, the querulous, honest smile fixed on his face.

" 'Cause if you are, I'm going to get me a knife, and I'm gonna come over here and cut off your nuts, cook them up, and make you eat them," Harper said.

"C'mon, Russ . . ."

Doug was peering at him, and then turned to look at Harper. "I don't know if he did it or not. But I'll tell you one thing: Shelly Carr couldn't find his own asshole with both hands and a flashlight. No matter who did it, we'd be safe enough if Shelly is doing the investigation."

"So?"

"So if something happened to that cop from Minneapolis . . ."

Harper put the lizard look on him. "If something happened to him, it'd be too goddamned bad, but a man'd be a fool to talk about it to anyone else," he said. *"Anyone else."*

"Right," said Doug. "You're right."

❈

When they were gone, the Iceman took a turn around the room, the beast rising in his throat. He ran a hand through his hair, kicked at a chair in frustration. "Stupid," he said. He shouted it: "STUPID!"

And caught himself. Controlled himself, closed his eyes, let himself flow, regulated his breathing, felt his heartbeat slow. He locked the door, turned off the lights, waited until the last vehicle had left the parking lot, then climbed the stairs again.

He could go to Harper's tonight, with the .44. Take him off. Harper had handled him like he was a piece of junk, a piece of garbage. *Yes, said the beast, take him.*

No. He'd already taken too many risks. Besides, Harper might be useful. Harper might be a fall guy.

Doug and Judy and Andy . . . so many problems. So many branching pathways to trouble. If anybody cracked . . .

Judy's face came to mind. She was a plain woman, her face lined by forty-five winters in the North Woods. She worked in a video rental store, and she looked like . . . anybody. If you saw her in a K Mart, you wouldn't notice her. But the Iceman had seen her having sex with the Harpers, father and son, simultaneously, one at each end, while her husband watched. Had watched her, watching the Iceman, as he taught her daughters to do proper blowjobs. She had seen her husband with their own daughters, had seen the Iceman with Rosie Harris and Mark Harris and Ginny Harris, the yellow-haired girl.

She'd seen all that, done all that, and yet she could lose herself in a K Mart.

He again approached the problem of what to do. Fight or run? This time, though, the problem seemed less like an endless snaky ball of possibilities and more like a single intricate but manageable organism.

He was far from cornered. There were many things he might do. The image of John Mueller came to mind: red spots on white, like the eight of hearts, the red in the snow around the boy.

John Mueller was an example.

Action eliminated problems.

It was time for action again.

CHAPTER

❋ ❋ ❋

11

Lucas stepped quietly into the house, pulled off his boots, and stopped to listen. The furnace had apparently just come on: the heating ducts were clicking and snapping as they filled with hot air and expanded. Weather had left a small light on over the sink. He tiptoed through the kitchen and living room, down the hall to the guest room, and turned on the light.

The room felt unused, lonely. The bureau had been dusted, but there was nothing on top of it and the drawers were empty. A lamp and a small travel alarm sat on a bedstand, with a paper pad and a pen; the pad appeared to be untouched. The room was ready for guests, Lucas thought, but no guests ever came.

He peeled off his parka, shirt, pants, and thermal underwear and tossed them on the bureau. He'd stopped at the motel and picked up his shaving kit and fresh underwear. He put them on the bedstand with his watch, took his .45 from its holster, jacked a shell into the chamber, and laid it next to the clock. After listening for another moment at the open bedroom door, he turned off the light and crawled into bed. The bed was too solid, too springy, as though it had never been slept in. The pillow pushed his head up. He'd never get to sleep.

❄

The bed sagged.

Somebody there. Disoriented for a moment, he turned his head, opened his eyes. Saw a light in the hallway, remembered the weight. He half-sat, supporting himself with his elbows, and found Weather sitting on the end of the bed. She was dressed for work, carrying a cup of coffee, sipping from it.

"Jesus, what time is it?"

"A little after six. I'm outa here," she said. She was stone-cold awake. "Thanks for coming over."

"Let me get up."

"No, no. Shelly's sending a deputy over. I feel silly."

"Don't. There's nothing silly about it," he said sharply. "And you should go somewhere else at night. Pick someplace at random. A motel in Park Falls. Tell us you're leaving, and we'll have somebody run interference for you out the highway to make sure you're not followed."

"I'll think about it," she said. She patted his foot. "You look like a bear in the morning," she said. "And your long underwear is cute. I like the color."

Lucas looked down at the long underwear; it was vaguely pink. "Washed it with a red shirt," he mumbled. "And this is not the goddamn morning. Morning starts when the mailman arrives."

"He doesn't get here until one o'clock," Weather said.

"Then morning starts at one o'clock," he said. He dropped back on the pillow. "John Mueller?"

"They never found him," she said. "When the deputy called, I asked."

"Ah, God."

"I'm afraid he's gone," she said. She glanced at her watch. "And I've got to go. Make sure all the doors are locked, and go out through the garage when you leave. The garage door locks automatically."

"Sure. Would you . . ."

"What?"

"Have dinner with me tonight? Again?"

"God, you're rushing me," she said. "I like that in a man. Sure. But why don't we have it here? I'll cook."

"Terrific."

"Six o'clock," she said. She nodded at the bedstand as she went out the door. "That's a big gun."

He heard the door to the garage open and close, and after that the house was silent. Lucas drifted back to sleep, now comfortable in the strange bedroom. When he woke again, it was eight o'clock. He sat on the edge of the bed for a moment, then staggered down the hall to the bathroom, shaved, half-fell into the shower, got a dose of icy water for his trouble, huddled outside the plastic curtain until the water turned hot, then stood under it, letting the stinging jets of water beat on his neck.

Harper. They had to put the screws on Harper. So far, he was the only person who might know something. He stepped out of the shower, looked in the medicine cabinet for shampoo. There wasn't any, but there were two packs of birth control pills. He picked them up, turned them over, looked at the prescription label. More than two years old. Huh. He'd hoped he'd find that they'd been taken out the day before. Vanity. He dropped them back where he'd found them. Of course, if she hadn't been on the pill for two years, she probably didn't have much going.

He looked under the sink, found a bottle of Pert, got back in the shower and washed his hair.

Harper wasn't the only problem. There was still the time discrepancy. Something happened there. Something was going on with the priest. He didn't seem to fit with the child-sex angle. There'd been a notorious string of cases in Minnesota of priests abusing parish children, but in those cases, the men had invariably acted alone. The standing of a priest in a small community would almost seem automatically to preclude any kind of ring.

"Aw, no," Lucas sputtered.

He should have seen it. He stepped out of the shower, mopped his face and walked down the hall to the kitchen, found the telephone. He got Carr at his office.

"You get any sleep?" he asked.

"Couple hours on the office couch," Carr said. "We got a search warrant for Judy Schoenecker's place. You can take it out there."

"I'd like to take Gene along. He was pretty good with Harper."

"I understand Russ might have a sore nose this morning," Carr said.

"It's the cold weather," Lucas said. "Listen, how many people live down Storm Lake Road, beyond the LaCourts' house? How many other residences?"

"Hmp. Twenty or thirty, maybe. Plus a couple resorts, but those are closed, of course. Nobody there but the owners."

"Could you get a list for me?"

"Sure. The assessor'll know. We can get his plat books. What're you looking for?"

"I'll know it when I see it. I'll be there in twenty minutes," Lucas said.

When he hung up, he realized he was freezing, hustled back to the bathroom, and jumped into the shower. After two more minutes of hot water, he toweled off, dressed, and let himself out of the house.

❄

Carr was munching on a powdered doughnut hole when Lucas got in. He pointed at a white paper bag and said, "Have one. Why do you want those names down the road?"

"Just to see what's down there," Lucas said, fishing a sweet roll out of the bag. "Did you get them?"

"I told George—he's the assessor—I told him we needed them ASAP, so they should be ready," Carr said. "I'll take you down."

George was tall and dark, balding, with fingers pointed like crow-quill pens. He pulled out a plat map of the lake area and used a sharp-nailed index finger to trace the road and tick off the inhabitants, right down to the infants. Three of the houses were lived in by single men.

"Do you know these guys?" Lucas asked Carr, touching the houses of the three single men.

"Yup," Carr said. "But the only one I know well is Donny Riley, he's in the Ojibway Rod and Gun Club. Pretty good guy. He's a retired mail carrier. The other two, Bob Dell works up in a sawmill and Darrell Anderson runs the Stone Hawk Resort."

"Are they married? Divorced, widowed? What?"

"Riley was married for years. His wife died. Darrell's gone off-and-on with one of the gals from the hospital, but I don't know much about him. Bob is pretty much a bachelor-farmer type."

"Any of them Catholics?" Lucas asked.

"Well . . ." Carr looked at the assessor, and then they both looked at Lucas. "I believe Bob goes to Sunday Mass."

"Does he come from here?"

"No, no, he comes from Milwaukee," Carr said. "What're we pushing toward here?"

"Nothing special," Lucas said. "Let's go back upstairs." And to the assessor he said, "Thanks."

Lacey was sitting in Carr's office, his feet on the corner of the sheriff's desk. When they came in, he quickly pulled his feet off, then crossed his legs.

"You're gonna ruin my desk and I'll take it out of your paycheck," Carr grumbled.

"Sorry," Lacey said.

"Now what the heck was all that about? Down there with George?" Carr asked Lucas as he settled into his swivel chair.

"There's a rumor around—just a rumor—that Phil Bergen's gay. That why I asked him last night if he'd ever had any homosexual contacts."

"That's the worst kind of bull," Carr blurted. "Where'd you hear that gay stuff?"

"Look: I keep trying to figure why he says he was at the LaCourts' when the LaCourts were dead," Lucas said. "Why he won't back off of it. And I got to thinking, what if he was somewhere else down the road, but can't say so?"

"Dammit," Carr said. He spun and looked out his window through the half-open venetian blinds. "You got a dirty mind, Davenport."

"Are you thinking about anybody in particular?" Lacey asked. Lucas repeated the three names. Lacey stared at him for a moment, then cleared his throat, edged forward in his chair, and looked at the sheriff. "Um, Shelly, listen. My wife knows Bob Dell. I once said something about he's a good-looking guy, just kidding her, and she said, 'Bob's not the sort that goes for women, I kinda think.' That's what she said."

"She was saying he's gay?" Carr asked, turning, pulling his head back, staring owlishly at his deputy.

"Well, not exactly," Lacey said. "Just that he wasn't the type who was interested in women."

"This is awful," Carr said, looking back to Lucas.

"It would explain a hell of a lot," Lucas said. "If people down there know that this Bob Dell is gay . . . maybe Bergen was down there, got caught in a lie, and then couldn't back off of it. Look at his drinking. If he's innocent, where's all the pressure coming from?"

"From this office for one thing," Carr said. He climbed out of his chair, took a meandering walk around the office, a knuckle pressed to his teeth. "We've got to check on Dell," he said finally.

"See if you can get his birthdate. Query the NCIC and Milwaukee, if that's where he's from," Lucas said. "And think about it: if this is Bergen's problem, then he's in the clear on the murder."

"Yeah." Carr spun and stared through his window, which looked out at a snowpile, a drifted-in fence and the backs of several houses on the next street. "But he wouldn't be clear on the gay thing. And that'd kill him."

They all thought about it for a minute, then Carr said, "Gene Climpt will meet you out at the Mill restaurant at noon." He passed Lucas a warrant.

Lucas glanced at it and stuck it in his coat pocket. "Nothing at all on John Mueller?"

Carr shook his head: "Nothing. We're looking for a body now."

❅

Lucas spent the morning at the LaCourts'. An electric heater tried to keep the garage warm, but without insulation, and with the coming and going of the lab crew, couldn't keep up. Everybody inside wore their parkas, open, or sweaters; it was barely warm enough to dispense with gloves. A long makeshift table had been built out of two-by-fours and particle board, and was stacked with paper, electronic equipment, and a computer with a printer.

The crew had found a badly deformed slug in the kitchen wall. Judging from the base and the weight, allowing for some loss of jacketing material, the techs thought it was probably a .44 Magnum. Definitely not a .357. The gun Lucas found the night of the killings had not been fired.

"The girl was alive when her ear was cut off, and also some other parts of her face apparently were cut away while she was alive," a tech said, reading from a fax. "The autopsy's done, but there are a lot of tests still outstanding."

The tech began droning through a list of other findings. Lucas listened, but every few seconds his mind would drift from the job to Weather. He'd always been attracted to smart women, but few of his affairs had gone anywhere. He had a daughter with a woman he'd never loved, though he'd liked her a lot. She was a reporter, and they'd been held together by a common addiction to pressure and movement. He'd loved another woman, or might have, who was consumed by her career as a cop. Weather fit the mold of the cop. She was serious, and tough, but seemed to have an intact sense of humor.

Can't fuck this up with Weather, he thought, and again, *Can't fuck this thing up.*

Crane came in, blowing steam, stamping his feet, walked behind Lucas to a coffee urn. "He used the water heater to start the fire," he said to the back of Lucas' head.

"What?"

Lucas turned in his chair. Crane, still wrapped in his parka, was pouring himself a cup of coffee. "The hot water faucet was turned on over the laundry tub, and a lot of premix was splashed around the water heater. The heater's a mess, of course, but it looks like there might be traces of charred cotton coming out of the pilot port."

"Say it in English," Lucas suggested.

Crane grinned. "He splashed his premix around the house, soaked a rag in it and laid it across the burner in the water heater. He had to be careful to keep it away from the pilot light. Then he turned on the hot water faucet, let the water dribble out. Not too fast. Then he left. In a few minutes, the water level drops in the tank, cold water refills it . . ."

"And the burner lights up."

"Boom," said Crane.

"Why would he do that?"

"Probably to make sure he could get out. We figure there were fifteen gallons of premix spread around the place. He might've been afraid to toss a match into it. But it does mean he must've thought about burning the place. That's not something that would occur to you while you were standing there . . . if it happened at all."

"If it did happen, that means there'd be a delay between the time he left and the time the fire started, right?"

"Right."

"How much?"

"Don't know," Crane said. "We don't know the condition of the water tank before he turned the water on—how hot the water already was. He didn't turn the faucet on very far, just a steady dribble. Could have been anything from four or five minutes to twenty minutes."

More delay, Lucas thought. More time between the killings and the moment the Jeep passed the fire station. There was no hope for a minor error anymore, a time mixup. The priest *could not have been* at the LaCourts'.

". . . through the surviving files . . ." Crane was talking about the search for the missing photograph.

"It wouldn't be in a file," Lucas said abruptly. "They would have stuffed it someplace where they could get at it—someplace both casual and safe. Where if somebody needed to see it, they could just pick it up and say, 'Here it is.' "

"Okay. But where?" Crane asked.

"Cookie jar—like that."

"We've looked through most of the stuff in the kitchen and their bedroom, the stuff that survived. We haven't found anything like it."

"Okay."

"We'll take it apart inch-by-inch," Crane said. "But it's gonna take time."

❋

Lucas made two phone calls and took one. The first call went to a nun in the Twin Cities, an old friend, a college psychology professor. Elle Kruger: Sister Mary Joseph.

"Elle, this is Lucas. How're things?"

"Fine," she said promptly. "I got Winston's preproduction beta-copy of the new *Grove of Trees*. I ran it with Sister Louisa over the weekend, and we froze it up right away, some kind of stack-overflow error."

"Dammit, they said they fixed that." *Grove of Trees* was an intricate simulation of the battle of Gettysburg that he'd been working on for years. Elle Kruger was a games freak.

"Well, we were on Sister Louisa's Radio Shack compatible," she said. "There's something goofy about that machine, because I ran the same disk on my Compaq and it worked fine."

"All right, I'll talk to them. We ought to be compatible with everything, though," Lucas said. "Listen, I've got another problem and it involves the Church. I don't know if you can help me, but there are people being killed."

"There always are, aren't there?" she said. "Where are you? And how does it involve the Church?"

He sketched the problem out quickly: the priest, the missing time, the question about the man at the end of the road.

"Lucas, you should go through the archdiocese of Milwaukee," Elle said.

"Elle, I don't have time to fool around with Church bureaucracy, and you know what they're like when there's a possible scandal involved. It's like trying to get information out of a Swiss bank. This guy—priest—Bergen is about our age, and I bet you know people who know him. All I'm asking is that you make a couple of calls, see if you can find some friends of his. I understand he went to Marquette. Get a reading. Nothing formal, no big deal."

"Lucas, this could hurt me. With the Church. I have relationships."

"Elle . . ." Lucas pressed.

"Let me pray over it."

"Do that. Try to get back to me tonight. Elle, there are people being killed, including at least one junior high boy and maybe two. Children abused. There are homosexual photos published in underground magazines."

"I get it," she snapped. "Leave me to pray. Just leave me."

A deputy came in as Lucas hung up. "Shelly was on the radio. He's on the way out, and he wants you to wait."

"Okay."

The second call went to the Minneapolis police department, to a burglary specialist named Carl Snyder.

❊

"If you were a woman casually hiding something in your house for a couple of days, a dirty picture, where drop-in neighbors wouldn't see it, but where you could get at it quickly, where'd you put it?"

"Mmm . . . got a pencil?" Snyder asked. Snyder knew so much about burglary that Lucas suspected that he might have done some field research. There had been a series of extremely elegant coin and jewel thefts in the Cities, stretching back twelve years. Nothing had ever been recovered.

"Don't talk to me," Lucas said. "There's a guy named Crane here, from the Wisconsin state crime labs. I'll put him on."

Crane talked to Snyder, saying *Yeah* a lot, his head nodding, and after hanging up, pulled on his parka and said, "Wanna come?"

"Might as well. Where're we going to look?" Lucas asked.

"Around the refrigerator. Then under boxes in the cupboard. Of course, there's not much left there."

The yard outside the house had been flattened by ice and the army of people working around it. They tramped across the frozen ground, pushed past a heavy canvas sheet, and went inside. Banks of tripod-mounted lights lit most of the interior; two refrigerator-sized electric heaters kept it vaguely warm. Most of the loose wreckage had been cleared away from the floors. Through the open door to the mudroom, Lucas could see a white chalk circle around the hole where they'd found the .44 slug.

"All right: around the refrigerator, on the kitchen counter," Crane muttered.

Wearing plastic gloves, he began sifting carefully through the wreckage on the kitchen counter top. The counter top had been yellowed by heat except where it had been covered. A bowl, a peanut butter jar, salt and pepper shakers left their bottom-shapes stenciled in white.

"No paper . . . how about the refrigerator?"

Crane found the remains of the photograph behind the magnetic message slate on the door of the refrigerator. He pried the message slate away from the door, was about to put it back and then said, "Whoa . . ."

"What is it?" Lucas felt a thump in his stomach.

Crane carried it to the window, held it to the light. A square of folded newsprint was stuck to the back of the slate, half of it charred black and imbedded in melted plastic. The other half was brown.

"I don't know; maybe we ought to send it down to Madison, have them separate it," Crane said. But as he said it, he slipped a finger under one edge of the newsprint and lifted. It broke at the burn line, and the browned part came free. Crane turned it over in his hand.

"It's kind of fucked up," he said. He looked at the paper melted into the plastic. "We might be able to recover part of that."

The browned portion of the paper was the left side of a photo, showing the back and buttocks of a nude man. The remaining caption under the photo said: LOOK AT THIS BIG BOY. DINNER.

Beneath the photo and caption was a series of jokes:

> *Guy walks into a bar, he's got a head the size of a baseball, says, "Gimme a beer." The bartender shoves a glass of Bud across the bar and says, "Listen, pal, it's none of my business, but a big guy like you—how'd you get a little teeny head like that?" The guy says, "Well, I was down in Jamaica, walking on the beach, when I see this bottle. I pull the top off, and holy shit, a genie pops out. I mean, she was gorgeous. She had a body that wouldn't quit, great ass, tits the size of watermelons. And she says I can have a wish. So I said, 'Well look, you know, what I'd wish for, is to make love to you.' And the genie says, 'Sorry, that's one thing I'm not allowed to do.' So then I say, 'Okay, how about a little head?'"*

"Who does this kind of shit?" Lucas asked. He held the paper on the flat of his open hands, peering at the type. There was no indication of where it might have come from.

"Anybody and everybody who can afford a Macintosh computer, a laser printer, and a halftone scanner. You could set up a whole magazine with a few thousand bucks' worth of equipment. Not the printing, just the type."

"Is there any way to run it down?"

Crane shrugged. "We can try. Do the best possible copies, circulate it, see what happens."

"Do that," Lucas said. "We need to see the picture."

✳

Crane put the photo into an envelope and they carried it back to the garage. Carr was walking up from the car park, and they waited for him at the garage door. Inside, Crane showed him the remnants of the photo.

"Damn," Carr said. "That could have made us, if we'd got all of it."

"We'll try to trace it, but I can't promise anything," Crane said.

Carr looked at Lucas and said, "Come on outside a minute."

Lucas pulled his parka back on, zipped it, followed Carr through the door.

"We got Bob Dell's birthdate off his DMV records and ran those through the NCIC," Carr said. "He was arrested a few times in Madison, apparently when he was going to school there. Disturbing the peace and once for assault. The disturbing the peace things were for demonstrations, the assault was for a bar fight. The charge was dropped before it got to court and apparently didn't amount to much. I called Madison, and it was just an ordinary bar, not a gay bar or anything. The demonstrations involved some kind of political thing, but it wasn't gay rights, whatever it was."

"Nothing there," Lucas said.

"Well, you remember what Lacey's wife said about Dell not liking women? I called her up, and asked her what she meant, and she hemmed and hawed and finally said yeah, there were rumors among the eligible women in town that you'd be wasting your time chasing Dell."

"How solid were the rumors? Anything explicit?" Lucas asked.

"Nothing she knew about."

"Where's this place he works?"

"Sawmill, about ten minutes from here," Carr said.

"Let's go."

Carr led the way down to the sawmill, a yellow-steel pole barn on a concrete slab. A thirty-foot-high stack of oak logs was racked above a concrete ramp that led into the mill.

Inside the mill, the temperature hovered just above freezing. A half-dozen men worked around the saws. Lucas waited in the work bay while Carr poked his head into the office to talk to the owner. Lucas heard him say, "No, no, no, there's no problem, honest to God, we're just trying to run down every last . . ." And then a cut started, and he watched the saws until Carr came back out.

"That's Bob in the vest," Carr said. "I'll get him when they finish the cut."

Dell was a tall man, wearing jeans and a sleeveless down vest with heavy leather gloves and a yellow hard hat. He worked with the logs, jockeying them for the cut. When the cut was done, they took him outside, away from the noise of the mill. The tall man lit a cigarette and said, "What can I do for you, Sheriff?"

Lucas said, "Did you have any visitors, or see anybody out around your place the night the LaCourts were killed?"

Dell shook his head. "Nope. Didn't see anybody. I came home, watched TV, ate dinner, and then my beeper went off and I hauled my butt up there."

Carr snapped his fingers. "That's right: you're with the fire department."

Dell nodded. "Yeah. I figured you'd be around sooner or later, if you didn't catch somebody. I mean, me being a single guy and all, and just down that road."

"We don't want to cause you any trouble," Carr said.

"You already have," Dell said, looking back at the mill.

"So you saw nobody that night. From the time you left work until the time you went to the fire, you saw nobody," Lucas said.

"Nobody."

"Didn't Father Bergen stop by?" Lucas asked.

"No, no." Dell looked mystified. "Why would he?"

"Aren't you one of his parishioners?"

"Off and on, I guess," Dell said, "But he doesn't come around."

"So you're not close to him?"

"What's this about, Sheriff?" Dell asked, looking at Carr.

"I gotta ask you something here, Bob, and I swear it'll go no further than the three of us," Carr said. "I mean, I hate to ask . . ."

"Ask it," Dell said. He'd stiffened up; he knew what was coming.

"We've heard some rumors in town that you might be gay, is what I guess it is."

Dell turned away from them, looked up into the forest. "That's what it is, huh?" And after a minute, "What would that have to do with anything?"

The sheriff stared at him for a minute, then looked at Lucas and said, "Sonofabitch."

"I never saw Father Phil," Dell said. "Think whatever you want, I never saw him. I haven't laid eyes on him for three weeks, and that sure doesn't have anything to do with . . . my sex choices."

The sheriff wouldn't look at him. Instead, he looked at Lucas, but said to Dell, "If you're lying, you'll go to jail. This is critical information."

"I'm not lying. I'd swear in court," Dell said. "I'd swear in church, for that matter."

Now Carr looked at him, a level stare, and finally he said, "All right. Lucas, have you got anything more?"

"Not right now."

"Thanks, Bob."

"This is gonna ruin me here," Dell said quietly. "I'll have to leave."

"Bob, you don't . . ."

"Yeah, I will," Dell said. "But I hate to, because I liked it. A lot. Had friends, not gays, just friends. That's gone." He turned and walked away, down to the sawmill.

❈

"What do you think?" Carr asked as he watched him go.

"It sounded like the truth," Lucas said. "But I've been lied to before and believed it."

"Want to go back to Phil?"

Lucas shook his head. "Not quite yet. We've got both of them denying it and nothing to show otherwise. Let's see what my Church friend has to say. I should hear from her tonight or tomorrow."

"We don't have time . . ." Carr started.

"If this is the answer to the time conflict, then it's not critical to the case," Lucas said. "Bergen would be out of it."

"It's a sad day," Carr said. He looked back at the mill as Dell disappeared inside. "Bob wasn't a bad guy."

"Well, he could hang on if he's got real friends."

"Naw, he's right," Carr said. "With his job and all, he's gonna have to leave, sooner or later."

✻

Lucas met Climpt at the Mill, a restaurant-motel built on the banks of a frozen creek. The old mill pond, below the restaurant windows, had been finished with a Zamboni to make a skating rink. A dozen men sat on stools at a dining counter, and another dozen people were scattered in twos and threes at tables around the dining room. Climpt was standing by the windows with a mug of chicken broth, looking down at the mill pond, where a solitary old man in a Russian greatcoat turned circles on the ice.

"Been out there since I got here," Climpt said when Lucas stepped up beside him. "He's eighty-five this year."

"Every day now, for an hour, don't matter how cold it is," a waitress said, coming up to Lucas' elbow. The old man was turning eights, building off the circles, his hands clenched behind his back, his face turned up to the sky. He was smiling, not fiercely, or as a matter of focus, but with simple distracted pleasure, moving with a rhythm, a beat, that came from the past. The waitress watched with them for a moment, then said, "Are you going to eat, or . . ."

"I could take a cup of soup," Lucas said.

The waitress, still looking down at the old man on the rink, said, "He's trying to remember what it was like when he was a kid; that's what he says, anyway. I think he's getting ready to die."

She went away, and Climpt, voice pitched low, asked, "You got the warrant?"

"Yeah."

"I brought a crowbar and a short sledge in case we have trouble getting in."

"Good enough," Lucas said. The waitress came back with a mug of the chicken broth, and asked, "You're that detective Shelly brought in, aren't you?"

"Yes," Lucas said.

"We're praying for you," she said.

"That's right," said a man at the counter. He was heavyset, and a roll of fat on the back of his neck folded over the collar of his flannel shirt. Everybody in the place was looking at them. "You just find the sons of bitches," he said. "After that, you can leave them to us."

❄

Lucas and Climpt rode to the Schoeneckers' house in Lucas' truck, hoping that it'd be less noticeable than a sheriff's van. "So what do you know about these people?" Lucas asked on the way over.

"They're private and quiet," Climpt said. "Andy's a bookkeeper, handles businesses in town. Judy stays home. They been here for twenty years, must be—come from over in Vilas County, I guess. You just never see them unless you see Andy going in or out of his office. They don't socialize that I know of. I don't know if they're church people, but I don't think so. Here, that's their driveway."

"Private house, too," Lucas said.

The Schoeneckers lived on an acreage at the north end of town, in a neat yellow rambler with blue trim. The lawn was heavily landscaped, dotted with clusters of blue spruce that effectively sheltered the house from both wind and eyesight. Lucas drove up to the garage and parked.

An inch of unbroken snow lay in the driveway.

"I got a bad feeling about this," Climpt said. "Nobody going in or out."

Lucas scuffed the snow with his boot. "They cleared it off after the last storm. This is all blown in."

"Yeah. Where are they?"

They went to the front door and Lucas rang the bell. He rang it twice more, but the house felt empty. "Got good locks," Climpt said, looking at the inner door through the glass of the storm door.

"Let's try the back, see if there's a door on the garage," Lucas suggested. "They're usually easier."

They followed a snow-blown sidewalk around to the back. The locks on the back door were the same as on the front. Climpt tried the knob, rattled it, put his weight against the door. It didn't budge. "Gonna have to break it," he said. "Let me get the bar."

"Hang on a second," Lucas said. A power outlet with a steel cover was set into the garage wall, just at light-switch height. Lucas lifted the cover, looked inside. Nothing. A post lantern with a yellow bug light sat at the corner of a back deck. He waded through thigh-deep snow to get to it, looked into the four-sided lantern, then lifted one of the glass elements, fished around, and came up with a key.

"Fuckin' rural-ass hayshakers," he said, grinning at Climpt.

The key worked on the door into the garage. The door between the garage and the house was unlocked. Lucas led the way in, found the inside of the Schoeneckers' house almost as cold as the outside. They walked through quickly, checking each room.

"Gone," Lucas said from the master bedroom. The closets and dressers were half-empty. A stack of wire hangers lay on the king-sized bed in the master bedroom. "Packed up."

"And not coming back in a hurry, either," Climpt said from down the hall. "Look at this."

Climpt was in the bathroom, staring into the toilet. Lucas looked. The bowl was empty, but stained purple with anti-freeze. "They winterized."

"Yup. They'll be gone a while."

"So let's go through it," Lucas said.

They began with the parents' bedroom and found nothing at all. The second bedroom was shared by the Schoeneckers' daughters. Again, they came up empty. They worked through the bathroom, the living room, the dining room, took apart the kitchen, spent half an hour in the basement.

"Not a goddamned thing," Climpt growled, scratching his head. They were back in the living room. "I never seen a house so empty of anything."

"Not a single videotape," Lucas said. He walked back down the hall to the master bedroom, checked the television there. A tape player was built into the base. In the living room, a bigger television was hooked into a separate tape player. "They've got two videotape players and no tapes."

"Could rent 'em," Climpt said.

"Even then . . ."

"Did those boxes in the basement . . . just a minute," Climpt said suddenly, and disappeared down the basement steps.

Lucas wandered through the still, cold house, then went to the garage, opened the door, and looked in. Climpt came back up the stairs, carrying two boxes, and Lucas said, "They've got two cars. The garage is tracked on both sides."

"Yeah, I believe they do."

"How often do families go on vacations and take two cars when there are only four of them?" Lucas asked.

"Look at this," Climpt said. He held the boxes out to Lucas. One was the carton for a video camera. The other was a carton for a Polaroid Spectra camera. "A video camera and no videotapes. And last night Henry Lacey said that Polaroid was taken with a Spectra camera."

"Jesus." Lucas ran his hand through his hair. "Okay. Tell you what. You go through that file cabinet with the bills, get all the credit card numbers you can find. Especially gas card numbers, but get all of them. I'm going back to the girls' room. I can't believe teenagers wouldn't leave *something*."

He began going through the room inch by inch, pulling the drawers from all the dressers, looking under them, checking bottles and boxes, paging through piles of homework papers dating back to elementary school. He felt inside shoes, lifted the mattress.

Climpt came in and said, "I got all the numbers they had, I think. They had Sunoco and Amoco gas cards. They also bought quite a bit of gas from Russ Harper, which is pretty strange when you consider his station is fifteen miles from here."

"Keep those slips," Lucas said as he dropped the mattress back in place. "And check and see if there's any garbage outside."

"All right."

A half-dozen books sat upright on top of the bureau, pressed together by malachite bookends shaped like chess knights. Lucas looked at the books, turned them, held them page-down and flipped through them. An aluminum-foil gum wrapper fell from the Holy Bible. Lucas picked it up, unfolded it, found a phone number and the name *Betty* written in orange ink.

He put the book back, walked into the living room as Climpt came in from outside. "No garbage. They cleaned the place out, is what they did."

"Okay." Lucas picked up the phone, dialed the number on the gum wrapper.

The call was answered on the first ring. "This is the Ojibway Action Line. Can I help you?" The voice was female and professionally cheerful.

"What's the Ojibway Action Line?" Lucas asked.

"Who is this?" The voice lost a touch of its good cheer.

"A county sheriff's deputy," Lucas said.

"You're a deputy and don't know what the Ojibway Action Line is?"

"I'm new."

"What's your name?"

"Lucas Davenport. Gene Climpt is here if you want to talk to him."

"Oh, no, that's okay, I heard about you. Besides, it's not a secret—we're the crisis line for county human services. We're right in the front of the phone book."

"All right. Can I speak to Betty?"

There was a moment of silence, then the woman said, "There's not really a Betty here, Mr. Davenport. That's a code name for our sexual abuse counselor."

CHAPTER

✳✳✳

12

Lucas parked in Weather's driveway, climbed out of the truck, and trudged to the porch, carrying a bottle of wine. He was reaching for the bell when Weather pulled the door open.

"Fuck dinner," Lucas said, stepping inside. "Let's catch a plane to Australia. Lay on the beach for a couple of weeks."

"I'd be embarrassed. I'm so winter-white I'm transparent," Weather said. She took the bottle. "Come in."

She'd taken some trouble, he thought. A handmade rag rug stretched across the entry; that hadn't been there the night before. A fire crackled in the Volkswagen-sized fireplace. And there was a hint of Chanel in the air. "Pretty impressive, huh? With the fire and everything?"

"I like it," he said simply. He didn't smile. He'd been told that his smile sometimes frightened people.

She seemed both embarrassed and pleased. "Leave your coat in the closet and your boots by the door. I just started cooking. Steak and shrimp. We'll both need heart bypasses if we eat it all."

Lucas kicked off his boots and wandered through the

living room in his stocking feet. He hadn't seen it in the dark, the night before, and in the morning he'd rushed out, thinking about Bergen. . . .

"How'd the operation go?" he called to her in the kitchen.

"Fine. I had to pin some leg bones back together. Nasty, but not too complicated. This woman went up on her roof to push the snow off, and *she* fell off instead. Right onto the driveway. She hobbled around for almost four days before she came in, the damn fool. She wouldn't believe the bone was broken until we showed her the X rays."

"Huh." Silver picture frames stood on a couch table, with hand-colored photos of a man and woman, still young. Sailboats figured in half the photographs. Her parents. A small ebony grand piano sat in an alcove, top propped up, sheet music for Erroll Garner's "Dreamy" on the music stand.

He went back into the kitchen. Weather was wearing a dress, the first he'd seen her in, simple, soft-shouldered; she had a long, slender neck with a scattering of freckles along her spine. She said, smiling, "I'm going to make stuff so good it'll hurt your mouth."

"Let me help," he said.

✳

She had him haul a grill from the basement to the back deck, which she'd partially shoveled off. He stacked it with charcoal and started it. At the same time she put a pot of water on the stove. A bag of oversized, already-shelled shrimp went into a colander, which she set aside. Herbs and a carton of buttermilk became salad dressing; a lump of cheese joined a pile of mushrooms, celery, walnuts, watercress, and apples on the cutting board. She began slicing.

"I won't ask if you like mushrooms; you've got no choice," she said. "Oh—get the wine going. It's supposed to breathe for a while."

The outside temperature had been rising through the afternoon, and was now approaching zero. A breeze had sprung up and felt almost damp compared to the astringent dryness of the air at twenty below. Lucas put his boots back on and tended the charcoal; the cold felt good on his skin, taken only a few seconds at a time.

✳

The salad was tart and just right. The shrimp were killers. He ate a dozen of them, finally tearing himself away from the table long enough to put the steaks on.

"I haven't eaten like this since . . . I don't know when. You must like cooking," Lucas said as he stood inside the glass doors, looking out at the grill.

"I don't, really. I took a class at the high school called Five Good Things," she confessed. "That's what they taught me. How to make five good things. This is one of them."

"That's a class I need," Lucas said, slipping back outside with a plate. The steaks were perfect, she said. Red inside, a little char on the outside.

"No Mueller kid?" she asked.

He shook his head, and the feel of the evening suddenly warped. "I can't think about it right now," he said.

"Fine," she said hastily, picking up his mood. "It's a terrible business anyway."

"Let me tell you a couple of things," he said. "But it can't go any further."

"It won't."

He outlined what had happened. The priest and the time problem, the homosexual question and Harper, the Schoeneckers' search.

She listened solemnly and finally said, "I don't know Phil Bergen very well, but he never struck me as gay. The few times I've talked to him, he seemed almost shy. He was reacting to me."

"Well, we don't know for sure," Lucas said. "But it would explain a lot."

"So what's happening with the Schoeneckers?"

"Carr's meeting with the sexual therapist right now to see if they can match any calls with the Schoeneckers' kids—the kids never actually came in, but they get a lot of anonymous calls that never develop into anything. The calls are taped, so there might be something. And we're checking credit cards, trying to find out where they are. They just took off, supposedly to Florida."

"If all this is true, the town'll be a mess," Weather said.

"The town'll handle it. I've seen this kind of thing happen before," Lucas said. "The big question is, how out-of-control is the killer? What is he doing?"

"Hey, you'll give me nightmares," she said. "Eat, eat."

Lucas gave up halfway through his steak and staggered off to an overstuffed couch in front of the fireplace. Weather put an ounce of cognac in each of two glasses, pulled open the drapes that covered the sliding glass doors to the deck, and dropped into an E-Z Boy that sat at right angles to the couch. They both put their feet on the scarred coffee table that ran the length of the couch.

"Blimp," Lucas said.

"Moi?" she said, raising an eyebrow.

"No, me. Christ, if somebody dropped a dictionary on my gut, I'd blow up. Look at that." Lucas pointed out the doors, where a crescent moon was just edging up over the trees across the lake.

"I feel like . . ." she started, looking out at the moon.

"Like what?"

"Like I'm starting out on an adventure."

"I wish I was," Lucas said. "All I do is lay around."

"Well, writing games . . . You said the money was pretty good."

"Yeah, like *you* came up here to make a lot of money."

"Not quite the same thing," she said.

"Maybe not," Lucas said. "But I'd like to do something useful. That's what I'm finding out. When I was a cop, I was doing something. Now I'm just making money."

"For now you're a cop again," she said.

"For a couple of weeks."

"How about going back to Minneapolis?"

"I've been thinking about it," Lucas said. He swirled his

cognac in the glass, finished it. "I had a case last summer, in New York. Now this. I sometimes think I could make something out of it, just picking up work. But when I get real, I know it'll never happen. There's just not *enough* to do."

"Ah, well . . . nobody said life'd get easier."

"Yeah, but you always think it will," Lucas said. "The next thing you know, you're sixty-five and living in a rundown condo on Miami Beach, wondering how you're going to pay for your next set of false teeth."

Weather burst out laughing and Lucas grinned in the dark, listening to her, delighted that he'd made her laugh. "The man is an incorrigible optimist," she said.

❊

They talked about people they knew in common, both in Grant and in the Cities.

"Gene Climpt doesn't look like a tragedy, but he is," she told him. "He married his high school sweetheart right after he got in the Highway Patrol—he was in the patrol before Shelly, way back, this was when I was in junior high school. Anyway, they had a baby girl, a toddler. One day Gene's wife was running a bath for the baby, running just hot water and planning to cool it later, when the phone rang. She went to answer it, and the kid climbed on the toilet and leaned over the tub and fell in."

"My God."

"Yeah. She died from the scalding. Then, when Gene was at the funeral home, his wife shot herself. Killed herself. She couldn't stand the baby dying. They buried them both together."

"Jesus. He never remarried?"

She shook her head. "Nope. He's fooled around with a few women over the years, but nobody's ever got him. Quite a few tried."

Weather had worked nights at St. Paul-Ramsey General for seven years while she was doing her surgical residency at the University of Minnesota, and knew eight or ten St.

Paul cops. Did she like them? "Cops are like everybody else, some of them are nice and some of them are assholes. They do have a tendency to hustle you," she said.

"A hospital's a good place to hang around if you're on patrol, and if the person you've brought in isn't a kid or your partner," Lucas said. "It's warm, you're safe, you can get free coffee. There are pretty women around. Most of the women you see, when you're working, are either victims or perpetrators. Nothing like having a good-looking woman tell you to stick your speeding ticket in your ass to chill off your day."

"They're right, cops should stick the tickets," Weather declared.

"Yeah?" He raised an eyebrow.

"Yes. It always used to amaze me, seeing cops writing tickets. The Cities are coming apart; people are getting killed every night and you can't walk downtown without a panhandler extorting money out of you. And half the time when you see a cop, he's giving a ticket to some poor jerk who was going sixty-five in a fifty-five zone. The whole world is going by at sixty-five even while he's writing the ticket. I don't know why cops do it, it just makes everybody mad at them."

"Sixty-five is breaking the law," Lucas said, tongue in cheek.

"Oh, bullshit."

"All right, it's bullshit."

"Don't they have quotas for tickets?" she asked. "I mean, really?"

"Well, yeah, but they don't call it that. They have *performance standards*. They say an on-the-ball patrolman should write about X number of tickets in a month. So a patrol guy gets to the end of the month and counts his tickets and says, 'Shit, I need ten more tickets.' So he goes out to a speed trap and spends an hour getting his ten tickets."

"That's a quota."

"Shhh. It's a hell of a lot more lucrative for the city than busting some dumb-ass junkie burglar."

❈

". . . wouldn't tell me what the guy wanted, she was just too shy, and about fifteen minutes out of nursing school. It turned out he wanted his foreskin restored, He'd heard that sex felt better with a foreskin and he figured we could just take a stitch here and put a hem over there."

Weather had a cop's sense of humor, Lucas decided, laughing, probably developed in the emergency room; someplace where the world got bad enough, often enough, that you learned to separate yourself from the bad news.

"There's just a thimbleful of cognac left and I get it," Weather said, bouncing out of the chair.

"You can have it," Lucas said.

When she came back, she sat next to him on the couch, instead of in the chair, and put a hand behind his head, on his opposite shoulder.

"You didn't drink hardly any of the wine. I drank two-thirds of the bottle, and now I'm finishing the cognac."

"Fuck the cognac," Lucas said. "Wanna neck?"

"That's not very romantic," she said severely.

"I know, but I'm nervous."

"I still have a right to some romance," she said. "But yes, necking would be appropriate, I think."

A while later she said, "I'm not going to be coy about this; I go for the aging jock-cop image."

"Aging?"

"You've got more gray than I do—that's aging," she said.

"Mmmm."

"But I'm not going to sleep with you yet," she said. "I'm gonna make you sweat for a while."

"Whatever's right."

After a while she asked, "So how do you feel about kids?"

"We gotta talk," he said.

❄

The guest room was cool because of the northern exposure, and Lucas put on pajamas before he crawled into the bed. He lay awake for a few minutes, wondering if he should try her room, but he sensed that he should not. They'd ended the evening simply talking. When she left for her bedroom, she'd kissed him—he was sitting down—on the lips, and then the forehead, tousled his hair, and disappeared into the back of the house.

"See you in the morning," she'd said.

He was surprised when, almost asleep, he heard her voice beside the bed: "Lucas." Her hand touched his shoulder and she whispered, "There's someone outside."

"What?" He was instantly awake. She'd left a hallway light on in case he had to get up in the night to use the bathroom or get a drink of water, and he could see her squatting beside the bed. She was carrying the .22. He pushed back the blankets and swung his feet to the floor. The .45 was sitting on the nightstand and he picked it up. "How do you know?"

"I couldn't sleep right away."

"Neither could I."

"I've got a bath off my bedroom and I went for a glass of water. I saw a snowmobile headlight angling in toward the house from out on the lake. There's no trail that comes in like that. So I watched and the headlight went out—but I could see him in the moon, still coming. The neighbors have a roll-out dock and it's on their lawn. He stopped behind it, I think. They don't have a snowmobile. There's a windbreak down there, those pines. I didn't see him again."

She was calm, reporting almost matter-of-factly.

"How long ago?"

"Two or three minutes. I kept watching, thinking I was crazy. Then I heard something on the siding, scratching-like."

"Sounds like trouble," Lucas said. He jacked a shell into the .45.

"What'll we do?" Weather asked.

"Call in. Get some guys down here, on the lake and on the road. We don't want to scare him off before we can get things rolling."

"There's a phone in my bedroom—c'mon," she said. She padded down the hall, Lucas following. "What else?"

"He's got to find a place to get in, and that's gotta make *some* noise. I want you down by the kitchen, just listening. Stay behind the counter, on the floor. I'll be in the living room, by the couch. If you hear him, just sneak back and get me. Let's call."

They were at her room and she picked up the phone. "Uh-oh," she said, looking at him. "It's dead. That's never happened . . ."

"He took the wires out. Goddammit, he's here," Lucas said. "Get on the kitchen floor. I . . ."

"What?"

"I've got a handset in the truck." He looked at the garage door; it'd take him ten seconds.

A loud knocking from the front room turned him around.

"What?" whispered Weather. "That's the doors to the deck."

"Stay back." Lucas slipped down the hall, stopped at a corner, peeked around it, saw nothing. They'd left the curtains open so they could see the moon, but there was no visible movement on the deck outside the house, no face pressed against the glass. Nothing but a dark rectangle. The knocking started again, not as though someone were trying to force the door, but as if they were trying to wake up Weather.

"Hey . . ." A man's voice, muffled by the tri-pane glass.

"What?" Weather had stood up, and was walking through from the kitchen toward the living room.

"Get the fuck down," Lucas whispered urgently, waving the pistol at her. "Get down."

She hesitated, still standing, and Lucas scuttled across the room, caught her wrist in his left hand, pulled her down and toward a wall.

"Somebody needs help," she said.

"Bullshit: remember the phone," Lucas said. They both edged forward toward a corner.

Another call, as if from a distance. "Hey in there. Hey, we got a wreck, we got a wreck," and there were three more knocks. Lucas let go of Weather's wrist and did a quick peek around the corner.

"It can't be him—that's somebody looking for me," Weather said. She started past him, her white nightgown ghostly in the dim reflected light from the hall.

"Jesus," said Lucas. He was sitting on the floor at the corner and reached up to catch her arm, but she stepped into the sightline from the deck, eight feet from the glass.

The window exploded, showering the room with glass, and a finger of fire poked through at Weather. Lucas had already pulled her back and she came off her feet, sprawling, okay, and Lucas yelled, "Shotgun, shotgun . . ." and fired three quick shots through the door, pop-pop-pop and pulled back.

The shotgun roared again, sending more glass flying across the room, pellets ripping through the end of the leather couch, burying themselves in the far wall. Lucas did a quick peek, then another, fired a fourth shot.

Weather, on her hands and knees, lunged toward the kitchen, came up with the .22 rifle she'd left there, and started back.

"Fucker!" she screamed.

"Stay down, that's a twelve gauge," Lucas shouted. Another shotgun blast, then another, a long five seconds apart, the muzzle flash from the first lighting up the front of the room. The flash from the second seemed fainter, the pellets ricocheting around the stone fireplace.

Five seconds passed without another shot. "He's running," Lucas said. "I think he's running."

He got to his feet and dashed into Weather's bedroom, looked out on the lawn. He could see the man there, a hundred feet away, twenty feet from the shelter of the treeline, fifteen feet. "Goddammit." He stepped back and fired two quick shots through the window glass, shattering it, then one more at the fleeing figure, a hopeless shot.

The man disappeared into the trees. Lucas fired a final shot at the last spot he'd seen him, and the magazine was empty.

"Get him? Get him?" Weather was there with the rifle. He snatched it from her and ran down the hall to the living room, out through the deck and into the snow. He floundered across the yard, through snow thigh deep, following the tracks, through the treeline . . . and saw the red taillight of a snowmobile scudding across the lake, three or four hundred yards away. The rifle was useless at that range.

He was freezing. The cold caught at him, twisted him. He turned and began to run back toward the house, but the cold battered at him and he slowed, plodding in his bare feet, his pajamas hanging from him.

"Jesus, Lucas, Lucas . . ." Weather caught him under the arms, hauled him into the house. He was shaking uncontrollably.

"Handset in my truck. Get it," he grunted.

"You get in the goddamn shower—just get in it."

She turned and ran toward the garage, flipping on lights as she went. Lucas peeled off his sodden pajama top, so tired he could barely move, staggered back toward the bathroom. The temperature inside the house was plunging as the night air roared through the shattered windows, but the bathroom was still warm.

He got in the shower, turned on the hot water, let it run down his back, plastering his pajama pants to his legs. He was holding on to the shower head when Weather came back with the handset.

"Dispatch."

"This is Davenport down at Weather Karkinnen's place. We were just hit by a guy with a shotgun. Nobody hurt, but the house is a mess. The guy is headed west across Lincoln Lake on a snowmobile. He's about two minutes gone, maybe three."

❋

"Weather, that's the damnedest, stupidist thing . . ." Carr started, but Weather shook her head and looked at the blown-out window. "I won't leave," she said. "Not when it's like this. I'll figure out something."

Lucas was wrapped in a snowmobile suit. Carr shook his head and said, "All right, I'll get somebody from Hardware Hank out here."

The gunman had come in on snowshoes, as the LaCourt killer had. By the time an alert had been issued, he could have been any one of dozens of snowmobilers still out on the trails within two or three miles of Weather's house. The two on-duty deputies were told to stop sleds and take names. Nobody thought much would come of it.

"When I got the call about the shooting, I phoned Phil Bergen," Carr told Lucas.

"Yeah?"

"Nobody home," Carr said.

There was a moment of silence, then Lucas asked, "Does he have a shotgun?"

"I don't know. Anybody can get a gun, though."

"Why don't you have somebody check on the sled, see if it's at his house? See if he's out on it."

"That's being done," Carr said.

The Madison crime scene techs were taking pictures of the snowmobile tread tracks, the snowshoe tracks, and were digging shotgun shells out of the snow. Lucas, still shaking with cold, walked through the living room with Weather. A double-ought pellet had hit the frame on one of the photographs of her parents, but the photo was all right.

"Why did he do it that way, why . . . ?"

"I have to think about that," Lucas said.

"About . . . ?"

"He wanted you by those windows. If he'd gone to a door, you might not have let him in. And he'd need a hell of a gun to shoot through those oak doors and be sure about getting you. So the question is, did he know about the doors?"

"I think the glass was just the way he wanted to do it,"
Weather said after a minute. "He could get access up from
the lake, nobody'd see him."

"That's possible, too. If you hadn't seen him, if we didn't
know about the phones, you might've walked right up to the
glass."

"I almost did anyway," she said.

Carr came back. "We can't find Phil, but his sled's in
the garage. His car is gone."

"I don't know what that means," Lucas said.

"I don't either—but I've got dispatch calling Park Falls
at Hayward. They're checking the bars for his car."

❄

The man from Hardware Hank brought three sheets of plywood and a Skil saw, broke the glass fragments out of the
glass doors and the window in Weather's bedroom, fitted
the openings with plywood, and set them in place with nails.
"That'll hold you for tonight," he said as he left. "I'll check
back tomorrow on something permanent."

By three o'clock that morning the crime scene techs were
packing up and the phone company had come and gone.
Bergen had still not been found.

"I'm going home," Carr said. "I'll leave somebody."

"No, we're okay," Weather said. "Lucas has his .45 and
I have the rifle . . . and I seriously doubt that'd he'd be back
again."

"All right," Carr said. He flushed slightly. Lucas realized
that he assumed that he and Weather were in bed together.
"Stay on the handset."

"Yeah," Lucas said. Then, glancing at Weather, said to
Carr, "C'mere and talk a minute. Privately."

"What?" Weather asked, hands on her hips.

"Law enforcement talk," Lucas said.

Carr followed him into the guest bedroom. Lucas
picked up his shoulder holster, took the pistol out. He'd
reloaded after he got out of the shower, and now he

punched out the chambered round and reseated it in the magazine.

"If we don't find Bergen tonight, he could get lynched tomorrow," he said.

"I know that," Carr said. "I'm praying he's drunk somewhere. First time for that."

"But the main thing I want to say is, we need to get Weather out of town. She's gonna fight it, but I've contaminated her. I can't quite think why, but I guess I have."

"So work on her," Carr said.

Lucas gestured to his bag on the floor, the rumpled bedclothes. "We're not quite as friendly as you think, Shelly."

Carr flushed again, then said, "I'll talk to her tomorrow, we'll work something out. I'll have a guy with her all day."

"Good."

When the last man left, Weather pushed the door shut, looked at Lucas.

"What was that little bull session about?" she asked suspiciously.

"I asked some routine questions and let Shelly get a good look at my clothes and my watch and the rumpled-up bed in the guest room," Lucas said. He shivered.

She looked at him for a moment, then said, "Huh. I appreciate that. I guess. Are you still cold?"

"Yeah. Freezing. But I'm okay."

"That was the stupidest goddamn thing I ever saw, you tearing through the snow like that in your bare feet. I honest to God thought you were in trouble when I got you back in here, I thought you were gonna have a heart attack."

"Seemed like the thing to do at the time," he said.

She walked back into the living room, looked at the damaged walls, and said, "I'm really cranked, Davenport. Pissed and cranked. I'm gonna have to reschedule the hysterectomy I had going this morning . . . maybe I can push it back into the afternoon. Jesus, I'm wound up."

"You've got about two quarts of adrenaline working their way through your body. You'll fall apart in an hour or so."

"You think so?" She was interested. "Hey, look at the holes in the walls—my God."

She called the hospital's night charge nurse, explained the problem, rescheduled the operation, unloaded then reloaded her .22, asked Davenport to demonstrate his .45, went repeatedly back to the buckshot holes, poking at them with an index finger, going outside to see if they'd gone through. She found three holes in her leather couch, and was outraged all over again. Lucas let her go. He went into the kitchen, made a bowl of chicken noodle soup, ate it all, went back into the living room, and fell on the couch.

"What about the shots you fired? Could you have hit somebody across the lake?" she demanded. She had the magazine out of his .45 and was pointing it at her own image in the mirror over the fireplace.

"No. Some people call a .45 slug a flying ashtray. It's fat, heavy, and slow. It'll knock the shit out of you close up, but it's not a long-range item. Fired from here, on the level, it wouldn't make it halfway across."

"Any chance you hit him?" she asked.

"No . . . I just didn't want him swarming through the door with the shotgun. I might of got him, but he would have got us, too."

"God, it was loud," she said. "The shots almost broke my eardrums."

"You lose a little high-frequency hearing every time you fire one without ear protection, and that's a fact," Lucas said.

She ran out of gas. Suddenly. She stopped talking, came over and slumped next to him on the couch.

"Snuggle up," he said, and pulled her down. She lay quietly for a moment, her back to him, then started to softly cry. "Goddamn him, he shot my house," she said.

Her body shook with the anger of it, and Lucas wrapped his arm around her and held on.

CHAPTER

✳ ✳ ✳

13

The Iceman rode wildly across the frozen lake, off the tracks, a plume of snow thrown high behind the sled when he banked through the long, sinuous turns that would take him to the Circle Lake intersection. He could see police flashers streaming down through the town, but couldn't hear them: and they certainly couldn't see him. He was running without lights, his sled as black as his snowmobile suit, invisible in the night.

The gunfight had surprised him, but not frightened him. He had simply seen the truth: not tonight. He couldn't get at her tonight, because if he stayed, if he fought it out with whoever was inside—and it was almost certainly the cop from Minneapolis—he could be hurt. And hurt was good as dead.

Time time time . . .

He was running out of it. He could feel it trickling through his fingers. Davenport and Crane had taken something out of the LaCourt house, and it was almost certainly the photograph. But they had sent it to the lab in Madison: maybe it had been ruined in the fire after all. He'd talked to the cops who'd been there when they were looking at it, but they had no precise details. Just a piece of paper, they said.

If Weather Karkinnen ever saw the photograph, they'd be on him.

Weather: why was Davenport at her house? Guarding her? Screwing her? Why would they be guarding her? Had she given them something? But the only thing she had to give them was the identification, and if she'd given them that, they'd be knocking on his door.

The intersection came up, marked by two distinctively pink sodium vapor lights. He was in luck: there were no other sleds at the crossing. If they saw him running a blacked-out sled, they'd be curious.

He bucked through the intersection, up the boat landing, down the landing road, onto the trail built in the ditch beside the road. A moment later he turned onto Circle Creek, ran under the road and two minutes later onto the lake. He turned on his lights in the creek bed but kept cranking. There were more snowmobiles on Circle Lake, and he crossed paths with them, moving south and west.

He worked through his options:

He could run. Get in the car, make some excuse for a couple days' absence, and never come back. By the time they started looking for him, he'd be buried in Alaska or the Northwest Territories. But if he was missing, it wouldn't take long for the cops to figure out what happened. And if he ran, he'd have to give up almost everything he had. Take only what would fit in the car, and he'd have to dump the car in a few days. And he still might get caught: they had his picture, his fingerprints.

He could go after the other members of the club, take them all out in one night. The problem was, some of them had already taken off. The Schoeneckers: how would he find them? No good.

He had to stay. He had to find out about the photograph. Had to go back for Weather. He'd missed her twice now, and he was uneasy about it. When he'd been a kid, working the schoolyard, there'd always been a few people he'd never been able to get at. They'd always outmaneuvered him, always foiled him, sometimes goading him into trouble.

Weather was like that: he needed to get at her, but she turned him away.

He bucked up over another intersection, down a long bumpy lane cleared through the woods by the local snow-mobile club, onto the next lake, and across. He came off the lake, took the boat landing road out to the highway, sat for a moment, then turned left.

❄

The yellow-haired girl was waiting. So was her brother, Mark. Mark with the dark hair and the large brown eyes. The yellow-haired girl let him in, helped him take off his snowmobile suit. Mark was smiling nervously: he was like that, he needed to be calmed. The Iceman liked working with Mark *because* of the resistance. If the yellow-haired girl hadn't been there . . .

"Let's go back to my room," she said.

"Where's Rosie?"

"She went out drinking," the yellow-haired girl said.

"I gotta get going," said Mark.

"Where're you going?" Smiling, quiet. But the shooting still boiled in his blood. God, if he could get Weather someplace alone, if he could have her for a while . . .

"Out with Bob," said Mark.

"It's cold out there," he said.

"I'll be okay," Mark said. He wouldn't meet his eyes. "He's gonna pick me up."

"And I'll be here," said the yellow-haired girl. She was wearing a sweatsuit, old and pilled, wished it were something more elegant for him. She plucked at the pants leg, afraid of what he might say; of cruelty in his words.

But he said, "That's great." He touched her head and the warmth flowed through her.

❄

Later in the evening he was lying in her bed, smoking. He thought of Weather, of Davenport, of Carr, of the picture; of Weather, of Davenport, round and round . . .

The yellow-haired girl was breathing softly next to him, her hand on his stomach.

He needed time to find out about the photo. If he could just put them off for a few days, he could find out. He could get details. Without the photo, there wouldn't be a link, but he needed *time*.

CHAPTER

* * *

14

The telephone rang in the kitchen.

Lucas let it ring, heard a voice talking into the answering machine. He should get it, he thought. He rolled over and looked at the green luminous numbers on the bedstand clock. Nine-fifteen.

Four hours lying awake, with a few sporadic minutes of sleep. The air in the house was cool, almost cold, and he pulled the blankets up over his ears. The phone rang again, two rings, then stopped as the answering machine came on. There was no talk this time. Whoever it was had hung up.

A minute later the phone rang twice again. Irritated, Lucas thought about getting up. The ringing stopped, and a moment later began again, two more rings. Angry now, he slipped out of bed, wrapped the comforter around his shoulders, stomped down the hall to the kitchen, and glared at the phone.

Ten seconds passed. It rang again, and he snatched it up. "What?" he snarled.

"Ah. I knew you were sleeping in," the nun said with satisfaction. "You've got a message on the answering machine, by the way."

Lucas looked down at the machine, saw the blinking red light. "I'm freezing my butt off. Couldn't . . ."

"The message isn't from me. I know you've got one because your phone's only ringing twice before the machine answers, instead of four or five times," she said, sounding even more pleased with herself.

"How'd you get the number?"

"Sheriff's secretary," Elle said. "She told me what happened last night, and that you're guarding the body of some lady doctor who's quite attractive. Are you okay, by the way?"

"Elle . . ." Lucas said impatiently, "You sound too smug for this to be a gossip call."

"I'll be gone for the day and I wanted to talk to you," she said. "I found a couple of Phil Bergen's friends. I didn't want to put it on an answering machine."

"What'd they say?"

"They say he was awkward around women but that he was certainly oriented toward them. He was *not* interested in men."

"For sure?" Lucas thought, *Shit.*

"Yes. One of them laughed when I asked the question. Bergen's not a complete 'phobe, but he has a distaste for homosexuals and homosexuality. That attitude wasn't a cover for a secret interest, if you were about to ask me that."

Lucas chewed on his lower lip, then said, "Okay. I appreciate your help."

"Lucas, these are people who would know," Elle said. "One was Bergen's college confessor. He wouldn't have talked to me if homosexuality had ever been broached in confession, so it must not have been. And it would have been."

"All right," Lucas said. "Dammit. That makes things harder."

"Sorry," she said. "Will you be down next week?"

"If I get done up here."

"We'll see you then. We'll get a game. By the way, something serious was happening at the sheriff's office. Nobody had any time to speak to me, something about a lost kid . . ."

"Oh, my God," Lucas said. "Elle, I'll talk to you later."

He hung up, started to punch in the number for the sheriff's office, saw the blinking light on the answering machine and poked it.

Carr's voice rasped out of the speaker: "Davenport, where'n the heck are you? We found the Mueller kid. He's dead and it wasn't an accident. I'm going to send somebody over to wake you up."

Just before the phone hung up, Carr called to someone in the background, "Get Gene over to Weather Karkinnen's house."

There was a motor sound outside. Lucas used two fingers to separate the curtain over the kitchen sink and looked out. A sheriff's truck was pulling into the driveway. Lucas hurried to Weather's bedroom. The door was unlocked, and he opened it and stuck his head inside. She was curled under a down comforter, and looked small and innocent.

"Weather, wake up," he said.

"Huh?" She rolled, half-asleep, and looked up at him.

"They found the Mueller kid and he's dead," Lucas said. "I'm going."

She sat up, instantly awake, and threw off the bedcovers. She was wearing a long-sleeved white flannel nightgown. "I'm coming with you."

"You've got an operation."

"I'll be okay, a few hours is fine."

"You really don't . . ."

"I'm the county coroner, Lucas," she said, "I've got to go anyway." Her hair stuck out from her head in a corona and her face was still morning-slack. She had a red pillow-wrinkle on one cheek. Her cotton nightgown hid all of her figure except her hips, which shaped and moved the soft fabric. She started toward the bath that opened off her bedroom, felt him watching her, said, "What?"

"You look terrific."

"Jesus, I'm a wreck," she said. She stepped back to him, stood on her tiptoes for a kiss, and Climpt began banging on the door.

"That's Gene," Lucas said, stepping back toward the hall. "Five minutes."

"Ten," she said. "I mean, it won't make any difference to John Mueller."

She said it offhandedly, a surgeon and a coroner who dealt in death. But Lucas was stricken. She saw it in his face, a quick tightening, and said, "Oh, God, Lucas, I didn't mean it."

"You're right, though," he said, his voice gone hard. "Ten minutes. It won't make any difference to the kid."

Lucas let Climpt in, and while the deputy looked at the damage from the night's shooting, went back to the bathroom for a quick cleanup.

When he came back out, Weather was coming down the hall, dressed in insulated jeans and a wool shirt, carrying the bag she'd had at the LaCourts'. "Ready?"

"Yeah."

"You were lucky last night," Climpt said. He was standing in the living room, smoking a cigarette, looking at the damage from the firefight.

"I don't think there was anything lucky about it," Weather said. "Look what he did."

"If'd been me out there, you'd a been dead. He should of waited until you were right at the door."

"I'll tell him when I see him," Lucas said.

❋

John Mueller's body had been dumped in an abandoned sand-pit off a blacktopped government road in the Chequamegon National Forest, fifteen miles from his home. A half-dozen sheriff's vehicles were jammed into the turnoff, and the snow had been beaten down by people walking into the pit.

"Shelly's freaked out," Climpt said, talking past a new cigarette. "Something happened at Mass today."

"They found Bergen?"

"Yeah, I guess. He was there."

They could see the sheriff standing alone, like a fat dark scarecrow, just inside the sandpit. "This is his worst nightmare," Weather said.

Climpt nodded. "All he wanted was a nice easy cruise up to retirement, taking care of people. Which he's pretty good at."

They parked and started up toward a cluster of cops at the edge of the sandpit. A civilian in an orange parka stood off to the side, next to a snowmobile, talking to another deputy. Carr saw them coming and walked down the freshly trampled path to meet them.

"How are you?" Carr asked Weather. "Get any sleep?"

"Very little," Weather said. "Is the kid . . ."

"Right there. We haven't called his folks yet." Carr looked at Lucas. "How long will it take to catch this guy?"

"That's not a reasonable question," Weather snapped.

But Lucas looked up the rise to the cluster of cops around the body. "Three or four days," he said after a few seconds. "He's out of control. Unless we're missing some big connection on this kid, there wasn't any reason to kill him. He took a hell of a risk for no gain."

"Will he kill more people?" Carr asked. His voice was a compound of anger, tension, and sorrow, as though he'd worked out the answer.

"He could." Lucas nodded, looking straight into Carr's dry, exhausted eyes. "Yeah, I'd say he could. You better find the Schoeneckers. If they're involved, and they're someplace where he could get at them . . ."

"We got bulletins out all over the south, from Florida to Arizona. We're interviewing their friends."

Weather was moving on toward the body, and Lucas trailed after her. Carr hooked his elbow. "You gotta figure a way to make something happen, Lucas."

"I know," Lucas said.

John Mueller's body had been found by the snowmobiler in the orange parka. He'd seen two coyotes working over the spot and assumed they'd killed a deer. He'd stopped to see if it was a buck and still had antlers. He chased off the dogs, saw the boy's coat, and called the sheriff's department. The first deputy at the scene had shot a coyote and covered the boy with a plastic tarp.

"Bad," Weather said when she lifted the tarp. Around them, the talking stopped as everybody looked at them crouched over the body. "Is that him?"

Lucas studied the child's half-eaten face, then nodded. "Yeah, that's him. I'm almost sure. Jesus Christ."

He walked away, unable to handle it. He hadn't had that problem since his third week on patrol: cops looked at dead people, end of story.

"You all right?" Climpt asked.

"Got on top of me," Lucas said.

He was halfway back to the cars when he saw Crane, the crime-scene tech from Madison, walking up the path.

"Anything for me?" Crane asked.

"I doubt it. The scene's pretty cut up and coyotes have been at the body. It'll take an ME to figure out how he was killed."

"I've got a metal detector, I'll check the site for shells. Listen, I got some news for you this morning. I tried to call and was told you were on the way out here. Remember that burnt-up page from the porno magazine that we sent down to Madison? The one with the picture you want?"

"Yeah?"

"We shipped it to all the major departments in Wisconsin, Illinois, and Minnesota, and we actually got a callback. A guy named . . ." Crane patted his pockets, pulled off a glove, dipped into one, and came up with a slender reporter's notebook. ". . . a guy named Curt Domeier with the Milwaukee PD. He says he might know the publisher. He says give him a call."

Lucas took the notebook page: something to do. He walked down to the truck, called the dispatcher, and was patched through to Milwaukee. Domeier worked with the sex unit. He wasn't in his office, but picked up a phone on a page. Lucas introduced himself and said, "The Madison guys say you might know who put out the paper."

"Yeah. I haven't seen this particular one, but he uses those little dingbats—that's what they call them, dingbats—at the ends of the stories. They look like playing-card suits. Hearts, diamonds, spades, and clubs. I've never seen that anywhere else, but I've seen it with this guy." Domeier's voice was rusty but casual, the kind of cop who chewed gum while he drank coffee.

"Can we get our hands on him?" Lucas asked.

"No problem. He works out of his apartment, up on the north side off I-43. He's a crippled guy, does Macintosh services."

"Macintosh? Like the computer?"

"Exactly. He does magazine stuff, cheap," Domeier said. "Makeup, layout, that stuff."

"We got four dead up here," Lucas said.

"I been reading about it. I thought it was three."

"There'll be another in the paper tomorrow morning, a little kid."

"No shit?" Polite interest.

"We think the killer might have hit the family because of the picture on that page," Lucas said.

"I can talk to this guy right now or you could come down and we could both go see him," Domeier said. "Whatever you want."

"Why don't I come down?"

"Tomorrow?"

"How about this afternoon or tonight?" Lucas said.

"I'd have to talk to somebody here about overtime, but if your chief called down . . . I could use the bucks."

"I'll get him to call. Where'll we meet?" Lucas asked.

"There's a doughnut place, right off the interstate."

❋

Carr was unhappy about the trip: "We need pressure up here. I could send somebody else."

"I want to talk to this guy," Lucas said. "Think about it: he may have seen our man. He may *know* him."

"All right. But hurry, okay?" Carr said anxiously. "Have you heard about Phil?"

"Bergen? What?"

"He showed up for Mass. We'd been looking for him, couldn't find him, then he drove up a half hour before Mass, wouldn't talk to us. After his regular sermon at

Mass this morning, he said he needed to talk to us as friends and neighbors. And he just let it out: he said he knew about the talk in town. He said he had nothing to do with the LaCourts or John Mueller, but that the suspicion was killing him. He said that he'd gotten drunk the night we found him, and said last night he'd gone to Hayward and started drinking again. Said he got right to the edge, right to the place where he couldn't get back, and he stopped. Said he talked to Jesus and stopped drinking. He asked us to pray for him."

"And you believe him?" Lucas asked.

"Absolutely. But you'd have to have been there to understand it. The man spoke to Jesus Christ, and while he was talking to us, the Holy Spirit was there in the church. You could feel it—it was like a . . . warmth. When Phil was walking away from the altar after the Mass, he broke down and began to cry, and you could feel the Spirit descending." Carr's eyes were glazing as he relived it. Lucas stepped away, spooked.

"I got a call from my nun friend," Lucas said. Carr wrenched himself back to the present. "She checked out some Church sources. They say Bergen's straight. Never had any sexual interest in men. That's not a hundred percent, of course."

Carr said, "Which leaves us the question of Bob Dell."

"We've got to talk to Bergen again. You can do it today or wait until I get back."

"We'll have to wait," Carr said. "After this morning, Phil's way beyond me."

"I'll try to get back tonight," Lucas said. "But I might not. If I don't, could you put somebody with Weather?"

"Yeah. I'll have Gene go on over," Carr said.

Weather declared John Mueller dead under suspicious circumstances and ordered the body shipped to a forensic pathologist in Milwaukee. Lucas told her he was leaving, explained, and said he would try to get back.

"That's a twelve-hour round trip," she said. "Take it easy."

"Gene'll take me into town. Could you catch a ride with Shelly?"

"Sure." They were standing next to Climpt's truck, a few feet from Climpt and Carr. When he turned to get in, she caught him and kissed him. "But hurry back."

On the way back, Climpt said, "You ever thought about having kids?"

"I've got one. A daughter," Lucas said. And then remembered Weather's story about Climpt's daughter.

Climpt nodded, said, "Lucky man. I had a daughter, but she was killed in an accident."

"Weather told me about it," Lucas said.

Climpt glanced at him and grinned. *He could have made a Marlboro commercial,* Lucas thought. "Everybody feels sorry for me. Sort of wears on you after a while, thirty years," Climpt said.

"Yeah."

"Anyway, what I was gonna say . . . I'm thinking I might kill this asshole for what he did to that LaCourt girl and now the Mueller kid. If we get him, and we get him in a place where we can do it, just sort of turn your head." His voice was mild, careful.

"I don't know," Lucas said, looking out the window.

"You don't have to do it—just don't stop me," Climpt said.

"Won't bring your daughter back, Gene."

"I know that," Climpt rasped. "Jesus Christ, Davenport."

"Sorry."

After a long silence, listening to the snow tires rumble over the rough roadway, Climpt said, "I just can't deal with people that kill kids. Can't even read about it in the newspaper or listen to it on TV. Killing a kid is the worst thing you can do. The absolute fuckin' worst."

❆

The drive to Milwaukee was long and complicated, a web of country roads and two-lane highways into Green Bay, and then the quick trip south along the lake on I-43. Domeier had given him a sequence of exits, and he got the right off-ramp the first time. The doughnut place was halfway down a flat-roofed shopping center that appeared to be in permanent recession. Lucas parked and walked inside.

The Milwaukee cop was a squat, red-faced man wearing a long wool coat and a longshoreman's watch cap. He sat at the counter, dunking a doughnut in a cup of coffee, charming an equally squat waitress who talked with a grin past a lipstick-smeared cigarette. When Lucas walked in she snatched the cigarette from her mouth and dropped her hand below counter level. Domeier looked over his shoulder, squinted, and said, "You gotta be Davenport."

"Yeah. You're telepathic?"

"You look like you been colder'n a well-digger's ass," Domeier said. "And I hear it's been colder'n a well-digger's ass up there."

"Got that right," Lucas said. They shook hands and Lucas scanned the menu above the counter. "Gimme two vanilla, one with coconut and one with peanuts, and a large coffee black," he said, dropping onto a stool next to Domeier. The coffee shop made him feel like a metropolitan cop again.

The waitress went off to get the coffee, the cigarette back in her mouth. "It's not so cold down here?" Lucas asked Domeier, picking up the conversation.

"Oh, it's cold, six or eight below, but nothing like what you got," Domeier said.

They talked while Lucas ate the doughnuts, feeling each other out. Lucas talked about Minneapolis, pension, and bennies.

"I'd like to go somewhere warmer if I could figure out some way to transfer pension and bennies," Domeier said. "You know, someplace out in the Southwest, not too hot, not too cold. Dry. Someplace that needs a sex guy and'd give me three weeks off the first year."

"A move sets you back," Lucas said. "You don't know the town, you don't know the cops or the assholes. A place isn't the same if you haven't been on patrol."

"I'd hate to go back in uniform," Domeier said with an exaggerated shudder. "Hated that shit, giving out speeding tickets, breaking up fights."

"And you got a great job right here," the waitress said. "What would you do if you didn't have Polaroid Peter?"

"Polaroid who?" asked Lucas.

"Peter," Domeier said, dropping his face into his hands. "A guy who's trying to kill me."

The waitress cackled and Domeier said, "He's like a flasher. He drops trow in the privacy of his own home, takes a Polaroid picture of his dick. Pretty average dick, I don't know what he's bragging about. Then he drops the picture around a high school or in a mall or someplace where there are bunches of teenage girls. A girl picks it up and zam—she's flashed. We think he's probably around somewhere, watching. Gettin' off on it."

Lucas had started laughing and nearly choked on a piece of doughnut. Domeier absently whacked him on the back. "What happens when a guy picks up the picture?" Lucas asked.

"Guys don't," Domeier said morosely. "Or if they do, they don't tell anybody. We've got two dozen calls about these things, and every time the picture's been picked up by a teenage girl. They see it laying there on the sidewalk, and they just gotta look. And if we got twenty-five calls, this guy must've struck a hundred times."

"Probably five hundred if you got twenty-five calls," Lucas said.

"Driving us nuts," Domeier said, finishing his coffee.

"Big deal," Lucas said. "Actually sounds kind of amusing."

"Yeah?" Domeier looked at him. "You wanna tell that to the mayor?"

"Uh-oh," Lucas said.

"He went on television and promised we'd get the guy soon," Domeier said. "The whole sex unit's having an argument about whether we oughta shit or go blind."

Lucas started laughing again and said, "You ready?"

"Let's go," Domeier said.

❄

Bobby McLain lived in a two-story apartment complex built of concrete blocks painted beige and brown, in a neighborhood that alternated shabby old brown-brick apartments with shabby new concrete-block apartments. The streets were bleak, snow piled over the curbs, big rusting sedans from the seventies parked next to the snowpiles. Even the trees looked dark and crabbed. Domeier rode with Lucas, and pointed out the hand-painted Chevy van under a security light on the west side of the complex. "That's Bobby's. It's painted with a roller."

"What color is that?" Lucas asked as they pulled in beside it.

"Off-grape," Domeier said. "You don't see that many off-grape vans around. Not without Dead Head stickers, anyway."

They climbed out, looked up and down the street. Nobody in sight: not a soul other than themselves. At the door, they could hear a television going inside. Lucas knocked, and the television sound died.

"Who is it?" The voice squeaked like a new adolescent's.

"Domeier. Milwaukee PD." After a moment of silence, Domeier said, "Open the fuckin' door, Bobby."

"What do you want?"

Lucas stepped to the left, noticed Domeier edging to the right, out of the direct line of the door.

"I want you to open the fuckin' door," Domeier said.

He kicked it, and the voice on the other side said, "Okay, okay, okay. Just one goddamn minute."

A few seconds later the door opened. Bobby McLain was a fat young man with thick glasses and short blond hair. He wore loose khaki trousers and a white crew-neck t-shirt that had been laundered to a dirty yellow. He sat in an aging wheelchair, hand-powered.

"Come in and shut the door," he said, wheeling himself backwards.

They stepped inside, Domeier first. McLain's apartment smelled of old pizza and cat shit. The floor was covered with a stained shag carpet that might once have been apricot-colored. The living room, where they were standing, had been converted to a computer office, with two large Macintoshes sitting on library tables, surrounded by paper and other unidentifiable machines.

Domeier was focused on the kitchen. Lucas pushed the door shut with his foot. "Somebody just run out the back?" Domeier asked.

"No, no," McLain said, and he looked around toward the kitchen. "Really . . ."

Domeier relaxed, said, "Okay," and stepped toward the kitchen and looked in. Without looking back at McLain he said, "The guy there is named Davenport, he's a deputy sheriff from Ojibway County, up north, and he's investigating a multiple murder. He thinks you might be involved."

"Me?" McLain's eyes had gone round, and he stared up at Lucas. "What?"

"Some people were killed because of one of your porno magazines, Bobby," Lucas said. A chair next to one of the Macintoshes was stacked with computer paper. Lucas picked up the paper, tossed it on the table, and turned the chair around to sit on it. His face was only a foot from McLain's. "We only got a piece of one page. We need the rest of the magazine," he said.

Domeier stepped over to the crippled man and handed him a Xerox copy of the original page. At the same time he took one of the handles on the back of McLain's wheelchair and jiggled it. McLain glanced up nervously and then went back to the Xerox copy.

"I don't know," he said.

"C'mon, Bobby, we're talking heavy-duty shit here— like prison," Domeier said. He jiggled the chair handle again. "We all know where the goddamn thing came from."

McLain turned the page in his hand, glanced at the blank back side, then said, "Maybe." Domeier glanced at Lucas and then Bobby said, "I gotta know what's in it for me."

Domeier leaned close and said, "To start with, I won't dump you outa this chair on your fat physically challenged butt."

"And you get a lot of goodwill from the cops," Lucas said. "This stuff you print, kiddie porn, this shit could be a crime. And we can seize anything that's instrumental to a crime. If we get pissed, you could say good-bye to these computers."

Bobby looked nervously at the Xerox copy, then turned his head to Domeier and said irritably, "Quit fuckin' with my chair."

"Where's this magazine?"

McLain shook his head, then said, "Down the hall, goddammit."

He pivoted his chair and rolled down a short hallway past the bathroom to the door of the only bedroom, wheeled inside. The bedroom was chaotic; pieces of clothing were draped over chairs and the chest of drawers, the floor was littered with computer magazines and books on printing. A high-intensity reading light was screwed to the corner of a bed; the windows were covered with sheets of black paper thumbtacked in place. McLain pushed a jumble of old canvas gym shoes out of the way and jerked open a double-wide closet. The closet was piled chest-high with pulp black-and-white magazines. "You'll have to look through it, but this is all I got," he said. "There should be three or four copies of each issue."

Lucas picked up a stack of magazines, shuffled through them. Half were about sex or fetishism. Two were different white supremacist sheets, one was a computer hacker's publication, and another involved underground radio. They all looked about the same, neatly printed in black-and-white on the cheapest grade of newsprint, with amateurish layout and canned graphics. "Which issue was this stuff in?"

"I don't know offhand. What I do is, I go down to the bookstores and get these adult novels. I take stuff out of them, type it up in columns—sometimes I rewrite them a little—and I put in the pictures people send me. I've got a post office box."

"You've got a subscription list?" Lucas asked.

"No. This goes through adult stores," McLain said. He looked up at Lucas. "Let me see that copy again."

Lucas handed it to him and he glanced at the bottom of the page, then said, "Just a minute."

"What about this Nazi shit?" Domeier asked, looking through it. "Does that go through the bookstores?"

McLain had wheeled himself to a bookcase next to the bed, and was going through a stack of *Playboys*, glancing at the party jokes on the backs of the centerfolds. "No, that's all commissioned stuff. The Nazi magazines, the phreak and hacker stuff, the surplus military, that's all commission. I just do the sex and fetish."

He scanned the backside of a blonde with blow-dried pubic hair, then checked the cover. "Here . . . I crib jokes from *Playboy* when a column doesn't fill up. This is the August issue, and here's some of the jokes on the bottom of your page. So you're looking for something printed in the last six months, which would be maybe the top fifty or sixty magazines."

Domeier found the picture ten minutes later, halfway through a magazine called *Very Good Boys:* "Here it is."

Lucas took it, glanced at the caption and the little-head joke. They were right.

The photo at the top of the page had a nude man, turned half-sideways to display an erection. In the background, a boy sprawled across an unmade bed, smirking at the camera. His hair fell forward across his forehead, and his chest and legs were thin. He looked very young, younger than he must have been. His head was turned enough that an earring was visible at his earlobe. He held a cigarette in his left hand. His left wrist lay on his hip, the hand drooping slightly. He was missing a finger.

The photo was not good, but the boy was recognizable. The man in the foreground was not. He was visible from hips to knees and was slightly out of focus: the camera had concentrated on the boy, made a sexual prop out of the man.

"You said the kid's dead?" Domeier asked, looking over Lucas' shoulder.

"Yeah."

"There ain't much there, man," Domeier said.

"No."

There wasn't: the bed had no head or footboard, nor were there any other furnishings visible except what appeared to be a bland beige or tan carpet and a pair of gym shoes off to the left. Since the picture was black-and-white, none of the colors were apparent.

Lucas looked at McLain. "Where's the original?"

McLain shrugged, wheeled his chair back a few inches. "I shredded it and threw it. If I kept this shit around, I'd be buried in paper."

"Then how come you keep this?" Lucas asked, pointing at the stack of paper in the closet.

"That's references . . . for people who want to know what I do," McLain said.

Lucas turned his head to Domeier and said, "If we slapped this asshole around a little bit, maybe threw him in the bathtub, you think people'd get pissed off?"

Domeier looked at McLain, then at Lucas. "Who're they gonna believe, two cops or a fartbag like this? You wanna throw him?"

"Wait just a fuckin' minute," McLain complained. "I'm giving you what you asked for."

"I want the goddamn original," Lucas snapped.

McLain rolled back another foot. "Man, I don't fuckin' have it."

Lucas tracked him, leaning over him, face close. "And I don't fuckin' believe it."

McLain moved back another foot and said, "Wait. You come out in the kitchen."

They trailed him back down the hall, through the living room into the kitchen. McLain wheeled his chair up to a plastic garbage bag next to the back door, pulled the tie off, and started pulling out paper.

"See, these are the pasteups for the last one. I output the stuff on a laser printer, scan the picture, paste it up and ship it. I shred the originals. See, here's an original." He passed Lucas several strips of shiny plastic paper. A shredded Polaroid. "Here's some more."

Lucas looked at the strips of plastic, which showed the back half of a nude woman, sitting on an Oriental carpet. Then McLain passed him a few more strips, which showed the front half of her, doing oral sex on a man, who, as in the Jim Harper photos, was cut off at hips and knees. McLain dumped a torn-up pizza carton on the floor, found a few more pieces of originals.

"What about the laser printer copies?" Lucas asked.

"I get the pasteups back and I shred those, too," Bobby said.

"Why do you shred them?"

"I don't want garbagemen finding dirty pictures and calling Domeier," McLain said.

"You don't keep any?" Domeier asked.

McLain looked up from the garbage bag. "Listen, you see so much of this shit, after a while they're like 29-cent stamps. And some of the people who contribute this stuff aren't so nice, so I don't wanna leave around any envelopes with addresses or that kind of stuff. I wouldn't want to bring any shit down on them."

"All right," Lucas said. He tossed the strips of Polaroid back at McLain. "You're saying you never saw the guy who took the picture of the kid."

"That's right. People send me letters and some of them have pictures. I'll put in the letter and the picture if it can be reproduced. You'd be amazed at how bad most of the pictures are."

✻

After a few more questions, they left McLain and walked back out to Lucas' four-by-four, taking McLain's four copies of the magazine.

"Did we do good?" Domeier asked.

"You did good, but *I* just shot myself in the foot," Lucas said. He turned on the dome light, opened a magazine again, and studied the picture. "The way things broke—the kid was murdered, then the LaCourts had gotten hold of the picture of him—I was sure there must be something in the picture.

Something. But there's not a fuckin' thing here."

Just a blurry picture of a man in the foreground and the kid in the background.

"Maybe you could figure out how long his dick is, go around with a ruler," Domeier said straightfaced. "You know, hang out in the men's rooms."

"Not a bad idea. Why don't you come on up?"

Lucas tore the photo page out of the magazine, threw the rest of the paper out of the truck into the parking lot, folded the page, and stuck it in his jacket pocket. "Goddammit. I thought we'd get more."

CHAPTER

✳ ✳ ✳

15

Just south of Green Bay, moving as fast as he could in the dark, Lucas ran into snow flurries, off-and-on squalls dropping wet, quarter-sized flakes. He paused at a McDonald's on the edge of Green Bay, got a cheeseburger and coffee, and pushed on. West of Park Falls on County F, he slowed for what he thought was a highway accident, two cars and a pickup on the road in the middle of nowhere.

A man in an arctic parka waved him through, but he stopped, rolled down his window.

"Got a problem?"

The man's face was a small oval surrounded by fur, only one eye visible at a time. He pointed toward a cluster of people gathered around a snowbank. "Got a deer down. She was walking down the road like she didn't know where she was, and she kept falling down. Starvin', I think."

"I'm a cop, I've got a pistol."

"Well, we're gonna try to tie her down, get her into town and feed her. She's just a young one."

"Good luck."

The snow grew heavier as he left Price County for Lincoln. Back in town, under the streetlights, the fat flakes turned the place into a corny advertisement for Christmas.

He found Weather and Climpt at her house, playing gin rummy in the living room.

"How'd it go?" Climpt asked. He dumped a hand without looking at it.

"We found the picture; not much in it," Lucas said. He took out the copy he'd ripped from the magazine, passed it to Climpt. Climpt opened it, looked at it, said, "That narrows it down to white guys."

Lucas shook his head and Weather reached for the photo, but Climpt held it away from her. "Not for ladies," he said.

"Kiss my ass, Gene," Weather said.

"Yes, ma'am, whatever you say," Climpt said with a dry chuckle. But he handed the photo back to Lucas. "Are you gonna bag out here again?"

"Yeah," Lucas said. "But I'd like to stick her somewhere that nobody knows about."

Weather put her hands on her hips. "That's right, talk around me—I'm a lamp," she said.

Climpt looked at her, sighed, said, "Goddamn feminists." And to Lucas: "You could put her at my place."

"Everybody in town would know about it in ten minutes," Weather said. "They know my car, they know your schedule . . . if there were lights in your place when you're supposed to be working, they'd be calling the cops."

"Yeah."

"I'm okay here as long as you guys are around," Weather said, looking from one of them to the other.

❋

When Climpt had gone, Weather took Lucas by the collar, kissed him, and said, "Show me the picture."

He got his coat and handed it to her.

"Quite the display," she said, peering at it. She shook her head. "I've probably got thirty patients who look more or less like that—the belly and the fat butt. How do you identify them from that?" She shook her head. "You won't get any help from me."

"Bums me out," Lucas said, running a hand up through

his hair. "We've got to find some way to crank up the pressure. I thought there'd be something in the picture. If it didn't ID the guy, there'd be *something.*"

"I'll tell you one thing," she said, poking the photograph at him. "If Jim Harper was involved in a sex ring, I can't believe that Russ wasn't aware of it. If blackmail ever occurred to anybody, it'd be Russ."

Lucas took the photo back, stared through it, thinking. Then: "You're right. We've gotta squeeze him. Squeeze him for public consumption. Maybe our asshole will come after him, or maybe Harper can put the finger on him." He wandered around the living room, touching her things: the photos of her parents, a Hummel doll, thinking. "If we play these Schoeneckers off against Harper . . . Huh . . ." He carefully folded the photograph, took his billfold out of his pocket, and stuck the photo in the fold, where he'd see it every time he paid for something. "How're you doing?"

She shrugged. "I'm tired but I can't sleep. I guess I'm a little scared."

"You should get out. Visit some friends in the Cities."

She shook her head. "Nope. He's not going to get on top of me."

"That's a little dumb."

"That's the way it is, though," she said. "How about you. Tired?"

"Stiff from the drive," Lucas said. He yawned and stretched.

"When I bought this place, the only big change I made was to fix up my bathroom. I've got a big whirlpool tub back there. Why don't you go in and lay in some hot water? I'll put together a snack."

"Terrific," he said.

The tub looked like it might be black marble, and was easily six feet long. He half-filled it, fooled with a control panel until he got the whirlpool jets working, then eased himself into it. He found he could rest his head on a back ledge and float free in the hot water. The heat smoothed him out, took him out of the truck.

The photograph had to be the key, and now he had the

photograph. Why couldn't he see it? What was it?

The door opened and Weather walked in, wearing a robe, carrying a bottle of wine. Lucas, embarrassed, sat up, but she pulled off the robe. Naked, she tested the water with her foot. She had small, solid breasts, a smooth, supple back, and long legs.

"Hot," she said, stepping into the far end of the tub. She might have been blushing or it might have been the hot water.

"What about the snack?" Lucas asked.

"You're looking at it, honey," she said.

❅

Fourth full day of the investigation: he felt like he'd been in Ojibway County forever. Felt like he'd known Weather forever.

Lucas made it into the sheriff's office a few minutes after eight. The day was warmer, above zero, with damp spots in the streets where ice-remover chemicals had cut through the snow. The sky was an impenetrable gray. Despite the clouds hanging overhead, Lucas felt . . . light.

Different. He could still smell Weather, although he wasn't sure if the smell was real or just something he'd memorized and was holding on to.

There was nothing light about Carr. He'd been heavy and pink, even at the LaCourt killing. Now he was gray-faced, drawn. He looked not hungry or starving, but desiccated, as though he were dying of thirst.

"Get it?" he asked when Lucas walked in.

Lucas handed him a copy of the porno magazine, folded open to the page with Jim Harper on it. "Is this it?" Carr asked, studying the photo.

"That's it. That's what the LaCourts had, anyway," Lucas said.

Carr held it to the window for extra light. Henry Lacey ambled in, nodded to Lucas, and Carr handed him the photo. "Who is it, Henry? Who's the fat guy?"

Lacey looked at it, then at Lucas. "I don't see anything. Am I missing something?"

"I don't think so," Lucas said. Carr put his thumb to his mouth, began nibbling his cuticles, then quickly put his hand back on his desk, his movements jerky, out of sync. Strung-out. "When was the last time you had any sleep?" Lucas asked.

"Can't remember," Carr said vaguely. "Somebody tell me what to do."

Lucas said, "How tight are you with the editor of the *Register*? And the radio station."

"Same thing," Carr said. He spun in his chair and looked out his window toward the city garage. "The answer is, pretty tight. Danny Jones is the brother to Bob Jones."

"The junior high principal?"

"Yup. We played poker most Wednesday nights. Before this happened, anyway," Carr said.

"If you just flat told him what you wanted in the paper, or on the radio, and explained that you needed it done to break this case, would he buy it?"

Carr, still staring out the window, thought it over, then said, "In this case—probably."

Lucas outlined his proposal: that they go to the county attorney with the photographs they'd found of Jim Harper and get an arrest warrant for Russ Harper. They would charge Harper with promoting child pornography, drop him in jail.

"He'll bail out in twenty minutes," Lacey objected.

"Not if we work it right," Lucas said. "We'll pick him up this afternoon, question him, charge him tonight. We won't have to take him to court until Monday. We tell the *Register* that he's been arrested in connection with a pornography ring that we uncovered during the investigation of the LaCourt murders. We also leak the word that Harper's dealing—that he's trying to make an immunity deal if he turns in other members of the ring. And we tell Harper that we'll give him immunity unless the Schoeneckers come in first. Anything about the Schoeneckers, by the way?"

"Nothing yet," Carr said, shaking his head. "What you're saying about Russ Harper is . . . we set him up. I mean, the charges wouldn't hold water."

"We're not setting him up. We're using him to make something happen," Lucas said. "And who knows? Maybe he has some ideas about the killer."

"If he doesn't, he'll sue our butts. He'll probably sue our butts anyway," Carr said.

"A good attorney would get him in court and stick those pictures of Jim right up his ass," Lucas said. Lucas leaned across the deck. "I'll tell you, Shelly, there's a possibility that the LaCourt murders and the Mueller kid and Jim Harper have nothing to do with this sex ring. Possible, but I don't believe it. There's a connection. We just haven't found it. And Weather said last night she can't believe a guy like Harper didn't have some idea of what his kid was up to."

"We've got to do it, Shelly," Lacey said somberly. "We've got nothing else going for us. Not a frigging thing."

"Let's do it then," Carr said. He looked up at Lucas, exhaustion in his eyes. "And you and me, we've got to go talk to Phil Bergen again."

❋

Bergen was waiting for them. Like Carr, he'd changed. But Bergen looked rested, clear-faced. Sober.

"I know what you're here for," he said when he let them in to the rectory. "Bob Dell called me. I didn't know he was homosexual until he called."

"You've never . . ." Lucas began.

"Never." Bergen turned to Carr. "Shelly, I never would have believed that'd you'd think . . ."

"He didn't believe it," Lucas said. "I brought it up. I looked at a plat map of the lake road, saw Dell's house, made some inquiries, and maybe jumped to the wrong conclusion."

"You did."

Lucas shrugged. "I was trying to figure out why you might claim that you were at the LaCourts' when you weren't, and why you couldn't tell us." They were standing in the entry, coats, gloves, and hats still on. Bergen faced them on his feet, didn't invite them to sit.

"I was at the LaCourts'. I was there," Bergen said.

Lucas looked him over, then nodded. "Then we've still got a problem," he said. "The time."

"Forget the time," Bergen said. "I swear: I was there and they were alive. I believe the killer came just as I left—maybe even was there before I left, and waited until I'd gone—and killed them and spread the gas around, but accidently set it off too soon. If the firemen are wrong by a few minutes, then the times work out and you're barking up the wrong tree. And you've managed to severely . . . damage me in the process."

Carr looked at Lucas. Lucas looked at Bergen for a long beat, nodded, and said, "Maybe."

Bergen looked from Lucas to Carr, waiting, and Carr finally said, "Let's go." To Bergen: "Phil, I'm sorry about this. You know I am."

Bergen nodded, tight-mouthed, unforgiving.

Outside, Carr asked, "Do you believe him now?"

"I believe he's not gay."

"That's a start." They walked to the car in silence, then Carr said wearily, "And thanks for taking the rap on Bob Dell. Maybe when this is over, Phil and I can patch things up."

"I'm going to get Gene and take Harper. Why don't you catch a nap for a couple of hours?"

"Can't. My wife'd be cleaning," Carr said. "That's pretty noisy. I can't sleep worth a damn when she's working."

Lucas called Climpt on the radio, got him headed back toward the courthouse. While Carr returned to his office, Lucas found Henry Lacey talking to a deputy.

"I need to talk to you for a minute," he said.

Lacey nodded, said, "Check you later, Carl." And to Lucas, "What's going on?"

"There're rumors that Shelly's having an affair with a lady at the church. I think I met her the other night."

"So . . . ?" Lacey was defensive.

"Is she married or what?"

"Widowed," Lacey said reluctantly.

"You think you could get Shelly over to her house? On the sly? Get him a nap, get her to stroke him a little? The guy's on the edge of something bad."

Lacey showed the shadow of a smile and nodded. "I'll do it. I should have thought of it."

✳

Lucas, Climpt, and the young deputy Dusty, who'd first talked to John Mueller at the school, took Harper out of his gas station at 4:30, just before full dark.

Lucas and Climpt ate a long lunch, reviewed the newest information coming out of the Madison laboratory crew at the LaCourt house, stalled around until the county judge left the courthouse, then picked up Dusty and headed out to Knuckle Lake. When they pulled into the station in Climpt's Suburban, they could see Harper through the gas station window, counting change into a cash register. He came out snarling.

"If you ain't got a warrant I want you off my property," he said.

"You're under arrest," Climpt said.

Harper stopped so quickly he almost skidded. "Say what?"

"You're under arrest for the promotion of child pornography. Put your hands on the car."

Harper, dumbfounded, took the position on the truck. Dusty shook him down, then cuffed his hands. A kid who'd been working in the repair bay came out to watch, nervously wiping his hands with an oily rag. "You want him to stay open or you want to close down?" Climpt asked.

"You stay open until the regular quitting time, and there better be every last dime in the register," Harper shouted at the kid. He turned and looked at Lucas. "You motherfucker." And then back at the kid: "I'll call you. I should be out real quick."

"There's no bail hearing until Monday. Court's closed," Climpt told him.

"You fuckers," Harper snarled. "You're trying to do me." And he shouted at the kid: "You're in charge over the weekend. But I'm gonna count every dime."

On the way back to town, Lucas turned over to look at Harper, cuffed in the back. "I'll say two things to you, and you might talk them over with your attorney. The first is, the Schoeneckers. Think about them. The next thing is, *somebody* is gonna get immunity to testify. But only one somebody."

"You can kiss my ass."

Harper called an attorney from the jail's booking room. The attorney ran across the street from the bank building, spoke with Harper privately for ten minutes, then came out to discuss bail with the county attorney.

"We'll ask the judge to set it at a quarter million on Monday, in court," the county attorney said. He was a mildly fat man with light-brown eyes and pale brown hair, and he wore a medium-brown suit with buffed natural loafers.

"A quarter million? Eldon, my lord, Russ Harper runs a filling station," said Harper's attorney. He was a thin, weathered man with long yellow hair and weather-roughened hands. "Get real. And we figure this is important enough that we can get the judge out here tomorrow morning."

"I wouldn't want to call him on a Saturday. He goes fishing on Saturdays, and gets quite a little toot on, sittin' out there in that shack," the county attorney said. "And Russ's station could be worth a quarter million. Maybe."

"There's no way."

"We'll talk to the judge Monday," the county attorney said.

"I'm told that this gentleman"—Harper's attorney nodded at Lucas—"and Gene Climpt have already beat up my client on one occasion—and this is more harassment."

"Russ Harper's not the most reliable source, and we're talking about child pornography here," the county attorney said. But he looked at Lucas and Climpt. "And I'm prepared to guarantee that Mr. Harper will be perfectly safe in jail over the weekend. If he's not, somebody else will be sitting in there with him."

"He's safe enough," said Lacey, who'd joined them. "Nobody'll lay a finger on him."

Carr was in his office, looking perceptibly brighter.

"Get some sleep?" Lucas asked. "You're looking better."

"Three, four hours. Henry talked me into it," he said, a ribbon of guilt and pleasure running through his voice. "I need a week. All done with Harper?"

"He's inside," Lucas said.

"Good. Wanna call Dan?"

❇

Dan Jones was the perfect double of the junior high principal. "We're twin brothers," he said. "He went into education, I went into journalism."

"Dan was all-state baseball, Bob was all-state football. I remember when you boys were tearing the place up," Carr said, his face animated. And Lucas thought: *He does like it, the good-old-boy political schmoozing.*

"Glory days," said Dan. To Lucas: "Did you play?"

"Hockey," Lucas said.

"Yeah, typical Minnesota," Dan said, grinning. Then he turned to Carr and asked, "Exactly what is it you want, Shelly?"

Carr filled Jones in about Harper, and Jones took notes on a reporter's pad. "We don't want to mislead you," Carr said, just slightly formal. "We're not saying Russ killed the LaCourts—in fact, we know he didn't. But as background, so you won't go astray, we want you to know that we developed the information about the porno ring out of the murder investigation."

"So you think the two are related?"

"It's very possible . . . if you sort of leaned that way, you'd be okay," Carr said.

"To be frank—no bullshit—we want the story out to put pressure on the other members of this child-molester group, whoever they are. We need to break something open, but we don't want you to say that," Lucas said. "We think there's a chance that Harper'll try to deal. Go for immunity or reduced charges. That could be significant. But we'd like to have it reported as rumor," Lucas said.

Climpt was digging around on his desk, found the porno magazine from Milwaukee, said, "You can refer to this, but you can't say directly what's in it," and passed it across to the newspaper editor.

Jones recoiled. "Jesus H. Christ on a crutch," he said. Then he remembered, and glanced up at Carr: "Sorry, Shelly."

"Well, I know what you mean," Carr said lamely.

"Horseshit reproduction," Jones said, turning the paper in his hand. "This is like toilet paper."

"In more ways than one," Carr said. "What about the story? Can you do something with it?"

Jones was on his feet. "Oh, hell yes! The Russ Harper arrest is big. The AP'll want that, and I can string it down to Milwaukee and St. Paul. Sure. People are so freaked out I've been talking to old man Donohue . . ."

Climpt said to Lucas, "Donohue owns the paper."

". . . about putting out an extra. With Johnny Mueller and now this, I'll talk to him tonight, see if we can get it out Sunday morning. I'll need the arrest reports on Russ."

"Got them right here," Carr said, passing him some Xeroxed copies of the arrest log.

"Thanks. Whether or not Donohue goes with the extra, we'll have it on the radio in half an hour. It'll be all over town in an hour."

✳

When Jones had gone, Carr leaned back in his chair, closed his eyes, and said, "Think we'll shake something loose?"

"Something," Lucas said.

CHAPTER

* * *

16

Weather Karkinnen threw her scrub suit into the laundry rack and stepped into the shower. Her nipples felt sore and she scratched at them, wondering, then realized: beard burn. Davenport hadn't shaved for an entire day when she attacked him in the bathtub, and he had a beard like a porcupine.

She laughed at herself: she hadn't felt so alive in years. Lucas had been an energetic lover, but also, at times, strangely soft, as though he were afraid he might hurt her. The combination was irresistible. She thought about the tub again as she dried off with one of the rough hospital towels: that was the most contrived entrance she'd ever engineered. The bottle of wine, the robe slipping off . . .

She laughed aloud, her laughter echoing off the tiles of the surgeons' locker room.

❋

She left, hurrying: almost six-thirty. Lucas said he'd be done with Harper by six or seven. Maybe they could drive over to Hayward for dinner, or one of those places off Teal Lake or Lost Land Lake. Good restaurants over there.

As she left the locker room, she stopped at the nurses' station to get the final list for the morning. Civilians sometimes thought surgeons worked every week or two, after an exhaustive study of the patient. More often, they worked every day, and sometimes two or three times a day, with little interaction with the patient at all. Weather was building a reputation in the North Woods, and now had referrals from all the adjoining counties. Sometimes she thought it was a conspiracy by the referring docs to keep her busy, to pin her down.

". . . Charlie Denning, fixing his toe," she said. "He can hardly walk, so you'll have to get a wheelchair out to his car. His wife is bringing him in."

As they went through it, she was aware that the charge nurse kept checking her, a small smile on her face. Everybody knew that Lucas was staying at her house in some capacity, and Weather suspected that a few of the nurses had, during the day, figured out the capacity. She didn't care.

". . . probably gonna have to clean her up, and I want the whole area shaved. I doubt that she did a very good job of it, she's pretty old and I'm not sure how clearly I was getting through to her."

The charge nurse's family had been friends of her family, though the nurse was ten years older. Still, they were friends, and when Weather finished with the work list, she started for the door, then turned and said, "Is it that obvious?"

"Pretty obvious," the nurse said. "The other girls say he's a well-set-up man, the ones who have seen him."

Weather laughed. "My God—small towns, I love 'em." She started away again. The nurse called, "Don't wear him out, Doctor," and as she went out the door, Weather was still laughing.

❉

Her escort was a surly, heavyset deputy named Arne Bruun. He'd been two years behind her in high school. He'd been president of the Young Republicans Club and allegedly had now drifted so far to the right that the Republicans wouldn't have him. He stood up when she walked into the lobby, rolled a copy of *Guns and Ammo,* and stuck it in his coat pocket.

"Ready to roll?" He was pleasant enough but had the strong jaw-muscle complex of a marginal paranoid.

"Ready to roll," she said.

He went through the door first, looked around, waved her on, and they walked together to the parking lot. The days were beginning to lengthen, but it was fully dark, and the thermometer had crashed again. The Indians called it the Moon of the Falling Cold.

Bruun unlocked the passenger door of the Suburban, let her climb up, shut it behind her, and walked around the nose of the truck. The hospital was on the south edge of town; Weather lived on the north side. The quickest route to her home was down the frontage road along Highway 77 to Buhler's Road, and across the highway at the light, avoiding the traffic of Main Street.

"Gettin' cold again," Bruun said as he climbed into the truck cab. Following Carr's instructions, she'd called for a lift home. Bruun had been on patrol, and had waited in the lobby for only a few minutes: the truck was still warm inside. "If it gets much worse, there won't be any deer alive next year. Or anything else."

"I understand they're gonna truck in hay."

They were talking about the haylift when she saw the snowmobile on the side of the road. The rider was kneeling beside it, working on it, fifteen feet from the stop sign for Buhler's Road. There was a trail beside the road, and sleds broke down all the time. But something caught her attention; the man beside it looked down toward them while his hands continued working.

"Sled broke down," she said.

Bruun was already watching it. "Yup." He touched the brake to slow for the stop sign. They were almost on top of the sled. Weather watched it, watched it. The Suburban was rolling to a stop, just past the sled, the headlights reflecting off the snowbanks, back on the rider. She saw him stand up, saw the gun come out, saw him running toward her window.

"Gun," she screamed. "He's got . . ."

She dropped in the seat and Bruun hit the gas and the window six inches above her head exploded and Bruun shrieked with pain, jerked the steering wheel. The truck skidded, lurched, came around, and the rear window shattered over her, as though somebody had hit it with a hammer. Weather looked to her left; Bruun's head and face were covered with blood, and he crouched over the wheel, the truck still sliding in a circle, engine screaming, tires screeching . . .

The shotgun roared again: she heard it this time, the first time she'd heard it. And heard the shot pecking at the door by her elbow. Bruun grunted, stayed with the wheel . . . they were running now, the truck bumping . . .

"Gotta get back, gotta get . . ." Bruun groaned. Weather, sensing the speed, pushed herself up in the seat. The side window was gone, but the mirror was still there. The rider was on the sled, coming after them, and she flashed to the night of the murders, the sled running in the ditch . . .

They were passing a tree farm on the road back to the hospital parking lot, the straight, regimented rows of pine flashing by like a black picket fence.

"No, no," she said. Heart in her throat. Looked into the mirror, the sled closing, closing . . .

"Gun coming up!" she shouted at Bruun.

Bruun put his head down and Weather slid to the floor. Two quick shots, almost lost in the roar of the engine, pellets hammering through the shattered back window into the cab, another shot crashing through the back window into the windshield, ricocheting. Bruun groaned again and said, "Hit, I'm hit."

But he kept his foot on the pedal and the speed went up. The shotgun was silent. Weather sat higher, looking out the shattered side window, then out the back.

The road was empty. "He's gone," she said.

Bruun's chin was almost on the hub of the wheel. "Hold on," he grated. He hit the brake, but too late.

The entrance to the hospital parking lot was not straight in. The entry road went sharply right, specifically to slow incoming traffic. They were there—and they were going much too fast to make the turn. Weather braced herself, locking her arms against the dashboard. A small flower garden was buried under the snow where they'd hit. There was a foot-high wall around it . . .

The truck fishtailed when Bruun hit the brake, and then hit the flower-garden wall. The truck bounced, twisting, plowing through the snow, engine whining . . .

There were people in the parking lot.

She saw them clearly, sharply, frozen, like the face of the queen of hearts when somebody riffles a deck of cards.

Then the truck was in the parking lot, moving sideways. It hit a snowbank and rolled onto its side, almost as if it had been tripped. She felt it going, grabbed the door handle, tried to hold on, felt the door handle wrench away from her, fell, felt the softness of the deputy beneath her . . . Heard Bruun screaming . . .

And finally it stopped.

She'd lost track of anything but the sensations of impact. But she was alive, sitting on top of Bruun. She looked to her left, through the cracked windshield, saw legs . . .

Voices. "Stay there, stay there . . ."

And she thought: *Fire.*

She could smell it, feel it. She'd worked in a burn unit, wanted nothing to do with burns. She pulled herself up, carefully avoiding Bruun, who was alive, holding himself, moaning, "Oh boy, oh boy . . ."

She unlocked the passenger-side door, tried to push it open. It moved a few inches. More voices. Shouting.

Faces at the windshield, then somebody on top. A man looked in the side window: Robbie, the night-orderly body-builder, who she'd not-very-secretly made fun of because of his hobby. Now he pried the door open with sheer strength, and she'd never been so happy to see a muscleman. He was scared for her: "Are you all right, Doctor?"

"Snowmobile," she said. "Where's the man on the snow-mobile?"

The body-builder looked up over into the group of people still gathering, and, puzzled, asked, "Who?"

❋

Weather sat on the edge of the hospital bed in her scrub suit. Her left arm and leg were bruised, and she had three small cuts on the back of her left hand, none requiring stitches. No apparent internal injuries. Bruun was in the recovery room. She'd taken pellets out of his arm and chest cavity.

"You're gonna hurt like a sonofagun tomorrow," said Rice, the GP who'd come to look at her, and later assisted in the operation on Bruun. "You can bet on it. Take a bunch of ibuprofen before you go to bed. And don't do anything too strenuous tonight." His face was solemn, but his eyes flicked at Lucas.

"Yeah, yeah—take off," Weather said.

❋

"Does *everybody* know?" Lucas asked when Rice had gone.

"I imagine there're a few Christian-school children that the secret's been kept from," Weather said.

"Mmmm."

"So what'd you find?" she asked.

"Just that you oughta be dead. Again. You would be if Bruun hadn't kept the truck rolling."

"And the asshole got away."

"Yeah. He waited in the trees by the stop sign until he saw you coming. After he fired the first shots, he followed you down the road to the spot where the power line cuts through the tree farm and then cut off through the trees. There was no chance of following him unless we'd been right there with a sled. He must've counted on that. He did a pretty good job setting it up. If Bruun had stuck the truck in the ditch, he'd of finished you off, no problem."

"Why didn't he shoot me through the door?"

"He tried," Lucas said. "Sometimes a double-ought pellet will make it through a car door, but most of the time it won't. Three went all the way through. One hit Bruun and the other two hit the dashboard. And we think Bruun got the arm hit through the broken window."

"Jesus," she said. She looked at Lucas. He was leaning against an exam table, his arms folded across his chest, his voice calm, almost sleepy. He might have been talking about a ball game. "You're not pissed enough," she said.

Lucas had come in just before she'd gone into the operating room, and waited. Hadn't touched her. Just watched her. She got down from the examination table, winced. Rice was right. She'd be sore.

"I was thinking all the way over here that I'm just too fuckin' vain and it almost caught up to me," Lucas said. He pushed away from the exam table and caught a fistful of hair at the back of her head, squeezed it, held her by the hair, head tipped up. "I want you the fuck out of here," he said angrily. "You're not gonna get hurt. You understand that? You're . . ."

"Why are you vain?" She'd grabbed his shirtfront with both hands, held on. Their faces were four inches apart, and they rocked back and forth.

He stopped, still holding her hair. "Because I thought he was coming after you because of me. I thought he went after the Mueller kid because of me."

"He didn't?"

"No. It's you he wants. You know him or you know something about him. Or he thinks you do. You don't know what it is, but he does."

She said, "Another snowmobile ran alongside my Jeep when I was coming back from the LaCourts' house, on the first night. I thought he was crazy."

"You didn't tell me."

"I didn't know."

He let go of her hair and put his arm around her shoulder, squeezed her, careful about her left arm. She squeezed with her right arm, then Lucas stepped back, took out his wallet, unfolded the photograph he'd stuck there.

"You know this fat man," he said. "He tried to kill you again. Who is he?"

"I don't know." She stared at the photo. "I don't have the foggiest."

CHAPTER

*** * ***

17

The priest said, "I'm okay, Joe. Seriously."

He stood in the hall between the kitchen and the bedroom. He was grateful for the call and at the same time resented it: he should be doing the ministering.

"I had a decent day," he said, his head bobbing. "You know all the talk about me and the LaCourts—I was afraid to say anything that might make it worse. It was driving me crazy. But I found a way to handle it."

His tongue felt like sandpaper, from sucking on lemon drops. He'd gone through two dozen large sacks the last time he went off booze. He was now working his way through the first of what might be several more.

Joe was talking about *one day at a time,* and Bergen only half listened. When he'd gone off booze the year before, he hadn't really *wanted* to quit. He'd simply had to. He was losing his parish and he was dying. So he'd gone sober, he'd stopped dying, he'd gotten the parish back. That hadn't cured the problems for which bourbon was medication: the loneliness, the isolation, the troubles pressed upon him, for which he had no real answers. The drift in the faith.

This time he'd sat down to write an excuse for himself, a pitiful plea for understanding. Instead, he'd written the strongest lines of his life. From the reaction he'd gotten at the Mass that morning, he'd gotten through. He'd touched the parishioners and they'd touched him. He felt the isolation crumble; saw the possibility of an end to his loneliness.

He might, he thought, be cured. Dangerous thought. He'd suck the lemon drops anyway. Better safe . . .

". . . I won't be going out. I swear. Joe, things have changed. I've got something to do. Okay . . . And thanks."

The priest dropped the receiver back on the hook, sighed, and returned to his work chair. He wrote on a Zeos 386 computer, hammering down the words.

There's a devil among us. And somebody here in this church may know who it is.

(He would look around at this point, touching the eyes of each and every person in the church, exploiting the silence, allowing the stress to build.)

The murders of the LaCourt family must spring from deep in a man's tortured character, deep in a man's dirty heart. Ask yourself: Do I know this man? Do I suspect who he might be? Deep in my heart do I believe?

He worked for an hour, read through what he had. Excellent. He picked up the papers, carried them to his bedroom, and faced the full-length dressing mirror.

"There's a devil among us . . ." he began. No. He stopped. His voice should be slower, deeper, reflective of grief. He dropped it a half-octave, put some gravel into it: "There's a devil among us . . ."

Should he show some confusion, some bewilderment? Or would that be read as weakness?

". . . deep in a man's dirty heart," he said slowly, watching himself in the glass. He wagged his head, as though astonished that these things could take place here, in Ojibway County, and then, yet more slowly, but his voice rising urgently into something like anger: "Do I know this man? Do I suspect who he might be?"

He would rally the community, Philip Bergen would.

And in turn the community would save him. He looked at the paper, relishing the flow of it.

But . . . he peered at it. Too many *hearts* there, too many *deeps*. He was repeating words, which set up a dissonance in the listener. Okay. Get rid of the last *deep* altogether and change the last *heart* to *soul*. ". . . in my soul do I believe . . ."

He worked in front of the mirror, watching himself through his steel-rimmed glasses, his jowls bouncing, trembling with anger and righteousness, his words booming around the small room.

Except for the sound of his own voice, the house was quiet: he could hear the Black Forest clock ticking behind him, the air ducts snapping as they expanded when the furnace came on, a scraping sound from outside—a snow shovel.

He went to the kitchen for a glass of water, caught sight of himself in a glass-fronted cabinet as he drank it. An older man now, permanent wrinkles in his forehead, hair thinning, paunch descending; a man coarsened by the work, a man whose best days were behind him. A man who would never leave Ojibway County . . . Ah, well.

He heard the ragged drag of a shovel again, went to the front window, parted the drapes with his fingertips, looked out. Across the street and three houses down, one of the McLaren kids was scraping at a sidewalk with a snow shovel. Small kid, eleven o'clock at night. The McLarens were a family in distress: alcohol again, McLaren himself gone most of the time. Bergen turned back to his work chair, made a few more changes on the word processing screen, then saved the sermon to both the hard disk and a backup floppy, printed a new copy for himself.

There's a devil among us. And somebody here in this church may know who it is.

Maybe he should harden it:

Somebody here in this church knows who it is.

But that might suggest more than he wanted.

❋

The knock at the door startled him.

He stopped in midsentence, turned, looked at the door, and muttered to himself, "Bless me." And then smiled at himself. Bless me? He *was* getting old. Must be Shelly Carr, coming to talk. Or Joe, making a check?

Stepping to the window, he parted the drapes again and looked out sideways at the porch. A man on the porch, a big man. Davenport, his interrogator, was a big man. With Lucas' face in his mind, Bergen went to the door, opened it, could see almost nothing through the frosted-over storm-door glass, pushed open the storm door and peered out. "Yes?"

❋

The Iceman's face was wrapped in a red-plaid scarf, the top of his head covered by a ski mask rolled up and worn like a watch cap. From the street, his face would be a furry unrecognizable cube, muffled and hatted, like everybody else. When he passed the time and temperature sign on the bank, it had been four below zero.

He was high from the attack on Weather, and angry. He'd missed again. Things didn't work like he thought they would. They just did not. He needed to plan better. He didn't foresee the possibility that the deputy would keep the truck rolling. Somehow, in his mind, the first shotgun blasts derailed the truck. But why would he think that? Too much TV?

Now the cops would focus on Weather. Who did she know that was involved in the case? He had to give them an answer, something that would hold them for a while.

And thinking about it, he became excited. This plan would work. This one would . . .

He stood on the rectory stoop, his left hand wrapped around the stock of the .44. Bergen was home, all right. The lights were on, and he'd seen a shadow on the drapes from where he'd been watching down the street. Facing the house, he reached up with his gloved right hand and pulled the ski mask down across his face. Then he knocked and half-turned to look back across the street, where some crazy kid was piling snow in a heap in his front yard. The kid paid no attention to him. He turned back to the house and gripped the storm-door handle with his right hand.

Bergen came to the door, pushed the storm door open two or three inches, leaned his head toward it. "Yes?"

The .44 was already coming up in the Iceman's left hand. With his right he jerked the door open, surged forward, the gun out, pointed at Bergen's forehead.

The priest reeled back, one hand up, as though to ward off the bullet.

"Get back," the Iceman snarled. "Get back, get back."

He thrust the oversized pistol at the priest, who was backing through his living room. "What?" he said. "What?"

The Iceman jerked the storm door shut, then backed against the inner door until he heard the latch snap.

"Sit down on the couch. Sit down."

"What?" Bergen's eyes were large, his face white. He made a broom-whisking motion with his hand, like he'd sweep the Iceman away. "Get out of here. Get out."

"Shut up or I'll blow your fuckin' brains out," the Iceman snapped.

"What?" Bergen seemed stuck on the word, uncomprehending. He dropped onto the couch, head tilted back, mouth open.

"I want the truth about the LaCourts," the Iceman rasped. "They were my friends."

Bergen stared at him, trying to penetrate the ski mask. He knew the voice, the bulk, but not well. Who was this? "I had nothing to do with it. I don't know myself what happened," Bergen said. "Are you going to kill me?"

"Maybe," the Iceman said. "Quite possibly. But that depends on what you have to say." He dipped into his parka pocket and took out a brown bag. "If you killed them."

"I tell you . . ."

"You're an alky, I know all about it," the Iceman said. He'd worked on this part of his speech. The priest must have confidence in him. "You were drinking again yesterday. You said so in Mass. And I asked myself, how do you get the truth out of a boozer?"

He stuck the brown paper bag in the armpit of the hand that held the gun, fumbled at the top of the bag with his gloved right hand, and pulled free a bottle of Jim Beam. "You give him some booze, that's how. A lot of booze. Then we'll get the truth out of him."

"I'm not drinking," Bergen said.

"Then I'll *know*, won't I?" the Iceman asked. "And if I know . . . I'll drop the hammer on you, priest. This is a .44 Magnum, and they'd find your brains in the next block." He'd moved around to the end of the couch, glanced down at the water glass on the end table. Excellent.

"Lean back on the couch," he ordered.

The priest settled back.

"If you try to get up, I'll kill you."

"Listen, Claudia LaCourt was one of my dearest friends."

"Shut up." The Iceman set the bottle on the table, turned the loosened top with his glove hand, took the top off and dropped it on the table. With his gun hand, he reached up, hooked his scarf with his thumb, pulled it down under his chin, then pushed his ski mask up until it was just over his upper lip.

With his glove hand, he picked up the bottle. He pointed the gun at the priest again, put the bottle to his lips, stuck his tongue into the neck of it to block the liquor, swallowed spit, took the bottle down, wiped his lips with the back of his gun hand. Bergen had to have confidence in the booze, too.

"I got you the good stuff, Father," he said, smacking his lips. He poured the water glass full almost to the top.

"Drink it down," he said. "Just slide across the couch, pick it up, and drink it down."

"I can't just drink it straight down."

"Bullshit. An alky like you could drink twice that much. Besides, you don't have much choice. If you don't drink it, I'm going to blow you up. Drink it."

Bergen edged across the couch, picked it up, looked at it, then slowly drank it; a quarter of it, then half.

"Drink the rest," the Iceman said, his voice rising. The gun waggled a foot from Bergen's head.

He drank the rest, the alcohol exploding in his stomach.

"Close your eyes," the Iceman said.

"What?"

"Close your eyes. You heard me. And keep them tight."

Bergen could feel the alcohol clawing its way into him, already spreading through his stomach into his lungs. *So good, so good*... But he didn't need it. He really didn't. He closed his eyes, clenched them. If he could get through this . . .

The Iceman picked up the bottle, poured another glass of bourbon, stepped back.

"Open your eyes. Pick up the glass."

"It'll kill me," Bergen protested feebly. He picked up the glass, looked at it.

"You don't have to drink this straight down. Just sip it. But I want it gone," he said. The gun barrel was three feet from Bergen's eyes, and unwavering. "Now—when was the last time you saw the LaCourts?"

"It was the night of the murder," Bergen said. "I was there, all right . . ." As he launched into the story he'd told the sheriff, the fear was still with him, but now it was joined by the certainty brought by alcohol. He was right, he was innocent, and he could convince this man. The intruder had kept his mask on: no point in doing that if he really planned to kill. *So he didn't plan to kill.* Bergen, pleased with himself for figuring it out, took another large swallow of bourbon when the Iceman prompted him, and another, and was surprised when the glass was suddenly empty.

"You're still sober enough to lie."

The glass was full again, and the man's voice seemed to be drifting away. Bergen sputtered, "Listen . . . you," and his head dropped on his shoulder and he nearly giggled. The impulse was smothered by what seemed to be a dark stain. The stain was spreading through his body, through his brain . . .

Took a drink, choking this time, dropped the glass, vaguely aware of the bourbon on him . . .

And now aware of something wrong. He'd never drunk this much alcohol this fast, but he'd come close a few times. It had never gotten on him like this; he'd never had this dark spreading stain in his mind.

Nothing was right; he could barely see; he looked up at the gunman, but his head wouldn't work right, couldn't turn. Tried to stand . . .

Couldn't breathe, couldn't breathe, felt the coldness at his lips, sputtered, alcohol running into him, a hand on his forehead . . . he swallowed, swallowed, swallowed. And at the last instant understood the Iceman: who he was, what he was doing. He tried, but he couldn't move . . . couldn't move.

✳

The Iceman pressed the priest's head back into the couch, emptied most of the rest of the bottle into him. When he was finished, he stepped back, looked down at his handiwork. The priest was almost gone. The Iceman took the priest's hand, wrapped it around the bottle, smeared it a bit, wrapped the other hand around it. The priest had sputtered alcohol all over himself, and that was fine.

The Iceman, moving quickly, put two prescription pill bottles on the table, the labels torn off. A single pill remained in one of the bottles to help the cops with identification. The priest, still sitting upright on the couch, his head back, mumbled something, then made a sound like a snore or a gargle. The Iceman had never been in the rectory before, but the office was just off the living room and he found it immediately. A yellow pad sat next to an IBM electric. He turned the typewriter on, inserted a sheet of paper with his gloved hand, pulled off his glove and typed the suicide note.

That done, he rolled the paper out without touching it, got the copy of the Sunday Bulletin from his pocket. Bergen signed all the bulletins.

When he got back to the living room, the priest was in deep sleep, his breathing shallow, long. He'd taken a combination of Seconal and alcohol, enough to kill a horse, along with Dramamine to keep him from vomiting it out.

The Iceman went to the window and peeked out. The kid who'd been shoveling snow had gone inside. He looked back at the priest. Bergen was slumped on the couch, his head rolled down on his chest. Still breathing. Barely.

Time to go.

CHAPTER SIX

CHAPTER

✳ ✳ ✳

18

Lucas woke suddenly, knew it was too early, but couldn't get back to sleep. He looked at the clock: 6:15. He slipped out of bed, walked slowly across the room to his right, hands out in front of him, and found the bathroom door. He shut the door, turned on the light, got a drink, and stared at himself in the mirror.

Why Weather?

If she was right about being chased on the night of the LaCourt murders, then the attacks had nothing at all to do with him.

He splashed water in his face, dried it, opened the door. The light from the bathroom fell across Weather and she rolled away from it, still asleep. Her arm was showing the bruises. She slept with it crooked under her chin, almost as though she were resting her head on her fists instead of the pillow. Lucas pulled the bathroom door most of the way shut, leaving just enough light to navigate. He tiptoed across the room and out into the hall, then went through the kitchen, turning on the lights, and, naked and cold, down into her basement. He got his clothing out of the dryer and carried it back up to the other bathroom to clean up and dress. When he went back to the bedroom for socks, she said, "Mmmm?"

"Are you awake?" he whispered.

"Mmm-hmm."

"I'm calling in. I'll get somebody down here until you're ready to leave."

As he said it, the phone rang, and she rolled and looked up at him, her voice morning-rough. "Every morning it rings and somebody's dead."

Lucas said "Just a moment" and padded into the kitchen. Carr was on the phone, ragged, nearly incoherent: "Phil's dead."

"What?"

"He killed himself. He left a note. He did it. He killed the LaCourts."

For a moment Lucas couldn't track it. "Where are you, Shelly?" Lucas asked. He could hear voices behind Carr.

"At the rectory. He's here."

"How many people are with you?" Lucas asked.

"Half-dozen."

"Get everybody the fuck out of there and seal the place off. Get the guys from Madison in there."

"They're on the way," Carr said. He sounded unsure of himself, his voice faltering.

"Get everybody out," Lucas said urgently. "Maybe Bergen killed himself, but I don't think he killed the LaCourts. If the note says he did, then he might have been murdered."

"But he did it with pills and booze—and the note's signed," Carr said. His voice was shrill: not a whine, but something nearer hysteria.

"Don't touch the note. We need to get it processed."

"It's already been picked up."

"For God's sake put it down!" Lucas said. "Don't pass it around."

Weather stepped into the hallway with the comforter wrapped around her, a question on her face. Lucas held up a just-a-moment finger. "How'd he do it? Exactly."

"Drank a fifth of whiskey with a couple bottles of sleeping pills."

"Yeah, that'd do it," Lucas said. "I'll be there as soon as I can. Look, it may be a suicide, but treat it like a homicide. Somebody almost got away with killing the Harper kid, making it look like an accident. He might be fucking with us again. Hold on for a minute."

Lucas took the phone down. "Do you know who Bergen's doctor is? GP?"

"Lou Davies had him, I think."

To Carr, Lucas said, "Bergen's doctor might have been a guy named Lou Davies. Call him, find out if Bergen had those prescriptions. And have somebody check the drugstore. Maybe all the drugstores around here."

❋

"Phil Bergen's dead?" Weather asked when Lucas hung up the phone.

"Yeah. Might be suicide—there's a note. And he confesses to killing the LaCourts."

"Oh, no." She wrapped her arms around herself. "Lucas . . . I'm getting scared now. Really scared."

He put an arm around her shoulder. "I keep telling you . . ."

"But I'm not getting out," she said.

"You could go down to my place in the Cities."

"I'm staying. But this guy . . ." She shook her head. Then she frowned. "That means . . . I don't see how . . ."

"What?"

"He would have been the guy who tried to shoot me last night. And the guy who was chasing me the first night."

"You were still at the LaCourts' when Shelly and I left, and we went into town to interview Bergen. Couldn't have been him," Lucas said.

"Maybe the guy wasn't chasing me—but after last night, I was sure that he was. I was sure, because it was so strange."

"Get dressed," Lucas said. "Let's go look at it."

❋

Seven o'clock in the morning, utterly dark, but Grant was awake, starting the day, people scurrying along the downtown sidewalks in front of a damp, cold wind. One city police car, two sheriff's cars, and the Madison techs' sedan were waiting at the rectory. Lucas nodded at the deputy on the door. Weather followed him inside. Carr was sitting on a couch, his face waxy. A lab tech from Madison was in the kitchen with a collection of glasses and bottles, dusting them. Carr wearily stood up when Lucas and Weather came in.

"Where is he?" Lucas asked.

"In here," Carr said, leading them down the hall.

Bergen was lying faceup, his head propped on a pillow, his eyes open, but filmed-over with death. His hands were crossed on his stomach. He wore a sweater and black trousers, undone at the waist. One shoe had come off and lay on the floor beside the couch; that foot dangled off the couch. His black sock had a hole at the little toe, and the little toe stuck through it. The other foot was on the couch.

"Who found him?" Lucas asked.

"One of the parishioners, when he didn't show up for early Mass," Carr said. "The front door was unlocked and a light was still on, but nobody answered the doorbell. They looked in the garage windows and they could see his car. Finally one of the guys went inside and found him here. They knew he was dead—you could look at him and see it—so they called us."

"You or the town police?"

"We do the dispatching for both. And the Grant guys only patrol from seven in the morning until the bars close. We cover the overnight."

"So you got here and it was like this."

"Yeah, except Johnny—he's the deputy who responded—he picked up the note, then he handed it to one other guy, and then I picked it up. I was the last one to handle it, but we might of messed it up," Carr confessed.

"Where is it?"

"Out on the dining room table," Carr said. "But there's more than that. C'mon."

"I'll want to look at him," Weather said, bending over the body.

Lucas took a last look at Bergen, nodded to Weather, then followed Carr through the living room and kitchen to the mudroom, then out to the garage. The back gate of the Grand Cherokee was up. A pistol lay on the floor of the truck, along with a peculiar machete-like knife. The knife looked homemade, with wooden handles, taped, and a squared-off tip. Lucas bent over it, could see a dark encrustation that might be blood.

"That's a corn-knife," Carr said. "You don't see them much anymore."

"Was it just laying here like this?"

"Yeah. It's mentioned in the note. So's the gun. My God, who would've thought . . ."

"Let me see the note," Lucas said.

❄

The note was typed on the parish's letterhead stationery.

"I assume he has an IBM typewriter," Lucas said.

"Yes. In his office."

"Okay . . ." Lucas read down through the note.

I have killed and I have lied. When I did it, I thought I did it for God; but I see now it was the Devil's hand. For what I've done, I will be punished; but I know the punishment will end and that I will see you all again, in heaven, cleansed of sin. For now, my friends, forgive me if you can, as the Father will.

He'd signed it with a ballpoint: *Rev. Philip Bergen.*

And under that: *Shelly—I'm sorry; I'm weak when I'm desperate; but you've known that since I kicked the ball out from under that pine. You'll find the implements in the back of my truck.*

"Is that his signature?"

"Yes. I knew it as soon as I looked at it. And there's the business about the pine."

Crane, the crime tech, stepped into the room, heard Lucas' question and Carr's answer, and said, "We're sending the note down to Madison. There might be a problem with it."

"What?" asked Lucas.

"When Sheriff Carr said you thought it could be a homicide, we got very careful. If you look at the note, at the signature . . ." He took a small magnifying glass from his breast pocket and handed it to Lucas. ". . . you can see what looks like little pen indentations, without ink, at a couple of places around the signature itself."

"So what?" Lucas bent over the note. The indentations were vague, but he could see them.

"Sometimes, when somebody wants to forge a note, he'll take a real signature, like from a check, lay it on top of the paper where he wants the new signature. Then he'll write over the real signature with something pointed, like a ballpoint pen, pushing down hard. That'll make an impression on the paper below it. Then he writes over the impression. It's hard to pick out if the forger's careful. The new signature will have all the little idiosyncrasies of an original."

"You think this is a fake?"

"Could be," Crane said. "And there are a couple of other things. Our fingerprint guy is gonna do the Super-Glue trick on the whiskey bottle and pill bottles, but he can see some prints sitting right on the glass. And except for the prints, the bottles are absolutely clean. Like somebody wiped them before Bergen picked them up—or printed Bergen's fingerprints on them after he was dead. Hardly any smears or partials or handling background, just a bunch of very clear prints. Too clear, too careful. They have to be deliberate."

"Sonofagun," Carr said, looking from the tech to Lucas.

"Could mean nothing at all," Crane said. "I'd say the odds are good that he killed himself. But . . ."

"But . . ." Carr repeated.

"Are you checking the neighborhood," Lucas asked Carr, "to see if anybody was hanging around last night?"

"I'll get it started," Carr said. A deputy had been standing, listening, and Carr pointed to him. He nodded and left.

Weather came in, shrugged. "There aren't any bruises that I can see, no signs of a struggle. His pants were undone."

"Yeah?"

"So what?" asked Carr.

"Lots of time suicides make themselves look nice. Women put on nice sleeping gowns and make up, men shave. It'd seem odd to be a priest, know you're killing yourself and undo your pants so you'd be found that way."

Carr looked back toward the bedroom and said, "Phil was kind of a formal guy."

"There's a knife out in his car," Lucas said to Weather. "Go have a look at it."

While she went out to the garage, Lucas walked back to the bedroom. Bergen, he thought, looked seriously disgruntled.

"We're checking the neighborhood now," Carr said, coming down the hall.

"Shelly, there's this Pentecostal thing," Lucas said. "I don't want to be insulting, but there are a lot of fruitcakes involved in religious controversies. You see it all the time in the Cities. You get enough fruitcakes in one place, working on each other, and one of them might turn out to be a killer. You've got to think about that."

"I'll think about it," Carr said. "You believe Phil was murdered?"

Lucas nodded. "It's a possibility. No signs of any kind of a struggle."

"Phil would have fought. And I guess the thing that sticks in my mind most of all is the business about the pine. We were out playing golf one time . . ."

"I know," Lucas said. "He kicked the ball out."

"How'd you know?"

"You told me," Lucas said, scratching his head. "I don't know when, but you did."

"Well, nobody else knew," Carr said.

They stood looking at the body for a moment, then Weather came up and said, "That's the knife."

"No question?"

"Not in my mind."

"It's all over town that he did it," Carr said mournfully. All three of them simultaneously turned away from the body and started down the hall toward the living room. They were passing Bergen's office, and Lucas glanced at the green IBM typewriter pulled out on a typing tray. A Zeos computer sat on a table to the other side, with a printer to its left.

"Wait a minute." He looked at the computer, then at the bookcase beside it. Instructional manuals for Windows, WordPerfect, MS-DOS, the Biblica RSV Bible-commentary and reference software, a CompuServe guide, and other miscellaneous computer books were stacked on the shelves, along with the boxes that the software came in. The computer had two floppy-disk drives. The 5.25 drive was empty, but a blue disk waited in the 3.5-inch drive. Lucas leaned into the hallway and yelled for Crane: "Hey, are you guys gonna dust the computer keys?"

"Um, if you want," Crane called back. "We haven't found any computer stuff, though."

"Okay. I'm going to bring it up," he said. To Carr: "I use WordPerfect."

With Carr and Weather looking over his shoulder, Lucas punched up the computer, typed WP to activate WordPerfect, then the F5 key to get a listing of files. He specified the B drive. The light went on over the occupied disk drive and a listing flashed onto the screen.

"Look at this," Lucas said. He tapped a line that said:

`Ser1-9 · 5,213 01-08 12:38a`

"What is it?"

"He was on the computer last night—this morning—at 12:38 A.M. That's when he closed the file. I wonder why he didn't compose his note on it? It's a lot easier and neater than a typewriter." He punched directional keys to select the last file and brought it up.

"It's a sermon . . . it looks like . . . Sermon 1-9. That would have been for tomorrow morning if that's the way he listed them." He reopened the index of files and ran his finger down the screen. "Yeah, see? Here's last Sunday, Ser1-2. Did you go to Mass?"

"Sure."

"Let's put it on Look." He called the second file up. "Is that Sunday's sermon?"

Carr read for a moment, then said, "Yeah, that's it. Right to the word, as far as I can tell."

"All right, so that's how he does it." Lucas tapped the Exit key twice to get back to the first file and began reading.

"Look at this," he said, pointing at the screen. "He's denying it. He's denying he did it, at 12:38 A.M."

Carr read through the draft sermon, moving his lips, blood draining from his face. "Was he murdered? Or did this just trigger something, coming face-to-face with his own lies?"

"I'd say he was killed," Lucas said. Weather's hand was tight on his shoulder. "We have to go on that assumption. If we're wrong, no harm done. If we're right . . . our man's still out there."

CHAPTER

* * *

19

The Iceman lay with his head on the pillow, the yellow-haired girl sprawled restlessly beside him. They were watching the tinny miniature television run through 1940s cartoons, Hekyll and Jekyll, Mighty Mouse.

Bergen was dead. The deputies the Iceman had talked to—a half-dozen of them, including the Madison people—had swallowed the note. They *wanted* to believe that the troubles were over, the case was solved. And just that morning he'd finally gotten something definitive about the magazine photo. The thing was worthless. The reproduction was so bad that nothing could be made of it.

At noon, he'd decided he was clear. At one o'clock, he'd heard the first rumors of dissent: that Carr was telling people Bergen had been murdered. And he'd heard about Harper. About a deal . . .

Harper would sell his own mother for a nickel. When his kid was killed, Harper treated it as an inconvenience. If Harper talked, if Harper said anything, the Iceman was done. Harper *knew* who was in the photograph.

The same applied to Doug Reston, the Schoeneckers, and the rest. But those problems were not immediate. Harper was the immediate problem.

Bergen's death made a difference, whether Carr liked it or not, whether he believed it or not. If the killings stopped, believing that Bergen was the killer would become increasingly convenient.

He sighed, and the yellow-haired girl looked at him, a worry wrinkle creasing the space between her eyes. "Penny for your thoughts," she said.

"Is that all, just a penny?" He stroked the back of her neck. Doug Reston had a particular fondness for her. She was so pale, so youthful. With Harper, she touched off an unusual violence: Harper wanted to bruise her, force her.

"I gotta ask you something," she said. She sat up, let the blanket drop down around her waist.

"Sure."

"Did you kill the LaCourts?" She asked it flatly, watching him, then continued in a rush: "I don't care if you did, I really don't, but maybe I could help."

"Why would you think that?" the Iceman asked calmly.

" 'Cause of that picture of you and Jim Harper and Lisa havin' it. I know Russ Harper thought you mighta done it, except he didn't think you were brave enough."

"You think I'm brave enough?"

"I know you are, 'cause I know the Iceman," she said.

✳

The yellow-haired girl's brother kept rabbits. Ten hutches were lined up along the back of the mobile home, up on stands, with a canvas awning that could be dropped over the front. Fed on Purina rabbit chow and garbage, the rabbits fattened up nicely; one made a meal for the three of them.

The Iceman pulled four of them out of their hutches, stuffed them into a garbage bag, and tied them to the carry-rack. The yellow-haired girl rode her brother's sled, a noisy wreck but operable. They powered down through the Miller tract and into the Chequamegon, the yellow-haired girl leading, the Iceman coming up behind.

The yellow-haired girl loved the freedom of the machine, the sense of speed, and pushed it, churning along the narrow trails, her breath freezing on her face mask, the motor rumbling in their helmets. They passed two other sleds, lifted a hand. The Iceman passed her at Parson's Corners, led her down a forest road and then into a trail used only a few times a day. In twenty minutes they'd reached the sandpit where John Mueller's body had been found. The snow had been cut up by the sheriff's four-by-fours and the crime scene people, but now snow was drifting into the holes they'd made. In two days even without much wind, there'd be no sign of the murder.

The Iceman pulled the sack of rabbits off the carry-rack, dropped it on the snow.

"Ready?"

"Sure." She looked down at the bag. "Where's the gun?"

"Here." He patted his pocket, then stooped, ripped a hole in the garbage bag, pulled out a struggling rabbit, and dropped it on the snow. The rabbit crouched, then started to snuffle around: a tame rabbit, it didn't try to run.

"Okay," he said. He took the pistol out of his pocket. "When it's this cold, you keep the pistol in your pocket as long as you can, 'cause your skin can stick to it if you don't." He pushed the cylinder release and flipped the cylinder out. "This is a .22 caliber revolver with a six-shot cylinder. Mind where you point it." He slapped the cylinder back in and handed it to her.

"Where's the safety?"

"No safety," said the Iceman.

"My brother's rifle has one."

"Won't find them on revolvers. Find them on long guns and automatics."

She pointed the pistol at the rabbit, which had taken a couple of tentative hops away. "I don't know what difference this makes. I kill them anyway."

"That's work—this is fun," the Iceman said.

"Fun?" She looked at him oddly, as though the thought had never occurred to her.

"Sort of. You're the most important thing that ever happened to this rabbit. You've got the power. All the power. You can do anything you want. You can snuff him out or not. Try to feel it."

She pointed the pistol at the rabbit. Tried to feel it. When she killed a rabbit for dinner, she just held it up by its back legs, whacked it on the back of the head with an aluminum t-ball bat, then pulled the head off to bleed it. Their heads came off easily. A squirrel, now, you needed an ax: a squirrel had neck muscles like oak limbs.

"Just squeeze," the Iceman coached.

And she did feel it. A tingle in her stomach; a small smile started at the corner of her mouth. She'd never had any power, not that she understood. She'd always been traded off and used, pushed and twisted. The rabbit took another tentative hop and the gun popped, almost without her willing it. The rabbit jumped once, then lay in the snow, its feet running.

"Again," said the Iceman.

But she stood and watched for a minute. Rabbits had always been like carrots or cabbages. She'd never really thought about them dying. This one was *hurting*.

The power was on her now, possibilities blossoming in her head. She wasn't just a piece of junk; she had a gun. Her jaw tightened. She put the barrel next to the rabbit's head and pulled the trigger.

"Excellent," said the Iceman. "Feel it?"

"Get another one," she said.

CHAPTER

* * *

20

Harper sat on the jail bunk, scowling, shaking his head, his yellow teeth bared. His attorney, wearing a salt-and-pepper tweed suit that might have been made during the Roosevelt Administration, sat next to him, fidgeting.

"That ain't good enough," Harper said.

"Let me explain something to you, Russ," Carr said. Carr's double chin had collapsed into wattles, and the circles under his eyes were so black that he looked like he'd lost a bar fight. "Eldon Schaeffer has to get *elected* county attorney. If he cuts a deal with you, and it turns out you're a member of some sex ring, and that you know who the killer is but you didn't tell us, and Eldon gives you immunity and you walk out of here a free man . . . Well, Eldon ain't gonna win the next election. He's gonna be out of a job. So he isn't going to cut that deal. He's gonna want some jail time."

"Then he can stick it in his ass," Harper said. He nodded at his attorney. "If Dick here is right, I'll be out of here in an hour."

"You'll risk going to trial for multiple murder to save a couple years in jail? You could do two or three years standing on your head," Lucas said. He was leaning on the cell wall, looking down at Harper. "And I swear to

Christ, if we tie you to the killer, if we even find a thread of evidence putting you two together, we'll slap your ass in jail so fast your head'll spin. For accessory to murder. You'll die in prison."

"If you're trying to cut me this kind of a deal, that means you ain't got shit on anybody," Harper said. His eyes flicked toward his attorney, then to Carr. "Take a fuckin' hike, Shelly."

❋

As they filed out of the cell, Carr looked at Lucas and said, "Slap his ass in jail so fast his head'll spin? Some threat. I'm gonna send it in to *Reader's Digest.*"

"I'll sue," Lucas said, and Carr showed a bit of a smile. While they were waiting for the elevator, Harper's attorney came out and joined them. As they were waiting, Carr looked at the attorney and asked, "Why'd you have to go and do this, Dick? Why'd you call the judge? You coulda waited until Monday and everything would have been fine."

"Russ has the right . . ." The attorney's prominent Adam's apple bobbed up and down. A large Adam's apple, big hands, rough, porous skin, and the suit: he looked like a black-and-white photograph from the Depression.

The elevator doors opened and they stepped inside, faced the front. "Don't give me any 'rights,' Dick, I know all that," Carr said as they started down. "But we've got five dead and Russ knows who did it. Or he has some ideas. He's the only thing we've got. If he takes off, and we get more dead . . ."

"He's got a *right,*" the attorney said. But he didn't sound happy.

Carr looked at Lucas. "Phil's body must be on the way to Milwaukee."

"Yeah. I'm sorry about that, Shelly—I really am," Lucas said.

Tears started running down Harper's attorney's face, and he suddenly snuffled and wiped his coat sleeve across his eyes. "God, I can't believe Father Phil's dead," he said. "He was a good priest. He was the best."

"Yeah, he was," Carr said, patting the attorney on the shoulder.

Lacey was walking through the halls, hands in his pockets, peering in through open doors. When he saw Carr, he said, "There you are. Two FBI men just arrived. A couple more may be coming from Washington—a serial-killer team."

"Oh, boy." Carr hitched up his pants. "Where are they?"

"Down in your office."

Carr looked at Lucas. "Maybe they'll do some good."

"And maybe I'll get elected homecoming queen," Lucas said as they started down the hall.

Lacey looked at him. "Did you know your new girlfriend *was* the homecoming queen?"

"What?" There was no longer any point in being obtuse about his relationship with Weather.

"That's right," Lacey said enthusiastically. "Around homecoming time, people still talk about the dress she wore on the float. It was like one of those real warm days and she had this silver dress. Oh, boy. They called her . . ." He suddenly snapped his mouth shut and flushed.

"Called her what?"

Lacey looked at Carr and Carr shook his head. "You can't get your foot any deeper in your mouth than it already is, Henry. You might as well tell him," he said.

"Um—Miss Teen Tits of Ojibway County," Lacey said feebly.

"Glad you told me—gives me an edge on her," Lucas said.

"I hope you got an edge on the feebs," Lacey said gloomily. "About two minutes with them, I felt like I had big clods of horseshit on my shoes and straw sticking outa my ears."

"Dat's da feebs," Lucas said. "That's what they do best."

❅

They talked for an hour with the two advance agents, Lansley and Tolsen. The two would have been hard to tell apart except that Lansley was the color of well-sanded birch plywood while Tolsen was polished ebony. They both wore gray suits with regimental neckties, long, dark winter coats with leather gloves, and rubbers on their wingtips.

". . . think there's some prospect that our man may be a traveler . . ."

Lucas, sitting behind Lansley, who was talking, looked past him at Carr and shook his head. No chance it was a traveler: none.

And after a while: ". . . name of the game is cooperation, and we'll do everything we can . . ."

Lucas broke in: "What we really need is computer support."

Tolsen was quick and interested. "Of what nature?"

"There are only about seven thousand permanent residents in this county. We can eliminate all women, all children, anyone with dark hair. Our man is obviously psychotic and may have a history of violence. If there's some way your computers could interface with the state driver's license bureau, process Ojibway County drivers and crosscheck the blond-male population with the NCIC records . . ."

Lansley and Tolsen took notes, Lansley using a hand-sized microcomputer. They came up with some ideas of their own and left in a hurry.

"What the heck was all that about?" Carr asked, scratching his head.

"They've got something to do," Lucas said. "It might even help if we need help three weeks from now."

A deputy knocked, stuck his head in the door. "Harper's out. Put up his gas station with Interstate Bond."

"That really frosts my butt," Carr said.

"Go home and get some sleep. Or check into a motel. You look so bad I'm seriously worried," Lucas said.

"That's a thought—the motel," Carr said distractedly. "What're you going to do?"

"Go someplace quiet and think," Lucas said.

❄

Weather got home a few minutes after six, came in with a deputy, and found Lucas staring into a guttering fire. "This is Marge, my bodyguard," she said to Lucas. The deputy waved and said, "You got it from here," and left. Weather shed her coat and boots, came over to sit beside him. He put an arm around her shoulder. "You ought to throw another log on," she said.

"Yeah . . . goddammit, there are fewer people in this county than there are in some buildings in Minneapolis. We oughta be able to pick him out. There can't be that many candidates," Lucas said.

"Still think Phil Bergen was murdered?"

"Yeah. For sure. I don't know why he was killed, though. Did he know something? Was he supposed to distract us? What?"

"Schoeneckers'?"

"Not a goddamn thing," Lucas said.

"Could they be dead?"

"We've got to start considering the possibility," Lucas said. "We were lucky to find the Mueller kid. He could've laid out there until spring. Hell, if the killer had driven him two minutes back into the woods, we might not ever have found him."

"Are you watching Harper?"

"That's impossible. Where're you gonna watch him from? We'll check on him every couple of hours, though."

Weather shivered. "The man scares me. He's one of those people who just does what he wants and doesn't care who gets hurt. Sociopath. I don't think he even notices if somebody gets hurt."

They sat quietly for a moment, then Lucas smiled, remembering, and glanced at her. She was looking into the fire, her face serious. "We've been having a pretty good time in bed, haven't we?" he asked.

"Well, I hope so," she said, laughing. She patted his leg. "We fit pretty well."

"Um . . ." He pulled at his chin, looking into the fire. "There's something . . . I've always wanted to do, you know . . . sexually . . . and I haven't been able to find a woman who could do it."

Her smile flickered. With an edge of uncertainty, she asked, "Well . . . ?"

"I always wanted to jump a homecoming queen wearing nothing but her white high heels and her crown. What do you think?" He pulled her closer.

"Those rotten jerks," she said, pushing him away. "I wasn't going to tell you until ten years from now."

"Miss Teen Tits of Ojibway County," he said.

"You should have seen me," she said, pleased. "The dress was cut fairly low in front, but *really* low in back. People said I had two cleavages."

"I like the image."

"Maybe we could work *something* out," she said, snuggling closer. "I don't know if I've still got the crown."

CHAPTER

❄ ❄ ❄

21

Harper was released at noon. He asked a deputy at the property window how he'd get back home, since the cops had brought him in.

"Fuckin' hitchhike, Russ," the cop said, and slammed the window down. Harper called his station. No answer. He finally found a kid smoking a cigarette outside a game parlor and offered him five bucks to give him a ride. The kid said ten, Harper argued, the kid tossed his cigarette in the street and told him to go fuck himself. Harper paid the ten.

The gas station was closed and locked. Harper went inside, checked the register. There was money in the till and a note: "Russ, had to close. People are pissed at you they think your in on it."

"Motherfucker." Harper crumbled the note, threw it in the corner, locked up and walked out to his truck. The tires were flat, all four of them. Cursing, he checked them, found no sign that they'd been slashed. That was something. He pulled an air hose out of the lube bay and filled the tires. Worried about his house, he drove down to it, parked, checked the front and sides. No one had been there since he left it. Okay. Inside, he made a fried egg and onion sandwich, and wolfed it down. The anger was growing. The cops would get them all if they didn't hang together. He'd done his part.

He picked up the phone, thought about it, put it down, got in his truck, drove to the station, parked and walked across the highway to the Duck Inn. There was a wall phone between the men's and women's restrooms, and he dropped a quarter.

The Iceman answered.

"This is Russ. We gotta talk."

"I heard you were in jail," the Iceman said.

"I bailed out. Where can we get together?"

"I don't think that's a good idea, Russ. I think we better . . ."

"Fuck what you think," Harper snarled. His voice had gone up and he looked quickly back toward the bar and dropped his voice again. "We gotta make some contacts. If anybody talks to the cops, if anybody cracks, we're all going down. They know about the Schoeneckers. We gotta figure out a way to find them, tell them to stay lost. I'll call Doug."

"Doug's gone. I don't know where," said the Iceman.

"Ah, Jesus. Well, they don't know about him. Maybe that's best. But listen: the cops don't have shit on anybody at this point. But if just one of us talks . . ."

"Listen. Maybe . . . you know yellow-hair?" asked the Iceman. "You know who I mean?"

"Yeah?"

"She's alone at her place. Why don't you stop by around four o'clock? I can get away for a while."

"See you then," Harper said and hung up. He walked back out to the bar, climbed onto a barstool. The heavyset bartender was wiping the counter with a rag; he had slicked-down hair, a handlebar mustache, and rode with the Woods Runners M.C. The mustard stains on his apron were turning brown. "Gimme a Miller Lite, Roy," Harper said.

"Don't want your trade, Russ," the bartender said, concentrating on his rag. There were three other men in the bar, and they all went quiet.

"What?"

"I said I don't want your trade. I don't want you in here no more." Now the bartender looked up at him. He had small black eyes, underlined with scar tissue.

"You're telling me my money's no good?" Harper pulled a handful of dollar bills from his pocket, slapped them on the bar.

"Not in here it ain't," the bartender said.

❄

"I hate the sonofabitch," the yellow-haired girl said. She sucked smoke from her mouth up her nostrils, looking cat-eyed sideways at the Iceman. "What're we going to do?"

"Well, the first thing is, he might of cut a deal with the county attorney," the Iceman said. He was sitting on the couch with a silver beer can in his hand. "He might be wearing a wire."

❄

Harper pulled into the driveway at the yellow-haired girl's house at five minutes to four. The sky to the west was shiny-silver, but the sun was hidden behind the thin overcast. Cold. He shivered as he got out of the truck. The Iceman's truck was already there, with an empty snowmobile trailer behind it. Harper frowned, stopped to listen. He could hear the music coming from the broken-down double-wide. Jim used to listen to it. Heavy Metal. Thump-thump.

The Iceman's snowmobile was sitting next to the house. Harper walked around it, knocked on the door. A little tingle, now: the yellow-haired girl was a little skinny for his tastes, but she had all the right sockets. He waited a moment, irritated, and pounded on the door.

The yellow-haired girl answered. "Come on in," she said, pulling the door back. Harper nodded, stepped inside, and wiped his feet on the square of carpet next to the door. The house smelled of burnt cooking oil and French fries, fatty meat and onions. "He's in the can," she said.

Harper wiped his feet, and as the yellow-haired girl backed away, caught her by the arm. "I'm gonna want some pussy," he said.

"Whatever," she said, shrugging. She backed into the front room, pulling him along, smiling, tongue on her upper lip. Harper went along, caught by her . . .

And the Iceman was there with a shotgun, the muzzle only a foot from Harper's face.

"What?" Harper blurted.

The Iceman put his finger to his lips, said, "Do it," to the girl. She stepped closer to him, unzipped his parka, pulled it off his shoulders, patted it down. Harper watched for a moment, confused, then said, "Oh. You think . . ."

The Iceman waggled the shotgun at his head, and Harper shut up, but relaxed.

"Shirt," whispered the yellow-haired girl. She unbuttoned his shirt, pulled it off. Untied his boots, pulled them free, looked inside. Unzipped his pants, pulled them down, pulled them off.

"As long as you're down there," Harper joked.

The Iceman half-smiled. The yellow-haired girl pulled down his underpants, then pulled them back up. Lifted his t-shirt, pulled it down. "Don't see nothing," she said.

"Okay," the Iceman said. This had worked with the priest. People *want* to believe. He kept the shotgun on Harper's skull. "Now, Russ, we want to talk, but we're not sure you didn't cut a deal. We're just trying to be careful. We want you to sit down on that couch and Ginny's gonna put a little tape around your hands and ankles."

"Bullshit she is." Harper was wearing nothing but his underwear and socks.

"I got the gun and I'm scared," the Iceman said. He blurted it out—let his voice rise and break. "If anything cracks, I'll go to prison forever. You could handle prison, Russ, but I'd die there. Man, I'm scared shitless."

"You don't need no tape," Harper said. He went to the couch and sat down. The shotgun tracked him. "Anyway, gimme my pants."

"We need to tape you up," the Iceman insisted. "I gotta

go outside and see if anybody came with you. You coulda made a deal."

"I didn't make no deal."

"Then the tape ain't gonna hurt, is it?"

Harper stared at the Iceman. The shotgun barrel never wavered. He finally shrugged. "All right, you motherfucker."

The yellow-haired girl was there with a roll of duct tape. "Cross your feet," she said.

"You're gettin' kinda bossy, ya little cunt," Harper said. But he crossed his feet. She taped them in a minute.

"Now your hands," she said. Harper looked at the gun, shrugged, and crossed his hands. "Behind you."

"Goddammit."

When he was taped, she stood up and looked at the Iceman. "Got him," she said.

"Go check," the Iceman said, tipping his head toward the door. "Go a half-mile up the road, both ways."

"What . . ." Harper began.

"Shut up," said the Iceman.

"Listen, motherfucker . . ."

The Iceman stepped close to him and hit him with the stock of the shotgun. The blow caught Harper on the ear and knocked him off the couch.

"You mother—" Harper groaned. He struggled to get up. The Iceman put a foot on his head and pressed. Harper thrashed, but the Iceman rode him, giggling. The girl pulled on a snowmobile suit, boots, ran out the door and started the snowmobile. She was back in five minutes.

"Nobody out there," she said.

"Is the tape strong enough to hold him?" the Iceman asked. He was sitting on Harper's head, Harper cursing weakly.

"That's all I got except for some of that paper tape," the yellow-haired girl said. Then brightened. "There's some wire that Rosie was gonna use for clothesline."

"Get it. And some pliers."

They wrapped the soft steel wire around Harper's wrists, and the yellow-haired girl turned it until Harper started to scream. "Fuckin' hurts, don't it," she said to him. She took three more turns, saw blood.

"Careful," the Iceman said. "Cops look for blood." Blood is evidence.

She nodded, and carefully wired his feet, wrapping it all the way to his knees. "That's got it," she said.

The Iceman stood up. Harper lay still for a moment, then tried to get to his knees. When he was halfway up, the Iceman kicked him in the middle of the back, and he pitched over on his face. "Motherfucker . . ."

"Hurts, don't it," the yellow-haired girl said, squatting next to him so she could look in his eyes. His eyelids flickered, showing the first sign of real fear. She reached down into his underpants. "You know what I think I'll do?" she asked playfully. "I think I'll get a knife and cut your dick off. How'd you like that?"

The Iceman, climbing into his snowmobile suit, said, "We don't have time to fuck around. You know how to get there?"

"Meet you in ten minutes," she said, intense, excited.

"Take it easy in the dark," the Iceman said.

Harper was thrashing on the floor again, managed to roll onto his back, tried to sit up. He was bleeding from his nose. The Iceman stooped, caught the wires between his ankles, and dragged him across the room, through the front door, down the porch. The yellow-haired girl was on the Iceman's snowmobile, waved, and pulled away. Harper's head banged off the stoop, and the Iceman pulled him through the snow to Harper's own truck, picked him up with some effort, and threw him in the back. Then he went back inside, gathered up Harper's clothes, got the truck keys, and went back out.

❄

The trip to the sandpit took seven or eight minutes. The Iceman took the right down to the pit, pulled off the road into the area beaten down by deputies' trucks when they'd found the Mueller kid. He climbed out, walked around in back, dropped the tailgate, and jerked Harper out of the back, letting him fall to the ground.

"You still alive?" he asked as Harper groaned. The temperature was below zero; in his underwear, Harper wouldn't last long. The Iceman dragged him around into the truck headlights as a snowmobile curved in from the trail. The yellow-haired girl stopped beside the truck and got down.

Harper, on his back, his face a mask of blood, spit once and then croaked, "You kill Jim?"

"Yup. Enjoyed it," the Iceman said. "Fucked him first."

"Thought you might of," Harper said. He thrashed for a moment, then began to weep, his body heaving. The Iceman walked back to the snowmobile, pulled his snowshoes off the rack, stepped into them and clipped them over his toes.

The yellow-haired girl was standing over Harper, watching him, her hand in her pocket.

"Got your gun?" the Iceman asked.

"Yup." She'd had it in her hand, and she pulled it out of her pocket.

"So shoot him."

"Me?" Harper tried to roll, but just managed to get facedown. She stared in fascination at the back of his head.

"Sure. It's a rush. Here." The Iceman stepped back from Harper, bent, grabbed his feet and rolled him in place until Harper was faceup again. Harper tried to sit up, but the Iceman stepped on his chest, pushing him flat.

"C'mon," Harper groaned. He saw the gun in the yellow-haired girl's hand. "C'mon—the cocksucker killed your school friends."

"Weren't no friends of mine. And besides, you're the one who just had to fuck me in the ass and hurt me. You remember that, Russ Harper? Me hurtin' and you laughin'?" She looked at the Iceman. "Where should I shoot him?"

"In the head's best," the Iceman said.

She leaned forward with the gun, holding it two feet from Harper's forehead. He closed his eyes, squeezed them. When she didn't pull the trigger, he said, "Fuck you then. Fuck you."

She still didn't pull the trigger, and he opened his eyes. As they opened, she pulled it, and the bullet hit in the left side of the forehead. He groaned, started to thrash.

"Again," said the Iceman. "Do it again."

She fired twice more, one bullet going through Harper's left eye, the other through the bridge of his nose. The second bullet killed him. She fired the third because it felt good. The gun snapped in her hand, like a gun should. She could feel the power going out.

"How's that feel?" the Iceman asked. Harper was still in the snow, his head at an odd angle; the blood running down his face looked purely black in the headlight.

"God . . . that was intense," said the yellow-haired girl. She knelt to look at Harper's face, squeezed his nose, then looked up at the Iceman. "Now what?"

"Now I carry him into the woods where they won't find him right away, and then I drive his truck out onto Welsh Lake by the fish shacks and leave it there. You pick me up."

"If we get another one, can I . . . ?"

"We'll see," the Iceman said, looking down at Harper. There was very little blood. "If you're good, maybe," the Iceman said. And he started to giggle.

CHAPTER

✳ ✳ ✳

22

On Sunday, Lucas and Weather slept late. For Weather, that was nine o'clock. After that, she was up, humming around the house, and at ten o'clock he gave up and got out of bed.

"There won't be much to do," she said. "Let's rent some skis and get outside."

"Let me check downtown. If nothing's happening, we could go out this afternoon."

"Good. I can go down to the Super-Valu and do some shopping. See you back here for lunch."

✳

Carr was sitting in his office, alone. When Lucas looked in, he said, "Harper's gone."

"Goddammit," Lucas said. "When?"

"We never even saw him once," Carr said. "Every time we check, nobody home. Nobody at the gas station. No truck. I put out a bulletin."

"We should have found a way to keep him inside," Lucas said.

"Yeah. What're you going to do?"

"Read the paper on the case, hang around. Wait. See if

I can figure out some other button to push. Nothing on the Schoeneckers?"

"I'd bet they're dead," Carr said. His voice was flat, as though he didn't care.

Climpt came by just before noon. "Not a damn thing going on," he said. "I was back out at the Schoeneckers', nothing there."

"Why'd he kill the priest?" Lucas asked half to himself.

"Don't know," Climpt said.

"There are about three or four knots in this thing," Lucas said. "If we could just unravel one of them, if we could find the Schoeneckers, or break Harper, figure out why Bergen was killed. If we could figure out that time problem when the LaCourts were killed."

"Or the picture," Climpt said. "You got that copy?"

"Yeah." Lucas dug his wallet out of his pants pocket, unfolded the picture, passed it to Climpt, who peered at it.

"Beats the shit out of me," he said after a minute. "There's nothing here."

Lucas took it back, looked at it, shook his head. The adult male in the picture might be anyone.

That afternoon Lucas and Weather rented cross-country skis and ran a ten-kilometer loop through the national forest. At the end of it, Weather, breathing hard, said, "You're in shape."

"You can get in shape if you don't have anything to do," he said.

❄

On Monday, Weather got up before first light. A morning person, she said cheerfully, as Lucas tried to sleep. All surgeons are. "Then if you've got two or three surgeries in a day, the hospital can fit them on one nursing shift. One surgical tech, one anesthesiologist, one circulating nurse. Keeps the costs down."

"Yeah, surgeons are famous for that," Lucas mumbled. "Go the fuck away."

"You didn't say that last night," she said. But Lucas

pulled the bed covers over his head. She bent over him, pulled the blanket down, kissed him on the temple, and pulled the cover back up and walked out, humming.

Five minutes later she was back. She whispered, "You awake?"

"Yes."

"Rusty's here to take me down to the hospital," she said. "I checked the TV weather. There's another storm coming up from the southwest and we could get hit. They say it should start late tonight or early tomorrow. I'm outa here."

✳

Lucas made it down to the courthouse at nine o'clock, yawning, face braced by the cold. The sky overhead was sunny, but a finger of slate-colored cloud hung off to the southwest, like smoke from a distant volcano. Dan Jones, the newspaper editor, was just climbing out of his Bronco as Lucas got out of his truck and they walked up to the sheriff's department together.

"So Bergen's not the guy?" he asked.

"I don't think so. We should hear something from Milwaukee today."

"If he's not the guy, how long before you get him?" Jones asked.

"Something'll break," Lucas said. The words sounded hollow. "Something'll give. I'd be surprised if it was a week."

"Will the FBI help?"

"Sure. We can always use extra resources," Lucas said.

"I meant *really* . . . off the record."

Lucas looked at him and said, "If a reporter screws me one time, I never talk to him again."

"I wouldn't screw you," Jones said.

Lucas looked him in the eyes for a moment, then nodded. "All right. The goddamn FBI couldn't find a Coke can in a six-pack of Budweiser. They're not bad guys—well, some of them are—but most of them are basically bureaucrats, scared to death they'll fuck up and get a bad personnel report. So they don't do anything. They're frozen. I suggested some computer stuff they could do and they jumped at it. High-tech, nothing to foul up, don't have to go outdoors."

"What'll break it? What are you looking at?"

"Still off the record?" Lucas asked.

"Sure."

"I can't figure out why Bergen was killed. He was involved right from the first day, so there must be something about him. He was seen leaving the LaCourts', admitted it, but they couldn't have been alive when he left. Or if they were, something's seriously out of whack. We've gone back to the firemen who saw him, and they're both solid, and there's no reason to think that they're lying. Something's screwed up and we don't know what. If I can figure that out . . ." Lucas shook his head, thinking.

"What else?"

"That picture I showed you. We think the killer was looking for it, but there's nothing in it," Lucas said. "Maybe he just hasn't seen it and doesn't know the top of his body's cut off. But that's hard to believe, 'cause it was a Polaroid."

"You need a better print than the one you're looking at," Jones said.

"The original was destroyed. So was the what-cha-callit, not the stickup . . ."

Jones grinned. "The pasteup?"

"Yeah, the pasteup," Lucas said. "They were shoved into a shredder and sent out to the landfill, like six months ago."

"What about the offset negative?"

"The what?" Lucas asked.

❉

Carr was unhappy: ". . . I don't want you leaving. Too much is going on," he said. He hunched over his desk, head down. A man confused, perhaps desperate. Mourning.

"It's the only thing I've got," Lucas said. "What am I supposed to do, go interview more school kids?"

"Then fly," Carr said. "You can be there in an hour and a half."

"Man, I hate planes," Lucas said. He could feel his stomach muscles contract at the thought of flying.

"How about a helicopter?" Lacey asked.

"A helicopter? I can deal with a helicopter," Lucas said, nodding.

"We can have one at the airport in twenty minutes," Lacey said.

"Get it," said Lucas, stepping toward the door.

"I want you back here tonight, whatever happens," Carr called after him. "We got a storm coming in."

Climpt had been standing in the doorway, smoking. "Take care of Weather," Lucas said.

❋

Domeier, the Milwaukee cop, had the day off. Lucas left a message, and the Milwaukee watch commander said somebody would try to reach him.

The Grant Airport was a single Quonset-hut hangar at the west end of a short blacktopped runway. The hangar had a windsock on the roof, an office, and plane-sized double doors. The manager told him to pull his truck inside, where four small planes huddled together, smelling of engine oil and gasoline.

"Hoser'll be here in five minutes. I just talked to him on the radio," the manager said. The manager was named Bill, an older man with a thick shock of steel-gray hair and blue eyes so pale they were almost white. "He'll put down right outside the window there."

"He's a pretty good pilot?" Lucas could handle helicopters because they didn't need runways. You could get down in a helicopter.

"Oh, yeah. Learned to fly in Vietnam, been flying ever since." The manager sucked his false teeth, his hands in his overall pockets, staring out the window. "You want some coffee?"

"A cup'd be good," Lucas said.

"Help yourself, over by the microwave."

A Pyrex pot of acidic-looking coffee sat on a hot plate next to some paper cups. Lucas poured a cup, took a sip, thought *nasty,* and the manager said, "If you get back late, the place'll be locked up. I'll give you a key for the doors so you can get your truck out. Here he comes."

The chopper was white, with a rakish HOSER AIR scrawled on the side, and kicked up a hurricane of snow as it put down on the pad. Lucas got the door key from the manager, and then, ducking, scurried under the chopper blades and the pilot popped the door open. The pilot wore an olive-drab helmet, black glasses, and a brush-cut mustache. He shouted over the beat of the blades, "You got pac boots?"

"Back in the truck."

"Better go get 'em. The heater ain't working quite right."

They took off three minutes later, Lucas pulling on the pac boots. "What's wrong with the heater?" he shouted.

"Don't know yet," the pilot shouted back. "The whole goddamn chopper's a piece of shit."

"Glad to hear it."

The pilot smiled, his teeth improbably white and even. "Little pilot joke," he said.

❋

A half hour after takeoff, the pilot got a radio call, answered, and then said, "You'll have a guy waiting for you. Domeier?"

"Yeah, good."

They put down at a general aviation airport at the north end of the city. The pilot would wait until ten o'clock, he said. "Got that storm coming in. Ten o'clock shouldn't be a problem, but if you were as late as midnight, I might not get out at all."

"I'll call," Lucas promised, pulling off the pac boots and slipping on his shoes.

"I'll be around. Call the pilots' lounge. There's a guy waving at us, and I think he means you."

Domeier was waiting at the gate, hands in his pockets, chewing gum.

"Didn't expect to see you," Lucas said. "I was told you were off."

"Overtime," Domeier said. "I got a daughter down at Northwestern, exploring her potentialities, so I need the fuckin' work. What're we doing?"

"Talking to Bobby McLain again," Lucas said. "About a thing called an offset negative."

❋

McLain was at home, with a woman in a red party dress. The woman sat on a couch, eating popcorn from a microwave bag. She had dark hair and matched her hair color with too much eye liner.

". . . suppose he could have it," McLain said. "He'll kill me if I send you out there, though."

"Bobby, you know what we're dealing with," Lucas said. "You know what could happen."

"Jeez . . ."

"What could happen?" asked the woman on the couch.

"Some people have been killed. If Bobby doesn't help us out, you could say he's an accomplice," Domeier said. He shrugged, and looked sorry about it.

The woman's mouth hung open for a minute, then she looked at Bobby. "Jesus Christ, you're dragging your feet about Zeke? The guy would trade you in for a fifty watt light bulb."

"Zeke?" said Lucas.

"Yeah. He's a teacher out at the vo-tech," the woman said. She tried a winning smile, unsuccessfully. "He does all our printing."

"At the vo-tech?"

"Sure. He's a teacher there. He's got all this great equipment. And if we're not using it, it just sits there all night, doing nothing."

"Who buys the paper?" Domeier asked.

McLain's eyes shifted. "Mmm, that's part of his price."

"Part of the price? You mean the vo-tech is buying your printing paper?"

McLain shrugged. "The price is right."

❊

McLain drove the grape-colored van; Lucas and Domeier followed him west through the suburbs. The vo-tech was a one-story orange-brick building surrounded by parking lots. A cluster of thirty or forty crows was settled around a heap of snow at one end of the building, like lost lumps of coal.

McLain parked and used an electric lift to get himself out the side door of the van. He was in a power chair this time, and rolled along in front of them, up a ramp, and down a long cold hallway lined with student lockers. Zeke was alone in his classroom. When McLain rolled through the door, he straightened, started a smile. When Lucas and Domeier followed McLain through the door, the smile vanished.

"Sorry," McLain said. "I hope we can maintain our business relationship."

Domeier said, "Milwaukee PD, Zeke."

❊

"I just . . . I just . . . I needed . . ." Zeke waved his hand, unable to find the right word, and then said, "Money."

They were standing in his office, a cool cubicle of yellow-painted concrete block, with a plastic-laminated desk and two file cabinets. Zeke was short and balding, wore his hair long and combed it in oily strands over his bald spot. He wore a checked sport coat and his hands shook when he talked. "I just . . . I just . . . Should I get a lawyer?"

"You gotta right . . ." Domeier started.

Lucas broke in: "I don't care about your goddamn printing business. I just don't have time to fuck around. I want the goddamn negatives or I'll put some handcuffs on you and we'll drag you outa the school by your fuckin' hair, and then we'll get a search warrant and we'll tear this place apart and your house and any other goddamn thing we can find. You show me the fuckin' negatives and I'm gone. You and Domeier can make any kind of deal you want."

Zeke looked at Domeier, and when the Milwaukee cop

rolled his eyes up to the ceiling, he said, "I keep the negatives at home."

"So let's go," Lucas said.

"How about me?" McLain asked.

"Take off," said Domeier.

Halfway to his house, Zeke, in the backseat of Domeier's Dodge, began to weep. "They're gonna fire me," he gasped. "You're gonna put me in jail. I'll get raped."

"Do you print for more than Bobby McLain or is he the only one?" Domeier asked, looking at him in the rearview mirror.

"He's the only one," Zeke said, his body shuddering.

"Shit. If there was more, you had some names, maybe we could work something out."

The weeping stopped and Zeke's voice cleared. "Like what?"

❊

An aging black labrador with rheumy eyes met them at the door.

"If I went to jail, what'd happen to Dave?" Zeke asked Domeier.

The dog wagged his tail when his name was mentioned. Domeier shook his head and said, "Jesus Christ."

The dog watched as they went through a closet full of offset negatives. The negatives were filed in oversized brown envelopes, with the name of the publication scrawled in the corner. They found the right set and the right negative, and Zeke held it up to the light. "Yup, this is it. Looks pretty sharp."

They trooped back to the vo-tech. The printer was the size of a Volkswagen, but the first print was done in ten minutes. Zeke stripped it out and handed it to Domeier.

"That's as good as I can get it," he said. "It's still a halftone, so it won't be as sharp as a regular photograph."

Domeier glanced at it and handed it to Lucas, saying, "Same old shit. You wasted your time."

The print was still black-and-white, but considerably sharper. Lucas put it under a table light and peered at it.

A man with an erection and a nude boy in the background. Nothing on the walls.

"The guy's leg looks weird." He took the folded newsprint version out of his pocket. The leg was so washed-out that no detail was visible. "Is this . . . whatever it is . . . is this the picture or is there something wrong with his leg?" Lucas asked.

Zeke brought a photo loupe over to the table, put it on the print, bent over it, moved it. "That's his leg, I think. It looks like it's stitched together or something, like a quilt."

"Goddamn," Lucas said. His throat tightened. "Goddamn. That's why he wants Weather. She must've fixed his leg."

"You got him?" asked Domeier.

"Got something," Lucas said. "Is there a doc around I can talk to?"

"Sure. We can stop at the medical examiner's on the way to the airport. There'll be somebody on duty."

"Can I go home now?" asked Zeke.

"Er, no," Domeier said. "Actually, we gotta go get a truck, the two of us."

"What for?"

"I'm gonna take every fuckin' envelope out of your house, and we're gonna find somebody to print them up for us. And I'm gonna want those names."

Lucas stopped on the way out of the house to call the airport, and got the pilot in the general aviation lounge. "It didn't take long. I'm on my way."

"Hurry. That storm's coming in fast, man," the pilot said. "I want to get out of here quick."

❄

The assistant medical examiner was sitting in his office, feet on his desk, reading a *National Enquirer.*

He nodded at Domeier, looked without interest at Lucas and Zeke. "Breaks my heart, what the younger women have done to the British Royal Family," he said. He balled up the paper and fired it at a wastebasket. "What the fuck do you want, Domeier? More pictures of naked dead women?"

"Actually, I want you to look at my friend's photograph," Domeier said.

Lucas handed the doc the print and said, "Can you tell what's wrong with his leg?"

Zeke asked, "You don't really have pictures of naked dead women, do you?"

The doctor, bent over the photo, muttered, "All the time. If you need some, maybe I can get you a rate." After a minute he straightened and said, "Burns."

"What?"

He flipped the photo across his desk to Lucas. "Your man's been burned. Those are skin grafts."

CHAPTER

✳ ✳ ✳

23

Lucas tried to get Carr or Lacey from the airport; the dispatcher said they were out of touch. He called Weather at home, got a busy signal. The pilot was leaning against the back of a chair, impatiently waiting to go. Lucas waited two minutes, tried again: busy.

"We gotta go, man," the pilot said. Lucas looked out the lounge windows. He could see airplanes circling ten miles out. "It looks pretty clear."

"Man, that storm is coming like a fuckin' train. We're gonna get snowed on as it is."

"Once more . . ." Weather's line was still busy. He punched in the dispatcher's number again: "I'm on my way back. Got something. And if the chopper crashes, a guy named Domeier has the negative. He's with the Milwaukee sex unit."

"If the chopper crashes . . ." the pilot snorted as they walked out of the lounge.

"Got the heater fixed?" Lucas asked.

✳

They lifted out of Milwaukee at seven o'clock, six degrees above zero, clear skies, Domeier standing at the gate with

Zeke until the chopper was off the ground. Zeke waved.

"Glad you called," the pilot said. He grinned but he didn't look happy. "I was getting nervous about waiting until ten. The storm's already through the Twin Cities. The weather service says they're getting three to four inches of snow an hour, and it's supposedly headed right up our way."

"You're not out of Grant, though," Lucas said.

"Nope, Park Falls. But we're both gonna get it."

The ground lights were sharp as diamonds in the dry cold air, a long sparkling sweep north and south along the Lake Michigan waterfront, fed by the long, living snakes of the interstates. They headed northwest, past the lesser glitter of Fond du Lac and Oshkosh, individual house lights defining the blankness of Lake Winnebago. Later, they could see the distant glow from Green Bay far off to the east; to the west, there was nothing, and Lucas realized that they'd lost the stars and were now under cloud cover.

"Do any good?" the pilot asked.

"Maybe."

"When you catch the sonofabitch, you oughta just blow him away. Do us all a favor."

They caught the first hint of snow twenty miles from Grant. "No sweat," said the pilot. "From here we're on cruise control."

They settled down five minutes later, Lucas ducking under the blades, fumbling for the key to the airport Quonset. As soon as he was inside, he could hear the chopper's rotors pick up, and a moment later it was gone.

He rolled out of the Quonset, locked the door, and started for town. The snow was light, tiny flakes spitting into his windshield, but with authority. This wasn't a flurry, this was the start of something.

Weather's house was lit up, a sheriff's Suburban in the drive. He used the remote to lift the garage door, drove in, parked.

Inside, the house was quiet. "Weather?" No answer. His stomach tightened and he walked through the front room. No sign of trouble. "Hey, Weather?"

Still no answer. He noticed that the curtain was caught in

the sliding door, walked over to it, and turned on the porch light. There were fresh tracks across the snow-covered deck. He pushed the door open.

And heard her laughing, and felt something go loose in his knees. She was all right. He cupped his hands around his mouth. "Weather . . ."

"Yeah, yeah, we're coming."

She came up the lake bank on skis, out of the night; fifty feet behind her, floundering, lathered with sweat, Climpt followed.

"Gene's never been on skis before," she said, laughing. "I've been embarrassing him."

"Never fuckin' again," Climpt rasped as he toiled behind in her tracks. "I'm too old for this shit. My goddamn crotch feels like it's gonna fall off. Christ, I need a cigarette."

Weather's smile faded. "Henry Lacey called. He said you might have something."

"Yeah. Come on in and get your skis off," Lucas said. He started to turn back to the house, but first stooped and kissed her on the nose.

"Now, *that's* embarrassing," Climpt said. "On the nose?"

❆

Lucas shook the photo out of the manila envelope onto the kitchen counter and Weather bent over it. "Better picture," she said. She looked at it, then up at Lucas, puzzled. "What?"

"Look at the guy's leg. It looks like a quilt. I'm told they might be skin grafts."

Weather peered at the photo, looked up at Lucas, stunned, looked at the photo again, then turned to Climpt. "Jesus, it's Duane."

"Duane?" asked Lucas. "The fireman?"

"Yeah—Duane Helper. The fireman who saw Father Phil. He was at the station . . . how'd he do that?"

❆

Carr had spent the afternoon at a motel, but still looked desperately weary. He was unshaven, his hair uncombed, his eyes swollen as though he'd been crying. He looked curiously at Weather and then back to Lucas. "What'd you get?"

Lacey came in just as Carr asked the question, and Lucas pushed the door shut behind him.

"Got a better picture," Lucas said, handing it to him across the desk. "If you look really close—you couldn't see it in the newsprint picture—you can see that his leg looks patched up. Those are skin grafts. Weather says it's Duane Helper."

"Duane? How could it be . . . ?"

"We've been talking, Gene and I, and we think the first thing we gotta do, tonight, is pick up Dick Westrom," Lucas said. "We don't know what he has to do with it, except that he backs up Helper's story. We put him on the grill. If we need to, we lock him up until we find out more about Helper."

"Why don't we just grab him? Helper?" Carr asked.

"We've been thinking about a trial," Lucas said, tipping his head toward Climpt. Climpt was rolling an unlit cigarette around his mouth. "Helper dropped the gun and knife on Bergen. A defense attorney will use that—he'll put Bergen on trial. All we've got is a bad picture, and the only witness we know for sure is Jim Harper, and he's dead. Nothing on the Schoeneckers?"

"No. Can't find Harper either," Lacey said. "They dropped off the earth."

"Or they're out in the goddamn snow somewhere, with coyotes chewing on them," Climpt said.

"Dammit." Lucas bit his thumbnail, thinking, then shook his head, looked at Carr. "Shelly, I really think we gotta get Westrom in here. We gotta figure out what happened."

Carr nodded. "Then let's do it. You want to go get him?"

"You should," Lucas said. "One way or another, we're gonna break this thing. Since you're an elected sheriff . . ."

"Right." Carr took a set of keys out of his pocket, opened his bottom desk drawer, and pulled out a patrol-style gun belt with a revolver. He stood up and strapped it on. "Haven't seen this thing in months. Let's go get him."

❋

Carr, Climpt, and Lucas went after Westrom while Lacey and Weather waited at Carr's office. "We'll bring him in the front so we don't have to go by dispatch," Carr told Lacey as they left. "We want to keep this quiet. We'll call you before we start back so you can open the door for us."

"Okay. What about his wife?" Lacey asked.

Carr looked at Lucas. "We oughta ask her to come along," Lucas said. "I mean, if Westrom's in this with Helper, then his wife's probably involved at some level. If she tipped Helper off, we'd be screwed."

"What if she doesn't want to come?" Carr asked.

Lucas shrugged. "Then we bust her. You can always apologize later."

Westrom was wearing blue flannel pajamas when he came to the door. He first peeked out, saw Carr, frowned, opened the inner door and pushed open the storm door. "Shelly? What's going on? Nothing's happened to Tommy?"

"No, nothing happened to Tommy," Carr said. He stepped forward, into the house, and Lucas and Climpt pressed in behind them. "We need to talk to you, Dick," Carr said. "You better get dressed."

If Westrom was guilty of anything, Lucas decided, he deserved an Academy Award for acting. He was getting angry. "Why dressed? Shelly, what the hell is going on?"

Westrom's wife, a small woman with pink plastic curlers in her hair, stepped into the room, wearing a robe. "Shelly?"

"You better get dressed, too, Janice. We need you to come down to the courthouse. We'll talk about it there."

"Well, what's it about?" Westrom asked.

"About the LaCourt killings," Carr said. "We've got more questions."

❋

While the Westroms were dressing, Carr asked, "What do you think?"

"They don't know what's happening," Lucas said. "Who's Tommy?"

"That's their boy," said Climpt. "He goes to college down in Eau Claire."

✳

The Westroms thought they wanted a lawyer. And they didn't want Weather in the room. "What's she here for?"

"She's another witness," Carr said, glancing at Weather.

"About a lawyer . . ."

"And we'll get you a lawyer if you really want one. But honestly, if you haven't done anything, you won't need one, and it'll be a big expense," Carr said. "You know me, Dick. I won't bust you just for show."

"We didn't do anything," Westrom protested. His wife, in jeans and a yellow sweatshirt, kept looking between Carr and her husband.

"What happened the night of the fire?" Lucas asked. "You were cooking and Duane was there, and he was looking out the window . . ."

"We've told you a hundred times," Westrom insisted. "Honest to God, that's what happened."

Lucas stared at him for a moment, then said, "Did you actually see Father Phil's Jeep? I mean . . ."

"Yeah, I saw it."

". . . could you have identified it from where you were standing if Helper hadn't been there? Could you have said, 'That's Father Bergen's Jeep'?"

Westrom stared down at the floor for a moment, thinking, then said, "Well, no. I mean, I saw the lights as it went by—and Father Phil admitted it was him."

"Like regular truck lights?" Lucas asked.

"Yeah."

"Bergen was pulling a trailer," Lucas said suddenly.

Westrom frowned. "I didn't see any trailer lights," he said.

Weather had been looking at Lucas and she picked up on him. "If you don't mind me asking, Dick, what were you doing before you were cooking? Just hanging out?"

Lucas glanced up at her and nodded, cracked a small smile. Westrom said, "Well, kinda. I came on, took a nap, then Duane called and I went down . . ."

"How long were you sleeping?" Lucas asked intently.

"An hour maybe," Westrom said. He looked around at them. "What?"

"Do you usually take a nap when you go on duty at the fire station?"

"Well, yeah."

"How often? What percentage of times?"

"Well, it's just my routine. I get out there around five, take a nap for an hour or so. Nothing to do. Duane's not much company. Maybe we watch a little TV."

"Duane's got a snowmobile?"

"Arctic Cat," said Westrom.

Lucas nodded, glanced at Carr. "That's it. It took timing, but that's it."

Carr leaned across his desk. "Dick, Janice, I hate to inconvenience you, but we'd like you to stay here overnight—for your own protection. You don't have to stay in jail—we could find an empty office and put some bedding inside—but we want you safe until we can arrest him."

Westrom looked at Lucas, at Carr, and then at his wife. Janice Westrom spoke up for the first time since she arrived at the courthouse. "We'll do anything you want if you think he might come looking for us," she said. She shivered. "Anything you want."

❋

When they were gone, Lucas said, "You want me to run it down?"

"Go ahead," said Carr, leaning back in his chair. He looked almost sleepy.

Lucas said, "Duane Helper finds out somehow that Lisa LaCourt has a picture of him with the Harper kid. He's seen the original, so he knows that his skin grafts are showing. But he doesn't know that the photo in the paper is so bad that his grafts are washed out of the picture. Or maybe he does know, but he's scared to death that once a cop sees the newsprint copy, we'll find a better one.

"Anyway, Westrom shows up for his shift at the firehouse and goes upstairs to bed. Helper climbs on his sled, goes on down to the LaCourts'. Someplace along the line, he sees Father Bergen, probably as Bergen leaves the LaCourts'.

"He kills the LaCourts, looks for the photo, doesn't find it, sets the place to burn—Crane tells me that he used the water heater to delay the fire—and he heads back to the firehouse. That's a three-minute trip on a snowmobile if you hurry."

"And dammit, we should have thought about that fire delay, about a fireman knowing that kind of stuff."

Climpt picked it up: "He gets back, parks the sled, pulls off his snowmobile suit, wakes up Westrom for dinner . . ."

Weather: ". . . He sees a car go by, any car, and says, 'There goes Father Bergen.' Westrom sees the lights, has no reason to think it's not Father Bergen, later has it confirmed that it was . . ."

"And it all gives Helper what he thought would be the perfect alibi," Lucas said. "He's in the firehouse, with a witness, when the alarm goes off. With the storm, he figures the priest won't know exactly how long it took him to get from one place to another, so that covers any little time problems. And he's right. He's only messed up because Shelly sees that the snow is too deep on Frank LaCourt's body, and then Crane finds the delay mechanism on the water heater."

Climpt: "He killed Phil because Phil kept insisting that the LaCourts were alive when he left, just like they were. And if they were alive, then the firemen had to be wrong . . . and if we looked at the firemen . . ."

"We still couldn't have resolved it," Lucas said. "We needed the picture."

"But we figured him out," Carr growled. "Now how're we gonna get the sonofabitch?"

CHAPTER

✳ ✳ ✳

24

Duane Helper—the Iceman—sat at the picnic table with the two lab techs, halfheartedly playing three-handed stud poker for dimes.

"Goddamn Jerry's had four hands in a row, Duane, ya gotta *do* something." The older of the two crime-lab people dealt the cards. They had almost finished the LaCourt house, they said. They'd wrung it out. Two more days, or three, and they'd be done. When they were gone, and the possibility of more developments began to fade, and the killing stopped, interest in the case would dwindle. He had to reach the Schoeneckers, but he'd thought about it. Before they came back, they'd almost surely call to talk. Bergen dead, Harper dead.

He'd done it.

The Iceman listened and played his cards.

A truck pulled into the parking area, doors slammed. Climpt came in, stamping snow off his boots. The Minneapolis cop, Davenport, was behind him, shoulders hunched against the cold. He hadn't shaved, and looked big-eyed, too thin.

Outside, in the early-morning light, snow swirled around

the fire building. The storm had begun in earnest just before dawn, thunder booming through the forest, the snow coming in waves. Almost nothing was moving on the highway except snowplows.

"Wicked out there," Climpt said. His face was wet with snow. He took off his gloves and wiped his eyebrows with the back of his hand. "Understand you got some coffee."

"Help yourself," said the Iceman. He pointed at an oversized coffee urn on a bench behind the lab people. "You out at the house?"

"Yeah. They're giving up for the day, tying everything down, getting back to town before the snow gets too bad," Lucas said. He looked at the techs. "Crane says to get your asses back there."

"Want to get my ass back to Madison," said the older of the two techs.

"Find a warm coed," said the younger one. "One more hand."

Davenport peeled off his parka and brushed off the snow. He nodded to the Iceman, took a cup of coffee from Climpt, and sat on the end of the picnic table bench.

"Anything new on the prints?" he asked.

"Nope. We're pretty much cleaned up," said the older tech. He dealt a round of three cards. "We've shipped in a few hundred sets, but hell, we printed Bergen after he croaked, and we can't even find a match to him. And we *know* he was there."

The younger tech chipped in: "The guy used a .44 and a corn-knife, took them with him. If it wasn't Bergen, he wiped the handles. And it was so cold, he had to have gloves with him. He probably just put them on after he chopped the kid."

Exactly, thought the Iceman. He sat and polished.

"Yeah. Goddammit." Lucas looked into the coffee cup, then sipped from it.

"You heard about the autopsy on Father Bergen?" Climpt asked. He was leaning against the cupboard by the coffee-pot.

"There were some problems, I guess," the tech said. He

flipped out another set of cards. "Duane's got ace 'n' shit, George's looking at shit 'n' shit, and I'm queen-jack. I'm in for a dime."

"They couldn't find any chemical traces of gelatin in his stomach. The sleeping pills he supposedly took with the booze came in gelatin capsules," Climpt said. "We didn't find any empty caps at the house, so he either flushed them or somebody dumped them in the booze and forced him to drink it . . . and forgot about the capsules."

The Iceman hadn't thought about the capsules. He'd flushed them, right here in the firehouse.

"So what does that mean?" the tech asked. "Sounds like it could go either way—either Bergen flushed them or somebody else did, but we don't know which."

"Yeah, that's right," Climpt said.

The tech ran out another round of cards: "Duane picks up an eight to give him a pair with his ace, George holds with his fours, and I'm looking at a possible straight. Another dime on the jack-queen-nine."

The second tech asked, "How about that picture? Do you any good?"

Lucas brightened. "Yeah. Maybe. Milwaukee found the guy who published the paper. He still had the page negative, and they made a better print. Should have been here today, but with this storm . . . should be here in the morning."

The Iceman sat and listened, as he had for a week, in the center of the only warm public place within miles of the LaCourt house. The cops had dropped in from the first night, looking for a place to sit and gossip.

"Anything in it?" the younger tech asked.

"Won't know until we see it," Lucas said.

"If you find time to look at it," Climpt snorted, burying his nose in his cup. His voice had a certain tone and the two crime techs and the Iceman all looked at Lucas.

Lucas laughed and said, "Yeah. Fuck you, Gene, you're jealous."

Climpt tipped his head at Lucas. "He's seeing—I'm choosing my words carefully—he's seeing one of our local doctors."

"Female, I hope," said the older of the techs.

"No doubt about that," said Climpt. "I wouldn't mind myself."

"Careful, Gene," Lucas said. He glanced at his watch. "We probably ought to get back to town."

The tech was still dealing the round of five-card stud, flipped another ace out to the Iceman. "Whoa, two pair, aces and eights," he said. He flipped over his own cards. "You can have it."

❄

When Climpt and Davenport left, the Iceman stood up and drifted toward the window, watched them as they stopped at the nose of the truck, said a few words, then got in the truck. A moment later they were gone.

"I guess we oughta get back," the older tech said. "God-damn, a couple more days of this shit and we're outa here."

"If anything can get out of here," said the other man. He went to the window, pulled back a curtain, and looked out. "Jesus, look at it come down."

❄

After the techs had gone, the Iceman sat alone, thinking. *Time to get out,* said a voice at the back of his head. He could start packing his trunk now, be ready to go by dark. With the storm, nobody would be stopping by the firehouse. He could be in Duluth in two hours, Canada in another four. Once across the border, he could lose himself, head north and west out to Alaska.

If he could take down Weather Karkinnen . . . But there'd still be the Schoeneckers and Doug and the others. But they were thousands of miles away. Nobody might ever find them. It could still work.

And besides, he wanted Weather. He could feel her out there, a hostile eminence. She *deserved* to die.

Get out, said the voice.

Kill her, thought the Iceman.

CHAPTER
❄ ❄ ❄
25

The Wisconsin state trooper had buried himself in a snow-drift across from the fire station. He wore an insulated winter camouflage suit that he'd bought for deer hunting, pac boots, and a camo face mask. He kept a pair of binoculars in a canvas bag with the radio, and a Thermos of hot chocolate in another bag. He'd been in place for two hours, reasonably warm, fairly comfortable.

He'd watched Davenport and Climpt go into the station to nail Helper down. After they'd been inside for a minute, the FBI man, the black guy, jogged up from the back, used a key to go through the access door into the truck bay. Two minutes later the FBI man slipped out and disappeared into the snow. Then Davenport and Climpt pulled out, followed by the crime techs from Madison. Since then, nothing. The trooper had expected immediate action. When it hadn't come, sitting in the drift out of the wind, he'd felt a bit sleepy; the winter storm muffled all sound, dimmed all color, eliminated odors. He unscrewed the top of the Thermos, took a hit of chocolate, screwed the top back on. He was pushing the jug back into his carry sack when he saw movement. The door on the far truck bay, where the

FBI man had gone in, was rolling up.

The trooper pulled the radio from the bag, put it to his face: "We got movement," he said. "You hear me?" The radio was unfamiliar, provided by the FBI, all talk scrambled.

We hear you. How's he moving?

"Hang on," the patrolman said. He studied the open door through the binoculars. A moment later Helper bumped out through the door on his snowmobile, looked right and left, then turned toward the highway.

"He's on the sled," the patrolman said into the radio. "He's moving, he's on the trail down 77. He's coming up toward your post . . . He's not moving too fast . . . wait a minute, he's moving now, he's really taking off."

Davenport, are you monitoring?

"Yes, I heard." Lucas was at the hospital, among the smells of alcohol and disinfectant and the stray whiffs of raw meat and urine. "Are you tracking him?"

We got him, and he's moving your way. The caller was the FBI man who'd provided them with the special handsets and the radio beacons now attached to Helper's sled and truck. *He's coming up on us. We'll let him pass and then try to hang on.*

"We're set here. Keep us posted," Lucas said. He looked at Weather. "He's coming." Lucas pulled the magazine from his .45, checked it. Climpt, who'd been sitting on an examination stool, picked up his Ithaca twelve-gauge and jacked a shell into the chamber. "He ought to be here in twenty minutes."

"If he's coming here," Carr said. The sheriff had buckled on his pistol again, but left it untouched in its holster.

"I got a buck that says he is," Lucas said. He slipped the magazine back into the .45 and slapped it tight with the heel of his hand.

"You're going to kill him, aren't you?" Weather asked.

"We're not trying to kill him," Lucas said levelly. "But he has to make his move."

"I don't see how you won't kill him," Weather said. "If he has a gun in his hand . . ."

"We'll warn him. If he opts to fight, what can we do?"

She thought for a moment, then shook her head. "If we had more time, I could think of something."

"Women shouldn't be involved in this sort of thing," Climpt said.

"Hey, fuck you, Gene," she said harshly.

"Take it easy," Lucas said mildly. He put the .45 up to his face and clicked the safety on and off, on and off, on. He saw the look on her face and said, "Sorry."

"I'm not being silly about this," she said. "Better he dies than anyone else. This ambush just seems so . . . cold."

"We ain't playing patty-cake," Climpt said.

The FBI came back: *He's passing us . . . Okay, he's past, he looked us over pretty good. No chance that we can keep up with him, Jesus, this snow is something else, it's like driving into a funnel . . . He must be doing forty down there in the ditch, he must be flying blind . . . we're doing thirty . . . Manny, he'll be coming up on you in five minutes.*

A second voice, the other FBI man: *Got him on the scope . . . Davenport, we're five minutes out, he's still coming, he's maybe two miles back.*

"Got that," Lucas said. To Climpt, Weather, and Carr: "Get ready. I'll talk to the twins." He ran down the hall, pushed open the double doors at the end of the corridor. Two cops were climbing onto snowmobiles, pistols strapped around their waists, one with a shotgun in a jury-rigged scabbard hung on the side of the sled.

"You been listening?"

"Got it," said one of the cops. Rusty and Dusty. In their helmets they were unidentifiable.

"All right. Stand off behind the lot, there. As soon as he gets off his sled, we'll bring you in. If something happens, be ready to roll. One way or another, we take him."

"Got it."

The two men took off and Lucas ran back down the corridor, clumping along in his boots, zipping his jacket over the body armor. Henry Lacey trotted down the hall toward him.

"Good luck," he called as he passed Lucas.

Carr was hanging up the phone when Lucas got back. "More stuff coming in on the sonofabitch. Lot of stuff from Duluth. He resigned there, just like he told us, but if he hadn't, the cops were gonna get him for ripping off homes after fires. A couple of arson guys think he might have set some of the fires himself."

"Good. The more we can pile up, the better, if there's a trial."

Davenport, you got it right. He's coming, he's past us, he's on the hospital road, he's on the hospital road, we're running parallel down the highway . . . Goddamn, it's hard to see anything out here.

"Shelly, you know where to go. Weather, get your coat on. Tighten up the straps, goddammit." He pulled the adjustments tight on the body armor, helped her with her mountain parka. She'd be cold without her regular jacket, but it'd only be for a minute or two. "You know what we're doing now."

"Pace it out, take it slow, stay with you. As soon as anybody yells, get down. Stay on the ground."

"Right. And everybody knows the panic drill if he decides to come inside." Lucas looked at Climpt and Carr, and they nodded, and Carr gulped and wiped his nose with the back of his hand.

"Nervous?" Lucas asked Weather, trying a smile.

"I'm okay." She swallowed. "Cottonmouth," she said.

❇

Even on a blizzard day, there'd be twenty or thirty people in the hospital—nurses, orderlies, maintenance people. Unless Helper had freaked out, he wouldn't try a frontal assault on

the building. And he knew that Weather had a deputy as a
bodyguard. His only chance was to snipe her with a rifle
or to get in close with a pistol or shotgun, shoot it out with
her bodyguard, like he'd tried when he ambushed Weather
and Bruun. They'd set up Weather's Jeep within a rough
circle of cars, they'd given him places to hide, places they
could reach with snipers on the roof. They'd show her to
him, just long enough.

As soon as he flashed a gun, they'd have him.

❋

He's thirty seconds out.

Anybody see a weapon?

*Didn't see a thing when he went by. He didn't show a
long gun on the machine.*

*He's ten seconds out. All right, he's slowing down, he's
slowing down. He's stopped right at the entrance to the
parking lot. Davenport, you got him?*

Lucas put the radio to his mouth, stared through the waiting room window out to the parking lot. He was looking
into a bowl of snowflakes. "We can't see a thing from in
here, the goddamn snow."

*He's still sitting there, can you guys on the roof see
anything?*

I can see him, he's not moving.

What's he doing?

He's just sitting there.

"Is he coming in?" Weather asked.

"Not yet."

*Wait a minute, wait a minute, he's moving . . . He's mov-
ing past the lot, he's going past the lot down the hospital
road. He's moving slow.*

Where's he going?

He's going on past the hospital.

Lucas: "You guys on the sleds, he's coming your way,
stay out of sight."

We're up in the woods, don't see him. Where is he?

Still coming your way.

Don't see him.

He's on the road by that gas thing, that natural-gas pump thing, he's just going by.

Wait a minute, we got him, he's moving slow. What do we do?

"Stay right there, let the FBI guys track him," Lucas said.

He's passing us. Boy, you can hardly see out here.

The FBI man's voice came in over the others: *He's stopped. He's stopped. He's two hundred yards behind the hospital, by that big woods.*

"Janes' woodlot," Climpt said. "He's gonna come through the woods, sneak in through the back door by the dumpsters."

"That's always locked," Weather said.

"Maybe he's got some way to get in."

He's not moving. Somebody's got to take a look.

Carr, fifty feet away, by radio: *Lucas, if he doesn't move in the next minute or so, I think the guys on the sleds ought to cruise by. If he's just sitting there, they can keep going, like club riders. If he's back in the woods, we ought to know.*

Lucas put the radio to his mouth. "You guys on the sleds—cruise him. Stuff your weapons inside your suits, out of sight. And be careful. Don't stop, keep going. If you see him, just wave."

Lucas turned to Climpt. "We better get set up by the back door. If he comes through, we should be able to see if he's carrying."

You guys on the roof—we might have to turn you around, he may come in the back. One of you go out

back right now, keep a lookout.
Got that.

"If we spot him coming in, we could have Weather just walk across the end of the t-corridor," Climpt said. "He'd be able to see her from the door, but he wouldn't have time to react. If he starts running down that way . . ."

They worked it out as they ran to the back of the hospital, Weather and Carr hurrying behind. Henry Lacey, pale-faced, stood by the reception desk with his .38. The nurses had been moved down to the emergency room, where they had concrete walls to huddle behind.

Rusty: *We just passed his sled. He's not here. It looks like he's gone up in the woods. Doesn't look like he's wearing snowshoes, Let's, uh . . .*

There was a moment of silence, then the same voice.

We'll cruise him again.

"What are they doing?" Lucas asked Climpt. "They're not going back . . . ?" He put the radio to his mouth: "What're you doing? Don't go back!"

Just coming back now.

There was a dark, abrupt sound on the radio, a sound like a cough or a bark, and a last syllable from the deputy that might have been . . .

He's . . .

Silence. One second, two. Lucas straining at the radio. Then an anonymous radio voice from the roof.

We got gunfire! We got gunfire from Janes' woodlot! Holy shit, somebody's shooting—somebody's shooting.

CHAPTER

✳ ✳ ✳

26

Weather was the key, the Iceman had decided after Davenport and Climpt left, but he couldn't go running off yet. Had to wait for the cops to clear.

He opened the green Army footlocker, took out the top tray, full of cleaning equipment, ammunition, and spare magazines, and looked into the bottom.

Four pistols lay there, two revolvers, two automatics. After a moment's thought he selected the Browning Hi Power 9mm automatic and a double-action Colt Python in .357 Magnum.

The shells were cool but silky, like good machinery can be. He loaded both pistols with hollow points, stuffed thirteen more 9mm rounds into a spare magazine for the automatic, and added a speedloader with six more rounds for the .357.

Then he watched television, the guns in his lap, like steel puppies. He sat in his chair and stared at the game shows, letting the pressure build, working it out. He couldn't chase her down, he couldn't get at her in the house. Wasn't even sure she was still at the house. He'd have to go back to the hospital again.

Weather usually left the hospital at the end of the first shift. She'd stay to brief the new shift on her patients. The fire volunteers would be arriving a few minutes after five. If he were going to pull this off, he'd have to be back by then.

A two-hour window.

He looked down into his lap at the guns. If he put one in his mouth, he'd never feel a thing. All the complications would be history, the pressure.

And all the pleasure. He pushed the thought away. Let himself feel the anger: they'd ganged up on him. Bullied him. They were twenty-to-one, thirty-to-one.

The adrenaline started. He could feel the tension rise in his chest. He'd thought it was over. Now there was this thing. The anger made him squirm, pushed him into a fantasy: *Standing in the snow, gun in each hand, shooting at enemy shadows, the muzzle flashes like rays coming from his palms.*

His watch brought him back. The minute hand ticked, a tiny movement in the real world, catching his eye with the time.

Two-fourteen. He'd have to get moving. He heaved himself out of his chair, let the television ramble on in the empty room.

Weather would walk out to the parking lot. Through the swirling snow. With a bodyguard. On any other day, a rifle would be the thing. With the snow, a scope would be useless: it'd be like looking into a bedsheet.

He'd just have to get close, to make sure, this time. Nothing fancy. Just a quick hit and gone.

❊

The ride to the hospital was wild. He could feel himself moving like a blue light, a blue force, through the vortex of the storm, the snow pounding the Lexan faceplate, the sled throbbing beneath him, bucking over bumps, twisting, alive. At times he could barely see; other times, in protected areas or where he was forced to slow down, the field of vision opened out. He passed a four-by-four, looked up at the driver. A stranger. Didn't look at him, on his sled, ten feet away. Blind?

He pushed on, following the rats' maze of trails that paralleled the highway, along the edge of town. Past another four-by-four. Another stranger who didn't look at him.

A hell of a storm for so many strangers to be out on the road, not looking at snowmobiles . . .

Not looking at snowmobiles.

❄

Why didn't they look at him? He stopped at the entrance to the hospital parking lot, thought about it. He could see Weather's Jeep. Several other cars close by; he could put the sled around the corner of the building, slip out into the parking lot.

Why didn't they look at him? It wasn't like he was invisible. If you're riding in a truck and a sled goes tearing past, you look at it.

The Iceman turned off the approach to the hospital, cruised on past. Something to think about. Kept going, two hundred, three hundred yards. Janes' woodlot. He'd seen Dick Janes in here all fall, cutting oak. Not for this year, but for next.

The Iceman pulled off the trail, ran the sled up a short slope, sinking deep in the snow. He clambered off, moved fifteen feet, huddled next to a pile of cut branches.

Coyotes did this. He knew that from hunting them. He'd once seen a coyote moving slow, apparently unwary, some three or four hundred yards out. He'd followed its fresh tracks through the tangle of an alder swamp, then up a slope, then back around . . . and found himself looking down at his own tracks across the swamp and a cavity in the snow where the mutt had laid down, resting, while he fought the alders. Checking the back trail.

Behind the pile of cuttings, he was comfortable enough, hunkering down in the snow. He was out of the wind, and the temperature had begun climbing with the approach of the storm.

He waited two minutes and wondered why. Then another minute. He was about to stand up, go back to the sled, when he heard motors on the trail. He squatted again, watched. Two sleds went by, slowly. Much too slowly. They weren't getting anywhere if they were travelers, weren't having any fun if they were joyriders. And there was nothing down this trail but fifteen or twenty miles of trees until they hit the next town, a crossroads.

Not right.

The Iceman waited, watching.

Saw them come back. Heard them first, took the .357 from his pocket.

He could see them clearly enough, peering through the branches of the trim pile, but he probably was invisible, down in the snow, above them. They stopped.

They stopped. They knew. They knew who he was, what he was doing.

The lifelong anger surged. The Iceman didn't think. The Iceman acted, and nothing could stand against him.

The Iceman half-stood, caught the first man's chest over the blade of the .357.

Didn't hear the shot. Heard the music of a fine machine, felt the gun bump.

The first man toppled off his sled, the second man, black-Lexan-masked, turning. All of this in slow motion, the second man turning, the gun barrel popping up with the first shot, dropping back into the slot, the second man's body jumped, but he wavered, not falling, a hand coming up, fingers spread, to ward off the .357 JHPs; a third shot went through his hand, knocked him backwards off the sled. And the gun kept on, shots filing out, still no noise, a fourth, a fifth, and a sixth . . .

And in the soft snow, the bumping stopped and the Iceman heard the hammer falling on empty shells, three times, four, the cylinder turning.

Click, click, click, click.

CHAPTER

✳ ✳ ✳

27

He's moving, he's moving, he's moving fast, what happened what happened?

The radio call bounced around the tile corridor, Carr echoing it, shouting, *What happened, what happened*—and knowing what had happened. Weather sprinted toward the emergency room, Lucas two steps behind, calling into the radio, *Stay with him stay with him, we might have some people down.*

The ambulance driver was talking to a nurse. Weather ran through the emergency room, screamed at him: "Go, go, go, I'll be there, get started."

"Where . . . ?" The driver stood up, mouth hanging.

Lucas, not knowing where the ambulance was, shouted, "Go," and the driver went, across the room, through double hardwood doors into a garage. The ambulance faced out, and the driver hit a palm-sized button and the outside door started up. He went left and Lucas right, climbed inside. The back doors opened, and a white-suited attendant scrambled aboard, carrying his parka, then Weather with her bag and Climpt with his shotgun.

"Where?" the driver shouted over his shoulder, already on the gas.

"Right down the frontage road, Janes' woodlot, right down the road."

"What happened?"

"Guys might be shot—deputies." And she chanted, staring at Lucas: "Oh, Jesus, Oh, Jesus God . . ."

The ambulance fishtailed out of the parking garage, headed across the parking lot to the hospital road. A deputy was running down the road ahead of them, hatless, gloveless, hair flying, a chrome revolver held almost in front of his face. Henry Lacey, running as hard as he could. They passed him, looking to the right, in the ditch and up the far bank, snow pelting the windshield, the wipers struggling against it.

"There," Lucas said. The snowmobiles sat together, side-by-side, what looked like logs beside them.

"Stay here," Lucas shouted back at Weather.

"What?"

"He might still be up there."

The ambulance slid to a full stop and Lucas bolted through the door, pistol in front of him, scanning the edge of the treeline for movement. The body armor pressed against him and he waited for the impact, waited, looking, Climpt out to his right, the muzzle of the shotgun probing the brush.

Nothing. Lucas wallowed across the ditch, Climpt covering. The deputies looked like the victims of some obscure third-world execution, rendered black-and-white by the snow and their snowmobile suits, like a grainy newsphoto. Their bodies were upside down, uncomfortable, untidy, torn, unmoving. Rusty's face mask was starred with a bullet hole. Lucas lifted the mask, carefully; the slug had gone through the deputy's left eye. He was dead. Dusty was crumbled beside him, facedown, helmet gone, the back of his head looking as though he'd been hit by an ax. Then Lucas saw the pucker in the back of his snowmobile suit, another hit, and then a third, lower, on the spine. He looked at Rusty: more hits in the chest, hard to see in the black nylon. Dusty's rifle was muzzledown in the snow. He'd cleared the scabbard, no more.

Climpt came up, weapon still on the timber. "Gone," he said. He meant the deputies.

"Yeah." Lucas lumbered into the woods, saw the ragged trail of a third machine, fading into the falling snow. He couldn't hear anything but the people behind him. No snowmobile sound. Nothing.

He turned back, and Weather was there. She dropped her bag. "Dead," she said. She spread her arms, looking at him. "They were children."

The ambulance driver and the attendant struggled through the snow with an aluminum basket-stretcher, saw the bodies, dropped the basket in the snow, stood with their hands in their pockets. Henry Lacey ran up, still holding the gun in front of his face.

"No, no, no," he said. And he kept saying it, holding his head with one hand, as though he'd been wounded himself: "No, no . . ."

Carr pulled up in his Suburban, jumped out. Carr looked at them, his chief deputy wandering in circles chanting, "No, no," both hands to his head now, as though to keep it from exploding.

"Where is he?" Carr shouted.

"He's gone. The feds better have him, because it'd be hell trying to follow him," Lucas shouted back.

The feds called: *We still got him, he's way off-road and moving fast, what's going on?*

"We got two down and dead," Lucas called back. "We're heading back to the hospital, gearing up. You track him, we'll be with you in ten minutes."

Lucas and Climpt took Carr's Suburban, churned back to the hospital. Lucas stripped off the body armor, got into his parka and insulated pants.

"Rusty's truck is around back, right? With the trailer?"

"Yeah."

"We'll take the sleds," Lucas said. "Right now we need a decent map."

They found one in the ambulance dispatch room, a large-scale township map of Ojibway County. The feds were using tract maps from the assessor's office, even better. Lucas got on the radio:

"Still got him?" he asked.

Yeah. We got him. You better get out here, though, we can't see him and we got nothing but sidearms.

Helper was already eight miles away, heading south.

"He could pick a farmhouse, go in shooting, take a truck," Climpt said. "Nobody would know until somebody checked the house."

Lucas shook his head. "He's gone too far. He knows where he's going. I think he'll stay with the sled until he gets there."

"The firehouse is off in that direction."

"Better get somebody down there," Lucas said. "But I can't believe he'd go there." He touched the map with his finger, reading the web of roads. "In fact, if he was going there, he should have turned already. On the sled, if he knows the trails, he probably figures he's safe, at least for the time being."

"So let's go."

They stripped the map from the wall, hurried around back to Rusty's truck. The keys were gone, probably with the body. Lucas ran back through the hospital, past the gathering groups of nurses, ran outside and got the Suburban. Climpt pulled the trailer off Rusty's truck, and when Lucas got back, hitched the trailer to the Suburban.

Ten deputies were at the shooting site now. The bodies still exposed, only one person looking at them; cars stopped on the highway, drivers' white faces peering through the side windows. Carr was angry, shouting into the radio, and Weather stood like a scarecrow looking down at the bodies.

Lucas and Climpt crossed the well-trampled ditch, climbed on the sleds, started them.

"Kill him," Carr said.

Weather caught Lucas by the arm as they loaded the snowmobiles onto the trailer. "Can I go?"

"No."

"I want to ride."

"No. You go back to the hospital."

"I want to go," she insisted.

"No, and that's it," Lucas said, pushing her away.

Climpt had traded his shotgun for an M-16, said, "I'll drive," and hustled around to the cab. Lucas climbed in the passenger side; when they pulled away, he saw Weather recrossing the ditch to the sheriff.

"Buckle up and hold on," Climpt said. "I'm gonna hurry."

✻

They took County Road AA south from the highway, a road of tight right-angle turns and a slippery, three-segment, two-lane bridge over the Menomin Flowage. Lucas would have taken the truck into a ditch a half-dozen times, but Climpt apparently knew the road foot-by-foot, knew when to slow down, when the turns were coming. But the snow was beating into the windshield, and the deputy had to wrestle the tailwagging truck through the tighter spots, one foot on the brake, the other on the gas, all four wheels grinding into the shoulders.

Lucas stayed on the handset with the feds.

He's either on the Menomin Branch East or the Morristown trail, still going south.

"We're coming up on you, we're on AA about to cross H," Lucas said.

Okay, we're about four miles further on. Jesus, we can't see shit.

Carr: *We're loading up, heading your way. If you get him, pin him down and we'll come in and finish it.*

Then the feds: *Hey, he's stopped. He's definitely stopped, he's up ahead, must be along County Y, two miles east of AA. We're about four or five minutes out.*

Lucas: *Find a good place to stop and wait. We're all coming in. We don't know what kind of weapons he's carrying.*

✻

"There's not much down that road," Climpt said, thinking about it. His hands were tight, white on the steering wheel, holding on, his head pressed forward, searing the snowscape. "Not around there. I'm trying to think. Mostly timber."

Carr came up: *Weather thinks he's at the Harris place. Duane was supposedly seeing Rosie Harris. That's a mile or so off AA on Y. Should be on the tract maps.*

"Goddammit," said Lucas. "Weather's riding with Carr."

Climpt grunted. "Could of told you she wouldn't stay put."

"Gonna get her ass shot," Lucas said.

"Eight dead that we know of," Climpt said, his voice oddly soft. A red stop sign and a building loomed out of the snow, and Climpt jumped on the brake, slowing, then went on through. "Can't find Russ Harper or the Schoeneckers, and I wouldn't make any bets on them being alive, either. Goddamn, I thought it only happened in New York and Los Angeles and places like that."

"Happens all over," Lucas said as they went through the stop sign.

"But you don't believe that, living up here," Climpt said. He glanced out the window. A roadhouse showed a Coors sign in the window. Three people, unisex in their parkas, laughing, cross-country skis on their shoulders, walked toward the door. "You just don't believe it can happen."

❊

The feds had stopped at a farmhouse a half-mile from where their ranging equipment said the radio beacon was. Visibility was twenty feet and was falling. In little more than an hour it would be dark. Lucas and Climpt pulled in behind the federal truck, climbed down, and went to the house. Tolsen met them at the door. "I'm gonna go down and watch the end of the drive, make sure he doesn't tear out of there in a car."

"Okay. Don't go in."

Tolsen nodded. "I'll wait for the troops," he said grimly. "Those two boys are gone?"

Lucas nodded, grimacing. "Yes."

"Shit."

A farm couple sat in the kitchen with a grown son, three pale people in flannel while Lansley talked on the telephone. He hung up as Lucas and Climpt came in, said, "We've got a hostage negotiator standing by on the phone from Washington. He can call in if we need him. If there's a hostage deal going down." He looked worn.

"We've got to do something quick," Climpt said. "If there's another sled in there, or if he gets out in a truck, we'll never find him."

"So what's the plan?" asked Lansley. "Where's Carr?"

"They're ten or fifteen minutes back," Lucas said. "Why don't you go down and back up Tolsen. Just watch the drive, don't get close. Gene and I'll go in on the sleds until we're close, then go in on foot. He can't see us any better than we can see him, and if we catch him outside, we can ambush him."

"You got snowshoes?"

"No. We'll just have to make the best of it," Lucas said.

The farmer cleared his throat. "We got some snowshoes," he said. He looked at his son. "Frank, whyn't you get the shoes for these folks."

＊

Lucas and Climpt unloaded the sleds and rode them through the farmyard. The farmer had given them a compass as well as the snowshoes. Fifty feet past the barn, they needed it. Lucas took them straight west, riding over what had been a soybean field, the stubble now three feet below the surface. The snow was riding on a growing wind, coming in long curving waves across the open fields. The world was dimming out.

Lucas had strung the radio around his neck, and turned it up loud enough to hear the occasional burp: *No movement . . . Nothing . . . Five minutes out . . . Get a couple more sleds down here, see if you can rent a couple at Lamey's.*

A darker shape shimmered through the snow. Pine tree. The farmer said there was one old white pine left in the

field, two hundred feet from the Harris's property windbreak. Lucas pointed and Climpt lifted a hand in acknowl-
edgment. A minute later the windbreak loomed like a curtain, the blue spruces so dark they looked black. Climpt
moved off to the left, fifteen feet, as they closed on it. At
the edge of the treeline, they stopped, then Climpt pointed
and shouted over the storm. "We're back too far. We gotta
go through that way, I think. Windbreak's only three or four
trees deep, so take it easy."

They moved back toward the road, Climpt leading. After
a hundred feet he waved and cut the engine on his sled.
Lucas pulled up beside him and pulled the long trapper's
snowshoes off the carry-rack.

"This is fuckin' awful," Climpt said.

Inside the windbreak, the wind lessened, but swirled
among the trees, building drifts. They plodded through,
and a light materialized from the screen of white. Window. Lucas pointed and Climpt nodded. They slid further
to the right, moving down the lines of pine, coming up on
the back of the double-wide mobile home. A snowmobile
track crossed the backyard, curved around the side and out
of sight.

"Let's get back a bit. I don't think they could see us."

Keeping the trees between themselves and the house,
they moved around to the front. A snowmobile sat next
to the door. A space had been cleared for a truck or a car,
but the space was empty.

"I'll watch the back," Climpt said. He'd slung the M-16
over his shoulder and now slipped it off into his hands.

"Sit where we can see each other," Lucas said. "We gotta
stay in touch."

Climpt moved back the way they came, stopped, beat out
a platform with the snowshoes, and sat down. He lifted a
hand to Lucas and put the rifle between his knees.

Lucas spoke into the radio. "We're here. We can see a
snowmobile parked in front. No other vehicle. The windows
are lit."

Any sign of life?

"Not yet. There're lots of lights on."

Carr: *We're here—we see you guys on the road.*

Feds: *Nothing's come out.*

Carr got with the agents. Deputies would block County Y in both directions. Others would filter into the treeline and occupy the abandoned chicken house in back of the Harris home.

We're talking about how long we wait for him. What do you think? Carr asked.

"Not long," Lucas said into the radio. "There's no vehicle here. I don't see any fresh tracks, but I can't see the other side of the yard. It's possible that he dumped his sled and took off on another one before we got here."

The feds have some kind of shrink on the line. He could call. We got some tear gas coming.

"Talk it out, Shelly. Talk to the hostage guy. I'm not a hostage specialist. All I can do from here is ambush the guy."

Okay.

A moment later Carr came back: *We've got a pickup coming in. Stand by.*

Two minutes later, from Carr: *We've got Rosie and Mark Harris in the pickup. They say their sister's in there, Ginny Harris. They say Helper's seeing* her, *not Rosie. They say there weren't any other vehicles there. They've got only this pickup and a sled, and the sled's in the back of the pickup. So they must be inside.*

"So we wait?" Lucas asked.

Just a minute.

Lucas sat in the snow, watching the door, face wet with melting snow, snow clinging to his eyelashes. Climpt was thirty feet away, a dark blob in a drift, his rifle pointed up into the storm. He'd rolled a condom over the muzzle to keep the snow out. From the distance, Lucas couldn't see the color, but back at the farmhouse, where Climpt had rolled it on, it was a shocking blue.

"Got neon lights on it?" Lucas had asked as they got ready to go out.

"Don't need no lights," Climpt said. "If you look close, you'll notice that it's an extra large."

Lucas, we're gonna have Rosie call in. We can patch her through from here. If Helper answers, she'll ask for Ginny. That's the young one. She'll tell the girl to go to the door when Helper's doing something, and just run out the front and down the driveway. Once she's out, we'll take the place apart.

Lucas didn't answer immediately. He sat in the snow, thinking, and finally Carr came back: *What do you think? Think it'll work?*

"I don't know," Lucas said.

You got any better ideas?

"No."

There was an even longer pause, then Carr:

We're gonna try it.

CHAPTER

28

The Iceman sat on the couch, furious, the unfairness choking his mind. He'd never had a chance, not from when he was a child. They'd always picked on him, victimized him, tortured him. And now they'd hunt him down like a dog. Kill him or put him in a cage.

"Motherfuckers," he said, knuckles pressed into his teeth. "Motherfuckers." When he closed his eyes, he could see opalescent white curtains blowing away from huge open windows, overlooking a city somewhere, a city with yellow buildings covered with light.

When he opened his eyes, he saw a rotting shag rug on the floor of a double-wide with aluminum walls. The yellow-haired girl had put a prepackaged ham-and-cheese in the microwave, and he could smell the cheap cheddar bubbling.

They'd set him up. They knew he'd done the others. The knowledge had come on him when he saw the deputies coming back, the knowledge had blown up into rage, and the gun had come up and had gone off.

He had to run now. Alaska. The Yukon. Up in the mountains.

He worked it out. The cops would call on every outlying farm and house in Ojibway County. They'd be carrying automatic weapons, wearing flak jackets. If he holed up, he wouldn't have a chance: they would simply knock on every door, look in every room in every house, until they found him.

He wouldn't wait. The storm could work for him. He could cut cross-country on the sled, along the network of Menomin Flowage snowmobile trails. He knew a guy named Bloom down at Flambeau Crossing. Bloom was a recluse, lived alone, raised retrievers and trained cutting horses. He had an almost-new four-by-four. If he could make it that far—and it was a long ride, especially with the storm—he could take Bloom's truck and ID, head out Highway 8 to Minnesota, then take the interstate through the Dakotas into Canada. And if he stuck the horse trainer's body in a snowdrift behind the barn, and unloaded enough feed to keep the animals quiet, it'd be several days before the cops started looking for Bloom and his truck.

By then . . .

He jumped off the couch, fists in his pants pockets, working the road map through his head. He could dump the truck somewhere in the Canadian wilderness, somewhere it wouldn't be found until spring. Then catch a bus. He'd be gone.

"Where'n the fuck are they?" he shouted at the yellow-haired girl.

"Should be here," she said calmly.

He needed Rosie and Mark to get back. Needed the gas from the truck if he was going to make the run down to Flambeau Crossing.

The yellow-haired girl had put the ham-and-cheese in the microwave and then she'd gone back to her bedroom and started changing. Longjohns, thick socks, a sweater. Got out her snowmobile suit, her pac boots, began to go through her stuff. Took pictures. Pictures of her mom, her brother and sister, found a photo of her father, flipped it facedown on the floor without a second look. She took a small gold-filled cross on a gold chain, the chain broken.

She put it all in her purse. She could stuff the purse inside her snowmobile suit.

Helper had told her about the cops. There had been nothing he could do about it. They were right on top of him. She could feel the sense of entrapment, the anger. She patted him on the shoulder, held his head, then offered him food and went to pack.

She heard the watch chiming, then the *ding* of the microwave. She carried her stuff to the kitchen, dumped it on a chair, took the ham-and-cheese out of the oven. The package was hot, and she juggled it onto a plate. She'd put a cup of coffee in with the ham-and-cheese, but it wasn't quite ready yet. She punched it for another minute and called, "Come and get it."

Her mom used to say that a long time ago. She sometimes couldn't quite remember her face. She could remember the voice, though, whining, as often as not, but sometimes cheerful: *Come and get it.*

The phone rang, and without thinking she reached over and picked it up. "Hello?"

The Iceman looked at her from the couch.

Rosie spoke, her voice a harsh, excited whisper. "Ginny—don't look at Duane, okay? Don't look at him. Just listen. Duane just killed two cops and all those other people. There are cops all around the house. You gotta get out so they can come in and get him. When Duane's in the bathroom or something, whenever you get a chance, just go right out the front door and run down the driveway. Don't put a coat on or anything, just run. Okay? Now say something like 'Where the heck are you?'"

"Where the heck are you?" the yellow-haired girl said automatically. She turned to look at Duane.

"Tell him we're still downtown and we wanted to know about the roads out there. Now say something about the roads."

"Well, they're a mess. It's snowing like crazy," the yellow-haired girl said. "The drive's filling up, and a plow came by a little while ago and plowed us in."

The Iceman was off the couch, whispering. "Tell her we

need them to come out. I gotta have the gas. Don't tell them I'm here."

She put a finger to her lips, then went back to the phone. "I really kind of need you out here," she said.

Rosie caught on. "Is he listening?"

"Yes."

"Okay. Tell him we'll be out in a while. And when you get a chance, you run for it. Okay?"

"Okay."

"God bless you," Rosie said. "Run for it, honey."

The yellow-haired girl nodded. Duane was focused on her, fists in his pockets. "Sure, I will," she said.

CHAPTER
✳ ✳ ✳
29

The snow was getting heavier and the thin daylight was fading fast. Climpt was a dark lump in the snow to his left, unmoving. Lucas had settled behind a tree, the pine scent a delicate accent on the wind. And they waited.

Five minutes gone since Carr had called on the radio: *Okay, the kid knows, she's gonna make a break for it. Everybody hold your fire.*

A man moved along the edge of the woods opposite Lucas, and then another man, behind him, both carrying long arms. They settled in, watching the door.

The radio kept burping in Lucas' ear:

John, you set?

I'm set.

I don't think there's any way he could get out this end—the storm windows got outside fasteners.

Can't see shit out back. Where's Gene and Lucas?

Lucas: "I'm in the trees about even with the front door. Gene's looking at the back." A shadow crossed the curtain over the glass viewport in the front door, stayed there. Lucas went back to the radio: "Heads up. Somebody's at the front door."

But nobody moving fast, he thought, heart sinking. The

kid wasn't running. The porch light came on, throwing a circle of illumination across the dark yard. Climpt stood up, looked at him. Lucas said, "Watch the back, watch the back, could be a decoy."

Climpt lifted a hand and Lucas turned back to the trailer home. A crack of brilliant white light appeared at the door, then the large bulk of a man and a struggling child.

"Hold it, hold it!" Helper screamed. He pushed through the storm door to the concrete-block stoop, crouched behind the yellow-haired girl. He had one arm around her neck, another hand at her head. "I got a gun in her ear. Shoot me and she dies. She fuckin' dies. I got my thumb on the hammer."

Lucas waved Climpt over and Climpt half-walked, half-crawled through the snow, using the trees to screen himself from the mobile home. "What the fuck?" he grunted.

Helper and the girl were in the porch light, dressed in snowmobile suits. Helper was wearing a helmet. "I wanna talk to Carr," he screamed. "I want him up here."

Carr, on the radio: *Lucas? What do you think?*

Lucas ducked behind a tree, spoke as softly as he could. "Talk to him. But stay out of sight. Get one of the guys on the other side to yell back to him that you're on the way. He can't see us—we're only about thirty feet away."

"I wanna talk to Carr," Helper screamed. He jerked the girl to the left, toward his snowmobile, nearly pulling her off her feet.

A few seconds later a voice came from the forest on the other side: "Take it easy, Duane, Shelly's coming in. He's coming in from the road. Take it easy."

Helper swiveled toward the voice. "You motherfuckers, the hammer's back—you shoot me and the gun'll blow her brains all over the fuckin' lot!"

"Take it easy."

Carr, on the radio: *Lucas, I'm walking up the driveway. What do I tell him?*

"Ask him what he wants. He'll want a truck or something, some way to get out."

Then what?

"Basically, if we get up against it, let him have it. Try to trade it for the kid. If we can get him away from the kid for a second, Gene's got one of your M-16s and he'll take him out. We just need a second."

What if he wants to keep the girl?

"I'd say let them go. I don't think he's figured out the tracking beacon yet. If the feds have another one, we could stick it in the truck, if that's what he wants."

The feds: *We got another one.*

Carr: *I can see the light from the porch, I'm moving off to the side.*

Lucas turned to Climpt. "How good are you with that rifle?"

"Real good," Climpt said.

"If he didn't have the gun on the girl, could you hit him in the head?"

"Yeah."

"With pressure?"

"Fuck pressure. Without pressure, I could hit him in one eye or the other, your choice. This way you might have to settle for somewhere in the face. You think I oughta . . ."

"When Shelly starts talking to him, I'm going to stand up, let him see me. I'm going to talk. You put your sights on his head, and if he pokes that gun at me, you take it off."

Climpt stared at him, suddenly sounded less sure. "I don't know, man. What if the kid's still in the way or . . ."

"We're gonna have a problem if he takes her," Lucas said. "I'd say it's fifty-fifty that he kills her, but even if he just dumps her somewhere, in this storm, she could be in trouble. She'd have a better chance with you shooting."

Climpt stared at him for a moment, then gave a jerky nod. "Okay."

Lucas looked at him and grinned. "Don't hang fire, huh? Just do it. I don't want him shooting me in the nuts or something."

Climpt said nothing; stared at his gun.

* * *

*

Lucas called Carr: "Shelly, where are you?"

I'm fifty feet down the driveway, sitting in the snow. I'm gonna yell up there now.

"When you're talking to him, I'm gonna let him see me. I'll be talking to him, too."

What for?

"Gene and I are working on something. Don't worry about it, just . . ."

Helper bellowed down the driveway, "Where in the fuck is Carr?"

"Duane . . ." Carr called from the growing darkness. "This is Shelly Carr. Let the little girl go and I'll come get you personally. You won't be hurt, I guarantee."

"Hey, fuck that!" Helper shouted back. "I want a truck up here and I want it in five minutes. I want it parked right here, and I want the guy who drives it to walk away. I won't touch him. But I don't want anybody else around it. I'll be watching from the house. When I come back out with the kid, I'll have the gun in her ear, and if there's anybody around the truck, I'll drop the hammer."

As Helper was talking, Lucas slid away to his right, then stood up. Carr shouted, "Duane, if you hurt her, you'll die one second later."

Helper laughed, a wild sound, weirdly sharp in the driving snow. "You're gonna kill me anyway, don't shit me, Shelly. If you don't kill me, you'll be digging ditches next year instead of being sheriff. So get me the fuckin' truck."

Helper backed toward the house, dragging the girl with him. She hadn't said a word, and Lucas could see her hair shining oddly yellow in the porch light. He remembered her from the school, the little girl who'd watched him in the hallway, the one with the summer dress and thin shoulders.

"Duane . . ." Lucas called. He shuffled forward. He knew he must be almost invisible in the darkness, away from the light. "This is Davenport. We got feds out here, we got people from other agencies. We wouldn't hurt you, Duane, if you let the girl go."

Helper turned, peered at him. Lucas lifted his hands over his head, spread them, palms forward, took three more steps.

"Davenport?"

"We won't . . ."

"Get away from me, man, or I swear to Christ I'll blow her brains all over the fuckin' yard, I . . . *get away* . . ." His voice rose to a near-hysterical pitch, but the gun never left the yellow-haired girl's head. Lucas could feel her staring at him, passive, on the edge of death, helpless.

"All right, all right." Lucas backed away, backed away. "I'm going, but think about it."

"You'll get the truck," Carr shouted from the dark. "We got the truck coming in. Duane—for God's sake don't hurt the girl."

Helper and the girl backed up to the door. The girl reached behind him, found the doorknob, pushed it, and Helper backed through, the pistol shining weakly silver in the porch light.

The feds, on the radio: *Got a beacon on the truck.*

Carr: *Get it up here. Get it up here.*

The feds: *It's rolling now.*

Carr: *Davenport—what the hell were you doing?*

"I was trying to get him to point the gun at me," Lucas said. "Gene was holding on his head with the M-16. If he'd taken the muzzle away from the girl, we'd of had him."

Good Lord. Where's that truck?

On the way.

The Suburban turned up the driveway, stopped with its headlights reaching toward the mobile home. The truck door slammed, the sound muffled by the snow, then it rolled forward again, its high lights on. It stopped where Helper had indicated, and Shelly Carr crawled down from the driver's seat, squared his shoulders as if waiting for a bullet, and walked back down the driveway.

"Idiot," Climpt said just behind Lucas' ear.

"Takes some guts," Lucas said.

"And if we get Helper, it sure as shit wraps up the next election. Here they come."

✳

The door opened again and Helper pushed through, his arm again wrapped around the squirming girl's neck. His free hand was bare, holding the revolver, his thumb arched as it would be if the hammer were cocked. The girl was carrying a gas can and what might have been aquarium tubing.

"What are they doing?" Climpt asked. He had the rifle up, following Helper's head through the sights.

The radio: *Girl's got a syphon.*

Helper was talking to her.

"Keep tracking him," Lucas said. They couldn't hear the words, but they could hear the rhythm of them. She unscrewed the gas cap on the truck, dropped it in the snow, stuck the tube in the gas tank, and pushed it down. She put the other end in the open top of the gas can, then squeezed a black bulb on the tube.

"Taking gas," Climpt said, and a moment later a vagrant wisp of gasoline odor mixed with the pine scent.

"He's going out on the snowmobile," Lucas said. "He's getting gas for it."

"Without that kid," Climpt muttered, tracking Helper with the rifle.

Lucas jabbed the radio: "He's taking gas out of the truck. I think he's going to refuel his snowmobile and take off. Gene and I left our sleds back a way, we better go get them."

Carr: *One of you better wait there until I get somebody up that side of the house.*

Lucas said to Climpt: "How're you doing? Gettin' shaky?"

"Just a bit," Climpt admitted. His eyebrows were clogged with snow, his face wet.

"You head back to the sled, let me take the rifle," Lucas said. "Where does it shoot?"

"Put it right over his ear," Climpt said. He held on Helper for another second, then said, "Ready?"

"Yeah."

Climpt handed him the rifle. Lucas put the front sight on Helper's helmet, right where his ear should be. He held it there, his cone of vision narrowing to nothing. He couldn't see the top of the girl's head, although it was only inches from Helper's ear. He could only infer its position.

"Come in as soon as you hear him start that machine. You can ride me back for the other," Lucas said, speaking around the black plastic stock. The stock was icy cold on his cheek, but he kept the sight on Helper's ear. "Can't be more than a couple hundred feet."

Climpt touched him on the shoulder and was gone in the snow.

The transfer of gasoline seemed to take forever, Helper leaning nervously against the truck while the girl stood passively in front of him, watching the syphon. Finally she pulled the tube out of the truck, dropped it on the ground, and she and Helper edged back to his snowmobile, the girl struggling with the can. Five gallons, Lucas thought, probably thirty-five pounds. And she wasn't a big kid. Next to Helper she looked positively frail.

The yellow-haired girl boosted the can up with her thigh, tilted it so the spout fit into the mouth of the gas tank. Again, it seemed to take forever to fill the tank, Lucas tracking, tracking, tired of looking at Helper over the sight.

The girl said something to Helper. Lucas caught one word, "Done." The girl tossed the can aside and Helper pushed her up on the driver's seat of the sled. A pair of snowshoes was strapped to the back, and Helper straddled them, sat down. His gun hand never wavered.

"Don't try to follow," Helper screamed, looking awkwardly over his shoulder as the girl started the snowmobile. They lurched forward, stopped, then started again. Helper screamed, "Don't try . . ." The rest of his words were lost as they started around the side of the house, heading toward the back. The forest was now almost perfectly dark, and silent except for the chain-saw roar of the sled. Lucas stood to watch them go, putting the rifle's muzzle up, clumping out into the yard, following the diminishing red taillight as long as he could.

The radio was running almost full time, voices . . .

He's going out the back.

Heading toward the flowage.
Can't see him.
And the feds: *We got the beacon, he's moving east.*

❋

Carr came running up the driveway. "Lucas, where'n hell . . . ?"

"Over here." Lucas waded through the snow to the driveway. Three other deputies pushed out of the woods, heading for them. Carr was breathing hard, his eyes wide and wild.

"What . . ."

"Gene and I'll go after them on the sleds. You follow with the trucks," Lucas said.

"Remember what he did to the other two, hit 'em on the back trail," Carr said urgently. "If he's waiting for you, you'd never see him."

"The feds should know when he stops," Lucas said. He realized they were shouting at each other and dropped his voice. "Besides, we've got no choice. I don't think he'll keep the kid—she'll slow him down. If he doesn't kill her, we got to be out there to pick her up. If she starts wandering around on her own . . ."

Climpt had come up on a single sled, and Lucas swung his leg over the backseat, holding the rifle out to the side. "Okay, go, go," Carr shouted, and Climpt rolled the accelerator forward and they cut back through the trees to the second sled. Lucas handed Climpt the rifle. Climpt slung it over his shoulder as Lucas hopped on the second sled and fired it up.

"How do you want to do this?" Climpt shouted.

"You lead, stay on his trail. Look for the kid in case he's dumped her. If you see his taillight . . . shit, do what seems right. I'll hang on to the radio. If you see me blinking my lights, stop."

"Gotcha," Climpt said and powered away.

❋

Helper was running four or five minutes ahead of them. Lucas couldn't decide whether he would be moving faster or slower. He presumably knew where he was going, so that should help his speed. On the other hand, Lucas and Climpt were simply following his track, which was easy enough to do despite the snow. Helper had to navigate on his own. Even if he stayed on the trails, the snow had gotten so heavy that they'd be obscured, white-on-white, under the sled's headlights. And that would slow him down.

They started off, Climpt first, Lucas following, and lost the lights around the house within thirty seconds. After that, they were in the fishbowl of their own light. When Climpt dropped over the top of a rise or into a bowl, Lucas' span of vision would suddenly contract, and expand again when Climpt came back into view. When Climpt suddenly moved out, his taillight would dwindle to almost nothing. When he slowed, Lucas would nearly overrun him. After two or three minutes, Lucas found the optimum distance, about fifteen yards, and hung there, the feds feeding tracking updates through the radio.

The snow made the ride into a nightmare, his face unprotected, wet, freezing, snow clogging his eyebrows, water running down his neck.

He's just about crossing MacBride Road.

Lucas flashed his lights at Climpt, pulled up beside him, took off his glove, looked at his watch, marked the time.

"You know MacBride Road?" he shouted.

"Sure. It's up ahead somewhere."

"The feds think he crossed it about forty-five seconds ago. Let me know when we cross it and we can figure out how far behind we are."

"Sure."

They crossed it two minutes and ten seconds after Lucas marked the time, so they were less than three minutes behind. Closing, apparently.

"Still moving?" he asked the feds.

Still moving east.

Carr: *He'll be crossing Table Bay Road by Jack's Cafe. Maybe we can beat him down there, get a look at him, see if he's still got the kid.*

❊

They were riding through low country, but generally following creek beds and road embankments, where they were protected from the snow. Two or three minutes after crossing MacBride Road, they broke out on a lake, and the snow beat at them with full force, coming in long curving lines into their headlights. Visibility closed to ten feet, and Climpt dropped his speed to a near-walking pace. Lucas wiped snow from his face, out of his eyes, drove, watching Climpt's taillight. Wiped, drove. Getting harder . . . Helper's track was filling more quickly, the edges obscured, harder to pick out. Four minutes later they were across and back into a sheltered run.

Carr: *We're setting up at Jack's. Where is he?*

He's four miles out and closing, but he's moving slower. How's it going, Lucas?

Lucas, tight from the cold, lifting his brake hand to his face: "We're still on his track. No sign of the kid. It's getting worse, though. We might not be able to stay with him."

All right. I've been talking to Henry. We might have to make a stand here at Table Bay.

"I wonder if the kid's with him. I can't believe he'd still have her, but we haven't seen anything that might have been tracks."

No way to tell until we see him.

Climpt stopped, then broke to his right, then turned in a circle, stopped. "What?" Lucas shouted, pulling up behind him.

"Trail splits. Must've been another sled came through here. I don't know if he went left or right."

"Where's Table Bay Road?"

"Off to the right."

"That's where he's headed."

Climpt nodded and started out again, but the pace grew jagged, Climpt sawing back and forth, checking the track. Lucas nearly overran him a half-dozen times, swerving to avoid a collision. He was breathing through his mouth now, as though he'd been running.

❄

The Iceman pounded down the trail, the yellow-haired girl behind him, on top the snowshoes. They'd stopped just long enough to trade places, and then went on through the thickening snow, along an almost invisible track, probing for the path through the woods.

They were safe enough for the moment, lost in the storm. If he could just get south . . . He might have to dump the girl, but she was certainly replaceable. Alaska, the Yukon, there were women out there for the asking; not nearly enough men. They'd do anything you wanted.

If he was going to make it south to the horse trainer's place, he'd have to get up on the north side of the highway, take Blueberry Lake across to the main stem of the flowage. He could take Whitetail Creek.

❄

The feds: *He's turning. He's turning. He's heading north, he's not heading toward Table Bay Road anymore, he's headed up toward the intersection of STH 70 and Meteor Drive.*

Carr: *We're moving, we're going that way.*

Lucas flashed Climpt, pulled alongside.

"They've just turned, heading north . . . wait a minute." He pushed the transmit button: "Do you know what trail that is? What snowmobile trail? Is it marked on the map?"

Feds: *There's a creek down there, Whitetail Run. We think that's it.*

"He's on a creek called Whitetail Run, heading up to Meteor Drive," Lucas said.

Climpt nodded. "That can't be far. This trail crosses it at right angles—we'll see the turn."

Carr: *We're coming up on the bridge at Whitetail. We'll nail down both sides.*

Another voice: *They'll see the lights.*

Carr: *Yeah. We'll let 'em. Henry and I been talking. We decided we gotta let him know that he can't get away. We gotta give him the choice of giving up the kid and quitting, or dying. The kid's gonna die if she stays with him. If he just leaves her out in the snow somewhere, she's gone. And if he stops someplace, gets a car, he can't leave her to tell anybody. Sooner or later he'll dump her.*

Feds: *If he realizes there's a beacon on him, he may look for it, then we'd lose him.*

Carr: *We're not going to let him go this time. And if he gets away somehow . . . heck, we gotta risk it.*

Feds: *Your call, Sheriff.*

Carr: *That's right. How far out is he?*

Feds: *Half-mile. Forty seconds, maybe.*

❋

The Iceman roared through the turn onto Whitetail, and he was almost to the bridge when he saw the lights, shining down through the snow. He knew what they were. The cops, and especially Davenport, had some kind of karma edge on him. They kept finding him when finding him was impossible.

"No!" He shouted it out as he hit the brake. The lights were there, big hand-held million-candlepower jobs, probing the creek. He slid to a stop, turned to the yellow-haired girl:

"That's the cops up there. They're tracking us somehow. If I had time . . . I'll have to try it on foot. I want you to take the sled back down the creek here, just ride around for a while. When they find you, tell them I'm heading for Jack's Cafe down by the flowage. Tell them that you think I'm going after a car. They'll believe that."

"I want to go with you," she said. "You're my husband."

"Can't do it now," he said. He pulled his helmet back, leaned forward, and kissed her on the lips. Her lips were stiff with the cold, her face wet with snow—she hadn't had a helmet—and a few tears.

"I tried, but we can't get through," he said. "You'll have to put them off me. But I'll come back. I'll get you."

"You'll get me?" she asked.

"I swear I will. And I'm counting on you now. You're the only woman who can save me."

She stood in the deep snow beside the sled, watched him snap into the snowshoes. He had his pistol in his hand, his helmet back on. With the snowmobile suit, he looked almost like a spaceman.

"Give me five minutes," he said. "Then take off. Just roll around for a while. When they find you, tell them I'm headed for Jack's."

"What'll you do?"

"I'll stop the first car coming down the road and take it," he said.

"Jesus." She looked up at the faint light, then cocked her head and frowned. "Somebody's coming."

"What?" The Iceman looked up at the bridge.

"Not that way . . . from behind us."

"Motherfucker," he said. "You go, go."

❄

Lucas and Climpt were moving again, the track filling in front of them, nothing in their world but a few lights and the rumble of the sleds.

Climpt's taillight came up and he leaned to the left, taking the sled through the turn. Lucas followed, pressed the radio button, trying to talk through the bumps. "How long will it take him to get from Whitetail to the bridge?"

Feds: *About two minutes.*

Lucas flashed Climpt, pulled up alongside, shouted, "We're coming up on him in maybe a minute. They're gonna let him see them."

He's stopped.

Carr: *Where?*

Two or three hundred yards out, maybe. Can't really tell that close.

Can he see our lights?

Maybe.

"I'll take the lead from here. I'll count it out. You get the rifle limbered up."

Climpt nodded, pulled the rifle down. Lucas started counting, rolled the accelerator forward with his right hand, touched the pocket on his left thigh where he kept the pistol. The pocket was sealed with Velcro, so he could get at it quickly enough once he'd shed his gloves . . . *one thousand six, one thousand seven, one thousand eight.* Seconds rolling away like a slow heartbeat.

Radio voice: *Don't see him, don't see him.*

Lucas slowed, Climpt closed from behind. *One thousand thirty-eight, one thousand thirty-nine . . .*

Lucas rolled forward, straining to see. His headlight beam was cupped, shortened by the snow. Looking into it was like peering into a foam plastic cup. They hit a hump, swooped down over the far side, Lucas absorbing up the lurch with his legs, beginning to feel the ride in his thighs. *One thousand sixty . . .* Lucas rolled the accelerator back, slowed, slowed . . .

There.

Red flash just ahead.

Lucas hit the brake, leaned left, dumped his speed in a skid, stayed with the sled, got it straight, headlight boring in on Helper's sled . . . and Helper himself.

Helper stood behind his snowmobile, caught in the headlight. Climpt had gone right when Lucas broke left, came back around, catching Helper in his lights, fixing him in the crossed beams. Lucas ripped his gloves off, had the pistol . . .

Helper was running. He was on snowshoes, running toward the treeline above the creek. Couldn't take a sled in there, too dense. Lucas hit the accelerator, pulled closer, closer. Helper looking back, still wearing his helmet, face mask a dark oval, blank.

❊

The Iceman lumbered toward the treeline, but the sound of the other snowmobiles was growing; then the lights popped up and suddenly they were there, careening through the deep snow. The lead sled swerved toward him while the other broke away.

He lifted his pistol, fired a shot, and the sled swerved and the passenger dumped off. The other sled broke hard the other way, spinning, trying to miss the fallen man, out of control.

The Iceman kept running, running, his breath beating in his throat, tearing his chest, running blindly with little hope, looking back.

❊

The muzzle blast was like lightning in the dark. Lucas cut left, came off the sled. Stunned, he thrashed for a moment, got upright, snow in his eyes and mouth, sputtering, put too much weight on one foot, crunched through to the next layer of snow, got to his knees, the .45 coming up, felt Climpt spinning past him.

Helper was at the treeline, barely visible, nothing more than a sense of motion a hundred feet away.

Lucas fired six shots at him, one after another, tracking the motion, firing through brush and brambles, through alder branches and small barren aspen. The muzzle flash blinded him after the first shot and he fired on instinct, where Helper should have been. And where was Climpt, why wasn't he . . . ?

And then the M-16 came in, two bursts at the treeline.

Radio: *Gunfire, we got gunfire.*

Carr: *What's happening, what's happening?*

❊

Snowshoes. They'd need the snowshoes.

Lucas' sled had burrowed into a snowdrift. He started for it, then looked back at Helper's sled, saw the yellow-haired girl. She was on the snow, trying to get to her feet. Struggling. Hurt?

Lucas turned toward her, pushed the transmit button:

"He's on foot—heading up toward the road—he's in the woods—we got the kid. She's here—we're on the creek just below the bridge. Watch out for him. We shot up around him, he could be hit."

Ginny Harris was squatting next to Helper's snowmobile, her hair gold-yellow in the lights of the snowmobiles, focused on the woods where Helper had gone. As Lucas ran up, struggling with the knee-deep snow, she turned her head and looked up at him, eyes large and feral like a trapped fox's.

❅

The yellow-haired girl crouched by the sled as the man on the first sled fired a series of shots into the wood. He looked menacing, a man all in black, the big pistol popping in his hand. Then there was a loud ratcheting noise from the man on the second sled, the stutter of flame reaching out toward her man like God's finger.

The first man said something to her, but she couldn't hear him. She could see his lips moving, and his hand came up. Reaching out? Pointing a gun? She rolled.

❅

She rolled away from him and he called, "You're okay, okay," but she kept rolling and her hand came up with what looked like a child's shiny chrome compact.

A .22, a fifty-dollar weapon, a silly thing that could do almost nothing but kill people who made mistakes. He was leaning forward, his hand toward her, reaching out. He saw the muzzle and just before the flash felt a split second of what might have been embarrassment, caught like this. He started to turn, to flinch away. Then the flash.

The slug hit him in the throat like a hard slap. He stopped, not knowing quite what had happened, heard the pop-pop of other guns around him, not the heavy bang-bang, but something softer, more distant. Very far away.

Lightning stuttered in the dark and flung the girl down, then Lucas hit the snow on his back, his legs folding under him. His head was downhill, and when he hit, the breath rushed out of his lungs. He tried to take a breath and sit up, but nothing happened. He felt as though a rubber stopper had been shoved into his windpipe. He strained, but nothing.

The snow felt like sand on his face; he could feel it clearly, the snow. And in his mouth, a coppery, cutting taste, the taste of blood. But the rest of the world, all the sounds, smells, and sights, were in a mental rectangle the size of a shoe box, and somebody was pushing in the sides.

He could hear somebody talking: "Oh, Jesus, in the neck, call the goddamn doctor, where's the doctor, is she still riding . . ."

And a few seconds later a shadow in his eyesight, somebody else: "Christ, he's dead, he's dead, look at his eyes."

But Lucas could see. He could see branches with snow on them, he could feel himself move, could feel his angle of vision shifting as someone sat him up, he could feel—no, hear—somebody shouting at him.

And all the time the rectangle grew smaller, smaller . . .

He fought the closing walls for a while, but a distant warmth attracted him, and he felt his mind turning toward it. When he let the concentration go, the walls of the square lurched in, and now he was holding mental territory no bigger than a postage stamp.

No more vision. No more sense of the snow on his face. No taste of blood.

Nothing but a single word, which seemed not so much a sound as a line of type, a word cut from a newspaper:

"Knife."

CHAPTER

✳ ✳ ✳

30

The Iceman was there, almost in the treeline, when the shot ripped through his back, between his spine and his shoulder blade. He went down facefirst, and a burst of automatic weapons fire tore up the aspen overhead. His mind was clear as ice, but his body felt like a flame.

There was another burst, slashing through the trees, then another, but the last was directed somewhere else. The Iceman got to his feet, pain riding his back like a thousand-pound knapsack. He pushed deeper into the woods, deeper. Couldn't go far, had to sit down. With the sudden profusion of lights below, he could see the vague outlines of trees around him, and he fought through them, heading at an angle toward the road. Behind him, his tracks filled with snow almost as fast as he made holes in it.

Then he was out of the light. Caught in the darkness, he probed ahead with his hands. The pain in his back grew like a cancer, spreading through him, into his belly, his legs, turning his body to lead. A tree limb caught him in the face mask, snapped his head back. His breath came harder: he pulled off the helmet, threw it away. He needed to feel . . .

He was bleeding. He could feel the blood flowing down

his belly and his back, warm, sticking between his shirt and his skin. He took another step, waving his hands like a blind man; another, waving his hands. A branch snapped him in the face, and he swore, twisted, tripped, went down. Swore, struggled to his feet, took another three steps, fell in a hole, tried to get up.

Failed this time.

Felt so quiet.

Lay there, resting; all he needed was a little rest, then he could get up.

Yukon. Alaska.

❋

Weather, coming up, saw Lucas on the snow and the blood on his face, screamed, "No, God . . ."

"He's hit, he's hit," Climpt screamed.

He was cradling Lucas' head, Henry Lacey standing over both Lucas and Climpt, Carr beside the yellow-haired girl, other deputies milling through the snow.

Like a scene shot in slow motion, Weather saw Lacey's teeth flashing in the snowmobile headlights, saw the face of the little girl, serene, dead, her coat puckered with bullet holes, and she thought, *Gone to the angels,* as she dropped to her knees next to Lucas.

Lucas thrashed, his eyes half open, the whites showing, straining, straining. She grabbed his jaw, found blood, tipped his head back, saw the entry wound, a small puncture that might have been made with a ballpoint pen. He couldn't breathe. She pulled off her gloves, pried open his jaws, and pushed one of the gloves into the corner of his mouth to keep him from snapping his teeth on her fingers. With his mouth wedged open, she probed his throat with her fingers, found the blockage, a chunk of soft tissue where there shouldn't have been anything.

Her mind went cold, analytical.

"Knife," she said to Lacey.

"What?" Lacey shouted down at her, shocked. She realized that he had a gun in his hand.

"Give me your fuckin' knife—your knife!"

"Here, here." Climpt thrust a red jackknife at her, a Swiss Army knife, and she scratched open the larger of the two blades.

"Hold his head down," she said to Climpt. Lacey dropped to his knees to help as she straddled Lucas' chest. "Put your hand on his forehead. Push down."

She pushed the point of the blade into Lucas' throat below the Adam's apple and twisted it, prying . . . and there was a sudden frightening croak as air rushed into his lungs. "Keep his head down—keep his head down."

She thrust her index finger into the incision and crimped it, keeping the hole open.

"Let's get him out—let's get him out," she shouted, slipping off his chest. Lucas seemed to levitate, men at each thigh and two more at either shoulder. "Keep his head down."

They rushed him out of the woods, up to the sheriff's Suburban.

With each awkward, bloody breath, Lucas, eyes closed now, said, "Awwwk . . . awk" like a dying crow.

✳

A siren screamed away down the road just above him. Helper was lying in the ditch below the road, he realized. All he had to do was crawl to the top, and when the cops were gone, flag a car.

A small piece of rationality bit back at him: the cops wouldn't be going. Not now. They knew he was here, now.

The Iceman laughed. They'd find him, they were coming.

He tried to roll, get up; he would crawl to the top, flag the cops. Quit. After he healed, he could try again. There was always the possibility of breaking out of jail, always possibilities.

But he couldn't get up. Couldn't move. His mind was still clear, working wonderfully. He analyzed the problem. He was stiff from the wound, he thought. Not a bad wound, not a killer, but he was stiffening up like a wounded deer.

When you shot a deer and failed to knock it down, you waited a half hour or so and invariably found it lying close by, unable to move.

If he was going to live, he had to get up.

But he couldn't.

Tried. Couldn't.

They'd come, he thought. Come and get him. The trail was only a couple of hundred yards long. They'd track him, they'd find him. All he had to do was wait.

✳

"If he's not hit, then going in there'd be suicide. If he is hit, he's dead. Just set up the cordon and let it go until daylight," Carr said. Lacey nodded, stepped to another deputy to relay the word.

"I want three or four men together everywhere," Carr called after him. "I don't want anyone out there alone, okay? Just in case."

✳

They found him lying in the ditch beside the road. Still alive, still alert.

The Iceman sensed them coming; not so much heard them, but simply knew. Cocked his head up; that was as far as he could move now. But still: if they got him right into town, they could save him. They could still save him.

"Help me," he groaned.

Something skittered away, then returned.

"Help."

Something touched his face; something colder than he was. He moved and they fell away. And came back. Nipped at him; there was a snarl, then a twisting flight, then they were back.

Coyotes. Brought by the scent of blood and the protection of the dark.

Hungry this year.

Hungry with the deep snow. Most of the deer dead and gone.

They came closer; he tried to move; failed. Tried to lift

his hand, tried to roll, tried to cover his face. Failed.

Mind clear as water. Sharper teeth at his face, snapping, ripping, pulling him apart. He opened his mouth to scream; teeth at his lips.

❄

Nine deputies were at the scene, four of them as pickets, guarding against the return of Helper. The rest worked over the scene, searching for blood sign and shells, or simply watched. The yellow-haired girl was a bump under a blue plastic tarp. Lacey and Carr stood to one side, Carr talking into the radio. When he signed off, Lacey was looking into the dark. "I still think if we went slow . . ."

"Forget it," Carr said. "If he's laying up, he'd just take out more of us. Keep the cordon along the road. Davenport got off a half-dozen shots at him, Gene chopped up the woods—I think there's a good chance that he's down. What we need . . ."

"Wait," Lacey snapped. He held up a gloved hand, turned, and looked northeast at an angle toward the road. He seemed to be straining into the dark.

"What?"

"Sounded like a scream," Lacey said.

They listened together for a moment, heard the chatter of the deputies around them, the distant muffled mutter of trucks idling on the road, and beneath it all the profoundly subtle rumble of the falling snow.

Nothing at all like the scream of a man being eaten alive.

Carr shook his head. "Probably just the wind," he said.

CHAPTER

✳ ✳ ✳

31

He was on snowshoes, working along the ridges across the access road to his cabin. After the first mile, he was damp with sweat. He took his watch cap off, stuffed it in his pocket, unzipped his parka to cool down, and moved on.

The alders caught at his legs, tangled him. They were small, bushy trees with thumb-sized trunks marked with speckles, like wild cherries. In some places they'd been buried by the frequent snowfalls. When he stepped over a buried bush, his snowshoe would collapse beneath him as though he'd stepped in a hole, which, in fact, he had—a snow dome, held up by the flexible branches of a buried alder. Then he'd be up to his knee or even his crotch, struggling to get back on the level.

As he fought across the swamp, a rime of ice formed on his sunglasses, and his heart thumped like a drum in the silence of the North Woods. He climbed the side of a narrow finger ridge; when he reached its spine, he turned downhill and followed it back to the swamp. At the point where the ridge subsided into the swamp, a tangle of red cedars hugged the snow. Deer had bedded all through the cedars, shedding hair, discoloring the snow. There were pinkish urine holes everywhere, piles of scat like liver-colored .45 shells; but no deer. He would have been as obvious to them as a locomotive, and they'd be long gone. He felt a spasm of guilt. He shouldn't be running deer, not this winter. They'd be weak enough.

His legs twitched, twitched against the pristine white sheets, white like the snow. The winter faded.

"Wake up, you . . ."

Lucas opened his eyes, groaned. His back was stiff, his neck stretched and immobile in the plastic brace. "Goddamn, I was out of it," he said hoarsely. "What time is it?"

"Four o'clock," Weather said, smiling down at him. She was wearing her surgeon's scrub suit. "It'll be dark in an hour. How're you feeling?"

Lucas tested his throat, flexing. "Still hurts, but not so bad. Feels more like tight."

"It'll do that as it heals. If it gets worse, we'll go back in and release some of the scar tissue."

"I can live with the tight feeling," he said.

"What? You don't trust me?" The .22 slug had entered below his jawbone, penetrating upwards, parallel to his tongue, finally burying itself in the soft tissue at the back of his throat. When he'd tried to inhale, he'd sucked down a flap of loose tissue not much bigger than a nickel and had almost choked to death. Weather had fixed the damage with an hour of work on the table at Lincoln Memorial.

"Trust a woman, the next thing you know, they're cutting your throat," Lucas said.

"All right, so now I'm not going to tell you about the Schoeneckers."

"What?" He started to sit up, but she pushed him down. "They found them?"

"Camping in Baja. This morning. They used a gas credit card last night, and they found them about ten o'clock our time. Henry Lacey called and said the folks don't know nothin' about nothin', but one of the girls is giving them quite an earful. Henry may fly out there with a couple of other deputies to bring them back."

"Far out. They can squeeze them on the other people in the sex thing."

"They? You're not going to help?"

Lucas shook his head. "Not my territory anymore. I gotta figure out something to do. Maybe go back to Minneapolis."

"Hmph," she said.

"Well, Jesus Christ," Lucas said, picking up her change of mood, "I was hoping you'd help me figure it out. One way or another, you'll be around, right?"

"We gotta talk," she said. "When you get out of here."

"What does that mean? You don't want to be around?"

"I want to be around," she said. "But we gotta talk."

"All right."

Shelly Carr knocked on the door. "Visiting hours?" He had a wool-plaid hunting cap in his hands, with earflaps.

"Come on in," Lucas croaked. Carr asked, and Lucas said he felt fine. "What's the word on Harper? Weather says you found his truck."

"Yeah—out on a lake. There's a big collection of fishing shacks. Lot of people around there. We think he might have met somebody, got a ride so we couldn't put out a bulletin on his license. God knows where he is now, but we're looking."

"You look pretty good," Lucas said.

"Got some rest," Carr said.

"Have you talked to Gene again?"

"Yeah. He's still up at your cabin," Carr said. "He just sits up there and watches television and reads. I'm kind of worried."

"He needs professional help, but there's no chance he'd talk to a psychiatrist," Weather said. "Big macho guy like that, no chance."

"Yeah, well . . . I know where he's at," Lucas said. "It's like the Church. If you don't believe, it won't do you any good to go. He's gonna have to work it out himself."

"The whole thing was odd," Carr said. "He was okay until he went to her funeral. He shouldn't have gone, I told him that."

"He might of had to," Lucas said.

"Yeah, I know," Carr said reluctantly. "But as soon as he saw her face, that was that. I mean, she looked like an angel. You know about his daughter."

"Yeah."

They sat for a moment, not talking, then Carr said, "I gotta go." He whacked Lucas twice on the leg. "Get better."

❋

When he was gone, Weather said, "Shelly's doing all right politically. Lacey's made sure that everybody knows about him walking up the driveway to deal with Helper."

"Took some balls," Lucas said.

"And somehow all the dead people are just . . . dead. Seems like nobody really talks about it that much. It's been less than a week."

"That's the way it goes," Lucas said.

"Did you see the paper?" she asked.

"A nurse brought it in this morning, just after you left," he said.

"Great picture, Shelly with the FBI guys, taking credit," she said. "Kind of made me mad."

"Shelly's just taking care of business," Lucas said mildly. He was amused.

"I know. I had a little talk with him about his wife, by the way. I suggested that they both might be better off divorced."

"What'd he say?"

"He said, 'Divorce is a sin.'"

❋

After a few minutes he said, "Push the door shut."

She looked at the door, then stepped over, pushed it shut, sat on the bed next to him, kissed him. He couldn't turn his head much, but he could move his arm, and he held her to him as long and hard as he could.

She finally pulled away, laughing, straightened her hair.

"Jeez, it's hard not to take advantage of you, a man in your condition," she said.

"Hey. I don't hurt all that bad. So come back here." He tried to reach for her, but she danced away.

"I wasn't referring to your getting shot. I was referring to the fact that you're falling in love with me."

"I am?"

"Take my word for it," she said. She stepped closer, bent over, kissed him lightly on the forehead. He tried to reach for her again, but she danced away. "Try to get some rest. You're probably gonna need it when you get out."

"You've got a sense of humor like a cop," Lucas said. "Nasty. And you hide behind it. Like a cop."

She'd been smiling, but now the smile narrowed, turned uncertain. "I guess I do."

"Because you're right. I am falling in love with you. You don't have to be funny about it."

This time she touched him on the tip of the nose and said, "Get well." She was smiling, but seemed to have tears in her eyes, and she left in a hurry.

Lucas drifted for a while, punched up the TV, turned it off, used the bed-lift control to raise his head. He could see out the window, across the lawn toward the town, with the small houses and the smoke curling out of the chimneys. Not much to see: white snow, blue sky, small houses.

And it was bitterly cold, everybody said, the worst cold of the winter.

From inside it didn't look so bad. From inside, it looked pretty good. He smiled and closed his eyes.